GAF 830

Tree Frog

Tree Frog

BY

Jason Charles

HAMILTON & Co. Publishers
LONDON

© Copyright 1998
Jason Charles

The right of Jason Charles to be identified as author of this work has been asserted by him in accordance with Copyright, Designs, and Patents Act 1988

All rights reserved. No reproduction,
copy or transmission of this publication may be made
without written permission.
No paragraph of this publication may be reproduced,
copied or transmitted
save with the written permission or in accordance
with the provisions of the Copyright Act 1956 (as amended).
Any person who does any unauthorised act
in relation to this publication may be liable
to criminal prosecution and civil
claims for damage.

All characters in this publication are fictitious and any resemblance to real persons, living, or dead, is purely coincidental.

Paperback ISBN 1 901668 50 9

Publisher

HAMILTON & Co. Publishers
10 Stratton Street
Mayfair
London W1X 5FD

Chapter 1

Marie-Record-Playback-Erase

You do not really know anything about me. I can tell you one thing about me, and that is that I mainly, no **always**, tell the truth. You learn a lot about lies in my line of work, and this makes you treasure the truth more than most.

I suppose that if you really want to hear all about it, the first thing you will want to know is where I was born, what my childhood was like, but you have asked all of these questions before, and how far did they get you then? If it is ages, dates, prices, shall we say numbers, that you want, then here is a good one for you, 2000.

This century is old. It is winding down. The process is irreversible. This century and this millennium go meandering onwards, ebbing out towards a new beginning, and a clean conscience. I do not have the kind of money that could insure my safety for the next thousand years but even I have started to make provisions. I am trying, by whatever means are available, to be ready for the future.

I am in it up to my neck. Believe me when I say that things are desperate. It might be that you haven't noticed yet. You might be happy. You probably are. Maybe it's just that nobody has told you. You have your life, a good life, and you have your partner, your work, your family, you have it all....then again maybe you don't. Maybe you are just like me. You can't quite work out what it's all about. You've tried to work it out. God knows I've tried...

We have failed to work out the answer because there is no answer. It is not that we've lost touch, or that there is no longer an answer, the truth is that there has never been an answer. So you have, or will soon have, arrived at the same conclusion as me. We are born and we die. We have no choice in that. The most that we can hope for is to enjoy the time in between, find love, and beauty, and live our lives with someone special. We are all looking for that special somebody because essentially we are alone. The answer, in the end, is simple enough. Love, that is true love, is what we should strive for in the time between birth and death. My conclusion is that love is all important. Through love we define ourselves and our hopes, dreams, and happiness, in fact our whole lives. The rest of the world seems to be intent on denying love, cheating on it, lying to it, casting it aside... They seem to know nothing of the conclusion that you and I have made.

I want love. No, I demand love. I want love, desire, and sensuality. I want it all. You want it all. I know you do. Somehow we are losing the ability to desire. We, well not we exactly, but somebody, has wrapped up desire in guilt, wrapped it up so tightly that it can no longer be experienced independently. Whatever you want, whatever you desire, is going to cost you. You have to be prepared to pay the price.

I straighten my arms, stretch back my neck, and watch desire extinguish itself below me. The woman below me is forty-two, very wealthy, still slim, beautiful in fact. I feel no pleasure, no desire. There is a grain of self-satisfaction somewhere inside at having wrung out a few last drops of life's pleasure from this arid senile century. I push my cold stomach flat onto her warm stomach. I reach down between her legs for my penis. I squeeze the collar of the condom tightly between my fingers and withdraw myself from her. I quickly, while she is still recovering, roll off the condom and wrap it in some white tissue paper. I have not orgasmed, but I may well have released a preliminary drop or two, but anyway, I do not want her to know that. I place the bundle out of her reach down by my side of the bed. I lie besides her joining in with her long deep breaths. She sighs, so I sigh. She moves over onto her side and comes up close to me. Her hand sweeps across my body.

"You're still erect," her eyes open.

"It stays like that sometimes. It's because you're such a good lover."

I speak with enough helplessness in my voice to reassure her. She kisses my face softly. She closes her eyes again and smiles a smile of what is, unknown to her, an unsound belief in a young man's virility. The smile turns inwards, to her pride the hard work she must put in to keep such a youthful figure. She moves even closer to me. Once again she brushes past my, still awake, but receding, penis with her hand; just for the sake of her smile. I do not fool myself. It is for this smile that I am here. My profit depends upon this smile, maybe more than the sex, maybe more than the orgasm. I tell her that I need the toilet and she rolls over onto her other side. I get out of bed. I pick up the evidence in the white tissue paper. I walk, naked, into the bathroom.

Alone, in the bathroom, with my reflection, I feel free. I watch my erection die in the full-length mirror. The cool straight surfaces of the bathroom appear to ricochet off the mirror and entrap me, entomb me. I did not expect the overhead neon light to be quite so bright. I suppose that I never do.

I pull down the toilet seat and sit down. The seat is cold on the backs of my legs. My arms get goose pimples all over, and I begin to piss. I hold the evidence, the tissue paper, tightly in my hand. The bathroom lacks comfort although it offers sanctuary. When I have finished I stand up and flush the evidence away. I watch the white ethereal paper soak up some of the blue water, swirl into the vortex, and then disappear, gone forever. I am safe in the knowledge that it will never return. I go back into the bedroom and back into bed. Marie is warm, but I am cold, and she is already asleep, and I do not want to wake her, so I keep my distance. I turn away from her to watch the bedside clock. I watch Sunday fade in minutes and seconds, and I lie uncomfortably in a perfect bed, with perfect covers. I move onto my back and remain still.

I think about the fading seconds. I think about the evidence vanishing forever. I think about today. I have to make today disappear. I have to erase it from my memory. I have to wipe out every thought, every sensation, the most minute details. I have to wipe my memory clean, like a palimpsest, or a child's Magic Slate. If I can remember every moment fully, truthfully, recall faithfully every sensation, isolate it, pore over it, then I can deal with it, remove it from my consciousness. I have to remember it all. But today is already yesterday, already beginning to fade as it is being absorbed by my mind. With no memory and no orgasm, I do not have to lie to Sally, my girlfriend, the one true love of my life, the idol of my affection. She is living proof that my conclusions are not unfounded. Before I continue I must play back the day to myself, play it back like a video recording, so that I can erase it, have a brand new blank cassette once again. I am going to tell you about earlier. What we did together

I arrived at Marie's house at around six o'clock this evening. The taxi left me at the foot of the drive. I walked up the tarmac drive and before I got to the door Marie had already opened it. She was wearing a white crepe trouser suit and flat, natural coloured, leather sandals. As I entered, I kissed her on the cheek. As soon as the door was closed she leaned forward and put her palms on my shoulders and kissed me fully.

"I've been thinking about your visit all day," she makes the first sound since my footsteps on the drive.

"And I have been thinking about visiting you all day," I smile to her, but inside I do not smile. To Marie I am a devoted lover but inside my head, I am insincere, a criminal feeding off her perception and goodwill.

Lying in bed now, beside Marie I am concentrating, trying to remember everything, the ring in our voices, the atmosphere in the room, the air in our lungs. I glance over at Marie, who is asleep, using her as an anchor in time. I am sure that I have captured our initial contact. The memory is gone. It is behind me. I go back to my remembering, to playing back the story.

The room was a collage of cool violets and tepid indigos. Marie brought me over a hefty single malt, with two cubes of ice that tinkled reassuringly against the glass. The room filled with the blue smoke from one of the two daily cigarettes that Marie allowed herself. She sat back on an antique chair that she bought from Woodbridge earlier this year. I stand up and move over to the French windows, catching the red remnants of the late afternoon, early evening, sun.

Marie is blonde. As a girl, her hair was probably natural, but not now. She spends most of her days having manicures, sun beds, and beauty treatments. She plays a hard game of squash, likes tennis, aerobics, and swimming, which is how she keeps her figure so youthful. Her speech is not affected by her husband's money or breeding. At the time when I arrived, she was quiet, quite unusual for her. I needed to pay her more attention. It had been a while since I last saw her. I knew exactly what to do. I walked up behind her, reached down to her collarbone, and then gently massaged her neck and shoulders. She began to relax, really enjoying her cigarette.

"I don't like it when I haven't seen you for a while. I keep thinking about what you're doing, where you are. Derek's regressing further and further into the small wonders of life, bloody cricket, and bloody electric train sets. Our own children were never that juvenile."

I lent down and kissed her neck right at the point where her hair turns into soft skin. She smiled and exhaled. I kissed her to take her mind off her husband. She can talk about him, bitch about him, to her friends, she does not need me for that. I increased the intensity of my caress. She responded by making her neck more accessible. I heard her legs rub together as she slid off her sandals. It was not quite right though, not how it should have been. The ashtray was just out of reach so she could not put out her cigarette, and the table was too far away so she could not put down the small gin that she had poured for herself. I took her drink with one hand, being as accommodating as possible, but I was no nearer to a receptive surface than she was. I needed to keep her attention. I continued kissing her neck and her gentle sighs told me that she was enjoying it, but I could tell that the burning cigarette was on her mind. I straightened up and moved over to the table. The ice cubes in the drinks tinkled against the cut crystal glass.

Remembering this sound brings me out of my memory and back into the bed, lying next to Marie. I glance around the room. My eyes are fully awake to the dark. The room is full of cosmetics and designer clothes. She has boxes that overflow with jewellery. She has fine perfumes and oils lined up in the most exotic bottles. She has piles of beauty and fashion magazines. I can see the cover of Vogue on the top of one of these piles. Sometimes we have sat in the garden and she has read these magazines from cover to cover, drawing rings around what she wanted to buy, underlining passages from the sex guides, reading out aloud from the social surveys, and etiquette pieces. Marie likes the perfect love scenes in films, impassioned moments of tasteful, uninterrupted body embracements. I contrive to move freely for her. There must be no seam showing in my actions, or in my conversations. I avoid ugly silences and clumsy fidgeting. I offer her Armani suits and Calvin Klein underwear. There is no physical benefit for her. It is just that seeing me in these clothes makes her feel worthwhile, desirable, that I have taste, and I have chosen her.

When I first arrived Marie was a little uncomfortable. It must be difficult for her, a mature woman of some beauty who is all but ignored by her inconsiderate husband. She dresses with style, always looking younger than her age, but never looking too old for what she is wearing. I put the drinks down and turned to see her hastily putting out her cigarette.

"You look very beautiful," I told her.

She laughed and her cheeks flushed with colour. The ease at which a compliment can do this to her makes me pity her situation with her husband. Even I must admit that she deserves better.

"I have been waiting for you to call," I told her.

I moved in front of her, crouched down, and began to rub her bare feet.

"I wanted to call you... Oh how I wanted to. We've had family staying. What could I do?" her voice was pleading with me, the pace of her speech increased.

"Where could we have gone? I did not know what to do."

"Hush," was all that I offered in return.

I took one foot in either hand. I pressed my thumbs into the soles of her feet and rubbed up and down, not too hard, but definitely not too gently. The more I did this the more she slid down into the chair. She raised her legs slowly with each circular push of my thumbs. She continued to make weak extenuations which were designed for me to ignore. She was working a facade, a conversation between two desperate lovers. It is a scene, and my role is to not listen, but to be overcome with desire, and allow passion to run its course. She began to repeat her excuses. The words that she vocalised were only so that she could meet the physical sensations with some mild resistance, just so that her resistance could be broken in a romantic entanglement of bodies and limbs.

I knelt right in front of her. She pointed her toes right at me, her feet were level with my shoulders. I looked right at her, whilst kneading the soles of her feet, her eyes were closed, her mouth trembling. I kissed her left ankle, pecking at the bone and sinew. She was quiet, her face serene and enigmatic. I became aware of her constricted breathing. She ran her polished nails through my chocolate brown hair. She moved down the chair into an uncomfortable horizontal position. I watched her; her chest beat up and down and her eyes were clenched tightly together. Marie gave out a long sigh of pleasure. I looked straight into her eyes, using my most penetrating gaze, and then we kissed each other.

"You are so, so, beautiful," I tell her again, moving my head slightly to feign sincerity.

I am thinking to myself how easy it all is. The word "beautiful" is easy. When I first started I used to think up different compliments, but they did not work. There would be a muted second or two, a seam in the script. It was not what was wanted. The word "beautiful" was what they wanted to hear anything else was not quite in the spirit of the story. It had to be simple, it had to be "beautiful".

We climbed up the stairs hand in hand, and entered her bedroom. I noticed an old grey suit of her husband's hanging off one of the handles on the wardrobe doors. We stood next to the bed kissing each other, holding one another rigidly in a prearranged lovers' clasp. She began to unbutton the Brooks Brothers shirt that I was wearing. The one she brought back for me from her trip to New York. I allowed her to finish. She ran her warm hands, and long fingernails, over my chest. I pushed her back, carefully, onto the bed. I slowly and carefully removed her clothes... She lay there in her ivory coloured silk underwear, which complimented her tight figure, tapered waist, soft brown skin tones, and perfectly applied makeup. She lay absolutely still for a moment, and I felt as if I were looking at a sensual portrait of a famous film star. Marie is well aware of her "goodside" though, her best pose, the angles that best help her to mask the irreparable damage of time.

She reached up to a cord and drew the curtains together, closing out the fading light of the early evening. I looked at her slightly crowned brown belly. Her silk panties felt cool and flimsy in my hand. I let them drop to the floor. I began to undress and I reached for a condom...

Marie was breathing fast. She had joined the oxygen race, when pleasure out paces your respiratory organs, your heart beats too fast, and you struggle for air, racing your lungs for more oxygen for your blood. I regulated my breathing with hers. Once I had done this, it was time to move on. When you follow someone else's breathing you have to keep up, but then as they get used to it they begin to rely upon you for the rhythm. At this point, you can take over. You keep it at their pace at first but then, as you move them closer to orgasm, you make your lungs work faster and faster, and they then follow you, trying to keep up in the oxygen race. I synchronized my breathing with hers, with my tongue on her nipple, with my hands on her body, with my intentionally vain attempts to enter her; my teasing increasing, and incensing, her desire. I could see the tendons in her body contracting with the effort, with the tight excitement, that was pumping through her arteries and veins. I maintained the synchronicity of my actions, except that I made them gradually faster, stronger.

She was meeting my body with a pushing all of her own, giving something back to her fairy tale lover. I wanted her to forget about any responsibility that she might feel that she had, and so I accelerated my forceful movement leaving her behind, abandoning her in the throes of ecstasy. How far she looked now from her favourite models, actresses, singers, and society queens. How inelegant her primal desire, moving her to the orgasm that she was paying for; that she paid for in magazines, health foods, aerobics classes, sun beds, saunas, designer clothes, designer underwear, and me. I watched the ghost of a forty-year-old's legitimate wrinkles surface from beneath her foundation, as her climax began to write its signature across her face. I sucked on her full nipple, and felt the tightening of her whole body around me. Then, as the taut waves of pleasure reached right down to the tips of her toes turning into warm and contented bliss, I watched the wires of tendon relax back into her now softened flesh.

I was pleased that it had been so easy. I find that the longer a client goes without having an orgasm the more difficulties they encounter when they see me. Then again, that is not always the case. Maybe the absence had been a good one, good for my account that is.

I relaxed, and stroked her soothingly, making sure of her developing smile, which was forming from out of her, now worn out, pink lipstick. I pinched the collar of the condom between my finger and thumb and walked into the bathroom. Marie, with a satisfied sigh and smile, slipped underneath the covers. I flushed away the evidence. All of this happened about six hours ago now. Later, as you already know, I would perform this act again. At that particular moment, I was pleased. There had been no problems, but Marie was always one of the most friendly, the most orthodox, of clients.

When I re entered the bedroom Marie was smiling at me. My penis had reduced enough so as not to arouse her suspicions. I moved in beside her. We talked, dressed, and ate. I watched her tiny idiosyncrasies. I listened intently to her conversation, as this is an important part of the service that I provide, it may well be the most important. She rattled off her eager external monologue and I replied with short, polite, retorts, and phantom nods, and shakes, of my head. A little while later a man arrived with the flowers that I had ordered. I always get Red Roses for Marie because she is a romantic. She loves the code that men and women have established in matters of love. It is not possible to send roses to most of my clients, as their husbands might become aware of what was going on. Often I send lilies, orchids, anything that can go unchallenged. Marie's husband, who is considerably older than she, does not notice roses in vases, behind ears, and, from what Marie tells me about him, he would not notice them if they sprung out fecundly from her cleavage. When I send flowers, and I send them maybe one in three visits, I always write their name on the card and nothing else. They love the secrecy and I do not have to think up different messages all of the time. I think that quite a few would rather me forget the sex than the flowers.

At some point in the evening, I took an envelope from out of the top drawer of her dressing table, the place where she always puts it. I am looking at her now, while she is sleeping, asking myself, how she sees it. Is she paying for the sex, or, for the smile. I examine her face. It is calm. It is beautiful. But it is sad. She really should not need me, but she does.

I have wiped out another memory; an early evening bout of choreographed, and purchased, sex. I too am tired, but I always find it difficult to sleep here in the middle of this glossy scene that I have created. I have another act to wipe out, but that will have to wait, because at the moment I do not feel like playing back another fleshy and hazy moment of limbs and lungs. The clock shows that her last orgasm was over a quarter of an hour ago. It has faded from her body, it has gone, a creation uncontained, unexplained, and soon to be erased. I watch the clock erasing time, spending seconds in a squandering circle. I turn to face Marie, the last act of today's, yesterday's, service.

Chapter 2

Virgin

It is Sunday. Two men are sitting in a car parked on the side of a road. It is a dry grey day that has drained the colour of the street and the lawns of the pristine detached estate houses. The man in the driving seat is wearing an unzipped, heavy looking, leather jacket which shows a plain navy sweatshirt underneath. He has his hands on the wheel, and his head is turned to face the man in the passenger seat. He is forty-five but looks older. The other man is slimmer and younger (around twenty-two, twenty-three) than the, would be, driver and is adjusting the mirror so that he can see out of the back window. He has short-cropped brown hair. When he is satisfied with his view in the mirror he reaches down and turns the radio on. The other man reaches down and turns the radio off.

Maurice (the driver): I don't even know if we should be doing this. I haven't even spoken to John.

Chris (consciously speaking slowly and softly, half soothingly, half mockingly): Look, shut up. You want to do it. You do want to do it. You just want reassurance right. You just want me to know that if there's any shit that I've gotta take the responsibility. Well this is your reassurance okay. For the last time. He phoned our room this morning. He told me to chill. He told me to tell you to take a couple of paid days off. He said to relax, and he did, he did, say to tell you to enjoy yourself.

Maurice: Then why ain't we at the races or a fucking casino. Why ain't we gone shopping. I'll get some things for Penny and the kids, and you can piss off and look for some of ya poncey clothes (exhales with disgust and distrust).

Chris (sternly): Moz, (he steadies himself) this ain't gonna be a big fucking secret. We're gonna tell John all right. We're gonna do the right thing. (proudly) We (pause, he looks in the mirror) are being enterprising.

Maurice: What! waiting for a couple of pakis to turn up on a housing estate in Birmingham. Enterprising, they're not even gonna show.

Chris (exhaling loudly): You've gotta stop thinking like that. You're fading man, fucking fading away. You've gotta change the way you think if you wanna survive the changes.

Maurice (loudly): What the fuck are you talking about. Why have you gotta speak in fucking riddles. We are leaving, right now, right this fucking minute.

He reaches down to turn the keys in the ignition. He stops dead in his action and draws his hand away as Chris, twisting his neck to get a better view out of the mirror, speaks.

Chris: Here we go Mozza, me old fucking beauty. Look who it is an'all. It's that fucking kid, and he's got the brightest grin you've ever fucking seen.

Maurice (puts his hand to his brow and looks down): Oh shit!

A young Indian boy, maybe twelve, walks up to the car. He talks through the window to Chris. The two men get out of the car. Chris follows the boy. Maurice locks the doors of the car and speedily looks around at the surrounding houses before pacing off quickly, following the other two. The boy leads the two men down the estate's concrete walkway which cuts through three cul-de-sacs. The boy and Chris walk side-by-side. Maurice, a step behind, constantly scans the areas to the side of the walkway, whilst habitually glancing over his shoulder every seven or eight paces. The boy leads them out of one cul-de--sac and they turn left at the top. Maurice catches his reflection in the windows of the passing houses, he hunches his shoulders a little and keeps plodding on belligerently.

As they turn the corner, the boy makes straight for the driveway of a house on the other side of the street. Chris turns to look at Maurice. They all walk up to the front door. The boy takes out a set of keys. He opens the door and they all file into the house.

Inside the boy opens a box to the left of the door and turns a key to switch off the burglar alarm. Maurice stands with his hands in his jacket pockets shuffling from left foot to right foot. He raises his eyebrows and looks at Chris as he addresses the boy.

Maurice: What's go'in on? Why are we 'ere? And why didn't ya just tell us to come 'ere? (pause) Why were we sent all over the place?

Chris gives Maurice a hard reprimanding glare, but Maurice steadfastly ignores it and turns to the boy

Said (with a noticeable Birmingham accent): You were not sent all over the place. I just gave Chris a different route okay. You must understand Mr. Maurice.

Maurice's annoyance visibly softens. He is still anxious but being called Mr. Maurice appeals to him. It should be Mr. Draufer anyway, but probably this kid, not being English, and probably because he's a fucking paki, doesn't know the difference between first and second names. He felt as if he knew what he was dealing with now. The boy's error pacified him.

Chris (trying to hide his embarrassment of Maurice): Well we're here for business "right" (he claps his hands together). So let's talk business. Exactly how much can you get your hands on.

Said: I can get an endless supply. I can get as much as you like, but not today.

Maurice: A wild fucking goose chase that's what this is. I've had enough, (to Chris) come on.

Said: Please Mr. Maurice, all I mean is that at such short notice you can't expect to become a millionaire.

Chris: 'Ear that Moz, milllionfuckinaires. That's good Said right? (Said nods). Too fucking right mate. See Moz this boy's got what it takes.

Chris is grinning and obviously very excited. Maurice is in the position where he knows that he cannot back down, and is annoyed that he has allowed himself to get into this situation. He knows that Chris is not everything that he let's on to be. In fact he knows that Chris has only recently been taken seriously by any of the others, and this is more to do with his socialising than business. Maurice resigns himself, grudgingly, to following through with this mess. He'd feel a lot better dealing with a white man. This is a kid though so at least there shouldn't be much trouble, even though he knew through experience how to solve that problem. He would follow through with the plan that they had made earlier.

Said: How much then gentlemen?

Chris takes a small wire coiled square pad of note paper out of the inside pocket of his cashmere blazer. Maurice digs into his inside pocket and hands him a pen. Chris writes something on the paper. He tears off a small line on which he has written a set of figures. Maurice has been looking on intently. He shows his satisfaction by not responding when Chris glances over to him. Chris fixes his gaze on Said. The silence reminds the two men that Said is only a boy. They move closer together and drop their intense stares down forcing the boy to look up. Chris holds out the piece of paper so that Said can read it. Said reaches out to take it.

Chris (solemn): Can you read it?

Said: Yes.

Said continues to reach out for the piece of paper. Chris takes it out of his reach and hands it to Maurice. Maurice squares his shoulders looks deadpan at Said and stuffs the piece of paper into his mouth. He chews on it slowly and widens his eyes to look as manic as possible. His jaw moves heavily in an elliptical cycle. The boy steadily gestures to take the notebook from Chris, so Chris gives it to him with the pen.

Said: I'm sorry I can't do that much today, next time for sure. How about this for today?

He flicks over the page, writes something with large swirling demonstrative strokes of the pen. He tears off the whole page and holds it up to the both of them. The two men nod to him. He then, concentrating totally on the piece of paper, follows his slow moving hands with his head, and gives the paper to Maurice. Then he looks up very slowly and expectantly, from the piece of paper that Maurice is now holding, to Maurice's mouth. Maurice looks down at the large piece of paper and furrows his brow. The boy acts unthreatened but curious, like a child looking in on one of the secrets of adults. Chris swallows and feels his Adam's Apple move up and down under the taught skin of his neck. He is trying not to look at Maurice who he knows will be looking confused and pathetic at this point. A loud noise can suddenly be heard, and before either of the men can recognize the sound, or notice that Said has moved, they hear his voice speaking into a telephone at the end of the hall. Maurice closes his hairy fist around the piece of paper and looks at Chris from underneath his furrowed brow. Chris avoids eye contact, squats down, and starts looking at the boxes that are piled up in the hall underneath the stairs. Maurice's interest is soon aroused and he follows suit.

Said: Yes Dad...
Yes they are...
We are just doing it now...
Yes...
Of course...
Are you sure? that doesn't leave me much time...
Okay...thanks Dad...
Are you coming later?...
Please try Dad... (respectfully)
Yes...
Yes...
Yes...
Yes I am Dad. You know I am...
Okay, okay...
I hope so...
Bye, bye.

Chris (turning around in his crouched position to look down the hall): How much are these computers?

Said (looking down the long hall, and looking sharply down at the two crouched men, Chris and Maurice fail to notice the boy's indulgent smile) I am sorry, I cannot sell them to you. There are some computers upstairs that may be of interest to you.

Chris: What's wrong with these?

Said: They've got to go back to the store. It's an insurance deal, you know. Some of my friends took them from the store. The deal is that we return them to the store manager. He's got something going, I'm not sure of the details. Would either of you like to have a look at the computers upstairs? Maybe I can get you a drink?

Chris (smiling at Maurice turns back to Said): 'Ang on, 'ang on. Your "friends" you mean people who work for your dad, right.

Said: Well yes, they have brought in everything that you see, and they do I suppose work for my father, although they've never met him. (with reverence) Have you?

Chris (quickly trying to answer the question so that he can ask one): Ehm... yes yes, yes I have. We both have. These friends though right, they're adults, I mean fifteen sixteen minimum?

Said: No.

Chris (holding his palms up, because he knows that he asking too many questions continues): Wait a minute. So, they're your age?

Said: Some of them.

Chris: This is some operation, (he looks around the hall at all of the boxes nodding his head) some operation. I mean, you've got my congratulations, not as you need it or anything, but you've got it anyway. Would you mind me asking one more question, and then I'd like to have a look upstairs, at the computers I mean, and discuss the price for our deal. What I want to ask is, I mean this is a low cost operation. One house, one son and a few "friends" so err... how much you paying them? Is it per item, or salary, or what?

Said (enjoying Chris's curiosity): You ask a lot of questions.

Chris: Yeah look I'm sorry. I don't mean any disrespect to your father or anything.

Said: It's okay, you work for Uncle John (Maurice's eyes shift instinctively to Chris, as the idea of his boss and this boy being related ricochets around his brain), that means that its okay (pausing and enjoying his deliberation) I suppose.

Chris: It's nice to hear you say that. (he turns to Maurice) It's nice ain't it Maurice (Maurice nods).

Said: Mr. Chris, we don't give them a penny.

Chris (feeling slightly insulted, raises his voice, and begins a protest): Hey, now come on, what do you think...

Said (interrupting): What I mean is: we do not pay them in money. I give them a stone for everything that they bring in.

Maurice (slightly outraged): Fuckin' jewels. (his mouth is hanging open incredulously) Jewels, like fucking diamonds and shit. You're giving (nodding his head to the rhythm of the repeated word) fucking jewels to fucking kids.

Said: No. Not Jewels. (pause) Crack.

Maurice becomes a little flushed and angry with himself for saying anything at all. Chris walks in front of him. He puts his arm around Said and walks him slowly towards the stairs.

Chris: You know Said, I've got a feeling that you're gonna be one of the greats in this business, one of the greats. Now, let's check out your stock, cos we've got a few birthday presents to get and stuff. Then how about we finish off our little deal.

Maurice and Chris are sitting in the car again. The car is now parked outside of the boy's house. The front door of the house is open.

Chris (excitedly): What about this kid? These people are sorted out, (nods in agreement with himself) totally sorted. This is going to be eeeeasy.

Maurice (staring harshly out of the windscreen at nothing): When we've got what we wanted I'll be happy all right!

Chris: See what I mean. He's a kid. A pissing kid. What can you do with him? He's polite and that. He just ran fucking circles around us. And he knows how to work it. He does us a deal and while we're round at his gaff he sells us a load of fucking gear: computers, fax machines, stereos. (firmly putting his point) See what I mean. He might be a paki but he's not fucking stupid. Jesus Christ Moz he even made sure we came here by a different route. Sheer professionalism that is. Total class. What an asset.

Maurice (shaking his head and leaving his mouth open after having spoken): He didn't give us the directions to get 'ere.

Chris (annoyed): He's our contact. He's sorted it all out. (looking out of the window at the sky, speaking slowly) There's more to this visit than we think. (to himself) Yeah. We didn't know about this until the last minute. John's got his eye on something. I feel good vibes from all this Moz, I'm telling ya.

The boy walks out of the front door carrying two large boxes that cover his head and face. He balances himself on his dangerously skinny legs, and begins to make small stuttering steps down the drive to the car. When he gets to the rear of the car Maurice, without diverting his attention to the boy, releases a catch from inside the car that opens the boot. The boy brings his knee up to help balance the boxes whilst trying to grip the handle of the boot. He manages to slowly open the boot but cannot help wobbling unsteadily on one leg. The boxes nearly slip off of his knee, but he opens the boot sharply and soon has two hands on the boxes and two feet on the ground. He arranges the boxes in the boot and goes back inside.

Chris: This is exactly what I meant Mozza. (holding the palms of his hands up to Maurice) I'm not fucking with ya. You've got things fucking beautiful back home. A family business, the girls who work for ya. I hear your Tony's doing great with Adam and Steve. Is it true he's gotta tattoo on his dick?

Maurice (surprised): Who? Our fucking Tony?

Chris: No Adam. I heard he'd got COBRA tattooed on his dick.

Maurice (smiling): Probably. A top man is Adam.

Chris: He's a fucking diamond geezer....Anyway as I was saying....You couldn't want for a better life mate, really. But, you know, ethnics are coming into the game. You can't ignore them any more. You gotta work with them. Do deals with them. They're emerging. They're gonna be part of the future. Why do you think we're here? Why do you think we were brought to the house yesterday, and taken to "this" warehouse and "that" restaurant, and all that shit that went on?

The boy comes out of the house with more boxes for the boot.

Maurice (looking straight at Chris): I don't care. I don't like them.

Chris : Pakis?

Maurice: I like white people. English people, from the South. John's a Brummie (pause). I like Brummies.

Chris: You don't like pakis. Fucking hell Moz, do you think they care? Do you think that kid cares? Those days are gone. These people make money. And we can make money with them. I don't like fucking Masters, well I don't fucking trust him, but he's a big part of our business. Anyway what about Serge?

Maurice (a little embarrassed at forgetting Serge): Well yeah! (quite positively) He's all right.

Chris (nodding at Maurice's error): Yeah he is "all right" (emphasising this word)... These pakis don't give a shit what we think about them. They just expect a bit of respect that's all. They fucking deserve it all right. A nice little operation like this, (he turns in his seat to look at the house) fucking marvellous it is.

The boy comes out of the house with a pile of clothes on coat hangers, all wrapped in thin clear plastic sheets.

Maurice (extremely irritated): Can we just get this over with.

Chris (mellow, realising that he has said too much): I'm sorry Moz. I just think that big things are going down that's all. And I think that we can learn a lot from this operation.

Maurice (realising his right to be offended): You're getting right on my tits. Just leave it alone. It's like having a fucking woman in my ear for fuck's sake. (flustered) Tell this little prick to get a move on and let's go and pick up the fucking money.

The boy brings out more clothes from the house, followed by a few more boxes. He then closes the boot and walks to Maurice's window.

Said: Would you like me to lock the boot for you?

Maurice (impatient): Just get in the back will ya!

Chris smiles to himself. The boy (still smiling) goes back inside for a moment, comes out with a coat on and gets into the back of the car. Maurice drives them off back to the hotel.

The car pulls onto the hotel car park. Maurice carefully parks the car and the two men get out.

Chris: I'll get the real thing. Said, be a good lad and help Moz out with the stuff in the boot.

Maurice (soberly): It's all right. You stay in the car. Don't get out! D'you hear me?

Chris runs off up to their room whilst Maurice fills his arms with clothes from the boot. Said sits perfectly still and relaxed in the back of the car. When Maurice returns from his first journey to the room Chris is with him carrying a small case. He puts the case on the front seat, leaves it there, and goes to help Maurice unload the boot. Maurice turns and stares at Chris, his eyes bulging with professional anger. Chris turned and got in the car with the case. Maurice picks up some boxes from the car. They look much smaller next to his large frame. He walks past Chris's window giving him a side-glance similar to the stare that he has just given him. Maurice is enjoying his chance to scorn Chris's basic error. Chris is suddenly aware of the danger that is always involved in any deal. How he had worried about every possible danger in every job that he had ever heard of being pulled off. How he had always told himself that he would never make an error because he was more aware of the dangers than anyone else. He had messed up only slightly but Moz knew now that he was not as professional as he let on. That he had never done anything like this before. He scolded himself silently and then decided to gloss over his mistake, not worry about it but just put it behind him, be cool and keep his mind on the moment.

Chris (watching Maurice he sighs to himself, but then turns to Said): So then (raising his spirits a little), where are we headed?

Said: Well we're going to an old broken down building. We'll meet some people, two of my cousins. They are good business people. They will like you and you will like them.

Chris (thinking about Maurice): Let's hope so.

Said: We can do more deals in the future. (playing his boy role) I think we have a very nice partnership Mr. Chris. I think this is only the beginning.

Chris is silent, the boy's accent was irritating him a little. He wants Maurice to hurry up with the unloading. Maurice comes steadily and heavily out of the hotel. His strides are solid and his natural bulky swagger intimates some of the physical power of this man. He takes out the final couple of boxes from the boot and slams it shut. He takes these boxes into the hotel. When he re-emerges, he has a mobile telephone in his hand. He opens the car door and tosses it to Chris. Not a word is said as he starts up the car and moves out of the car park.

Maurice and Chris stand up and kick away the splintered wooden frames that they have been sitting on. They are in an old derelict warehouse. There is broken glass on the cold concrete floor. The noise of a car braking, and stopping, on gravel fills the empty building. Four doors closing and the crunch of footsteps approaching follow this. Maurice positions himself square on to the entrance and tilts his head back so that he must look down on whoever is about to enter. Chris shuffles his feet, realises that this is a nervous reaction and becomes more nervous. He thinks that he cannot be so nervous though because he was at least able to analyse why he shuffled his feet. He feels uncomfortable, as if his body is covered with some clammy glue that is being over produced by some primordial internal gland. He tries to tell himself exactly why he feels like this. His mind works quicker and quicker, and his eyes are trying to look everywhere at once. He starts to find his confidence. He tells himself not to move or fidget, not to give anything away. He does not look at Maurice but knows that at this moment he will be as solid as granite, totally unmoveable. He brings to mind a huge cube of granite the same size as Maurice, and tells himself not to let go of this image for a second. Said is eagerly awaiting his two cousins who are his heroes. They are his image of young manhood. They are exactly what he wants to be himself. He is wearing the same make of tracksuit that Sanjeed wore last time that he saw him. His heart is beating fast beneath his chest. When the men finally walk in, he wants to run over to greet them. He starts to walk over to them but he cannot hide his pride and pleasure. He breaks into a light jog. His chest puffed out in front of him, blood and adrenaline pumping through his veins making him feel lighter than air, leading his feet swiftly bouncing across the concrete.

"Cousin, cousin," he calls out in his need to try to impress. Two of the young men greet Said stoically, and then along with the other two fix their gaze at Maurice and Chris.

Said: These are the men (pointing to Maurice and Chris), cousin (he emphasises this word, enjoying the sound that it is making in everyone's ears).

Cousin 1 (nodding at the case that Chris is carrying, and speaking with a thick Birmingham accent): If that's what your buying with you'd better slide it over here.

Chris (the huge block of solid brilliant white granite is firm in his mind, he has made his face as flat as possible by drawing into himself any emerging flicker of emotion): Here (he puts the case down on its side and shoves it across with his foot).

The larger of Said's cousins motions to one of the others. He is then handed an empty sports bag, which he opens. He opens the case and looks at the ten thousand pounds that is arranged in neat bundles inside. Each bundle is pinched, neatly in the middle, by a small elasticised strap, as if it had a waistline that it wanted to show to the world. The man who handed the bag over kneels down and takes the money bundle by bundle and places it in the sports bag. Said's cousin kneels down heavily but managing to control his stocky frame with his bent squat legs. He withdraws random notes from the bundles and takes what looks like a small torch out of his jacket pocket. He flashes the torch at each of the chosen notes. When he is satisfied he puts the notes in the bag along with the others, and puts the torch back into his pocket. Chris can feel that his throat is dry and tight. He notices the clothes that the men are wearing are all the same as the ones that the kid had just sold to them. These men are covered in gold. Large gold rope chains lie over Reebok and Ellesse sweatshirts, and they all have fat gold earrings in both ears that shine next to their black brilliontined haircuts. He thinks that their style is rather crass and cheap, and this makes him feel superior. And it makes him begin to feel ready for these men, as if they might have put him in this position of hating them because of their tacky dress sense. He suddenly felt ready to kill every one of them if he had to. He felt as if he were growing inside, as if he were ready for anything. He was proving himself to Maurice and he began to feel a sense of anxious optimism, coupled with delirious palpitations, at being so very close to fulfilment. He was pulling off something that he could not believe he was capable of, but had been telling anybody who would listen, that he had managed a thousand times, and now he no longer had to carry the black satchel of fear that he had opened in his fantasies only to find it empty, his mind, or spirit, or balls, empty of the confidence and conviction he needed to call upon just once, just for that first time. He had learnt a lot. Enough to pay attention to what was not being said as much as what was being said, or what was being celebrated, or what they were raising their glasses to. He knew how to pitch a story (a brag or exaggeration), or a lie (a practical story to someone outside of the group), or a scratch (a lie to someone within the group). He had learnt about physical confrontations, about not backing down to challenges, about how to confront a member with a higher standing without causing them embarrassment. He had learnt everything that he needed to survive and prosper. He had everything he needed he just had to get through this test of his faith in himself. Said was smiling still, and looking up to his cousins. He was happier now than ever. These moments, when he earned respect from the young men who his cousins took as friends, were precious. He knew that service, to these older and wiser men, was the best way to be accepted. His cousin stared into Said's eyes for a second and then looked away.

Said (loud and well rehearsed): Gentlemen, I am going with Nayim and Sanjeed my cousins. You must wait here. They will check that everything is okay and will return in two to three hours. In the event of any unforeseen delay we will not telephone you for reasons of our own security, but we will get here you can be assured of that. It is imperative that no matter what happens, or however long any delay might be, that you remain here. I will not see you again, not until your next visit. It has been enjoyable doing business with you. I hope that you will be satisfied with your purchase, and I look forward to us all doing business again, thank you.

The men all turn around to leave. Said walks in between his cousins.

Maurice (projecting his voice effortlessly in the large building, making it echo enough for his words to take longer than usual to be recognised by the brain): Three hours. I'll see you in three hours.

Said (turning around, speaking without a hint of compromise): It is imperative.... that you remain here Maurice (he smiles to himself for using the man's first name only).

Chris is sitting on a wooden box. He can hear Maurice's loud voice filling the whole building. He is talking to Chris or rather yelling at him. It is over three hours since the men left, Maurice is telling him that it is now nearer to four hours. Chris is not listening to Maurice, but he knows that Maurice has a valued position in the scheme of the action back home. Chris knows that he cannot respond to Maurice, that he must endure this moment, that when the men return with their merchandise his non-retaliation will be remembered and admired by Maurice, who will in turn retell it as a story to everyone else. Maurice's face is getting closer and closer to Chris's. Chris knows that he cannot retreat, and cannot look back at him. Maurice's face is twisted in his rage, and white creases in his middle-aged skin run through his furious blood-red features. Maurice takes a step back lowers his booming voice and delivers his poignant conclusion.

Maurice (with disgust): You've really fucked this up.

Chris: Moz....they said they might be late. Come on they'll be here any minute mate. We know where that kid lives don't we. They've gotta show.

Maurice: We don't know what's going on with these people. John has set something up. We can't go round there splitting open 'eads. This could be a major incident. This could jeopardise whatever John's doing with these people. (shouting, carefully enunciating word by word) WE SHOULD NEVER 'AVE GOTTEN INVOLVED.

Chris: Come on Moz...(he wanted to say how these things always went like this, that people always left you hanging around, but he knew that Maurice knew that he was inexperienced and that he had pretty much shit his pants earlier; he hoped that when everything was over Maurice would look back and laugh, that this was what all of the men's stories were like when you were involved, and that afterwards they grew into tales of camaraderie over drink and drug binges spoken within earshot of women and young girls)...it's gonna be all right. They'll be on their way. We just need to occupy our minds.

Chris paces up and down, keeping on the move so that he never has his back to any part of the building for more than a couple of seconds. He creased his brow and told himself to keep in control. He gave himself fantastic incentives of images of London hotel rooms, and card games, and of Maurice and the old guard laughing at the intricacies and discomforts that are a part of every deal, or job, that is ever pulled off.

Chris (earnestly): Please Moz, I know that they're going to show. Come on they even said about what to do if they were late.

Maurice: Yeah stay here and give them enough time to disappear...(looking at Chris)...Look you know that this is serious, I can see that. You want to get involved right. (Chris tries to interrupt) I know what it is, I know. You've never been in on a deal before.

Chris: Yeah, of course Moz...

Maurice: I'm not talking about selling draw to fucking students. I know, I've seen people go through this before. You want it right? You want it because you're a virgin...

Chris (realising the futility in denying this): Well I wouldn't say virgin....I mean I have a good operation but you know I need to do more. I need to get involved in more...

Maurice: It's difficult. I know.

Chris (rubbing his sweating palms on his trousers): I need this to work Moz. I suppose that I've taken too many risks. I know that they're gonna show though. They've gotta, they don't want any problems on their side, just like us. Come on Moz see this through with me. I'll be fully responsible.

Maurice: You can't be. I don't know why John brought you on this trip. I mean its all been kept quiet yet you're a new kid, you know. If John brought you along then we're all now liable for everything that you do. This trip is your acceptance but you haven't worked that out. So, you see now that you can't be responsible, not alone.

Chris (humbly): I'm sorry Moz. You know for being a right cunt earlier. I was so fucking...into making this deal you know. It being the first big one as well.

Maurice (to himself): I suppose that it was easier for me. I was just a hardcase. (shouting) THAT DON'T EXCUSE IT THOUGH. Things were easier then. I used to just turn up with the people who'd organised the job and then kick fuck out the biggest bloke on the other side.

Chris (relishing the chance to pick Maurice's mind, remembering the stories he'd heard of his friendship with John, he hopes to appeal to Maurice's sense of nostalgia): Is that how it started for you then? You and John like?

Maurice (laughing assuredly to himself): John wasn't even around when I started. I used to work alongside my brother Barry. He was the one with all of the connections. No John then, no Masters either. The whole game was different then, you're right about that. But in the main essentials, it hasn't changed.

Chris (cajoling enthusiastically): So how'd you and John meet then?

Maurice: He'd sort of come on the scene, but he was just a poxy student talking about "hashish" then. He was a kid you know. He wasn't taken seriously cause he hadn't done nothing in order for anyone to take him seriously. I was inside, but my reputation was still walking the streets if you know what I mean. I'd been in and out for just about as long as I can remember. I'd got collared for a post office job that Barry had put me in touch with. Four of us went down. Barry wrote to me about this kid John, only he didn't talk about him like a kid. I didn't even realise it was the same person for six months. Anyway, he remembered me. (Chris is relieved at the flow of the conversation, pleased to have pacified Maurice's attention) He talked to Barry, asked him how I was doing. He knew that with me inside that it must have been hard for Penny. He wanted to talk to me and help out Penny and the kids under the supervision of Barry. He was very smooth err...tactful like. When he came with Barry to see me, I couldn't believe it was that kid. He must have been doing something, taking big risks I suppose, maybe he just made it big cause of the eighties, I dunno, but he offered me a deal. Nobody but family had been near. I wasn't earning in jail, well not big money anyway, so I went for his deal. He looked after my family. When I came out, he was waiting for me. I'd never seen anything like it, I mean for the first three days I hardly slept a wink, and I didn't see Penny, or the kids. I thought it was going to be champagne parties and all that shit, the return of one of the lads, you know how people carry on when they first get out. It wasn't like that for me. I was working solid. I was running around with him, and others, I couldn't stop to think. But I did realise how serious he was. He was careful, quiet, he kept his mouth shut. He preferred listening to talking. I cracked a few heads for him. He gave me a nice wad to start myself off with, and after the three days he paid for me, Penny, and the kids to go to Spain for a week. Fucking marvellous he was. I mean by this time Penny thought he was great.

Chris: It must be nice being close and that. I mean you know you're one of the respected members.

Maurice: Yeah, but you know I've always been straight within the group. And I've always done my share of the shit jobs. But I understand that its different for you new blokes. There's still a place for hard men but the money's in the deals not the hold ups.

Chris: I suppose in a way that John's the start of the new way?

Maurice: He knows both ways. I think there's some who are beginning to wonder. You know what I mean? I'm all for pushing Masters right out. Get rid of him. I ain't scared of him and his fucking wanky suit boys.

Chris: Don't you think that we can all make money together? There's room for us all.

Maurice: Not when he gets the nod from London. Then he'll come looking for us all. Maybe he'll move on, but I don't think so. He knows what he's doing. If he does get the nod, it'll be the end of me.

Chris (concerned): What?

Maurice: I've seen him. You can't work for him. He don't play it right you know. With John, you know that as long as you don't fuck up you're all right. He'll look after you. Masters's men are shit scared of him. They don't know who's gonna get it next.

Chris (with respect): Yeah, but you gotta make people scared of you.

Maurice: Too much fear. He ain't right. He ain't nothing. I mean I know a couple of the older boys who work for him. They're making, don't get me wrong, but he's a risk taker they all know that. He's done more than anyone in such a short space of time, even I'll admit that. He's come out of nowhere, but all these risks will catch up with him.

Chris: Do you think he whacked Zak?

Maurice: If he did, we'll eventually find out? And then there'll be fucking trouble...

Chris (probing): What does John think about him getting the nod from London?

Maurice: He ain't said nothing to me. Anyway, I'll just retire from the big stuff. I'd keep the girls on and the small bits of business but apart from that, I'd leave it. And I'd keep my lads out of it as well. He makes too many people feel uneasy, it just wouldn't be worth the hassle.

Chris: It's a good sideline the girls?

Maurice: Oh yeah. We all do all right out of it.

Chris (suggesting sexual benefits): I bet you do.

Maurice: In the past yeah (smiles). But you know that's all a part of the job, the women. I can't say that I'm bothered any more. Penny never found anything out in all our married years. I've had my share of women but I never got involved. It was always just a part of what was going on, the parties, or the weekends working in the city. The women who work for me, you know who do the thieving and all that, well, they still want some from time to time, and usually they get it. I think that they just want more money. In some ways, I'd rather give it to them but people lose their self respect when they get handouts. That's the reason why I still fuck them from time to time. It's better that I don't get involved. They're better off sticking to the shoplifting. To tell you the truth Penny really is the only one for me. I try to be fair with all the girls, after all, they're my steady income, but sometimes I have to put them back in line. Me and Penny are rock solid and I can't have nobody fuck about with that. When we do an overnight, and Penny can't make it, it's a fucking nightmare (laughs)...

Chris (joins in):...beating them off with a shitty stick eh Moz?

Maurice (fighting off the laughter): Well they do all right. I suppose we only hurt the shops really. We owe Mark's and Spencer's a tidy fucking packet mind you... (more laughter from both of them).

Chris (realises that this is his chance to find out about the men at the top, he treads carefully feigning innocence, he allows his laughter to taper off): You must have some good stories about you and John in the old days?

Maurice (making a flat statement): Yeah.

Chris (realising that Maurice will not answer any questions about John): I mean you know piss ups and women and stuff (slightly flushed with embarrassment at his new error)?

Maurice (smiling again): Some good times.

Chris: (in his most respectful tone): There's a lot of people talking about those old days in the pub...Well at the card games or whatever... (nodding) really Moz...

Maurice (aggressively suspicious): I know what they fucking say. They don't say it in front of me, I'll tell you that fucking much.

Chris (finally getting to the crunch question, lowering his voice slightly, trying to distance himself from everything that has been said about John and Harry): Some of them are always talking about Harry...and Serge...

Maurice: Not in my presence, they fucking don't. Loyalty is the best thing you can have Chris. Don't forget that... Fucking wankers...

Chris: I keep out of it.

Maurice: I know who fucking says it. Masters and those little fucking bastards who follow him around. If you want to get on like you say then listen to me: I trust John he'll sort everything out for you if you're on a level with him. He handles his own life, so you're best to keep out of it. I'll tell you this much, Serge is a part of the operation as a whole an overview, that's all. And as for Harry, have you ever met Harry? Have you ever seen Harry? I don't believe any of it. If Harry does exist, he's just some bloke like you or me, somebody with different connections. It ain't like what they say.

Chris (worried): Like I said Moz, I don't have anything to do with all that shit. Fucking kids that's all they are.

Maurice: You want to stop drinking with those Masters pricks. I serve them drinks but they never, FUCKING NEVER, get out of order in my boozer.

Chris: I just hang around sometimes, you know, just to see what they've been up to.

Maurice: What they say they've been up to? They're all fucking bullshit.

Chris (having half suspected this himself, but also aware that he has been guilty of exaggerating): Yeah Moz, you're right.

Maurice: You just be patient you're turn will come. They'll tell you anything. They think that they're scoring points. Truth is Masters doesn't give a fuck about them.

Chris: You know Moz (with respect) you've got it all worked out mate. I've learnt a lot from you. You've probably got the best set up there is. A nice group of birds doing over all the respectable shops. You've got the connections to pick up the credit cards...yeah fucking lovely mate...

Maurice (full of his own worth): You'll learn. Mind you you've soon changed your tune you little fucker. You were all set to trade me in, for a gang of fucking pakis, this morning...

Chris (embarrassed and apologetic): Yeah well you're a real fucking pro mate. I can see that now. I'm sorry for acting like a prick. (smiling) I suppose that I've just got a weakness for Asian women that's all.

Maurice (quietly composing a serious question): Funny that in it?

Chris: What?

Maurice: Asian. They say that on the news and that. What's it mean? Does it mean pakis or fucking chinks. I mean they're both in Asia ain't they? So it's not really telling you much is it? (resolutely) Why don't people just say pakis or fucking chinks, eh? Why not? I mean there is a difference.

Chris: Yeah well when I said Asian, what I meant was pakis, all right? (grinning) You'd know exactly what I mean if you'd fucked a few paki women.

Maurice (laughing): How do you know that I haven't?

Chris: Well have you?

29

Maurice (exhaling): Nah...Well I wouldn't go as low as a paki mate. I've had a nice black woman. And I'll tell you something I know why a black man wants a white woman, its because he can't handle a black woman....She nearly ripped it off she did, let me tell you...

Chris (pretending to choke on laughter): Fucking hell...(continues laughing)

Maurice: So don't you get talking about "Asian" women...

Chris: Well it's like they know how to make you happy....I mean they're into everything, and anything that you want, anything.

Maurice (slightly more interested): What are we talking about here, wearing no knickers? Nurse's uniforms? Leather? Rubber? I mean what?

Chris: It isn't a matter of them wearing a basque on your birthday and a black line down the back of their stockings, its more than that Moz. It's in your imagination, you want it out of your imagination and in your bed, or on your floor (laughs)....They're a mix, a mix of naivety and a will to please. These women are not allowed out of the house as girls. They don't know nothing about the world. As girls they sit around wanting to be women and all they know is magazines and T.V. Next thing they know they're at college, or are allowed to go out to work, they have no idea how people their own age have been living. They've read about all kinds of shit, fucking blow jobs and sixty-nine and a load of other shit and they just want to get out there and do it all. They want everything that they have been hearing about, and they want to please you, so that you don't know that they've never had a life before. They're willing to do what ever you suggest. You just have to be in to them, like they're some fucking model or Madonna or something. They can't give you enough of what ever you want as long as you treat them like they're half famous or some kind of star, but....but they never get above themselves they always, I mean fucking always, want to make you happy.

Maurice: Dirty bitches eh?

Chris: You bet Moz...They don't even know what dirty is, all they know is what they see in films and fucking Women's Own. They all want to be the best fuck that you have ever had. They love it when they think that they have done something that has impressed you. They'll stop at nothing. Every Asian woman I have ever 'ad 'as sucked my cock. They fucking love it. Anywhere I have wanted to fuck they've bent over backwards to make me happy. (smiling) I've had them tied down and all sorts Moz.

Maurice: It's like a fucking drop of curry for them...(they both laugh together, Maurice slaps Chris on the shoulder)

The two men converse in virtual darkness, laughing at, and applauding, one another's experiences. It is very dark now although the men have not noticed. Outside of the building a short brown man, in a heavily weathered anorak, gets out of a taxi that he has been driving. He takes out two straining plastic carrier bags out of the boot of the car. He takes these heavy loads one in each hand, and, finally managing to balance himself, he walks carefully into the building. The two men are laughing loudly, almost intolerably, in the echoes of the large concrete and brick skeleton of a building. His jacket makes a synthetic rustling noise as he walks. The two men are a long way from the man. He notices how little the distance between them decreases with each step that he takes. He wonders if he will ever get near to them. He decides to put down the straining bags. The two men swivel around sharply. Maurice stands immediately and Chris follows suit.

The bag carrier (in an unmistakable Indian accent, speaking before they can): Excuse me sirs. I am bringing you that which you have been purchasing from my boss. He sent me here to give this to you. And I must be apologizing for this delivery being so late as it is. I hope that I have been inconveniencing you for too long (he stops, has he made a mistake? he thinks about what he has just said, he is not sure but decides that he probably has not made an error, he continues) Here is that which you asked for...

Maurice and Chris look at one another. They are suddenly very aware of their surroundings again. Chris hopes that Maurice is going to speak.

Maurice: Who are you? You're fucking late.

The bag carrier (concentrating): I am a humble taxi driving sir. (as if rehearsed) I am only working under the instructions of my boss. I am only trying to be doing my job.

The bag carrier shuffles across the room and the rustling begins again. He fears proximity to the two men and feels as if he is moving very quickly now. He regards the men with a respect that he expects they presume to be their right. He wants to leave the building. He puts the bags down in front of Maurice and Chris and takes a step back.

The bag carrier: Everything is here that you are asking for. (as if rehearsed) My boss sends you good lucky for the future, (as if quoting) please be enjoying fortune too much.

Maurice kicks over the two bags and heavy bundles of crisp ten pound notes and twenty pound notes fall out onto the floor. Chris unable to hold himself back kneels down draws a note from the middle of a bundle of twenties. He looks at both sides of the note and smiles to Maurice. The two men have widened eyes. Maurice kneels down to inspect the money.

Chris (excited and relieved): It's fucking beautiful.

Maurice: It's all here too by the looks of it...lovely.

They start to gather all of the notes together. They hear the sound of an engine starting and when they look up the man has gone.

Maurice (with a strain of paranoia, looking at the notes and then looking around the empty building): Come on let's get going for fuck's sake.

Chapter 3

Marie-Playback-Erase

I wake up in my bed. It is ten o'clock. I wipe my watery eyes, knowing that I have slept too long. My room is extremely untidy, magazines and books scattered everywhere, all lying in dangerous spine splitting positions. I get up to go to the toilet, on the way accidentally stepping on Oscar Wilde's *The Picture of Dorian Gray*. I stretch out in the bathroom in front of the mirror. It seems like an average everyday kind of morning, but the blank fatigue that I can read in my eyes tells me that it is not that kind of morning, but rather a morning after a night of work, of pretence, of lies and deception.

I pick up my copy of The Guardian that is delivered every morning. I take it into the bedroom and I spread it out across my unmade bed. I am reading the supplement, looking for suitable employment. There seems to be nothing for me. I have a degree in English Literature and I am halfway through a Masters course in American Literature. I want a job in which I can exercise my knowledge, use my expertise. I do not want to read the newspaper, I want to be in it. I read about life in the classics. I do not need to read about political sleaze, scandal, innuendo. I do not care about infidelity polls, orgasm surveys, sex guides... I want a life that is real, that is pure, not sensationalised, and not full of commercials. We are sold sex in a variety of forms; perverse, homicidal, suicidal, romantic, daring, technical, pornographic, athletic, career threatening, life wrecking... The sex that I sell is quiet, and discrete, set with polished coffee spoons and middle-aged cake crumbs, in the rural, and semi-rural neighbourhoods of Essex, Suffolk, and Norfolk, in houses full of silence, and mockery, and ridicule. There is British Sex, and Hollywood Sex, and French Sex, and Oriental Sex, but where is the love? What has happened to love? Why can't we be obsessed by love? The country, the whole western world in fact, is full of marriages that are based on what Douglas Coupland calls the "Divorce Assumption", that if things do not work out then there is no problem, you can just get a divorce. How sad that marriage, that love, is worth so little. How sad that all we read, and watch, are stories about infidelity, about the quick ephemeral thrill of sex snatched selfishly at the expense of our partner's, our loved one's, feelings.

I want to get married. I want to marry Sally as soon as possible. Maybe nobody believes in love any more; they certainly do not believe in marriage, but I do. I have a problem though. I am a young man who has come from nothing. My family are good people, but they are working people. I am educated, over-educated, to the point that I am detached from them. I have had to leave one social sphere only to find that I am not welcome in the next one. Sally is different. She only knows education. Sally's world is different. There are different expectations. The first time that I brought up the subject of marriage she laughed and told me that she doubted whether a student of Literature could ever earn enough money to marry her. I am trying. I have saved up a sizeable sum. I get most of my clothes bought for me. I spend money on books, newspapers, and food, only. The only things that I do other than study, read, and work, are, physical exercise and letter writing. I will finish my M.A. and enjoy the new status whilst having a decent sum of money tucked away in the bank. It will be a sign, undeniable proof to Sally of my commitment to her. Then, I am quite sure, she will marry me.

I am being helped by Gillian, one of my professors. She helped me to get this work. She gave me the chance to earn all of this money, and she is helping me to make a name for myself, giving me opportunities in Academic Circles, introducing me to the right kind of people. Soon I will be able to stop this work and go straight, so to speak. I will have enough money saved to show Sally that I am serious. She will see that I have made somebody of myself through my post-graduate study. I will have some savings to back me up, something to offer her, something to prove that I am a man of action, who has resources from which he can draw.

The envelope, which I removed from Marie's drawers, is on top of my bookshelf, resting between collections of poems by Emily Dickinson and William Butler Yeats. It is still full of money. I remember that I have to pay it into the bank, and that I still have to erase the second of last night's two encounters with Marie. You are probably thinking that I am making a big deal out of nothing. Maybe all I am doing is having sex but I do not see it that way. All that I, that we, have left in this world is love and passion. There are very few other pleasures that do not shorten your life expectancy, or destroy your brain cells, or put added strain on your heart. I refuse to compromise my love with images of glamour that I have had no part in creating. I will not be prey to pin-ups, hunks, and goddesses that I never asked for. I will not be told what to like, or who to desire. I have made my choice and have it instilled in me right through to my soul. I want Sally and nothing, and nobody else, will do... It is time to think about Marie, to rid myself of last night, to keep my love clean for Sally, for when we are together again.

You may think that I am lying to you. How can I not enjoy these women? How is it possible to stop myself from orgasming? How can I simply wipe out these memories? Well it took time, hard work, good research, and patience. I went back to a book I read some years ago called *The Cities Of The Red Night* by William Burroughs. I remembered the Brotherhood, and how in order to join the Brotherhood you had to be able to exercise total body control, which includes total sexual control. His guidelines set me on my way.

"To accomplish sexual control, I abstained from masturbation. In order to achieve orgasm, it is simply necessary to relive a previous orgasm...

I did not want to have an orgasm, so essentially I went about trying to achieve the opposite, which I managed to do by doing exactly what he did not. I soon realised that with intense concentration I could prevent myself from orgasming, and then all I had to do was relive my unfulfilled excitement. The more that I practised the easier it became. I have managed to keep my passion clean. I have nothing to fear. I have everything under control.

I am imagining Marie. I am going back into the depths of my memory so that I can pull the whole episode out by its roots. I must leave no stone unturned. I wonder whether she felt any guilt when she withdrew the money that she needed to pay me with. Perhaps it excited her, perhaps it gives her a sense of revenge over her inanimate husband. How does she feel when she is getting herself ready to see me? There are some things that I cannot know, that I have not been witness to, but as for the rest of it I must go back...

I have to worship Marie. I have to tell her the right things, treat her in the right way. She has to have that mature sophistication that attracts young men to older women. I have to play the game like children who have long since burst the myth of Santa Claus, but who maintain their belief in front of their parents just in case the presents dry up.

Marie was lying naked on her bed, her belly down, her head tilted slightly to one side. I was massaging her back, having already effleuraged and petrissaged her legs and buttocks. I rolled my thumbs up and down her spine. She was making a deep humming noise that seemed to come from within her chest and then rise out, taking all of her tension and stress with it. I pushed my knuckles into her shoulder blades leaving tiny white imprints on her back that lasted for a few seconds before disappearing. I brought my head down and gently brushed my lips against the skin at the bottom of her back. She allowed her legs to relax and open a little more while I began to rub oil into her shoulders and neck. I pinched and plucked the flesh and then used the tiger's mouth technique up her arms, and over her shoulders, onto her neck. I pushed my knee between her legs and she began to move, to rub her crotch gently against it, breathing out slowly as she did this. I turned her around and rubbed oil into her breasts. She raised her stomach up as I dug my fingertips into her flesh and combed them down her body. Marie's body shivered and she brought her feet up to push against my chest. I pulled her feet apart and laid her legs back down upon the bed. Then I took her hand and kissed it. I licked the tip of her index finger, and then I began to suck it on the very end, and slowly I slipped all of it into my mouth, then another finger, and then another. I rolled my tongue in a circle across the palm of her hand. I kissed the inside of the joint in her arm, the other side of her elbow. She groaned and I flicked my tongue in and out of the groove. My condom was already on and I put my belly on hers, and kissed her mouth forcefully, desperately running my fingers through her hair. I kissed her until she could not breathe and then I gave her some respite, a handful of seconds before I did it again. I wanted to keep her out of breath. Marie's whole body squirmed beneath me. She had her mouth fully open trying to swallow as much air as she could. I would not let up though. I changed my position to approach her from the side. I pushed my fingers into her, pushing hard, making her scramble up the bed, and then I pulled her back down, as she gave out short sharp invitations and protests. I smiled to myself it was all so easy... I rolled her over without any warning....I pressed my hand between her buttocks... Marie winced with delight at this promise, but that was all it was - a promise. I pulled her up onto her knees, not saying anything, acting as if I was some kind of aroused monster that had to have his own way. I reached for her and squeezed her flesh and I moaned out loud as if she was the most exquisite being the world had to offer.

Marie is a regular up and down woman, which means that she likes her clitoris rubbed up and down. This does not mean that this is the only way in which she likes it to be touched, it is just her preferred action. Some of my clients like it regularly rubbed, or licked, form side to side, others just like it to be randomly stimulated, in any direction, in an abandonment of form and emotion. Marie likes all of these, but I know, from experience, that she prefers it to be up and down, and as she has not seen me for a while it is important, I think, to give her exactly what she likes best, remind her of what she has been missing out on these last few weeks.

My body slid across her oiled skin. I turned her around and took her. Soon the bed was creaking enviously. I began to regulate my breathing with hers. I raised her bottom half up from the mattress so that I could get her at a more penetrative angle. She gave a shriek as I touched deep inside her. I began to increase the speed of our breathing. I complemented her thrusts with low bestial grunts. Her voice comes into her breathing, a higher shriek than before, almost a whistle. Each and every sound is followed by an intake of breath. She strained to raise her head up and then let it fall back onto her pillow; again and again her head thumped down as my body pressed against hers. Her neck began to tighten. There were rows of tendons popping up from beneath the tight skin of her neck, arranging themselves in a delirious fan shape. I moved harder. I moved faster. She was trying to say something, trying to shout, to scream, but she could not get the words out. She used all of her energy trying to make one obliterating scream but all that she managed was a gossamer whisper, "Now, Now, Now..." I grabbed the pillow that was at my side and pushed it underneath her back and buttocks jacking her body up so that I could push into her even further. She called out another perfunctory "Now." Her body quivered in shock. She settled into her climax, sinking into her bed, collapsing into orgasmic comfort. Her "Now" settled on her contorted face, slowly radiating throughout her entire body. The blood of the moment had already left her arteries and entered her veins...

I made my way back in the early hours of this morning. The taxi was on time. I sat in the back. Something was playing on the radio. I asked the driver to turn it up. She did, and, smiling, asked if it was worth a tip. I returned her smile and listened intently to the words. I was trying to find the meaning of the lyrics and then apply this meaning to me, to my life, to yesterday, to last night, to how I felt at that moment, but as much as I tried I could not quite do it. I sat listening, puzzled, wanting to erase it all.

Is this too much? Maybe it should be. We all define ourselves through what we do. You have to know what I do. It is not the sex. I am telling you that it is not the sex but you do not believe me. You do not understand. You have been blinded by too much too soon. I have to show you how I can be. I can change with each situation, with the wishes of each client, in every separate encounter.

The memory has gone. I remembered every detail, and every sensation, and it is now washed clean away from my mind. All of the details have gone. I am untainted, untouched, by the shallow acts that I have been involved in. I feel very little, nothing in fact, for any of these women except for maybe pity. I do not enjoy these encounters but they are necessary. I need the money. I need a life that is full of real love, and real passion, and not games of lust, or idle play. I want Sally and I must pull myself up from the canvas again and again before I am counted out. I have to make myself a desirable partner by any means possible.

What I do is dangerous, psychologically dangerous. I take my chances and limit the damage as I have explained. My major soul saving principle is that I love Sally, and I will do whatever it takes to make her mine. I love her totally and unconditionally. I am devoted to her. All of the money that I earn goes towards us and our future together. I erase these encounters so that I do not have to lie. It may seem strange, impossible even, but I open the door of the dark room and let in the light, destroying every moment, every image. I scrutinise every detail until it fades to nothing, to clean vacuous whiteness.

Sally has no idea what I do. She thinks, because I told her (a lie I know), that I work in some dusty warehouse, working evening shifts, making only a little money. This is what I have told everyone. When she asks where I got all of my money from I will show her some article that Gillian has had published for me, and that will be the end of it. Soon all of this will be lost forever.

I am still staring at the job pages, looking for some position, maybe at a university, teaching in some literature department. There is nothing. I am staring without looking so that all of the words have jumbled into one great big clutter of meaningless shapes. My eyes are focused on nothing. I cannot continue reading it. I am losing all hope. The sheets are all grey and I can feel my spirit dissipating with every page that I turn. I stand up and throw the newspaper in the bin. I had better check my answer machine. The light is not flashing. There are no messages. The cassette is blank.

Chapter 4

Lisa

She was that kind of girl. You remember her. She held a monopoly on all of your, pubescent, fairy godmother three wishes. She was in your class. You could think of no one else. You woke up in the middle of the night with every pore of your body weeping for her. You talked to her, and you agreed with her, whenever she gave you the chance. Every boy in the year wanted to be on speaking terms with her. She spoke to just about everyone, bringing a warm glow to the cheeks of each of your friends. You watched them compete with each other in conversation each wanting to keep her engaged. You scorned their pathetic attempts at holding her interest, each trying to make her think about them. You knew that as soon as anybody made such an advance that they were doomed to failure, but you fell over, fell over yourself, in your own pathetic demonstrations of masculine power.

You got older together, only she seemed to accelerate towards womanhood, whilst manhood, for you, was postponed. She was still very friendly to you, and to everyone, but the time was approaching when you would both leave school, and part forever. You planned a proposal of marriage on the last day of your school life, but you saw the same hopeless hope in the red spots, of sexual insomnia, in the eyes of every young man present on that last morning. You admonished yourself at night, alone without her, for not shouting out the words that you had rehearsed in your mind, but you cling to the memory of sharing a short straw, drinking from your Ribena carton, and you never forget the taste of her glistening warm viscous saliva, that she left for you, just for you. She is gone.

You can no longer see her legs beneath the desk in Geography. You know that you will begin to forget the contours of her calves that you had committed to memory. It is over, and it never happened. One night, with friends in a pub, you hear how she pursued some career in modelling and that it never quite worked out. You remember her as being stupid and you spend the evening with your friends, reminiscing, and creating a caricature out of her two dimensional personality. Of course, that night alone you remember her differently. You still feel insignificant when you see her on the High Street and you avoid her glance so that you can stealthily study the way she walks. You married her a thousand times, and spent a thousand times the number of your weddings with her in your marital bed. The sex that you have enjoyed with your girlfriends was always very special, but you know that it can never come close to the love making that you should have had together but were denied by your, and all young boys', fatal lack of experience.

One day you have finally forgotten all about her. You have achieved beyond the dream you had of her. You know that it was only the circumstances of youth, and the dynamics of adolescent girls' attraction to confidence, and a teenage boy's callow anxiety, that prevented your union. She is no longer a mystery because she is no longer a girl and you are no longer a boy. If only all of those old friends and enemies could see you now, now that you have everything that you know they can only dream about. You have made it. You are staying in the best room in the best hotel in the city. People present themselves to you like fruit on a tree, like animals in a zoo. You are confident and secure in your ability to do whatever you please, and nobody matters as much as that girl did because there is nothing that is so out of your reach. You stride down the expensive feeling carpet of the corridor outside your room. The cut of your suit is dazzling, the fabric is uniquely compelling to the eyes of people that you walk past. You walk out into the lobby and it seems that everybody is there for you. But its not quite that simple, because you become another of these spectators, as suddenly She walks across your path one more time...

Uncanny John could not believe it. It was as if the lobby and reception desk were freeze-framed. Everybody, and everything, seemed to be completely still, and all noise had turned to silence. He felt as if, for a few seconds, he was looking at a large photograph. The elevator doors opened and he did not have to look at her to know who she was. He recognized the picture before him; how all possibilities lead to her. The way that every piece of furniture, every outstretched arm, every line of depth on the picture before him pointed to her. For the people and objects that surrounded her, wherever she was, there seemed to be no alternative to the gift of her mere existence.

She was talking to a receptionist at the desk. She had her back to John. Her hair still shone blonde. She stood on her left leg straight and taut, with her knee locked. Her right leg was torpid and bent at the knee, it swivelled back and forth on the axis of her right toe. John walked into the silence of the photograph hearing every muffled step that he made on the carpet's deep pile. This was the only sound that he could hear in the midst of the busy lobby. As he approached her she began to turn in a kind of timeless slow motion that distorted everything else around her. He could see that a smile of recognition was already on her face as though she already knew that he was going to be there.

He tried to make his eyes sparkle and his voice overflow with surprise and enthusiasm. It was she who spoke first though.

John...John? It can't be...can it...but it is...Oh John I'm so happy to see you again...

When she spoke it was as if she had given her permission for all of the noises of the hotel to be suddenly released on his unexpecting ear. But then a moment later the migrainous din subsided as all ears stopped to listen to her perfect words and every person, animal, plant and machine rolled out an invisible blanket of silence for her to speak in. The two of them spoke to each other with immediate openness. He made as much eye contact as he could muster in the presence of this face of his adolescent worship. Her voice was slightly lower than he remembered, and he liked that. He also realised that he had underestimated the grace with which she undertook every action.

She asked him to wait in the bar a while whilst she finished up her details with reception. She would join him in a few minutes. As if hypnotized he began his short walk to the bar, obeying the instructions from her smile and eyelashes like the over excited school-boy that he had once been.

He went into the bar, ordered their finest Irish Whiskey, and drank it down. Then he ordered another which he sipped as if he enjoyed nothing more than the warm smoothness of its trickle down the throat. He noticed a strange cardboard display behind the bar showing a frog sitting squat next to two fluorescent green apples. The sign, also in fluorescent green, said: *CroakCroakRibbit, Pommetizer the new sparkling apple drink, made with French Apples and British KnowHow*. They were giving away free scratch cards with every bottle of Pommetizer. John looked at the picture of the frog. He decided that it looked more like a toad. The whole cardboard display was painted in vivid gloss but the frog (toad) stood out as being glossier than the rest. It almost seemed as if the frog was wet and this made it look alive. He watched it suspiciously, recognition skimming hastily through his mind. He had probably seen it in another bar somewhere. He sat fidgeting for a few moments and then began to make plans. He had the upper hand now. He had money and power and confidence and men that worked for him and the right clothes and opinions and access to the finest clubs and restaurants and he had something more knowledge. Knowledge is power. It also intimates experience and experience is what makes us interesting and unspoken experience makes us mysterious. Thinking about this made him feel good, as if he could not fail to impress her. He took stock of the situation and was annoyed with himself, here he was already waiting around for her, already unable to think of anything else but the dreams that she made possible. He had to salvage what he could from this situation. He had to be able to control everything in order to keep her attention. He had changed from that fumbling teenager into a man who controlled operations that brought him and his associates hundreds of thousands of pounds a year. He had to make all that he knew, and that she did not, bear down upon them both, but he had to do it without appearing to be trying to impress. If she was certain of what he wanted, of what he was, then there would be no need for her to maintain her interest in him. He had lost the initiative but he had caught hold of himself before he had stammered his way through a round of drinks with her. He had to move slowly and keep her thinking about him. He had to be careful not to be too interested in her but he had to remember not to appear to be flippant about seeing her again, after all she still knew that he had loved her because everybody had loved her. He knew to try and pretend that he had not loved her, or that he had forgotten that he had loved her, would only make her think that he had learned nothing, that he was still an insecure immature male.

He had to get out of this situation. He had to make sure that this time he did not let her slip out of his life. He decided to leave a message with the bar man and retire quietly to his room where he could arrange a trap that she would find irresistible despite its dastardly posture. He had made up his mind. He drank down the second drink and left his message, instructing the bar man to recount his message word for word. He showed his appreciation discretely to the bar man and embarked upon the most hazardous part of his plan: getting to his room without seeing her.

It was nice to see him again after all the years and all of the life that passed since school. He had grown filled out nice suit nice smile hair still lovely no fumbling, fidgeting, shuffling softened accent (like herself) interesting. She had to contact her agent to see if he had set her up with new work. She held and held and got an answer machine. She wanted to shout "pig" into the microphone but knew that she would not be helping herself if she did. She left a message trying to strike a balance between politeness and pressure with an appealing hint of desperation. She went to the bathroom to look in the mirror but could not resist peeking into the bar before quickly examining herself. He was still there. She had underestimated just how nice that suit was on him. He wore it well which meant that he was used to wearing suits... She saw him drink off his drink. She smiled and pondered over his life story as she went to the bathroom. How much could she guess about him and how much of his life would shock her?

She leaned over the hand basin in the bathroom so that her face would be nearer to the mirror. She inspected her faultless makeup and decided to touch up her lipstick out of intrigue and love for the endless combinations of life that were constantly showing themselves to her and then hiding again. The design of existence seemed to be one huge game of peekaboo that forever realigned itself so that you never knew who it was, or what it was, or where it was. She had decided that to be happy you had to move forwards and backwards, and move in and out of focus of the camera that watches us all. She stepped back from the mirror to look at her clothes and how they hung. She pushed up close again and squeezed two handfuls of hair just so. The handfuls of soft shining blonde curls flamed up from between her fingers. She opened her hands and the impish curls wafted perfectly down to her tanned head like swooping cherubs. She thought for a second about her miserable agent but decided to go out into the bar, have a little fun, and leave him to worry about her for a change.

In the bar she could not see John. She sat down and waited. The barman, a slim grey-haired middle-aged man, walked over to her table.

"Excuse me Ms. The gentleman Mr. John Tomilary has asked me to convey his most sincere pleasure at seeing you again after all these years. He apologizes for having to leave without seeing you but he has been unavoidably called away. He has honourably requested permission to contact you in your room to arrange another meeting that could occur at your earliest convenience. Mr. Tomilary could not impress upon me enough how much an acceptance of his apology, by yourself, would please him. He would like you to help yourself to anything you might like from the bar, and has asked me to inform him of your room number so that he may call you when he gets back from his untimely meeting. Madam,..." The barman stood back awaiting a reply. The man had a nice accent, Spanish, Italian, or Greek, she couldn't tell, but she did appreciate it. The barman's words made her realise how different John was to the boy she remembered. She ordered a Gin and Tonic and said that of course she would accept the gentleman's apology, and she gave her room number to the barman after she had finished flicking through a magazine having enjoyed her drink. She contemplated another drink but she felt a little encumbered drinking alone so she went to her room, having no choice but to await a call from her agent.

What the fuck was he playing at? She's waiting downstairs and he blows the whole thing out. They could be drinking and talking and smiling right now. He had run away from her because, and he was certain of this, he remembered, for a split second, the way it felt when you were not in control. He did not have the confidence to sit and talk to her as he is because he could not get over what he was. He sat on the sofa in his plush room his left hand to his head. It could all be salvaged. He could put it all right. There was no damage done. She was, hopefully, a little pissed off, and if not then he was in no less a situation than he had been ten minutes ago. He would show her style and respect, give her as few facts as possible. He would show his wealth, his power, his knowledge rather than talk about them. He would ask questions about her life and he would listen to the answers. When they discussed the old school days he would always compliment her in some way and be at ease with laughing at himself as an adolescent. He had to show no weakness to her. He ran through all of this in his mind leaving himself mental notes for the conversations that would follow between the two of them.

He thought about tonight. Tonight he would take her out but he would have to get in contact with her soon so that she wouldn't make other arrangements, but if he contacted her too soon it would be obvious that he had fled from their earlier encounter. He didn't want to think about this at the moment it was his mistake and it made him uneasy. He would deal with other details first, and later it would be time to contact her, and then he could do just that without having worried about it in the meantime. Where were they going to go? He remembered that they had, for security reasons, hired a car for the journey; an inconspicuous blue, top of the range, Rover. He couldn't take her out in that and he knew that Maurice looked like a gangster, and Chris had never driven for him before. They were all supposed to be going back tomorrow. In fact their business was complete they could have gone home now but he liked being away from the pressure and was taking this, an extra night, Saturday night, for himself so that he could travel back fresh. No car, no driver, no reservation, this was all bad, and he was leaving tomorrow and then there was Harry...shit, shit, shit, shit. Maybe Maurice and Chris would somehow pick up on his weakness for Lisa and see it as a sign of the end of his career. He put both hands up to his head now. He jumped tensely drenched in anxious perspiration and paranoia as the phone buzzed urgently like a killer hornet. He breathed in allowing the phone to continue before picking up the receiver.

Voice (Mediterranean accent): Hello Mr. Tomilary...[Yes]...Ms. La Truen says that of course she accepts your apology and would be delighted to hear from you. Although she will be checking out tomorrow morning, she would like to get chance to speak to you. Her room number is ___. She asks you to call at any time...[Thank you].

He writes down the number of the room scoring over the digits again and again, and decides to call Hanif.

She lounged over one of her magazines with extreme indolence. She sat on the bed, her shoes off, her legs and feet curled up beneath her. She stared for a few seconds at a strange advertisement that showed two men, surrounded by lush overgrown foliage, in just their briefs, holding pistols up to one another. The men were young, golden in colour, well muscled, and their bodies were hairless. They both held their pistols in their left hands. She noticed nothing strange in all this. She wondered if they were cold, the models, when the shot was taken. She flicks rapidly through the rest of the magazine so that it plays like a fragmented film of glamorous images. She finds this interesting enough to do it again and then flips the magazine from off her bed. She opens a notebook to a page that has her agent's number on it. She looks at the number, at the telephone, and back at the number, and then back at the telephone, "ringring, ringring, ringring," she mimics. She picks up the book that her younger sister gave to her for her birthday in order to show her what she was studying. She was trying to read it. She was determined to read more and was going to begin by appreciating her little sister's studies. Lisa sighs and then stares at the strange name on the cover of the book OVID. She opens to where she left off. She reads about Salmacis and her sisters. How the sisters urged Salmacis to get a javelin. How Salmacis wanted only to wear see-through gowns and lie in splendour amongst the leaves and grass. She decides to take a bath. She puts the book down, relieved, but proud of her sister's achievement, and proud of herself for being able to keep up her promise to read the book. She got up to run the hot water.

...yeah Said was really happy seeing you again....it'd been far too long...

You've got a great kid there. He's turning out well. It was nice to see Dena too...she looked as lovely as ever...shame that the little ones don't remember me...

Well we should be seeing a little more of you John...

This has been a great couple of days away from the aggro down there...not that I can't handle it...it's like I said they don't understand professionalism...they still rob because they enjoy it. (laughing) That has always been your biggest problem in this business...our white cousins have always taken pleasure form the dirtier side of the operation...(laughing)it's a burden that comes with your superiority...but don't worry I think that, from now on, things are going to be a little easier...you know John when you get back to your position you should be taking things easier. I'm not saying that you become slack, you just need people that can get the job done, so that you can observe in the back seat. You need to make the crossover...become untouchable...the sleeping partner...sleeping with your eyes open of course. Our little business arrangement should ease your passage...

Hanif, it's just like old times again talking to you...

I have to make it special for you back in your old town...

Thanks again for everything...

Just enjoy your evening...make sure that you call me before you leave.

I will.

(laughing)Goodbye Godfather

(laughing)Goodbye Godfather

John is tingling with excitement as he puts the phone down. He moves straight to the wardrobe and starts looking for the right outfit for tonight. He is ready now, well prepared, to meet Lisa. He runs through it all in his mind, and reads off his note pad.

1   Meeting and Greeting (in the lobby).

2   In the Jag make a gag (note: think of joke).

3   Sitting at the table be amiable (ask questions; listen; be interested in her).

4   Dine with wine (memorize the requests that Hanif suggested eg. specific grapes, regions and vintages, appear to know all about the wine list).

5   Don't be a fool when you talk about school (remember to chuckle about yourself as a schoolboy, it makes you appear to be different now, familiarity running alongside mystery a perfect combination; when talking about her as a young girl use words like "pretty", "admire", "fun", "mischievous"; do not make any sexual references or clumsy compliments).
He counted them off on the fingers of his left hand whilst reciting his rhymes in a loud preoccupied whisper.   Hanif has managed to secure a place at a top restaurant. He is also supplying an old Jag (the old model that is his pride and joy, a bigger car would be too obviously a show of lookatmemanship) and an experienced driver. He knew exactly, exactly, how to be with her. How to present himself. It had been a long time since he had made love to a woman. Of course Harry wouldn't understand. Harry would never understand...but then things with Harry weren't going well. Harry didn't know and Harry must never know. He decided to forget about everything else for a while, everything, he owed himself a good time and he was going to have one. He wanted to feel Lisa all over him; covering him and soaking him. He ran a shower and took off his clothes as he tried to think up a joke.

Lisa finished painting her fingernails black. She put the top back on the varnish and put the bottle on the dressing table. Her long slender legs were stretched out before her. She looked at her feet and the blue styrofoam toe separators that she was wearing so that her painted toenails could dry properly. John was so easy to talk to, even after all these years. He seemed to be successful, happy, not bitchy like the other old friends that she sometimes caught up with. She guessed that he was a manager now or maybe he worked in a bank. He was always clever at school. Where did he get that suit from? She wondered. Maybe she was underestimating him. Maybe he was a solicitor or a business whizz-kid. He was probably a newly promoted sales rep. She thought about whether she should think about his intentions, but couldn't sustain the thought and instead cursed her agent again. She had looked at every page in her magazines even if she couldn't muster the energy to focus her eyes on some of the pictures. The book that her sister had given her was not an evening option, just an attempt to feign interest in her sister. Lisa's mother had suggested the idea. Lisa didn't mind reading. It was better than daytime TV, but it was not going to happen on a

Saturday night, no way. She found the grass that Bridget had given her and decided to "turn on" whilst waiting for Baywatch to come on.

John had put on his favourite suit. His shirt was white and stiff. His underwear was tight and secure. His hair had fallen correctly and would not trouble him now. His suit, that he loved so much, was fastened up high and when unbuttoned revealed a superbly tailored waistcoat. He tied his shoes up tight and hard, and in a double bow, so that they pinched him, that way he knew that they would remain on his feet, or maybe that his feet would remain inside of them. He had been called up to say that the driver was downstairs. He had called Maurice and Chris and told them to wait by the phone in case he needed them, and that he expected to return at some time after eleven and that they would be in the bar when he got back to the hotel. He wanted them there for security and because a part of the Lisa La Truen fantasy was that you had to be seen with her in front of as many other men as possible. He also wanted to make sure that this was all really happening so he needed the witnesses.

He left his room and locked the door. He walked as a total whole, a single being, solid within the perimeters of his suit. His tie did not move, his hair did not move, his handkerchief did not move, neither did his collars, his lapels, his shoelaces, or his features. His legs and arms moved mechanically as he walked towards the elevator but even then his clothes were crisp enough not to crease, or sway, or stretch. He stepped into the elevator and pressed number __, Lisa's floor. He began to unbutton his jacket. When he had finished the jacket opened about half an inch but did not hang it just stood rigid and solid as before.

Lisa opened the door. John felt as though the skin on his face was going to rip open as he fought to make his features still and unmoving. It was as if she had read his mind and picked out the exact clothes that he had always imagined her to wear. He could see how white blonde her hair was. Her skin and makeup looked immaculate, and she was wearing a long black dress with two simple loose straps that hung over her shoulders. Lisa noticed his strange grimace when she first opened the door. It seemed, though, that as soon as she noticed this grimace he opened up a large smile, and leaned forward to embrace her warmly. John allowed himself to squeeze her very lightly and his hands touched momentarily on the soft black silk of her dress. Lisa was pleased at how friendly John seemed to be. She felt happy with him, unthreatened and appreciated. He seemed to be very comfortable not like the boy she used to sit next to in Geography. She suddenly realised that she was very, very, slightly impressed by him.

She left her room and locked the door. She walked elegantly along to the elevator. Her dress moved steadily around her, sometimes clinging to her slender waist with a gentle ruffle as she swayed, sometimes swishing and unfolding down her thigh or calf as she stepped. It seemed to John that she was constantly moving. Her dress changed its shape revealing a little of her body for a moment, and then it swung away, reforming itself over and over. John tried to re-establish his mind's image of her with unsuspicious subtle glances but she seemed to have no fixed shape. She seemed to repeatedly move out and in, as if her body was polymorphous and merely flirted with an idea of a round hip, and then a smooth calf, and then a tapered waist, and then she just seemed to be a busy hive of curves and flesh, and then...

Lisa shimmered as she stepped out of the elevator into the lobby and for the first time and he realised, for the first time, what it was to be with Lisa in public. It was a totally new experience. He was told that the car was ready. Lisa took his arm. He felt no weight from her hands on his arm. It was as if she had no shape and no weight and now he felt as if she were violating his hard singularity and he could not feel his legs working but he seemed to be moving quickly towards the doors. He was moving as if on wheels only too fast and he felt a little sick. Lisa was smiling leading him leading her. He could see the car outside getting nearer as they approached the glass doors by what seemed like an act of will. The driver was standing by their door and he opened it for them as they approached. He smiled at John and Lisa, as they got into the car, and he greeted them courteously. He was from Sri Lanka. Lisa noticed his bright brown eyes sparkling with subtlety. She thought that his beautiful imperially correct English, and perfect intonation, put both her and John to shame, and in appreciation she sent him a warm smile. The man was happy to be dressed so smartly and to be given such an important job. He, and his family, needed the extra money such jobs brought in. He had to make sure that there was no room for complaint. He knew that this man was very important. He would enjoy dressing up for the evening and chauffeuring these two beautiful people around. He saw his reflection in the windows of the car as he walked around to the driver's seat, he was handsome. He would savour this while he could because tomorrow he would be back in the heavily weathered anorak, and short shuffling steps, making late deliveries of fake bank notes, and pretending that he could not speak fluent English, that he was the humble immigrant. Never mind, he thought, these seemed to be important people, so he must be moving in the right direction.

Inside the car John asked her, "What do you call a sheep with no legs?"

Dinner.

No...

Breakfast?

No.

An easy lay?

No.

Anything you want because it won't run after you.

No.

I give up....What do you call a sheep with no legs?

A cloud.

The only thing that she ate all night, as far as he noticed, was desert. She ate chocolate and pistachio ice-cream from a long androgynous spoon. The rim of her wine glass carried the spectre of her painted lips. He had watched her drink. His eyes followed her unblemished neck as she drank down the wine. He watched her fingers curl around the brightly transparent glass. He focused on the shining wetness of wine on her lips that remained for a few exquisite moments after every time she finished tasting her drink. He liked watching her. He liked being so close to her. Everything seemed to be happening exactly how he had planned, exactly how he had always imagined. They both seemed to be flashing smiles at one another all evening. He watched her move her spoon languidly up to her mouth and then tilt her head back slightly so that the ice-cream would effortlessly slide down her throat. He imagined the green and brown trail that the ice-cream must be leaving in her mouth, throat, and passageway to her stomach.

The rumour was right she had become a model. She had done a few shows....but she hadn't got the kind of figure that was fashionable....she had problems with her curves....they were looking for coat hangers with pimples for breasts....she had moved into music videos....you know all tight leather and high heels, mainly heavy metal bands....she had got a big break....appearing in scenes on Baywatch....she met Pam....and she was a wonderful woman....very shrewd....a great sense of humour....she didn't stay on....she enjoyed it but she decided against the boob job...

He had to admit that he was impressed by her. She had succeeded.

She had decided to return to England....she missed her mom....she would like to work abroad again though definitely.... maybe Australia, or even Japan....she was waiting on her agent....he, they, were always very unreliable....they were the worst thing about her kind of work....queers or perverts all of them....the queers were easier to work with....they got more work and were only demanding in a professional capacity, but they had more girls on their books....she had worked with women agents....in America....it was a woman who got her the Baywatch contract....but she had taken a larger cut than usual....the woman lost interest after she refused the boob job....she might get a boob job when she was good and ready but not because someone else told her so, especially not some fat bitch from L.A...

He didn't want to get her hopes up on false promises but he knew people who had contacts in London with that kind of thing. He would see if he could help her, put some work her way or maybe just give her an address, or telephone number, or something. In fact he knew that Masters had a few contacts and he was up for a promotion. He was going to be swallowed up by the Big Time London outfits who would all be too happy to help out their new member, and Masters would, no doubt, enjoy demonstrating his new power to old associates and undeclared rivals. He filed this away in his memory to use later.

She remembered how lovely he was as a young boy. Always smiling and always cheerful...he was clever too. He must be doing really well for himself. She had felt a little embarrassed when he insisted on ordering champagne as an aperitif. It was sweet of him though. It was nice that he was interested in what she was up to after all of these years....and he didn't make judgements about her work. He seemed to realise that it wasn't all glamour....and he appreciated all of the hard work that had helped to get her to where she was. He mentioned that he might know somebody who could help her get some work....and he didn't act as if he knew the whole fucking world of showbiz, he just said that he might be able to help no fucking bullshit, no "I am" and he left it at that. He ordered the best from the menu....and he ate with good table manners and a fine appetite. He didn't drone on about himself or his work....and he didn't just witter on about people, that they used to know, or memories and stories that used to seem so important. When he did talk about the past it was with a tone of contentment....and he used such beautiful words, and he spoke so well.

She had had an interesting evening. She was very thankful for such a good time. She felt so comfortable with him. He didn't stare at her hands every time she touched the stem of her wine glass. He didn't patronize her, or her achievements. He didn't pretend to know about anything that he didn't know about. He asked her questions. He listened to her answers. She liked spending time with him....well she enjoyed the evening.

When they arrived back at the hotel she clung to his arm as they got out of the car. John's hands moved quickly as he picked out notes from an attractive pile of cash and handed them to the driver. She smiled at the money that John handed to the grateful driver. John said something to the driver: a thank you, and a message to give to somebody. The champagne and wine were flowing through her body making her hold onto John's arm even tighter. John walked her into the hotel and they both felt very warm, too warm.

John was ready to relax. He had asked Lisa if she smoked. She laughed at his bashful invite to puff with him. He had asked if she had ever drank before smoking because it could make you feel a little....ill if you weren't used to it. She told him that she worked on Rock Videos, had lived in California, and was generally tuned in to what was going on. She decided against telling him about the extent of her drug experience. She didn't want to shock her new old friend. She didn't want to offend him and his clean cut vice, and it was always a mistake to let men know that you knew more about something than they did. She would sit and smoke his little piece of executive hash, and he would think that he was the most exciting man on the planet.

John suspected that she knew the whole scene but wasn't experienced in the harder side of it all, probably she liked a little hash and a little grass. She was beautiful enough to be turned on to just about anything, but he thought that her beauty also meant that she would have been shielded from the more harmful images of illegal substances. As far as John was concerned she had agreed to smoke with him and that was virtually agreeing to sleeping with him. They would both get off their heads and the memories, his money, her dress, and the fact that it was night time, would do the rest.

They entered the hotel. John went to the desk to get his key and then half remembered that it was in his pocket. Lisa giggled with intoxication. John was aware that, although he wasn't as drunk as Lisa, he was, none the less, a little merry. They turned to get the elevator when two men, seeing them from the bar, walked towards them. John remembered who they were and why they were there. Lisa noticed them approaching. Later she couldn't remember much about them other than, them being very polite to her, and that John spoke to them very differently than he spoke to her. She somehow would recall that he commanded them as much as spoke to them, and that his tone sounded good at the time, quite sexy. There was something in the way that he spoke to them that presumed that they would pay her no attention other than courtesy and respect. She didn't quite understand this but it all seemed to be mildly funny. If John had presumed how they would act he was right. The whole scene, and it seemed like a scene from a film that she was not a part of but rather a spectator of, was slow and hazy but it made John appear to be very powerful (and this also seemed to be mildly funny because she remembered him as a young school boy) and totally in control of the situation. John did not seem to worry about Lisa being regarded by these men. This was a new experience for her. She had never met anybody before who did not protect her from the gaze of other men. She could not work out then why she found this to be so compelling but later, after she had thought about it, she realised that he must be a very secure man who appeared to be content in the knowledge that he had no rivals, or at least no rivals who were on equal terms. This was also an attractive character trait: total confidence, total belief. Then later, when they were alone, in the elevator she thought that he appeared to be annoyed with the two men as if they had offended her by daring to stand in the same corridor as her. If she had not been drunk it might have all been very confusing.

The elevator stopped at floor __, his floor. She didn't make any comment about this. Then he remembered that he had already explained that he needed to be available for any telephone calls that he might get. He could not believe that Maurice and Chris had been downstairs quite obviously waiting like a couple of minders. He feared that she had put all the clues together and had worked him out. There was the possibility that she had not thought about it, or that she was drunk enough not to find the situation strange, or that he could possibly get her so fucked up that she would not remember it anyway. They walked to his room

He was still stiff in his suit. He moved straight and solidly. She was still moving in a perpetuation of unfolding silk, constantly changing her shape to fit the space that she was in. He opened the door to his room. Lisa was expecting a room like the one that she was staying in, of course John's room was much bigger and much more expensive than the standard rooms. Lisa found this even more amusing than the nice men downstairs. She went straight to the bathroom where she laughed even louder at the sunken bath and Jacuzzi, the marble wash basin, and cold tiled floor. John heard her heels trip trap across the cold tiled floor and he went straight to the bar to take out a Gin for Lisa and an Irish Whiskey for himself, typically they did not have what he wanted and he had to take a Scotch instead. He took out an inconspicuous looking small piece of hash from one of his bedside drawers. He moved to one of the rigid armchairs and began to roll a joint. He could hear Lisa's hot pee falling in with the rest of the cold toilet water. He heard her flush out the old water and wash her hands. He thought about the water, that he could hear, for a moment. He thought about the finest undetectable sprays of water that covered everything. Every tiny droplet enough to see the filthiest roach through its prenascent incubation, enough to germinate the foulest of fungi and the most merciless virus, enough to stain the fairest of skin with pissyellow blots. He casually wondered whether there was any escape from it. Lisa re-entered the room and flopped onto the large circular bed that seemed to flow with cushions, pillows and concertinaed silk sheets. Lisa got up to put on a lamp and turn off the bright lighting that had invaded the room. John, continuing his efforts to appear as an amateur, sat trying to authentically roll an imperfect joint, whilst at the same time putting in as much hash as he could. Lisa was back on the bed her arms and legs stretched out underneath her dress in an array of concupiscent curves and arcs.

They smoked the joint between them and John remembered to cough gently and with embarrassment the first time that he inhaled. He told himself over and over and over: She's here, she's here... Lisa unfastened the ankle straps and kicked her shoes off. John watched her do this and watched her stretch her legs out and gently rotate her newly freed ankles and feet. She made a sigh of relief that John could only decode as a play to the erogenous frequency of the ear. He felt the alcohol deadened tingle of arousal as he looked at her now shoeless feet. The ankle strap left behind a red crease on her skin and an identical black crease on the black transparency of her outer hose. He couldn't help wishing that she had not taken her shoes off despite the eroticism of the act and the positive willingness that had now leaked into any interpretation of her words or gestures. The simple movement, rotating her foot, was one that he had never seen before. This new movement seemed to suggest a power that he had not even considered, as if she could tear down the wall with one flex of her ankle, or disappear under the tiniest crack of the door by stretching her foot out to a point. He had already noticed the straps that had been fastened around her ankles and he had taken comfort from them. They were gone now. She was lying back on the bed. Her eyes were closed and she drew in long and slowly on the large joint. She lay smiling indulgently to herself scratching her left calf with her right toe. John tried to read her mind... She was probably running her mind back over the evening and the fact that he had subtly mentioned connections that could help her career. And here she was now in the lavish hotel room of that handsome connection who she knew had loved her as a child. A prime target for her pragmatism and a fine test of her ego's will to prove beyond doubt that she has the measure of any man, regardless of wealth, or position, or power.

He had swiftly managed to get a second joint together and he had got two more drinks from the bar and set them down. He took the lit joint from her long flat fingers and finished it off before handing her the second joint. Once again she lay back, eyes closed in reticent pleasure, and smoked the joint, and once again he tried to read her mind. She had to call him over with her eyes closed because she remembered the pathetic juvenile that he must have been. He had to erase that memory from her mind and replace it with this new man that he has presented her with. She was a model, an actress, she must have turned enough tricks to have been even modestly successful, but she had too much pride left to voice her play for his help, she wanted him to still want her, needed him to still want her, too much, for that... She wanted him to have, and exist in, all of her favours but he had to take them for himself he only had to believe in his belief to pass this final test. He had to believe it not only in his new life but in his old life too. He had to be able to visit the past without cringing, without bowing down to those who appeared to be his superiors. He had to take her for his own like he had all of the other beautiful women he had met since he had made it... like all the men who had wanted to climb onto and into her without knowing, or wanting to know, that she was the finest queen of women... He watched her tense inhale and languid exhale, and the apparition of pleasure on her face. He continued to read her mind. He held his forefingers to his tightly creased temples and focused entirely upon her. She began to dig her feet into the soft mattress and push back on her heels so as to fulfil an itch that she couldn't quite find between her shoulder blades. He watched the ease of the movement of her effortless pushes and stretches. The seemingly unpiloted drifting of her body between the silk sheet, that was rippling like some billowing epidermis, and her own silk dress, that had stretched loosely over her back as if it were her own skin. He stood up in one whole, single, motion and, with fingers still at his intense temples, he began the slow journey to the bed. She bent her elbow and took another long hit off of the joint and then pushed her back into the bed in firm slow swerves of her body as she continued to search for that itch. He moved in hope that her dress would fold underneath her, or snag on some invisible hook, so that as she writhed up and down the bed, to satisfy her itch, she would suddenly move up and out of her dress as if she were moving out of it and shedding it behind her and at once expose her full orbicular breasts that would deliver him from his anxious approach, but this did not happen. She lay in her dress and the fabric seemed to move with her, moving out from her and then rushing back and enveloping her flesh with its soft coolness. He got nearer and nearer until he was sure that her expression and pleasure and thoughts were all obviously directed at him. His fingers moved from his temples as he got to the end of his journey across the room and stood silently for a moment above her.

She tried desperately to finish off that fucking itch but she couldn't quite get at it. She was far too fucked up to reach over her shoulder, and this made her smile. She felt particularly comfortable on the large circular bed, which was also making her smile. The whole scene and it almost felt as if she were watching a film about two other people was funny. She even found the joint hilarious with its phalic kink and loose roach. Here she was fucked off her head with some old school friend who she had once flirted with over a carton of Ribena. She didn't even want to think about what the fuck was going on in his head. She still couldn't reach the itch. He was nice though. Maybe he was the man for her? She spoke this thought in her head in the most ironical tone that she could imagine. She wanted to laugh and laugh, but then she was here in his luxury suite. Oh maybe she should try, give it a go. She knew, because she had learned from experience, that the narrative that we perceive when we meet and interact with others could be beautiful but she didn't trust any story completely. You could never tell. Divorced family and friends could never tell. She knew that she could never be sure. She could never be sure until she had put herself into the living pulse of sex. She knew that she never knew until the moment of penetration, and then with the man, this man, pressing himself into her, and forcing his hardness into the rhythms of the force that they would unleash, would she ever be able to even guess at their chance of love. She had enjoyed his story but it was not enough. She always enjoyed every story. She loved loyalty, and excitement, and sensitivity, and she loved the stories of romance that men created for her: exotic dark chocolates, blood red roses, honest flowing verse and sheer silk stockings. This was all beautiful but she knew nothing after eating the chocolates, smelling the roses, reading the verse or admiring her calves, they were all very important, but they were all invalid. They told her nothing. Only life could give her the clues, the prompts, that she needed and she, like anybody else, could be deceived but not in an act that was in harmony with the motoring pump of the heart and the connected circuits of her physical senses.

When he touched her she moved slowly around to accommodate him. Her smile became a grin as he moved her dress carefully up and over her body. She stretched her arms out over her head and he removed the dress which then seemed to trickle out of his hands as if he could not grasp its smooth shining fluid form. She started to hold back the laughter that was winding up inside her. She wanted to try out this modern fairy tale; this childhood sweetheart boy next door story. She wanted to know if he was right, if they could be right. The champagne, and wine, and Gin, and the hot smoke of the cannabis, filled her body. There seemed to be no alternatives, none that required less effort or offered any greater achievement. She kept her eyes closed and breathed in more of the stimulating joint. She turned herself around and around for him and joined him in an incipient embrace.

Beneath her silk dress Lisa offered more silk. She wore a black strapless bra, with a lace trim, which held her firm pert breasts up high so that they could be seen at their very best. John looked at her orange tan skin through the lacy trim. His fingers smoothed over the lace, following it up and around each breast. She sighed her approval. His hands stroked her flat tanned stomach running over her black crushed velvet suspender belt. This beautifully decadent garment was also trimmed with suggestive black lace. It was a real work of art. There were tiny black bows of silk decorating the top of each suspender, and a shiny silver metal clip at the end. It was fair to say that this suspender belt was Lisa's most favourite item of clothing. John had never witnessed anything quite so elegant. She was warmed by the attention that he was giving it. The suspenders were attached to sheer silk black stockings. The stockings had lacy tops and were made from the finest silk so that they were, when not being worn, almost weightless. John fingered the lace on her stocking tops. He ran his hands slowly down her smooth black stockinged legs. Lisa smiled to herself. She knew what men liked. She enjoyed the power that this gave her. She liked to watch men squirm with anticipation, and tremble with longing. John began to kiss her thighs and knees. He watched tiny kinks appear and disappear from around her knees and on the soles of her feet. He wondered how many times he had dreamed about this? How many times had he looked at her shapely legs and wished to be one of those tiny kinks in her stockings just so that he could be next to her skin? He put his hands on the naked flesh above the tops of her stockings. Her flesh was warm to the touch. Lisa gave out a long throaty invitation. John, urged on by Lisa's slow seductive moans, focused on her black pure silk panties which were tight and tastefully narrow and cut high up on her leg, garter style. The kind of panties that he didn't really think that real women wore. Her sex was visible through the black silk mesh. He could see her fine blonde pubic hairs neatly clustered in thick comfortable curls, around the edges of the thin crotch of the black silk, looking like tiny foaming lilies. They were framed in a square, below that mystically powerful suspender belt; between two tight elasticated suspenders; and above those black lace stocking tops which had made men shake with desire and promise their wearer the earth and everything in it. John pressed his hand into this frame and touched the cool silkiness of Lisa's sexy panties. He could still hear his heart beating from over ten years ago. Lisa's underwear was extremely beautiful but Lisa herself far surpassed any definition of beauty. She made everything that she wore scheme to enhance her perfect figure. Lisa's round firm breasts, her smooth full hips, and her erotically plump behind, all wrapped in the finest black silk was too much for any man, even John.

He felt ready to take off his clothes. His unbuttoned shirt fell to the floor. He took off his trousers revealing lightly haired muscular thighs. She welcomed his nakedness. She reached out for the impervious singularity of him. She wanted his oneness. He made himself naked and moved to her. John had grown into an attractive man himself. His dark eyes were calm but full of emotion. His chest was swarthy and muscular with tight brown button nipples. His shoulders were broad and powerful. What Lisa was most surprised by, most interested in, was his firm, well muscled, bum. It was round and really tidy, just right for a girl to squeeze as he moved on top of her.

As John began to touch all that he once thought to be untouchable, Lisa gave out a sharp breath of pleasure, and pointing her toes, stretching her legs, arching her back and pushing out her chest, she offered him her breasts to fondle. They were covered in a fine damp mist. In fact all of her exposed flesh was doused in tiny droplets of moisture that could only be sweat. It had seeped through her skin and now onto his, constantly combining itself with whatever it touched losing its old form and making a new. It reacted with everything around it. She had perspired through her skin and as he ran his palms down her tight stockings he noticed that she had also perspired through this silken skin making the fabric sticky, making it feel unlike any fabric that he had ever touched. He looked at her closed eyes and touched her damp hairless skin and delighted in it all. It was perfect.

Again he began to run his hands over her stomach and thighs, and then he moved a hand in between her legs over her explicit panties. She closed around his hand hugging his arm with her soft thighs. He looked over her body intently. He looked at her harder and harder looking for something. There was something in the way that he imagined remembering her father picking her up from school that made him think, or expect, that she would, when naked, reveal her secrets in ugly self-gouged scars on her arched back or rounded buttock. If not then maybe he would witness thin accurate parallel razor cuts in some secret pit of the arm or consciously covered shoulder. He could find none of these although he was sure that they were there. He was not looking in the right place, or in the right way, or he just hadn't managed to work out the signs yet. Lisa's breasts moved to him and then away rocking back and forth with the sway of their bodies. His hand was wet from the increased perspiration inside her thighs. Her movement troubled him. It seemed to cut through the story that he had created. It seemed to make light of their shared experiences of youth. It was as if her oscillating rhythms scribed a pattern, a wave-length, from a different frequency that he could not recognize from their evening together, or from their school days together, or from his secret screaming adolescent yen for her in those lonely sleepless nights. He looked up from stroking her and from making a circle around her navel with his tongue using a now inseparable combination of his saliva and her sweat; he looked up, he was sweating now and he was covered in his own perspiration and hers' too; he looked up and looked at their reflection together in the mirror on the table beside the bed. He looked up at the mirror's tiny fragmented image of the two of them. It was hot and beads of condensation rolled down the smooth cool surface. He looked up for a moment and saw, as her lack of scars had made him conclude, that she cast no reflection. He had known. He had been sure. He was right. There were no scars, and the only way that she could have survived without mutilating herself was if she was the kind of woman who cast no reflection. It was the only possible explanation for the absence of thick rubbery cicatrix, of red disfigurements. He looked back at her creeping writhing body and flesh. He looked back at the mirror and saw her this time right next to him. He could not explain why he had thought that he could not see her, maybe he had just not seen the scars. He looked closely at the reflection of Lisa and saw that her black sweat moistened silk underwear was reflecting the reflection in the mirror. Her glistening wet skin reflected the mirror too and he could see the depthless image of the room on her body broken up only by the few rigid straps of the underwear that she was still wearing. The light would not fall in the room on any one point, or on any one centre. It seemed to move back and forth from Lisa, the mirror, and the windows, but it never seemed to rest anywhere, for any amount of time. The light was somewhere between them all. It could not be sustained on these reflective surfaces. He made himself concentrate on Lisa's constantly reforming body. He moved onto her, and resolutely held onto her as close as he could. Every fluid that they had on their skin now became one fierce intoxication. They began to move together. Lisa tried to make the life that she could not understand, that nobody can perceive, unfold for her now. John had to stop. He would not have unprotected sex and neither would Lisa. He searched for a condom. It was cold and uncomfortable and their wet bodies became clammy for a time. She held her eyes tightly shut as he touched her where she wanted to be touched. They began to move together again. The moment continued.

John awoke, his nose was hot and he moved his hands up to try and take away the dry heat. He saw small dry specks of blood on his fingers. He looked around from his sitting position on this large circular hotel bed. He was alone. He remembered. He began to remember the coke that he had been funnelling into his nose all night. It must have been shit because his nostrils were on fire. The white powder was sitting on a piece of white paper on the bedside table. It was a dull white next to the intense droplets of splashed crimson blood. His head hurt. He decided to put some cold water on his raw nose. The floor was covered in fine black garments all askew as if whatever had left them behind had pulled themselves out of this shedded skin, or outer shell, and had just kept on moving. A pair of black stockings lay torpid on the floor like two charmed cobras. He splashed cold water onto his nose and it hurt even more. Lisa was sitting in the bath surrounded by white foam. She was repainting her nails. She was pleased and relieved to see his body was nice even though his demonstration and gesticulation of his pain was comical, but she could smile at that for now. He turned to her squinting and trying to smile. His nose was twice as big as it had been.

Good Morning.

You must be allergic to something that it was cut with.

She tried to hide her snigger.

John went to the phone. Lisa laughed into her second Gin and Tonic of the morning. John dialled Maurice and Chris's room.

Chris was smoothing his hair down in front of the mirror. He stared at himself as if he were confronting a rival; trying to register how intimidating he could be. He began to speak to himself in a threatening tone.

I don't think that you want to say that to me...do you? [pointing at his reflection]

Huh...do you really want to say that to me?[pointing at himself]

I don't think that you quite understand what I'm saying to you.

He repeated this to himself trying to be more menacing. He continued with other litanies, but he was always aware that Maurice would be up from buying a Sunday paper from the reception desk at any moment. The telephone rang. Chris was startled he checked himself out in the mirror. He smiled smugly at himself mugging his reflection as if it were a camera lens. He rolled a threatening sneer off of his top lip and picked up the telephone with all of the violent attitude that he had been attempting to master.

Hello Maurice?

No. This is Chris.

He was pleased with his straight firm no-nonsense answer, but he was unprepared for the reply.

Yes, well this is John. Remember me?

Yes Boss. Sorry Boss.

He saw that his brow had furrowed and was quivering nervously. His whole head was beginning to glisten in the light. He inspected himself for any weakness that John might detect. He realised that his hair was still in the style that he had been smoothing down before the telephone had rung. His hands moved, almost trembling, through his hair and he checked himself again more strictly than before.

We're staying here for a few more days okay.

A few more days...

Yes that's right...well done...a few more days...

John's voice sounded like a roar on Chris's end of the telephone.

Is there anything you want us to do Boss?

No.

John's answer was followed by a harsh silence which made Chris scramble for something to say. He had angered John and he searched his mind for the right words whilst looking at his severe paranoid reflection.

Do you want us to stay around the hotel Boss?

No.

The veins in Chris's temples were throbbing as he stood mentally chastising his own nervous image.

..Is there anything that you want us to do Boss?

I don't give a fuck what you do...Do you understand?...Go out enjoy yourselves...find a casino...Maurice can get some things for the kids and Penny and you can buy some poncey clothes...I don't give a fuck okay...be enterprising...I don't want to see you or hear from you okay.

Yes Boss....of course...

He realised that John had already put the telephone down. That was it, he had to go through with it now. He had made a prick of himself with John. He had to follow through with it to prove something, if only to himself. And he had to get Moz in on it too. He looked at himself and swore that he would do this. Somebody had mentioned the possibility of forged bank notes. He found the number that he had been given and made the call. He was going to do it. He was going to set up his first ever major deal.

John's nose had splashed a little blood on the floor as he had got irate, and one small drop had hit the telephone and was now smeared across the buttons. He clenched his fists as hard as he could. Then he realised that Lisa could have heard the whole conversation, maybe she had guessed already. He had to have her again and again to make sure that he already had, that last night had happened. He had to be sure. The memory of their sex had already faded. He needed something that would never fade, something that would never wear down to a simple but charming silhouette. He had a few days to make the act stick in his mind forever.

Chapter 5

Masters

The man, whoever he was, was talking, too loudly, and in monotone. He was talking about people and figures, and he was talking, too loudly, in monotone. Why was he talking? He would not shut up. He would not. He was sitting on his left. The man was middle-aged and overweight. There was another man on his right side. He was nodding, smiling and agreeing with all of the drawling sounds of the other man. The man was middle-aged, balding, and overweight. Why were they talking loudly? Why so loudly? And why was the other man smiling? Why was this happening? He was in a bar. He was in a bar? He held onto the sides of his stool and exhaled. He tried to listen, but the flat drone would not let him. He could not remember what he was drinking. He picked his drink up and tried it. Both of the men suddenly broke into laughter that was too loud. Why were they laughing? Why were they laughing at him? What was he drinking? He tried to smile at the other two men. They were still, still, laughing. The man on the left had a bright fat pink face and neck that spilled out over his white collar. Tiny particles of spittle were sparking off his bottom lip as he laughed. The voice began again droning and droning. Why was he here?

He folded his swollen red hands onto his lap and tried to concentrate on looking forwards. He stared belligerently at his reflection, at his dark face, that looked so foreign to him, and he looked at his harsh pocked cheeks. He tried some more of his drink, but he found it hard to swallow and he still could not tell what his drink was. It was in a large bulbous glass that had a short leg on the bottom. The drone was getting louder and louder. He stared at the bar. He looked at a ship in a bottle. He could see that the ship was called the *San Dominick*. He stared at the mirror behind the bar. He stared at himself between the two men. He saw them looking at one another and then at him. The man's voice sounded Spanish. They were talking Spanish. Why was he here? Why were they here? Why was he talking? Why was the man talking in Spanish? As he thought about this he furrowed his brow and he felt drops of sweat falling down his creased forehead. Why had they done this too him? Why had they sent him here? He saw the other two men reach for their drinks and they seemed to have no difficulty in drinking. He felt as if he should take a drink too, just like the other two, but he could not reach out to the bar. He knew that.

He knew a lot of things. He knew about JohnTom (John Tomilary) and Harry. That was John and Harry, he had heard John speak to Harry on the telephone. He knew that John fucked Harry. He knew about JohnTom and his nigger. He knew that. He knew how they did it too. He knew how they fucked. The nigger on his back. He was the taker. That was how they did it. He could see that. He could see it all in his mind. They did it just as their names suggest. They did it like a nigger and his john. That was how they did it. He moved over the nigger and he fucked him. He knew that. He knew how they fucked. He knew how the nigger would lie on the stiffest whitest sheet to show his black black skin. That faggot slime white shit would throw talcum powder all over his nigger skin. It would show large white blotches on the nigger's skin as if he was full of holes. White sheet, white powder, white cock and the black black nigger were fucking and fucking. He had seen them do it. He had seen them. He had seen them a million fucking times. They were doing their dirty filth together; their filthy cocks were fucking. That filthy white shit was pushing his cock into the nigger, his nigger. And the nigger's cock stuck up into the air and rubbed against the queer white stomach of his white master. They were dirty, fucking, men. After they would kiss each other, that's what John and his nigger did. The nigger probably cooked his meals. He was fucking sure of that. He could see him doing it. He probably shaved him too. The nigger shaved him with a cut throat razor and white red foam, and the long black fingers that the nigger pushed into his white open arse when he was getting fucked held that long cut throat razor. When he pulled his limp cock out of the nigger their two selves would touch and entwine. He was watching them now. He could see their vile erections. He could fucking well see their dirty dirty bodies. He was no longer in the bar. He was watching their two fat cocks entwining like huge serpents. He felt safer watching this. He was holding a large staff in his hand and it made him feel in control. And he beat the two serpents. He beat them and he beat them. He felt his own body change constantly moving from one other to another other. He did not like to be an other at all but when he struck there was a single instant when he thought that he had escaped. He watched the men writhe together their black and white filth all over each other. Wasn't the white captain fucking his nigger slave, wasn't he his nigger attendant? Who was he? Was it not true? Was he incorrect? He thought that he was screaming at everything. He wasn't screaming. Wasn't he listening? He couldn't not try his drink again, because he still didn't know anything about his drink did he?

Masters could not see the silvergrey haired man. He was looking for him but he could not see him. Maybe he wasn't there. No he was always there. He could never get rid of him.

Masters hated the silvergrey haired man who wasn't there. He hated him but he was scared of him too. How much did he know? He could not be sure of how much the silvergrey haired man knew.

He was afraid of listening to Spanish or English. He was afraid of listening to that one flat sound that the man was making. Why was he making that sound? They were looking at him. They were looking at him because he had not taken a drink and they were looking at him because he did not know what he was drinking. He felt as if he was sea sick. They had stopped talking. They were silent. And they were drinking and he wasn't. He knew that if he looked at the bar they would talk again. He wanted them to talk now because they were always talking, and he was afraid of their silence. It worked. They were talking again. He looked at the bar. There was a cut out figure of a frog, that looked like a toad, on the bar. The frog looked to be covered in a wet translucent slime. It was covered in it and the slime from the frog (toad) had formed a pool by the frog on top of the bar. It was thick, very thick, and he could see it all oozing from the frog's skin all over the bar. He began to feel frantic. He did not want to see the frog, not here. Why was it here? What was the man saying to the frog in Spanish. How could the frog understand Spanish when next to the frog was a cut out sign. It said: *CroakCroakRibbit, Pommetizer the new apple drink, made with French Apples and British know how*. There was a lot of slime coming from the letters on the cardboard sign.

He looked at the barman. He was pouring drinks for the other two men from a bottle. They were all making noises. Why had he put the frog (toad) on the table? Why did he put it in front of him? How did he know? The barman was dribbling white milky fluid from the corner of his mouth. He turned to look at the man on his left who was making noises at him. He looked at the man. The man's head had gone. The frog's head was there. The man's collar had swollen to accommodate the frog. There was a heavy milky liquid falling from the frog's front legs that looked like hands. He moved one of these giant wet green hands to pick up the drink from the bar. A heavy string of milky liquid slowly made its way from the frog's hand and arm to the floor. A pool of this liquid had gathered around the stool. Why was the other man laughing? He was laughing throwing his head back and looking mockingly at him. The giant frog was also laughing at him. The barman laughed and the milky froth poured out of his mouth as if his face had been burst by a slow snigger. They all knew. They fucking knew. They all knew everything...

The man on the left was drinking with his head held back when it happened. He was just about to order another for himself and the other two. He did not see this. He could see his warted skin; his yellow facial markings; his red fire coloured neck that was squeezed into clothes that were now saturated by the milky white fluid that was pouring from the frog. He hit him hard as he was drinking. It was awful. The foul shit was now all over his hand and the frog was only temporarily knocked to the floor. He had to get the shit off of his hand but he had to kill the frog. He moved over him, leaned down and rammed his fist repeatedly into the frog's head the man on the right finally processed the information sent to him by his eyes and moved away, he began to tremble five seconds later when he realised that Russell was probably going to be murdered, and he lost control of his bladder when he realised who was going to kill him and who was going to be murdered next. The beating continued. He was using both fists now like two huge clubs. The frog was small on the floor and was having problems moving. He beat the frog like he had beat the two cocks. It gave him the same joy. He had moved his fists hard and fast until they blurred in front of his eyes and made the frog try to cover itself. He could tell that it was dazed. He was angry now. It would soon be over and he was angry about that. He was angry that the frog was not resilient. He would have to go beyond punishment in order to ensure that the frog would not do this to him again. His arms and fists hurt and so he began to kick the frog. The man on the right could see that Russell was out on the floor like a cracked egg with no chance of getting out of the way. He was now stamping on Russell's face. The metal rimmed heel of the left foot was gashing his face and blood was shooting out in tiny geysers. There was blood now all over the floor. The barman had ran out into the other bar, maybe he was getting some help. This man was huge and Russell was...not a part of this. The undefended skull was making a terrible beat against the foot of the bar. The sickening throbbing dead sound continued louder and faster until he had made the beat race at the exact tempo of everybody's accelerated, and identical, heartbeat. Everybody could feel the thump of the skull sharply in their chest for a few unearthly hideous moments and then his men intervened.

They called out, " That's it, that's it Boss." They tried to get him off Russell but he was still aiming kicks at his unprotected torso. The man on the right could hear Russell's ribs cracking. He looked at the red pulp that was Russell's head, his associate, his friend. He looked at his eyes and he saw an eerie vacuum where his right eye should have been. The left eye was hanging out of its socket half of it had slid down to his cheekbone the other half was stuck to the heel of the man's shoe. The metal heel had cut the eye in two. The cut was perfect. As if it had been cut by a great artist with a sharp razor. The men moved him away so that his kicks could no longer reach. The man, the frog, Russell, threw up. The group of men pushed Masters out of the bar. He was now screaming hard and looking around for the cocks and the frog and the greyhaired man. He was struggling with the men. The four of them managed to push him into a car whilst people, aroused by his abusive screams, looked on. He tried to break free. They all swayed and over balanced as they tried to hold him back but he was a giant man and could not be held back. The car was rocking with him inside. The car pulled off the car park quickly. The engine's purr did not cover the screams coming from inside. The two men who had jumped in the back to restrain him were easily outfought. He opened the window shouting and cursing the frog and threw his shoe, that he saw was covered in the frog's slime, out onto the street. The driver picked up the telephone and called someone back at the hotel bar.

You'll have to send someone onto the street to pick up a shoe...

He was screaming from the back seat, "I don't want the fucking shoe...I DON'T WANT THE FUCKING SHOE." He didn't want the shoe, he didn't want any more of that shit to touch him. The men were close to restraining him now. They let his hands free so that he could shake them. He was crying now, desperately crying and he shook his red swollen hands as hard as he could to get that shit off.

...so that it can be burnt.

Okay, okay, take him back to the house. I'll clean this shit up. It's all okay. I don't see there being any problems.

The man on the right looked at Russell. He felt guilty. He felt bad for seeing him like this. It was as if he were naked, or found in his own silence wearing women's clothes, or leather bondage, such was the shame and embarrassment of being assaulted, your being invaded and abused by another. Maybe Russell was so stunned that he had been found out he had become temporarily speechless .... There were bubbles of blood coming from where his nose and mouth used to be. He was still moving in erratic shaking spasms and he was making a ghoulish whistling noise. He was banging his head weakly against the bar trying vainly to keep up with the earlier vicious beat, then he threw up again and stopped. The man on the right wanted to tell Russell that he would be all right. He didn't know why he wanted to say it, and so, in the end, he didn't.

Chapter 6

Sonya-Playback-Erase

The main difference of course, and it may sound politically incorrect, is that I am male. There is no pimp, or potential pimp, hovering in the background. I am not in any immediate physical danger. None of my clients have the ability to overpower me or to force me into doing something that I really really do not want to do. The biggest problem that I face is disease. I always wear a condom. I would not even contemplate having unprotected sex. None of my clients are put off by condoms, in fact I think that they prefer to have sex with condoms than without, no inconvenient bodily fluids I suppose not that I ever orgasm with any of them anyway. Also, of course, being a man means that I have control in just about every situation. This seems to be similarly politically incorrect I know, but it is my erection and if I am not happy then it would not occur. I suppose that it is the unfortunate flip side of the maxim that all men are potential rapists. That is the main difference. It sounds as if I am being a myopic bigot. I am not. It is just that I think that I am not as vulnerable as a female prostitute. I can fake orgasms like a woman, and so protect myself emotionally. I record every tiny detail so that I can erase it like a VCR, or a HiFi, or a machine, and so protect myself spiritually. And I am responsible for the erection and so cannot be manipulated physically. I am always in control. The erection is not always the main factor. The last

73

woman who Gillian introduced me to, Elaine, finds penetration very uncomfortable and so she receives her pleasure orally.

The erection is not really the attraction it is just what I use to work with. Marie really wants to be appreciated. She wants to be loved, admired, adored. She has me to do all of those things. Having sex with her reassures her that she is still beautiful and desirable. If we did not have sex then how could she believe in the compliments and the gifts. I am happy to play my puppet sex with these women. I want them to be happy. A part of me wishes that they did not need me. If they had good relationships then they would not need me. I suppose that this is another difference. A happily married man might have sex with a prostitute, but a woman would have no need to. They might flirt but that is an ego thing totally different. I never flirt. It is a sour message to anyone that your life is inadequate, that you are incapable of making for yourself a life that you want to live. And I love Sally. She is the only person that I want to flirt with.

The coach that I am sitting on is leaving the motorway. I am looking around at the passengers who are in my line of vision. I wonder about their lives. What celebrations will they make for the new millennium? The smokers will smoke more and the fat people will eat more. Do the other people on this coach have perfect sapphires and rubies and emeralds at the centre of their worlds? Do they cherish their gems or are they neglected? I know that the brightest light shines from my centre, and I know that I am the bright light of Sally's centre. We have our brilliant love that is untainted; that is pure. Why do other people neglect their partners? Why do they covet the woman on television or the man in the film? It does not make sense to me. The only thing that we are all equal in is love. We can all make our love grow, and blossom, and be splendid, but this does not seem to be important to some people. What can be more important than love? The women who call me know this. I am not their answer and I think that they are selfdeluding fools, but I do feel something for them. I wish them happiness, and I do think that I bring them some relief from the empty internal lives that they live.

All of these women are different. There are those like Marie who really just want to make some contact with someone who is prepared to treat them in a way that they deserve to be treated. There are others though like Gillian who needs to use me for herself. There are those like Sonya who need the right man with the right look to help make them happy. Sonya is the woman who is left in my memory at the moment. I have erased most of our encounter. There is a little left for me to playback to myself. She is a very successful woman when it comes to business, but not so successful when it comes to love. I know that she divorced her first two husbands and then she had some crisis, ever since she has needed the company of young men to maintain her image, and to maintain her lifestyle. It is obvious really; that young men like myself are fashion accessories for women like her. There is not much wrong with that as long as the young men are all willing. Sonya needs names and labels. She needs to have the best of everything and she needs to be seen to be having the best of everything. She has to wear the same clothes as the famous mature women that I see in the glossy photographs taken at film premieres. She likes me to be around. She likes me to say the word "fuck" rather than "have sex" or "make love". I make different stories for her to the ones that I make for Marie. I "fuck" her as if I am some kind of sycophant, as if I never think of anything else. Every encounter that we have has to be created in the jaws of some lusting beast. She has to be the electrifying source of a thousand expensive fantasies. She pays me so that I will have those fantasies of her. She pays me so that I will wake up in the middle of the night my body covered in nasty cold sweat and my thoughts smothered by her angular limbs and spongy flesh.

I put away a collection of William Carlos Williams's poetry that I am studying for my M.A. I have just read *Romance Moderne.*

Childhood is a toad in the garden, a happy toad.

I put the book into my bag and make sure that it is in a position where the pages cannot get creased or ripped. I have been studying very hard. I need to study hard because I have to be successful. I do not want to continue with my current means of earning money. I want to be successful because of my intellect. I want to be challenged and I want to be of some importance to somebody, whether that somebody is a corporation, or a government, or a business, or a group of students eager to learn. I need to make Sally proud of me. I need to make her see that I am worthy of her love. This is why I am doing this M.A. I cannot afford it really but my part-time work pays very well compared with other student jobs. I have to feign poverty to my family, and I have to make sure that I visit Sally and that she does not visit me. It is only for one year and that is partly over now. It is all a means to an end. I will walk away quite anonymously at the end of it all, but I will have a strong qualification. I will have the chance of a desirable future. Then, when I have proved to Sally that I can make it as a professional, we will be together. Marriage is a possibility I am sure. I want to marry Sally more than anything. We are good together. She is everything that I want from the world. I have no interest in any distractions. Sally is my dream. She is my vision. When the new century arrives we will be inseparable.

I have no option but to continue with what I am doing. I have to pay University fees, my rent and my living costs from no grant, no savings and no welfare support. I rely on my acting and my ability to create an intriguing story. More than this I rely on my selfcontrol and my perfect reconstruction of dialogue, action, and sensation. I have to suffer some disorientation after I wipe out my memory and so I usually try to playback my encounters before sleeping, or at least during the evening when I do not have to function in any social or professional context. I have no choice but to recall and playback now, despite the small risk, because I am on my way to spend the weekend with Sally at Keele University. I must erase the memory of my two days with Sonya.

It is not easy to do this. It is draining. It wears down the batteries but it is effective, actually imperative, for keeping me sane and for maintaining my inner dignity. Sonya was actually my first client. I cannot erase this piece of information, not yet. I have to wait until I leave Essex and end this source of employment otherwise it would all be too confusing. It is obviously important for me to know how I got involved in this line of work so there are some things that I have to live with, for a while, until I can be rid of it without risking detrimental confusion. I met Gillian at a party given for staff and students. She is a professor. We spoke at length. She offered me a research grant. The next day I went to see her about her proposal. She told me that she wanted somebody lively, experimental, discreet and dependable. Then she told me what it was that she wanted. She doubled the research grant and promised that if I played her game that I would get accredited with a major role in her latest research project. She has also made sure that I have all my essays and dissertations published in very reputable journals and periodicals. The first time that we, or rather she, consummated our deal is the only memory that I have kept of all the encounters that I have had. Gillian recommended me to Sonya when Sonya needed an escort to a party. In this way Sonya became my first client. Gillian was happy to get me more work. I have been introduced to many women since. Eventually I will erase Gillian and Sonya completely but at the moment I fight to keep them as ghosts at the back of my mind. I fight to keep them from finding any substance or any material with which to manifest themselves in the forefront of my consciousness.

The coach, coming down from Manchester, is only half full. I have a seat to myself. I could have taken the train. I could have afforded first class but I must be careful. Sally must not think that I am anything but a temporarily poor postgraduate. I am travelling down from Manchester because I have spent a few days with Sonya at some kind of textile convention for the High Street Fashion Market.

I walked over to Sonya who was sitting at a table in the corner of the bar. It was around ten o'clock. I felt fresh having just showered. I strode over to the bar. Sonya was sitting with some man who she was flirting with. He was in his mid-thirties I would guess, probably older, but I was pretty sure, almost certain, that he was younger than Sonya. He was wearing light grey trousers and a black polo-neck sweater. His hair was very short, in a style that looked younger than he did. Sonya was drinking mineral water. I could hear the man trying to talk her into having a drink and loosening up. I ordered a mineral water too even though the barman suggested that if I wanted a soft drink I should try their new carbonated apple drink. There was no need to drink anything. We were both buzzing quite pleasurably as we had both taken E's, which Sonya got so that we could fuck on (Sonya likes to do this because it highlights the physical sensations and she says that ecstasy represses the male orgasm and so we can do it for longer), these E's were working well and so we were not interested in drinking anything other than water. I could see Sonya in the mirror behind the bar. She had put on her heather coloured Ghost dress. It was not exactly low-cut but much of Sonya's soft white chest was on show. The dress did show her shape perhaps more than she should allow, but even if her feminine curves had drifted, or dropped, over the last ten years she was not drastically overweight, it was just that her flesh hangs now she has lost her firmness. Her legs are still very attractive and the dress was short enough to make this observation but not too short so as to be obvious. She had crossed her legs invitingly showing an extra inch of thigh that the man opposite her was appreciating. She was wearing raven black hose, stockings of course, and high heeled white horizontally strapped sandals. The white patent leather clashed fashionably with the black hose, and almost even more startling were the brightly painted red toe nails that were lined up like tiny phantoms of anatomy peering through the ethereal outer layer of the taut artificial skin of black lycra. She was running a finger over her knee scoring a meaningless circle over and over again. Every few seconds she would look up from her absorbing activity and look at her table companion to make sure that he was still watching her. He always was. She had a wide grin on her face that she flashed like bait at the man before she moved her attention back to the circle. I picked up the drink that I had ordered. I liked the feeling of chilled water in my mouth but I really did not want to swallow it.

The man shuffled his chair around the table so that he was no longer opposite Sonya. Sonya was drawn into conversation again. She crossed her legs over in the opposite direction which was right over left rather than left over right. She shook her right foot expertly in time with the gentle background music of the bar. The man watched her dangling foot move with the music. He watched her ankle twisting, shaking and rotating. He looked encouraged by her leg crossing that had now brought her one revealed thigh closer to him. I could not quite hear what they were talking about but he was having problems maintaining the conversation. When he was managing to get any kind of response from Sonya, and he seemed to be struggling to do this, she would talk at him constantly, her mouth moving uncontrollably. This would be followed by a short silence as he fumbled attempts to take up one of the loose ends of Sonya's soliloquy. At times he was baffled and was probably unable to continue with any of Sonya's random babble. Then she would use her ecstatic fidget as a pretext to slipping her dress a quarter of an inch up to reveal a little bit more of herself.

I looked at my own reflection for a moment. I had a large tooth filled grin that I could not stop. I could feel that the muscles in my cheeks were stiff from the over use of a permanent smile. I took a tiny sip of water for the coolness of it on my tongue. I straightened myself up from my Chandleresque bar slouch and whilst tapping my foot on the floor in time with the gentle music, in time with Sonya, I made sure that I was presentable. I have to make sure that I, because the "I" is all that I have to work with, am looking as fine as I possibly can. I have ironed my collars in the set fashion that Sonya prefers at the moment. I have aligned the legs of my pinstriped narrow legged trousers, and on the leather of my square toed shoes I can see a mass of colour that is presumably a reflection, a representation, of my face. I could see now that the man was sitting right next to Sonya. His hand was a split second's touching distance from her hand. I watched him lean back in his chair after taking a long extravagant drink. He leaned back so that their shoulders were pressing against one another. He moved his hands to stroke her hair. He was trying to act as if he did this all of the time, as if it were a reflex, as if it were his own inimitable way of connecting, but he looked awkward. I could see the seams in his movements, in his involuntary predatorial glances at the exposed thigh. Sonya is enjoying the attention though and has her head back proffering her throat. I stared at myself, my face. I stared into my own eyes rehearsing the look that would penetrate Sonya's eyes, the look that she was paying for. I accepted my stare as being of a quality that would have the desired effect. I was ready to turn around.

You must... that is right you; do not pretend that you are not there, you have always been a part of it; you cannot, will not, move away; you have to be watching, listening, hearing, computing, etc...do not be as foolish to think that nobody is aware of you ...by now you should have realised the game, the story, that we are playing out. You must have guessed Sonya's secret secret. The story is an easy one, it is an obvious one, but it is irresistible to Sonya. I turned at the bar with a drink in my hand like a young actor playing a young outlaw.

Sonya had pulled up her dress enough to show this man the beginning of the black lacy frill at the top of her stocking. He had one arm around her and the hand from this arm was employed in stroking her neck. He was whispering something in her ear whilst brushing his fingers up and down that leg. Sonya had a small visible patch of damp purple on the front of her dress. I looked at this and agreed that it was very hot. I could not tell if Sonya was listening to the man. She was flushed in the cheeks and was sucking and blowing hard on the cigarette that she had lit. With her free hand she was running her fingers through her hair fast and hard, digging her fingers and nails into her scalp, and then she pulled harder and longer on her cigarette, and then she began running her fingers through her hair again. I began my walk over to their table and made sure that I locked my eyes on Sonya as I approached, staring her relentlessly into the ground just as she liked. I had to concentrate on walking slowly because I, the ecstasy, wanted to bounce across the floor dancing, leaping and running to the table but for Sonya's story I had to be focused, and cool, and moody. I walked over to their table and sat down. Sonya's eyes flickered their focus all over my body. Her eyes were anticipating and enjoying my entrance into her film. I sat down and looked directly at Sonya. I did not move from this position whilst we were at the table. When I had to address this man I would not move my eyes. I did not, could not, take my eyes off Sonya.

Sonya looked at me and then away. She was smiling; the E making her appear adolescent, the smile making it all too predictable.

I have been waiting for you.

The man has now turned around. He was, until I spoke, unaware of me. He did not like me being there.

Do you know him?

She smiles a no at him and then looks at the table sniggering to somebody. He gathers himself together and musters all of the confidence and scorn that he can.

Do you want something?

I moved my voice slowly but impatiently towards him. I look straight at Sonya.

I think that we both know exactly what we want.

I smile at her warmly enjoying our pretence, but with enough directness that it appears that we do not know one another. Her smile is high up on her face. She pulls her dress down just a little. She is slightly bashful, and I know from our previous meetings that her vagina is twitching. She likes to tell me whenever her vagina twitches. It might be whilst watching a film or merely walking past a garage and smelling the mechanics hard at work. I recognized the expression on her face, and her sudden sense of modesty gave it away.

Look I don't know who you are but we don't want you at our table. Please go and annoy somebody else.

He turns his back on me and begins to whisper to Sonya and moves his hand to hitch her dress up to where it was before I sat down. Sonya finds his new impunity hilarious and she starts to laugh uncontrollably to me. The man thinks that she is laughing at me. He turns around aggressively.

Are you still here? Do I have to have you removed? I have no reservations about having you thrown out on your arse!

His tone was as pompous and affected as could be expected from the people who use this bar.

That is a really bad idea.

You are bothering my friend. Do I have to get the doorman?

If you call the doorman you will only get very embarrassed.

I took my time.

You see when this man, this doorman, comes over to our table then you are forcing a choice on this.... so beautiful lady.... and then she has to decide what she wants....and she wants me....and she is going to have to sacrifice whatever friendship that you have, and any respect that she may have for you, because she will not risk the certainty that she will never see me again....she will not want to make you look foolish but you will have given her no choice.

I could see that Sonya was liking this. She pulled as hard on her Silk Cut as her lungs would allow. She inhaled off it one last time before putting it out, and then she lit another and she tried to inhale even more than she had off the last one. She was grinning, nodding her head to the soft tune playing in the background, and she had crossed her legs tightly reversing their position again.

You do not have to make yourself look any stupider than you do.

Pause.

Why not go and talk to some young impressionable teenager....I'm sure that there are plenty who would talk to you all night if they thought that you were paying for the drinks. Now run along before something happens that is beyond your control.

We'll see about this....you insufferable prick.

He said prick rather uncomfortably, as if he did not know the meaning of the word, as if he was trying to compete or impress. It resounded as "pwick" in our ears and Sonya coughed out bluegrey clouds of laughter. She stifled the sound with her hand and sucked hard on her cigarette and raked her finger nails across her scalp. He got up from the table. I could see that his collar was damp from where it had rubbed against his bloated neck and double chins. He said that he was some kind of important guest. He made some attempt at a full blooded macho promise to Sonya, one that he would fulfil on his return. He went to find the doorman. Sonya put out her freshly lit cigarette repeatedly stubbing it against the hard glass ashtray in the centre of the table.

Do the same thing, exactly, as we did last month in Edinburgh.

I made a wide eyed frown that asked her to remind me, but, as far as she was concerned, my expression was letting her know that I knew exactly what she wanted. I had no idea of what she wanted. I must have erased whatever happened in Edinburgh. I cannot be sure when. She grinned a come on lets go grin. She grabbed my hand and we walked quickly towards the elevator.

I held her and kissed her open mouth in the elevator. She pushed her dry nicotined tongue onto mine and I responded by forcing my tongue against hers, and I continued to do this whilst making deep noises of fake sexual hunger. I heard a light swish of friction, the sound of stockinged legs moving, and not an entirely altogether unpleasant sound, as she stood on her left foot and hinged her right knee up as far as she could, resting it on my body. She did this as invitingly as she could. I held her leg and pushed my tongue deeper into her mouth. I held her right leg as she leaned onto me. Her pose was of the kind I experienced as a teenager. She was like a young girl showing off her limited sexual language, as performed by the body, to a boy her own age who has virtually no experience. She was impressing me, so of course I was impressed. I held onto her leg tightly as if I depended upon it for support. I stretched my other arm around her side and clenched the palm of my hand around her flabby buttock. I squeezed hard and recklessly as if I would lift her off the floor with my aroused enthusiasm.

The elevator doors opened and we ran down the corridor hand in hand to her room. Sonya's room was large. It had a modern four-poster bed in neutral beige and lightly stained pine. She opened the door breathlessly telling me, in a tone that suggested that it was a reminder, that I should get the chair. I moved the armchair, which was designed in the same fashion as the bed, from the corner by the television, into the middle of the room. Sonya was hurriedly removing her jewellery and putting it down on the huge dressing table beside her bed. The dressing table had a mirror that was not quite ceiling to floor but still big enough to reflect an image of someone from their head to their toes. Sonya wanted me to position the chair in front of the dressing table. I wheeled the chair in front of the dressing table. Then she impatiently told me to turn it around so that the chair faced the other way. I did this. She asked me if I liked her shoes. I looked at them and said that I thought they were fantastic. She smiled and began to kiss me again. We kissed for a few seconds and then Sonya turned around. She started to push out her bum at lascivious angles and beckoned me forward. It was about to begin. She told me to remove her dress. She was really out of breath and the ecstasy made it easy for me to be out of breath too. I could feel my pulse jolting through the blood vessels in my neck. I reached down and pulled her dress right over her head. She continued to have her back to me. I held her hands. She was now moving her hips like a fat drunk woman on a package holiday. I moved my hands over her stomach and up to her breasts as I kissed her neck hard and fast. I squeezed her breasts rougher than usual because I could tell by her movements that I was supposed to be frenzied. I began to unfasten her bra but she resisted. She said no. She does not like to take her bra off. She does not like to see, or for anyone else to see, her large shapeless sacks of jiggling fat. I pleaded with unnerving sincerity that I wanted her breasts. She turned ninety degrees towards me so that I was facing her side. She smiled to herself and whilst still grinding her bum and hips she pulled down the cups of her bra with her two hands and pushed her breasts out towards me. I met her invitation as she wanted and I flicked my tongue over her nipples. They soon became erect, and I managed a seemingly authentic, but futile, attempt to suck both of them at the same time as she pushed them closer together. She said that that was enough and tried to push me away, but I did what I know she wanted and continued to stimulate her with my tongue and mouth. I built up my counterfeit pleasure by dextrously unfastening her bra. She began to breathe faster and faster and louder and louder. Here she was, paying for some man, and she is twice his age, to do what she bids but when they are together he is so turned on, even though he is young and handsome and athletic, that he cannot help but please himself. She sighed slowly and then gasped as she tried to get enough air back into her lungs. She did this without feeling any remorse as her black bra fell down her flesh onto the carpet. Her wrinkled white shapeless tits hung down the front of her body. I attempted to squeeze them into my mouth with my hands. I tried savagely to push them all in. I tried to act as if they were not sagging flaps of flesh but as if they were young, firm, and unavoidably erotic. She enjoyed the attention for a few more moments. And she enjoyed the electrifying sensation of having her nipples sucked whilst on E for a few moments more, but she would not be without her bra for long. Then she breathed heavily into my ear reminding me of the chair. She flopped down onto the chair. And with her muscles twitching tensely with sexual energy she picked up the discarded bra and tried to put it back on as quickly as she could so as not to break the excitement. I made no false appeals this time. I took off my clothes as if I were thinking only of her, abandoning them as they fell. This gave her a few extra moments during which I unwrapped a condom and slid the cool rubber sheath onto my penis which I was just about managing to keep erect. She sat back for a moment. I undressed. I moved forward naked and stretched over and kissed her gently as she sat in the chair. I told her that she looked beautiful. I told her that more than that, she turned me on. She began kissing me harder and our tongues were together again. I moved my head down and kissed her breasts again through her bra but this did not seem as interesting to her as it had been. I looked at her black lace panties and could see how as her buttocks came out over the end of the elastic that they spread out and up far above the flesh that was tightly held underneath the material. Sonya's figure was well sculptured by the fashion world. Her behind was made to look acceptable by fabrics that compressed her body. Her hold up black stockings cut a similar wedge into her thighs. They helped to support the few deposits of fat that were on her legs. Her underwear shaped her figure, pushing it, and pulling it, in the right directions, and her black hose hid all of the wobbling cellulite at the back of her calves and thighs. I fingered the nylon lace at the elasticated top of each stocking and I begin to roll one of them down her leg to remove it. She closed her eyes and whispered that I did not have to take them off if I did not want to, she said that they were my special treat. I understand, despite her flesh creasing and bloating, and her shape falling and swelling, that Sonya's legs still have the firm salient curves of a younger woman. I know that these are her only haven of self--admiration. I always, always, remove lingerie. It is to be enjoyed but my clients must never, not even for a moment, think that they are anything but the sole object of my passion. Lingerie, especially basques, suspenders and stockings, is difficult to put on and take off. It must be removed very slowly and carefully. I always pay extreme attention to the lady. These garments are so difficult to remove because they are there to slow you down, to allow you to spend time simply enjoying the beauty of your lover. I never make the mistake of tearing through such clothing. I never make the mistake of persuading my clients not to remove such clothing. I have to make them forget their fat, or old, or wrinkled, bodies. They are always desirable women, and dressing up in what look like ridiculous fancy dress costumes is not the point. They, them, their bodies and their personalities, are always the point of every encounter. I do not like these lingeried women fetishized by men. I find this whole softporn phenomena to be disturbing. I wonder about the images that are being sent out by the tabloids, all lingeried women and lottery cards. The model in the centrespread weekly feature for women, are they features, or advertisements for designers and stores, or are they paper mops for all of the unfuckable men that read that shit. These garments, when I try to consider a woman's point of view, look as though they are uncomfortable to wear. I have to conclude that they are then selected as suitable apparel for the right lover to enjoy and admire. They are worn as a gesture of romance, and every gesture of romance demands a gesture from the recipient. This time I understand. I thanked her in a whisper. I told her how exciting she looks dressed this way. I told her how jealous I was in the bar because I knew that the man she was talking to found her very sexy. I told her that even the barman pointed her out to me. I told her that I do not like any other man seeing what great legs she has. And I made her promise not to pull her dress up so far next time because I do not want anybody else to see her thighs. I told her that I had dreamed about her the night before. "I dreamt about you Sonya. I dreamt that I was fucking you and sucking....really hard and I was biting... And at one point I opened up your legs and licked you. And I opened you and teased you until you were all wet and bright red with excitement and I put....and... ...inside you....and I... it out.. and put it back in. You were dressed just as you are now. I fucked you Sonya. I did it to you in my dream. Unbelievable? It is like you are my fantasy." I began to whisper descriptions of lurid acts into her ear. I used lots of dirty words just the way she likes. She started breathing heavy again as I spoke to her. She loves to be spoken to in this way. She was smiling and her breathing sounded as if it were trying to find a meaning and tell me what that meaning was. I continued by telling her that I had not been able to stop fantasising about her since our last meeting. She told me to stand up. I want it like Edinburgh she repeated in a pleading tone. I stood up because she made an effort to stand up. She took my hand and stepped up onto the arms of the chair. The heels of her white shoes sank like daggers into the cushioned arms of the chair leaving deep hard black marks on the fabric. Sonya was facing her dressing table, looking at herself in the mirror. She asked me to put some music on. We both laughed. This is so fucking intense she gasped smiling. I turned on the stereo unit. Sonya said that she wanted the radio on. She wanted rave music. She wanted to fuck to some rave music was what she said. I found one channel but it was no good. Then I went through another channel and Liam Gallagher was singing:

As he faced the sun he cast no shadow...

Sonya liked that. She repeated that we were going to do it to Oasis. Oasis and on E she kept saying this over and over again like an over salacious mantra. Oasis and on E. That's what we're going to do it to. Liam continued to sing. I moved forward. I moved forward and began kissing her pantied buttocks, that were dimpled with cellulite, whilst running my hands up and down her unctuously stockinged legs. She began to grind again and I moved one hand up between her legs. We managed to find a slow rhythm that we could maintain and still be in tune with the song. The ecstasy helped us. Sonya laughed loudly when the DJ began to talk about Noel and Liam, and then began to introduce the next song. I watched her in the mirror watching herself. I watched her ecstatic grin. She was very happy up in the air above me. She looked at her own breasts, held pert in her bra, and now she approved of their high moulded shape. I started to touch her vagina through her panties. She bent her knees a little lowering herself onto my hand, swaying her pelvis to the music and groaning in delight to the fast beat of the new song that I did not recognize. I knelt down on the chair underneath her. I watched her wild abandonment, her drug induced dance, and her ecstatic sexual pleasure. I watched her perform to herself, to her audience, maybe even to you. I stroked her through her panties with both hands now. I kept my fingers flat and stroked firmly up and down from the base of her vagina up to her clitoris. Her body began to shudder with anticipation and her legs shook as she remained standing, one foot on either side of the chair. I watched her high heels sink into the upholstered chair. The long tall heels were unstable, constantly swivelling on their sharp metal points. Her whole body came down to just two small points. It looked frightening, to be stuffed into two tightly bound odd shaped shoes. Sonya's feet bulged out between the straps. This tension and the pressure, that I could see in the tips of her heels, was sharply defined by the violence that these shoes suggested. She had squeezed into them, had puled the straps tight, and now she could not keep her balance. I could not look any longer. She tottered. She fought gravity by locking her knees and by making her legs into an upside down "V" which would then support her torso. This made her porcine flesh quiver, and this quiver became more and more exaggerated every time my hands got to the end of their stroking cycle and touched her clitoris. She had steadied herself but she was not totally comfortable. She was enjoying herself and she started trying to push down harder on my hands but was finding it difficult to balance and so she had to lean forward a little and hold onto the mirror. She was kind of stooping down now rubbing her crotch against my hands as much as I was rubbing my hands across her crotch. In a breathless whisper she implored me to continue. I began to tease her, holding up the elastic of her panties, as if I was about to push one of my hands up inside her, or as if I was about to snatch them down and expose her naked sex to my attention. She raced her lungs to catch up with the oxygen that she needed. She told me that they were in her briefcase. She told me that I was not to do it like that, that what I needed was in the briefcase. I walked over to the briefcase that was on the desk on the other side of the bed. Sonya caught her breath and crouched now with her hands on her knees. I opened the briefcase and inside there were samples of fabrics with patterns and textures, all of different sizes. There was a pair of long steel scissors. I picked them up. They were very cool on the palms of my hands, and I knew that they would chill any skin that they might touch. I walked back over to Sonya who stood up straight again. She was moving her jaw fiercely from side to side and she asked for a drink of water, and so I fetched one for her. She drank the water down. Her body was damp and hot, drizzled in perspiration. I restarted my touching. I rubbed her clitoris from side to side (she is a side-to-side woman) through the black lace until Sonya was fighting for air again. I pushed the closed cold steel blades of the scissors carefully up and down her crotch, as I had my hands a few minutes before. She groaned out the zenith of her stimulated sensations, it sounded as if she could not possibly take any more physical pleasure. I slipped one of the cold steel blades inside her panties. She inhaled sharply as the metal touched the lips of her vagina, and then she exhaled long and slowly as I brushed her clitoris, with the utmost care and attention, using the blunt edge of the cold steel blade. The loose wobbling fat indicated that underneath the cellulite Sonya was tightening what little flesh she had not lost to alcohol, full-fat cream, and gravity. I made a clean crisp cut and snipped a perfect line through the crotch of her panties. Then I cut them at the waist band and pulled the remnants down onto the floor. Sonya squealed like a fat juicy piglet being roasted alive. I explored more of her sticky pudendum with my hands and fingers. I held the scissors up and cut through the straps of her bra. She was not expecting this and enjoyed its spontaneity even though her shamefully torpid breasts were hanging out above my observing head. I peeled off her stockings with my free hand. They ruffled around her ankles and fell over her white patent leather sandals. I moved my head down and began to stroke her between the legs with my tongue. I steadied her body with my hands. She opened her eyes to look down at me for a while. She grinned appreciatively to me and then watched herself in the mirror for a while, watching her own movement and face. She watched me in the mirror too. She watched, probably telling herself that it was happening; watching it happen, feeling it happen. I moved my tongue slowly to bottom of her vagina. Then I licked slowly up, parting her lips for a moment and darting inside with my tongue before coming out again teasingly and then moving my mouth up to gently suck her bright red swollen clitoris. I continued this for a while whilst I regulated my breathing with hers. I synchronized our breathing and although I did not quicken the pace of my tongue I did begin to quicken the pace of my breathing. I punctuated my breathing with lingering groans of fulfilment. Sonya's breathing was now linked to mine and she could not help but breath at my pace. She had entered the oxygen race. I kept my tongue strokes slow but I increased the pressure that I was exerting with my tongue. She began to moan her gratitude each time I scooped my tongue in to her, and each time I sucked hard on her. When she got used to the rhythm I began to delay the licking and the sucking for a split second teasing her expectations. This made her very excited. She had now lost total control. She was standing on the arms of a chair facing a mirror with her eyes tightly held shut. She was naked all but for her shoes and hose that was down over her ankles. She had me, between her legs, in control of her breathing, and holding back, just for a split second, her paid for pleasure. Her body was beginning to show signs of tightening again. I did not relent in holding back the pace of my licking and her groans became shouts of relief as slowly her climax raised itself. It held out agonizingly for an extra licking and sucking sensation that was slow and deliberate and just enough to pull her through to a full and pulsating orgasm. She screamed out her tension holding onto me for support. Her body was then a mass of uncontrollable flab that seemed to move in all directions in slow flaccid waves. She repeated, "Oh God, Oh God..." over and over. I helped her down from the chair. She asked me to my pleasure if I thought that I could come. I told her that I thought that I would have no problem. She dug her finger nails into my back as I began to viciously thrust in and out of her with my semi-stiff penis. I counted to one hundred in my head as I did this. And then I stiffened my whole body as if I were experiencing the orgasm of my life. We nursed each other through the fragile phase of post-orgasm. We lay kissing for a while until I pulled out my penis to deposit my condom in the bathroom. I flushed the empty condom down the toilet basin. I put the toilet seat up. I knelt down already retching. I threw up in the toilet bowl, over and over....I wiped my mouth on my hand and stood up.

In the bathroom I felt safe. I pulled down the toilet seat. The seat was at first cold on the backs of my legs. I held my cramped and injured stomach. I was sweating a lot and the cold seat was sticking to my legs and rear. I sat on the toilet until my penis looked as if it were convalescing and then I went back into bedroom. Sonya had recovered. She had put on another bra. She had turned the volume up on the stereo. We were now listening to a song by a group introduced as Garbage. The singer repeated the words "Stupid Girl." Sonya was laughing, chewing unnervingly quickly, and smoking a cigarette. She pointed at my penis and joked that ah! it was all deflated now. I told Sonya that there was no chance of me not orgasming with her, the E made no difference to my climax. She seemed to like this. Sonya took her clothes off so that we could be naked together. We danced bouncing on the bed's mattress.

Sonya does not commit the same crime against herself as Marie does. Marie creates the illusion of love that she has not achieved in her marriage. Sonya does not want something else; she wants herself. She wants herself to be the target of adoration. Marie likes the images of love. Sonya wants to be the image of love. The headturning girlwoman who wears the right clothes in the right way. She wants the right friends and she wants to be wanted by the right kind of man. She wants to elicit uncontrollable urges. She wants to tap into some primitive lust that once activated cannot be stopped. In this way she invents herself out of male images of the female. It does not matter how expensive her clothes are, or the hotel that she is staying in, she always looks like a slut. She always looks deliberately contrived so as to appeal to men. I do not mind the guise of the slut. It is obvious but at least it is not hopeful of much, it is not self-deluding. I suppose that I can help Sonya in a way that I can never help Marie. It is because of this that Sonya is so alluring. Marie is much more beautiful, much more elegant, but Sonya is getting everything that she wants. She becomes who she wants to be. She has her designer clothes, and designer drugs, and she designs her own sexual identity through her sexual adventures. There is no self-delusion. I do not orgasm with her I never have. I never will. I have no real wish to be with any of these women, but sometimes it is not that simple. I have control and I am not interested in anyone but Sally. Nevertheless I have had to practice to make sure that I am impregnable. I have masturbated during the quiet of night slowly taking myself to the point of climax before stopping and controlling. I used this well known exercise as a kind of back up, extra insurance. I have had to make sure that I am clean for Sally. I am always on my guard against whatever Sonya can dream up. She is already fading now. The whole episode vanishing like unravelled film held up to the light.

It is gone. My memory is clear. The coach stops in Newcastle-under-Lyme. I get off in this familiar town. I get the bus to Keele University. I look around the bus. I am alone. It is empty.

Chapter 7

Return Journey

Lisa had on a tight pair of pale lime green flares made from thin mole skin, light brown stack soled platform sandals, and an open- necked, white, strategically creased silk shirt. She was sitting, no she was lying, in the reclined passenger seat of the car. Her mouth was open and her head was back, and she was breathing conspicuously as she slept. John did not mind her unglamorous pose. He still liked her. He liked her a lot, and he was very happy that they had met up. It was a kind of reward from the past. Of course there was nothing more between them. He had enjoyed spending a few days with Lisa. He had watched intently as his hands had clutched at her flesh. He had watched the stark evidence of himself entering her, and he had carefully scrutinized the presence of himself inside her as it materialized on her face. He liked her but he loved Harry. There was no way that Harry would understand what had happened. No, as much as he was fond of Lisa, he had to make things work with Harry. He would help Lisa as much as he could. Give her a few leads, help push her career, he would do whatever it took. She might have been a dream from a time when things were simple, or at least seemed simple, but now he had Harry and he had to make things right. He had counted down the months, and now it was only weeks, until the deals could be made so that he could be free to concentrate on Harry, and Harry alone. He wanted to make everything right with Harry. He would do his best. But Lisa had reminded him of some of the joys of intimacy. There had been a meaning to their meeting, or at least there was once he had sat and thought about it. He wanted to share these kinds of feelings with Harry. Lisa had helped him to realise what was worth saving, he was grateful for that. He would have a go at making things work between himself and Harry but he would not waste his life waiting. Lisa had also reminded him of the beauty of life and he would not let it pass him by as he had been doing. He would make things right, and if he couldn't then he would deal with Harry and get on with things. He had been emotionally stagnant for too long. He looked over at Lisa's contorted sleeping face. He had a lot to thank her for. So much that she would never know. He decided to ask one more favour of Masters. He would make sure that she got the break that she deserved, and Masters had all of the connections. He might as well use him while it was still possible, whilst he still had the contacts.

John smiled. It was so nice to be in a hired car. You didn't have to have the radio on. He looked at the fuel gauge and made a mental note to stop at the next service station for fuel.

John knew that as soon as he got back he would again be subject to all of the pressures and stresses that came with his position. Everybody was edgy. People around him were acting out of character. The influence of the top men in London was unsettling John's operation. They wanted to take in a successful local and promote him as their man. They wanted an interest in the area, and whoever they picked out would have their protection. This meant that this chosen individual could make unreasonable demands of everybody else and there would be no right of appeal.

The word was that Masters was going to be the lucky guy. There were only two people who it could be: John or Masters. John, as far as he knew, had done nothing wrong, but there were rumours. Masters was more their kind of man. He was a criminal right through to his toe nails. He looked menacing, which helped, and more importantly he acted like a criminal, as if he had something to hide. This somehow made him more acceptable. John, and Serge for that matter, had started out selling drugs to students. It had been profitable and successful but it hardly sent a shiver up your spine. Sure they could slap students around, organize their men so that they could branch out, make money, but if they were ever up against it, up against someone like Masters, nobody could be sure that they had what it took. As far as most people were concerned John and Serge were good earners, good suppliers, good profiteers, but they could not be expected to out fight men like Masters.

John was worried about the future, as was anyone not directly connected to Masters. The common feeling amongst the men was one of caution. John was on good terms with Masters, but, then again, Masters was not sure that he was going to be chosen and so he was probably just playing safe for the moment. Once the decision was made things would be different. If Masters was chosen he would come looking for John, and John knew it. Masters would try to take from him the drug import business which he had worked so hard to build up over the past five years. If things went wrong, If Masters got the nod from London, then John and his partner Serge would need a quick escape.

There were other problems to consider too. Zak, John's main runner, who was responsible for keeping the contacts in Amsterdam happy, had gone missing. Zak's boyfriend Stuart, or Fat Stuart as he is known to most people, had been spotted once since the disappearance at a club in London. Masters and his men were denying having anything to do with it. If Fat Stuart wasn't already dead, and John was not ruling out this possibility, he would know where Zak was, or at least what had happened to him. If Fat Stuart could be found, and if he pointed the finger at Masters, then John could sit down with the big men from London and have Masters killed. Nobody liked people who bumped off major runners, especially if they didn't replace them with someone else. It was a foolish thing to do. When the money stopped flowing people got angry, and there were too many people making too much money to allow such shoddy practice to go unpunished.

This Zak thing played heavily on John's mind. Serge was sure that it was Masters's work. He was already trying to weaken their power base. If John and Serge were unable to bring anything into the country for a while their usefulness to their associates would be severely reduced, and this would make it easier for Masters to get the approval of others and have them murdered. The more John thought about it the more he realised that Serge was right. He was pretty much always right. Zak was the key to all of this. If they could just find out what happened to Zak before any decision was made.

It was a tense situation. John still had Moz who was a zealously loyal servant. He also had Adam Bishop, also known as The Bishop, or just plain Bish. He was one of the most promising young career criminals that John had ever met. Adam Bishop was a natural bully, intimidation was second nature to him. He was a massive brute of a man. Adam occasionally did work for Masters but he was strictly a member of John's crew. John certainly did not approve of some of Adam Bishop's business interests but he tolerated them, that is what he knew of them. John did not like the sex industry. It was wrong but as long as it was just magazines, videos and whores well it was better that they were making money off it rather than someone else. John had given Adam his big break. He had nurtured him, held him back when he was about to do something rash, and pushed him forward when he was ready to handle bigger jobs. He could count on Bish. He was sure of it.

There was Harry too. His Harry. John had carefully kept Harry away from the action at home. It was a shrewd move. Nobody really knew who Harry was and that was the way John liked it. It was common knowledge that they were somehow involved together but nobody was quite sure what their relationship was. Nevertheless it would have made it dangerous to have Harry around. If Masters, or anyone else, wanted to get at John, and there were always enemies, then Harry would be the easiest and most vulnerable target. Harry, because of being virtually unrecognizable, was in effect invisible, an enviable attribute in the world in which they lived. Masters may well be in the superior position but John was still holding some good-looking cards.

John took the turn off for the service station. He eased the car to a halt and quietly opened the door so as not to wake Lisa. Something woke her up though. She squinted at him through creased eyes and a suspicious scowl. It took a second for her dream to recede and to remember who he was, and when she did remember she said, in a demanding yet childishly disarming tone, that she wanted a white chocolate Magnum. She finished her sentence and rolled over onto her side and covered her head with John's coat.

Maurice was buttoning up his shirt. He began with the top buttons. His hairy stomach was on show, tattooed around his naval was the legend 'MADE IN ENGLAND", in a circle like some kind of corporation branding. Maurice was talking to Chris who was sorting through the clothes and boxes which contain all of the electrical appliances that you can think of. They are talking about Adam Bishop the most feared and respected member of the new generation of "businessmen". Moz, without warning, answers a question that has not been asked.

Yeah. He likes all that strangulation an'all that....you know....before he shoots his fucking whack....like that woman in that film.

What that film with....what's it called now?....err....I know the one you mean....It's supposed to make it even better right.

Yeah that's it....he's in to all that like....he get's all is birds into it an'all.

Do you reckon that Bish strangles all of his girlfriends?

That's what he says....That's Bish for you though....great fucking geezer....the great Adam Bishop....dirty fucker though mind you.

They both laugh together. Chris is counting money, all tens and twenties. He looks at Maurice.

Right Moz....These are tenners, legit right....these are twentys, legit right. We'll split these. These are moody tenners.... and these are moody twentys. We should do a bit in the towns that we pass on the way back?...

Country boozers mate....that's what we want....no fucking spotlight on the till, no fucking bother.

Okay....whatever you say....that box is full of your stuff you bought from the kid. Did you get that shirt for Tony?....and that dress for little Mary?....she'll love that you know....all the fucking rage at the moment you know ….

Yeah got it all. (Looking suspiciously at Chris because of the way he mentioned Mary).

The rest of the stuff we know about….right.

Yeah don't worry.

Great I'll just go and check to see if the car's downstairs, and we'll be off…Eh, err Moz…. what do you reckon's going on with that bird we saw him with the other night? I mean we ain't seen him since. And I mean fucking hell she was a looker all right. And now he's taking her back home....

Well he ain't said nothing to us about it 'as he? Don't get saying nothing to anybody, not if you want to come on a trip again....know what I mean?

Oh definitely Moz....I mean this is where my education started you know. I just mean it makes all of those sniggering fuckers look like the cock suckers they are you know....All that talk about Harry and John this, and Harry and John that....And here he is banging the best piece of cunt I've ever seen.

Just goes to show ya....keep your opinion to ya fucking self....Stupid pricks.

Yeah....Fuck me even Bish would be jealous of this catch....Fuck me though I'm sure I've seen her somewhere before... Okay Moz, I'll go and check on the motor, and then I'll start moving all this shit down okay.

Chapter 8

Sally

> Sent to me from heaven
> Sally Cinnamon
> You are my world

The sound of our voices echoes in the darkness. It is three o'clock in the morning. We all start again.

Until Sally I was never happy...

I have been drinking Guinness all night. Sally started on Diamond White but moved over to Blackcurrant Hooch as soon as we all started skinning up. I feel really good, really high. It was good being back in the Union Bar. Sally lives over at Horwood which is not far from the bar or the old Dance Hall. We have been drinking and puffing in there all night. I liked seeing all of the old faces. I still have a lot of friends here. Some are here now, slouched against the wall, making loud arrangements for tomorrow's fun. Karen and one of the barmen are all over one another. They had been flirting all night. Mark, the other Mark, Juliette, Rob, Carl and Sue have just set a time, for tomorrow, with Sally who can hardly remember the way back to her room. I say goodbye to them all. We hug and laugh and everybody is happy to see me. I take Sally's arm and we walk over to her block. Somebody shouts out of a window telling the others to fucking shut up. They respond with a new song.

And so Sally can wait
She knows it's too late

The sound is muffled by the block that they have just turned behind. A light has just flickered in the sky. Sally and I are laughing. There is a low booming sound. Sally and I are still laughing. A cloud bursts overhead. Sally and I....

We go upstairs and Sally puts on her favourite tape at the moment Alannis Morrisette. You don't know Alannis like I do she is telling me. I want you to get to know her like I do. It is very important that we have the same likes. I want you to be listening to the same music as me, watch the same films and soaps, and I want to do all the things that you do. I think it is important. We need to stay in synch with one another. I stand up. I am standing up moving towards her. I am looking at her smile and her blackcurrant stained lips and teeth. I move closer and I kiss her forehead, her nose, her eye lids and her mouth. She is telling me that she has been waiting for that all night. I thought you had forgotten all about us girls, maybe you've forgotten what we like. I thought maybe you had lost your memory or had it wiped out. I kiss her again with more force. We bounce down on the bed which is about three feet away from the tape player which was where we were standing. Sally starts to laugh which breaks one of our kisses. She laughs again I presume at my startled face. It's okay I've put the wrong side on. Kate Bush has started singing. The cassette now turned over we begin kissing again with soft wet lips and warm caressing tongues. Oh dear my head keeps spinning when I close my eyes to kiss you. Keep them open then, is my reply. My tone and smile are cheeky and she likes them. She makes a constricted low moan as I kiss her neck. She feels my bum, squeezes my buttocks. She moves her hand between my legs in a manner that invites me to do the same. I take the encouragement to heart and tentatively explore through her Levi's.

It has been so long since I last made love. The last time I visited was about two months ago which was the last time I made love. Sally is so strikingly beautiful. She is a woman to be cherished and adored. I am planning all the time for our future, our wedding, our lives. I will stop at nothing to get this woman of my dreams. I want to spend the rest of my life treating her like a queen.

We have had such a wonderful time, drinking cans and smoking reefers down by the lakes, and then shuffling off to the bar. Sally and I, and the others, dancing next to the jukebox, and then going off into the dance hall and drinking and puffing until two-thirty. Sally had been happy to introduce me to all of her new friends, parading me proudly amongst all of the eager young girls. She used a tone when introducing me to someone that seemed to say here he is, and I told you so. We had a tray of chips each and more when we left the dance hall. We held hands everywhere we went. She asked for drinks, and spliffs, and chocolate, and I attended to her as if she were an adorable girl. We all talked, and laughed, and saturated ourselves in our own superiority, mimicking and insulting those around us for being pompous, or pretentious, or having long-at-the-back wrestlers' haircuts. Sometimes Sally and I would look at one another in the midst of some larger conversation that we may, or may not, have been involved in. We would stare transfixed into one another's eyes, talking to each other without speaking, promising each other our eternal love. I felt, at these moments, as if I could hear her every heart beat. I could feel how much she had missed me, and how much she now wanted me. I want to be with her and nothing else really matters.

Sally is trying to move herself so that my hand is actually touching something beneath the denim. She is moving impatiently. Her fine strands of blonde hair stick to my velcro-like stubble covering our mouths as we kiss. I know that Sally's cassette is playing but I am not listening. Sally is kissing my face very lightly and she whispers to me to take off my clothes. I remove my Ben Sherman shirt as provocatively as I can, bringing my arms up over my head, stretching out my chest and stomach that I have been working on solidly for the past two months. My torso is a mass of twitching muscle and I am proud to say that beneath my tight black curly chest hairs I have cultivated the beginning of a cleavage of sorts, a hard space of sanctuary that separates my well developed chest. As I lift my shirt off, with erotic nonchalance, I stand next to the bed, I stare into space waiting for Sally's admiring purr. Sally has her back to me and is diligently brushing her teeth over the sink. Where's your toothbrush she growls through her clenched foaming teeth. I go through my bag for my toothbrush trying to shrug off my disappointment. I find my toothbrush and stand behind Sally. I begin to brush my teeth whilst looking at our reflections in the mirror.

Sally washes and undresses and jumps underneath her quilt into the bed. She remarks that I am looking very fit, that I must have been exercising a lot. I try not to smile. I take off my Vans that Sally picked out for me at the end of last summer. I take off my jeans and stand in front of her bed in my Midnight Blue boxer shorts that Sally bought me for Christmas. I take them off slower than I normally would when I am alone. Sally tells me to hurry up and get in. I slide in next to her naked. We grasp each other in a warm embrace underneath the warm quilt. We kiss more and more and we move our tongues rapidly against one another in the darkness. Sally moves her leg up against mine. I can feel the half inch long hairs on her legs that are coarser than mine because she shaves them occasionally and I do not. I run my hand up and down her bristled leg. I stroke her cheek with my finger tips. She takes my finger tips and kisses them lightly. We stretch out and hold each others limbs and kiss each others bodies. I can smell tobacco in Sally's hair and I know that she can smell it in mine too, but our breath is fresh. I can feel her perfect skin all around me, enveloping me. Our kisses are desperate and hungry. I am beginning to kiss her breasts, and I cannot help myself from hastily sucking the very tips of her nipples. She writhes at my side. Her hands are entangled in my hair, and she is pushing her breasts out for my attention. I am gasping for air. I need to put on a condom before things get past the point of caring. I tell her this. Sally looks a little shocked. I'm still on the pill she says, don't forget. I reassure her. I am telling her that I am losing my mind over her. She makes a soft Mmmmmm sound and sinks herself, a little, into the mattress and quilt. She brings her foot up, pointing her toes, and pushes in between my legs. My body seems to be going through a weird fluctuation, one moment I think my insides are going to explode through my skin and the next moment I feel as if I am going to implode and suck Sally into myself along with the rest of the unsuspecting world. I am tenderly kneading fistfuls of Sally's breasts and she is telling me how good this is. How much she wants me. I am very excited; aroused to the point where I feel as if I am about to go off at any moment. Sally is running her index finger up and down the shaft of my penis. She is whispering I love the things you do to me, over and over but so that I can barely hear her. I rub frantically around her crotch trying to get a firm grip on her clitoris with my fingers. I cannot quite grasp it but keep moving my hand in the general area. Sally is responding by squeezing my throbbing self in her hand and pushing her tongue into my ear. She begins to enjoy my hands' haphazard stimulation of her. She is breathing heavily and this is exciting me. Inside Me, Inside Me, INSIDE ME, INSIDE ME NOW, NOW, INSIDE ME PLEASE. I anxiously grab Sally and myself. I hold her open her and thrust myself into her. I'm inside I tell her and I speedily pull myself out and thrust myself back in again whilst Sally makes syncopated noises of passion....Oh my god I can feel my thrusts getting deeper and deeper inside her and I feel as if I am losing control of my balance even though I am lying down and I can see Sally's hair has fallen all over her face and she is grunting and I realise that I am grunting loudly and that I am finding my way further and further inside her and...oh....she is beautiful is my thought, I love her, I love you I chant............................What, no, no, oh that's just fucking great. That's just fucking brilliant. The stupid bastard was probably thinking about his mother again. For FUCK'S SAKE WHAT DO I HAVE TO DO TO GET A DECENT FUCK? He's only just got his pants off. This is getting past a joke. Look at him. He's got that pathetic shiteatinggrin that he gets, which is so annoying, as if he's never had sex before. I'm telling him, "me too." I hope he just goes to fucking sleep now the inconsiderate prick...same old fucking story.

What's the point. We hardly ever see each other. And when we do he goes around announcing how much we are in love together, Wanker, and scares off just about any genuinely good shag that might have been coming my way. I know that he means well. I know that he's a good boy but I need to have my buttons pressed at least once a year. He's always talking about *real love*, true love as opposed to....as opposed to what, a good satisfying fuck that loosens you up relieves the stress and makes you beam all over. I don't know what his problem is, I think he just loves his mommy too much. The constant compliments and gifts that he can't afford....what do they prove? Fuck all that's what. It's not that I'm ungrateful, I do love the attention but its all just like hot air or something. Yeah he does literature, yeah he knows all about feminism, yeah he's right fucking on! Wanker, Wanker, WANKER. "...Yes it was great," I'm telling him... Why can't I just be a normal girlfriend? Why can't he enjoy me physically? Why can't he enjoy anybody physically and simply? It always has to be that women are betraying their sisters, whether its dyed hair, or permed hair, or makeup, or nail varnish, or tight clothes, or poster nudes, or dieting, or aerobics or some lucky fucking bitch getting what she wants, exactly what she wants, whilst not looking like some cave woman in Doctor Marten's. I'm so bored by his self-righteous no risk, no fun, sex. I mean we wouldn't want to turn anybody on now would we. I wish he'd go out and fuck a few older women, somebody who would not put up with his bullshit, somebody who'd sort him, and his limp dick, out....

Poor bastard he'll be lying awake all night worrying about whether he has done his duty, as a *man*, a conscientious *man*, and managed to bring me off sorry I should have said, *bring my emotions to a natural, loving and secure, climax, where I can examine my identity as a heterosexual woman*. I really shouldn't be so bitter. It's just difficult to remember his good points at times like this....He's living in Colchester, doesn't even know anybody down there. He stays in pining, huffs and puffs about our *ideal* relationship and how we both have space to be the people that we want to be, and we don't have to conform to sexual stereotypes....but can he act on any of it? Can he fuck. I mean like what is the point. I don't go around telling everyone that I'm this or that, or that I can do this or that, especially when I'm not, and when I can't. It's like this fucking M.A. thing. Well done. Great idea. But he can't really afford it. "...Oh yeah amazing, probably the best ever," I'm telling him... Anyway, off he goes, promising that he's going to do all of this, and get himself a good job, with his M.A., and everything is going to be peachy. No thought that, however great his poxy course might be, I might just want him to be able to keep something between my legs for longer than five seconds. The way I feel if he could manage fifteen it would probably be enough. Why does he think that I am going to be happy ever after once he's got another degree? He has to prove something to himself. A fucking martyr that has had to start something like a Masters Degree that he can't afford just to show much he loves me....me the sweet little blonde girl looking down from her pedestal. "...Just go to sleep," I'm telling him, "I'm just turning over to get more comfortable....sorry I'm really sleepy, we can talk in the morning..." I wish he would go to sleep so that I could at least finish myself off without having to listen to his droning romantic bullshit....

Chapter 9

Friends

Two men are sitting in an office. They have spread themselves out on their black leather swivel chairs. They both have glasses of rum beside them and there is a freshly opened bottle standing next to their glasses. One of the men is recognizable as John Tomilary. He is relaxed and smiling. He is wearing a brown knitted T-shirt with a soft orange collar, loose linen trousers and navy suede Adidas trainers. Sitting opposite him is a black man. He is laughing. He is laughing at John. The man is slim and athletic but not ostentatiously muscular. He is wearing a white and purple plaid Ted Baker shirt, soft natural cotton trousers and neutral coloured Timberland boots. The two men, we can tell by their gestures and voice tones and body language, have a close bond. John grins as he sips his rum. He looks at the other man as if he is going to say something, as if he is going to explain, but he remains silent and the other man folds himself along his stomach and laughs and laughs and laughs and laughs....

John (trying to be genuine through all of the laughter): Honest to God Serge. I promise. I wouldn't make this shit up.

Serge (allowing his laughter to die down): ....Let me see....hmmmm....so, this childhood sweetheart, she comes....(he begins to smirk)...she comes....and then she fucking ejaculates....she actually fucking ejaculates all over you. So does she foam through those little see-through panties she was wearing?...(he falls into whole hearted laughter)....Was there a lot of this creamy shit? I mean did you save some for me?(his laughter is now uncontrollable).....(John is pretending to be offended)....I'm sorry....I'm sorry....(insincerely)....I really am (more laughter).

John: Come on Serge, I wouldn't tell you a lie.

Serge (controlling himself, composing himself): So who the fuck made her wear all of this shit you've been talking about. You ask her to put on your favourite pervy bra and panties. Don't tell me, don't tell me, she doesn't usually cream up all over her men it was just that your such a great fuck....(he bursts into more laughter)....You must know all of the tricks my man (he makes a mocking attempt to hold back his laughter and then falls back into his chair and bangs the desk with his hand revelling in his own fun).

John: I didn't make her, or ask her, to wear, or do, anything.

Serge: So who did? Come on....come on....what's going on? I've met a lot of good looking women, but this is the nineties. Women don't run around tripping over heels and suspender belts and shit....Come on women don't pick out these clothes man, not anymore. Sure, Adam's whores dress up like that for his films and for their work but that's Adam man it's not them....So if you aren't the one getting her to do this then who is? It can't be her. I mean come on....who's pulling the strings John?...Who is the one making her wear all of this shit?

John: Maybe she's into it.

Serge (unconvinced): Maybe....but I don't think so. I've seen her....she's a beautiful woman, no doubt about it....but think about it....you come in here telling me about the biggest wet dream you ever had, turning up in Birmingham, in the same hotel, at the same time, as you....She turns up for a night out as if she's stepped straight out of a wank mag, and then bang you bring her off and she drips her hot come all over you....all I can say is that if I live for a thousand years I'll never get lucky enough to meet a woman like that. And of all the people that it could happen to … there's women available to you all the time …. so what's going on? Are you changing?

John: Okay so it seems a little far-fetched....but I'm telling you that that is how it all happened. I don't know why she's wearing this or doing that – it's not up to me…..But it was great to make love to a woman again. That's why I stayed a few extra days....I just sat back and enjoyed myself. It's funny you know even now it's almost like I can't exactly remember what it was like with her....I mean I know that it was great....I watched her titties swell out between my fingers when I squeezed them....I watched her arch her back when she came and I did, I did, I fucking swear it, see and feel her come....I fucking swear....but now its like I can't really remember what it was like and it wasn't just because of the coke and shit, you know? It's like once its gone, that's it, and you've got to do it again to remember, and then you'll only forget it again.

Serge (still slightly mocking): So what's going to happen to Harry? Are you going to have a complete new life?

John (seriously): Harry is to know nothing about it - NOTHING. Lisa's a very beautiful woman. I am happy that we met up (Serge begins to chuckle, but does not impose on John's speech). She is a part of my past. It had nothing to do with Harry, or how things are between Harry and me. Everything is going to be just right between Harry and me again. We just need some time together. Harry is what really matters.

Serge: I must admit I was shocked when you told me that you were fucking a woman up in Birmingham. It must have been a change?

John (sternly): It was. It's over now though. I've got to concentrate on Harry.

Serge (seriously): Well how was Hanif?

John: He was as great as ever. Everything is just perfect. He's agreed to do the transport. He's agreed to keep it exclusive. He's just waiting on a word from us. No more shit with couriers. No more shit with anything. It was like I'd seen him only yesterday you know.

Serge (respectfully): He's a real fucking pro. An amazing man.

John: He showed us his operation. Total fucking hospitality. Maybe he was the one behind the whole Lisa deal (laughs)....Chris and Moz even got in amongst the action. They bought a load of moody tenners off his family.

Serge: What Moz buying off a load of Asian dudes?

John: No problem. Even Moz can't grumble at the way their business is conducted....Now the factory is able to sort out just about whatever we need. They can replicate any set of conditions.

They'll be no more sleepless nights, no more big risks. There's a distance between us and the action. We are moving out of the frame. Hanif is never going to get pinched, no fucking way. The ethnic situation is such that all of his work force would never, I mean fucking never, point the finger at him. They all owe him so much. I mean with him delivering as well its like we're further away from it than even he is! Fuck Masters, he can get the nod from the smoke. We won't be dealing with him for much longer. He can own fucking London for all we'll care....Has there been any word on Zak?

Serge: Not a word, nothing....nobody wants to say anything....

John: Have you had any more thoughts on his disappearance?

Serge: Nothing new....we've got to presume that it's got something to do with Masters and be on our guard....we've got nothing to go on.

John (nodding his head in agreement): Okay, okay....Have you heard from Adam and Steve?

Serge: Yeah....they came to see me with an idea....two ideas actually....He wants you to help him set something up in Goa. He wants you to get Hanif to sponsor a project to set up a studio over there. He says that there'll be a lot of fucked up desperate types who'll do all kinds of shit for the kind of drugs he's going to be holding out there, which of course will be bought from you. He likes the idea of buying up all the girls from the poor families and making a lot of Snuff films....

John (annoyed): He wants me to sponsor it because he knows that I've been back to Brum.

Serge: I don't know how he found out, but it sounds as if he wants to let us know that he's aware of what's happening.

John: He doesn't know shit....Moz has been talking that's all....he'll have told the kid, Tony. He still works for Bish....And?....And what's this second idea?

Serge: He wants to sell his club and move into London. Or maybe even keep the club and open another in London. He wants you to help, talk to Masters, be kind of unified on the whole idea. He wants to use Masters's potential in London and his contacts with the rich and famous, well the agents of the famous, to promote the place. He wants to open a club with a theme restaurant and all kinds of shit. He thinks that we need to get more involved now it's becoming common knowledge that Masters is in line for the nod.

John (suspicious and angry): Since when did The Bishop (sarcastically) ask me about his dealings with Masters. He's always been a part of our team, but he's always done his own thing with Masters.

Serge: Be fair now John he has been an exceptional servant, and he has made you a lot of money and done a lot of dirty work on his way up. He deserves special treatment and he knows it.

John (with a raised voice): He thinks he's too big you mean....He thinks he's the new man....(he exhales loudly)

Serge (pacifying): Come on John don't fucking blow this, just leave it.

John (takes two swigs of his drink, pours himself another and tops up Serge's glass): Do they think I'm some kind of fucking idiot? ...We'll see (takes another drink).

Serge (purposely changing the subject): Forget about that shit....it's all in hand right (reassuring tone)....Tell me more about this woman who's caught up with you....Why is she here?

John: I told you about her. She's a model, and she's done some acting.

Serge: Yeah but introducing her to Masters....is that a good idea?

John: She can run rings around suckers like him. I mean it's like she's just stepped out of page three, right up his street. He won't be able to help himself. He'll be jumping through hoops for her. And he is connected. He won't be able to resist her.

Serge (concerned): What about if something goes wrong? What about if he fucks her?

John (trying not to be startled): He probably will. But she's not going to hang around for long. She'll get what she wants, I'll have helped her along the way and that'll be that, end of the fucking story. She'll screw him until she gets what she wants. (Serge looks at him harshly half disbelieving)....Look Serge, she knows what she's doing. She's seen the old casting couch....with real men of power....a clumsy prat like him isn't going to trouble her....now is he?

Serge: What about if he starts fucking her around and shit?

John (irritated at having to keep trying to convince Serge): He won't! For fuck's sake....she won't let him. She's an old friend who turned me onto something that I haven't had for a long time. I'm fond of her. She's helped me out. She's a good fucking omen, lighten up....I'm not interested in her. She doesn't know about Harry. Harry is going to benefit from my experience. I'm going to be a better partner now that I have experienced intimacy with a special person again. I don't have enough time to worry about some fucking bimbo woman. She'll be fine. She won't be around for long. The first serious person that he introduces her to will either see that she's got what it takes, or will be so eager to have the chance to fuck her that he won't have her hanging around here for long. She's gorgeous, she's talented (smiling), she's too good for around here.

Serge: What if the only person that he introduces her to is Adam? He's got a film studio. What about if he's the one that she starts screwing? Him and all of that strangling and shit....you know like in that film where they get off on choking as they climax. You know that he's into that kind of shit.

John: That's just films and books, doesn't mean shit. Adam might do that shit to frighten his whores....suffocating them or whatever they did in that film....what was it called?.... but he isn't going to fuck around with a friend of mine.

Serge (cautiously): I hope that you're sure....

Chapter 10

The Big Deal

He was meeting the queer for lunch. The queer was bringing some woman along who needed his help. This meant that there was time for him to eat a late breakfast and get changed. He walked barefoot into the kitchen. The linoleum floor was cold. The white metallic surfaces were lifelessly cold, about the same temperature as his naked body. The chrome finish to the appliances reflected bright light into his eyes. He squinted. His penis swung heavily between his legs. He is a huge man. His body is a paragon of physical perfection. When he moves you can see every muscle roll or tighten with the the flow of energy. He was not graceful but very steady, very balanced. He moved slowly but with the self-assurance that he could not be stopped, not by anything. He turned his palms up and looked at his swollen hands. He turned them over again and looked at his dark skin and his black body hairs, and then moved simianlike to the refrigerator. He took out a box of six eggs. He took the frying pan off the hanging rack and poured in some oil, watching the oil form a reflective membrane in the pan. He stared at his reflection in the oil. He closed one eye and watched his reflection in the pan do the same. He watched himseld for seconds, minutes, for what seemed like forever. He watched himself watching himself.

      He turned on one of the rings on the cooker. He put it on high. He put the pan on the ring and listened to it sizzle gently. He picked up an egg from out of the box. He studied the egg rolling it around in his hand, absorbed by its perfect form. He brought the egg, that looked tiny in his massive hand, near to his face, near to his eyes. He inspected the shell. He felt its smoothness. He dropped it.

The egg cracked on the floor. He looked down at the broken egg. He got down on all fours to look closer at the egg, because the strangest thing had happened. The linoleum felt as cold as his hands and knees felt. He felt conspicuous with his penis and scrotum so exposed, and he felt some trepidation at examining the broken egg. He got closer to it finding the angle at which he was able to see his reflection on the yolk only there were two yolks. He looked down to see his reflection one eye in one yolk and one eye in the other, or maybe his face distorted by the uneven bulges of the double yolk. He did not see this. He saw himself twice. He saw himself twice. One face in one yolk and another in the other yolk. He flinched. He moved back. He stood up distancing himself from this unpleasant image. His breathing, and his heart beat, had quickened. He grimaced disgusted at the mess on the floor. He scored a spiral in the wet egg with his big toe. He shivered dejavu and moved back to the box of eggs and the hot oil in the frying pan.

He cracked open another egg into the hot pan. Two perfect yellow yolks formed around the sizzling white in moments. The yolks glared the light up into his face. He stepped away from the pan, never taking his eyes off it. Then, reaching for the eggs on the adjacent work surface, he stepped back into the numbed egg on the linoleum. His perfect chest heaved. His senses sharpened. He dropped another egg on the floor and another and another and another and that made....two, four, six, eight....and then with all the eggs cracked open it made....it made thirteen, and then he dropped the box and then he tried to run as far from that place as he could but his feet slid violently on the linoleum and he was then on all fours and, covered in these chilled chicken foetuses, he could not get enough grip to move the few feet needed to get out of the kitchen. He worked his arms and legs furiously, trying to gather enough momentum to deliver himself, away from this enmeshing double vision and too bright reflective light, into the warm corridor. He finally scratched his way across the linoleum slamming the door behind him. He sat outside alone, with his back to the door and with his lungs burning in their fight to claim oxygen.

There was a definite nip in the air. She decided to fasten up another button on her electric blue satin shirt. She looked out of the window again. It was not warm but she was not taking off her cyan suede miniskirt. The legs were very very important, and she had great legs, they had to be on show. Bare legs would be best. Clinique's self-tan is a twentieth century miracle, but it would not keep you warm no matter how much you put on. She held her favourite tights in her hand, the softest cotton lycra mix in terry nappy white. Two hours in those though and she would definitely get Thrush. Trousers were out of the question, ditto long skirt, because of that "must be something to hide" bullshit. She certainly didn't want to go dressed up like a prostitute, not yet. If they did get to sex, which she would avoid, she didn't want him to think that she was soft porn material, or worse. No. She threw the tights down. She could wear her baby blue brushed leather mules. She jumped off the bed to get them. It would be great if the guy was genuine. If he wasn't some creep. She looked at her legs in the mules. She sniggered. John would be here soon. Soon, when all things will become much more.... She picked up the book that her sister had sent to her. She felt a temporary wave of self-admiration probably for her endurance in this gesture to her sister. Echo was getting her first glimpse of her love.

John and Lisa step out of the car and are immediately escorted by a large, square headed, man. John called the man Jimmy and started asking some friendly questions about his kids. The man looked surprised by the questions, by the topic of the questions. Lisa noticed the man's ugly burst nose and his harsh pocked skin. John seemed to know a lot of these hard faced people. Jimmy led them into the restaurant. The interior was grand, a little old-fashioned, but nevertheless impressive. The walls and upholstery were deep pure colours in shimmering silks and plush velvets, eye-catching and extremely unusual but not unattractive. It was the kind of place in which your own shadow could fall upon your face. Everybody in there having lunch seemed to be somehow cloaked in a darkness that did not hang in the room but settled in recesses and corners. There were not too many people dining but more than she had anticipated as it was lunch time and it was an expensive looking place. In the middle of the first row of tables from the front of the restaurant near the kitchens a strikingly handsome man with black wiry hair was sitting alone. On the next table, facing the handsome black haired man, there was a small TV. Lisa watched this man watching the film. They got nearer and nearer to the table so that she was able to make out more of the man's features. The shadows of the room seemed to scheme around him blackening out one half of his face and shrouding the other. Lisa knew that this was the man that they had come to meet.

John and Philip, as he had just asked her to call him, shook hands firmly and they all sat down. She could see more of this man now. John and Philip were talking and exchanging pleasantries. The man was very smartly dressed in a suit and open shirt that showed dozens of tight black curls on his chest. She could see that his hair was very dark and full of capricious waves. He looked strong enough for anybody to fear him and she could tell that John was not so relaxed around him. As his jacket fell back a little from his chest she could quite easily make out his two large and threatening pectorals. She watched them heave up and then settle down with his breathing. She was in awe of his great frame, he made her feel so small. She imagined lying on that hard cruel chest surrounded by his giant limbs. He looked like a cradle of strength to her. She looked down at her feet as she was only half listening to the two men's comments. She had not dressed too smartly but she was cute, and most of all she did not look easy. She could already tell that this man could handle anything, money, power, beautiful women, she had never seen such a person before. She thought about his connections to the world of showbiz and she thought about some of the men that she had regrettably had sex with so that she could get some work, any work. She was sure that this man, this Philip, had no need to screw the ambitious, he was too certain of himself. She knew that he had too much of everything to be bothered in some sleazy deal of sex and ambition. The idea of getting work was suddenly not a priority anymore. She looked at his face hearing him ask John about some guy called Harry and she thought that she saw a million things of importance that she knew nothing about. And she thought that she could see the attention of a million of the most beautiful women all having failed to make an impression on his vague countenance. She knew already that she was very attracted to him and there weren't many men that she could say that about. She also knew that he had enough appeal to women to be able to pick and choose his lovers. She thought of all of the women who would have thrown themselves at him in her situation and she knew how cynical he must be to their reckless sexual propositions. She wanted him and this was a new feeling. She didn't want anything other than him, for the first time that she could remember she wanted a man for nothing more than himself. The irony of this, she admitted to herself, was sharp as he was at this time talking to John and had not shown her as much as a side glance. He appeared to have no interest in what she was doing or even that she was sitting there at the same table. This lack of attention was something that was new to her. She looked around the restaurant for a moment, the waiter had moved closer to their table and was definitely giving her the eye. She decided not to notice him. She paid closer attention to Philip. He had no rings on his fingers, although she knew that that meant nothing anyway. Maybe he had some beautiful woman at home who he cared form, she didn't know, but she felt a knot in her stomach forming as she looked at the princely gestures of this mysterious man. Then she looked at his hands again not for a ring, or a promise, but at the skin, and the way he used them. He had huge hands and as she sat there observing she wondered how they'd feel on her naked body. She thought about just how manly and strong this man's giant hands could caress her. She thought about how he could squeeze her and take her and make her do anything that he wanted. She thought about how she would be unable to resist this man's powerful and dangerous embrace. She watched his hands and imagined them squeezing her breasts through electric blue satin and then she imagined one of his hands coming up between her legs from behind. She realised then that his hands were bright red and covered in sores as if he had psoriasis or eczema. She wanted to touch them and kiss them. She watched him wring out his hands time and time again as if something else was on them, something invisible covering them. Then she thought about him, and his thoughts, and she decided that he moved his hands because of her. She made him want to hold something. He was talking to her, it was body language. She had read about this in magazines. He was displaying his tense sexual energy. He was feeling the same way that she was. She knew then that there was an intoxicating chemistry which existed between them, and that he was a victim of it too. He was fighting it harder than she was though, probably for the sake of decency. She looked down at her feet again for a moment. She wished that she had dressed more modestly but at least she was not looking as if she had come here to get fucked. He was too much of a great powerful man to be interested in some cheap slut who wanted to suck his cock so that he would like her. He was too shrewd for that and too experienced. She had to be sweet and charming. He was not a vulgar man she could tell. She crossed her legs tightly to prevent any scent of her aroused vagina from reaching his nose. She had to play this, on one hand, like a lady and, on the other, like a charismatic young girl. She sat with her legs crossed as tightly as was comfortable planning to get their attention as meekly as she could...

He looked at the sick prick sitting opposite him at the table. He was disgusted by his proximity. So the queer bastard had brought some fucking bimbo with him and was asking for his help, his help to help her out. The fucking cocksucker thought that this was some kind of disguise, some way of hiding his fucking perversion, dirty, dirty, dirty bastard....and who was she? ...some tits and arse bitch with dumb blonde hair....but there was more to it than this wasn't there....dirty bastard....he could tell that she was beautiful however you looked at it; she was beautiful, and she was here, right here....that dirty, dirty fucker had brought her....what for? ...some sick test for some of his faggot shit games....was he thinking of his nigger now....or of Harry....or about him....he was probably thinking about him....yes, yes, this was a setup...

He could not help but notice how everybody seemed to be looking at her. She was beyond any comprehension of beauty, drawing all eyes to her. He had tried to pretend that she was not there, a totally insignificant being. Then she had ordered only icecream and he had been forced to look at her. He could see that she was an elaborate and perfectly calculated trap but he knew that he had no choice. He knew now that this shitstabbing freak was waiting to see what he would do. The dirty bastard had pushed her out to him and was waiting to see what was going to happen. He would have to play along.

He was going to have to fuck the fucking bitch for the sake of the queer....and for the sake of himself....he had no choice....but he had that cocksucker's number....he had it now....and he was sure that cocksucker's queer grin was trying to laugh at him....trying to laugh right in his face....that bastard was in big trouble, deep fucking shit; he was going to finish him and his gay bastard practices, and all of his sperm drinking boyfriends....it would be all over very soon.

Masters was worried about the silvergrey haired man. He had not seem him for a while, but if he thought that he could just turn up and dictate to him, tell him how to run things, well he'd show him. If the man with the silvergrey hair thought that he could push him around he was wrong. Masters didn't have to put up with any of his shit, not anymore.

He could hear the TV. It was on too loud but nobody else seemed to be hearing it as if they were conspiring to fool him. They were pretending that there was nothing wrong with the sound to make him think that he was mad or something, but he knew who was really fucked up, he knew that alright. The sound was beginning to hurt his ears and the voice on the TV was calling out abusively to him....at him. He rubbed his hands together trying to make the pain go away. He looked up at John as if he had turned the volume up on the TV. John looked at him as if he was awaiting an answer to something but all that he could hear was the TV and its evil suggestions. Why was it so loud? The voice made him feel dishonest but as if everybody knew about his dishonesty. They could all, including the queer bastard, see him far better than he could see himself. They all knew about him. They all knew everything. He had no choice but to accept this nasty bitch that was being paraded before him. He took his handkerchief from out of his pocket and dabbed the sweat from his brow trying desperately to think, to work it all out. Eventually after enough silence had passed to make him feel that everybody else thought him strange and that everybody else hated him, he called over the waiter to turn down his TV. The waiter picked up the remote control that was next to him and turned the sound down so that it could be barely heard above the voices in the restaurant.

Is that okay sir?
He nodded.

Excuse me. Do you have any Pommetizer? With the cute little froggy on the front?

He covered his mouth with his hand, and he began to sweat in terror, as he nervously cleared his throat. He watched her closely from the corner of his eye as if he was paying her no mind. He couldn't be sure now. Maybe she knew something. His throat clearing turned into an unstoppable cough that made sure that everybody had to turn to look at him. This was all bad.

I know this film.

She had swivelled in her chair to watch the TV that nobody had been watching but which he thought that everybody had been observing, waiting for their moment.

I do, I do....that's Henry and that's....that's....Tommy, Tommy right....oh this is a great film....Oh I remember this bit....oh yes....Tommy is angry at Henry....look, look.....but he's not really angry.....well he might be, and Henry isn't sure if Tommy's joking or not, and I think that Tommy is not sure either....whether he's angry at Henry or not I mean....it's great....I thought that he was going to shoot Henry but he does not know what's going on he....I mean Tommy....has to cover his back, you know....

She took a short deep breath and continued to speak.

Anyway if neither of you two want any desert why don't you order ice-cream. I'll eat it. I promise.

She did look convincing. He looked at John with disbelief. John tried to change the subject.

See she knows her films. A superstar ready for the picking.

Oh I'd love to work in a film. I've done some acting, I'm confident that I could do it.

Maybe you'll get your chance?

They both looked at him. They stared at him. He was not sure what they were expecting, but he knew what they wanted the queer and the bitch. He was going to make sure that both of them would regret their little plan, their vicious little plot, for the rest of their short lives....

John was being driven back to his home. He could feel the tension leaving his body after having had lunch with his archenemy, who of course was not really his archenemy in public, but actually his best friend. They both wanted each other out of the way, but Masters had taken a lot of risks and they had, so far, all worked. At first it seemed that it was only a matter of time before he got careless or unlucky. Now John suspected that there was a pay off going to some shitbag in the police because so far they hadn't been able to get near him. Masters hated him. He could not stand it that John's operation was so tight and so successful. Masters and his men spent most of their time badmouthing John and his associates. They wanted to fuel some kind of shoot-out or gang war, all rather distasteful really. Masters had too much power and too many connections for John to have him whacked. He couldn't be seen to do anything until Masters had raised his hand.

The thing that pissed Masters off the most was that John made too much money for too many important people, and he virtually controlled the drug imports for the area. He had courted Amsterdam for a long time and now he not only imported for himself but he acted as a negotiator for people in London.

John's problem was that for all of his work for the big men in London it was Masters who was the running favourite to be accepted into the big man community, the select club. Masters had a lot of important friends. He knew all of the right people and those who didn't know him showed him respect, the kind of respect that grows out of fear. It didn't matter how John conducted business, or how efficient he was, he was the college boy criminal. He was thought to be lacking the strength of the others, the leaders in the other towns, who were brought up on fists and boots. He had chosen his career because he happened to be dealing as a student. He got himself closer and closer to the source whilst avoiding unnecessary confrontations. He watched what went on and then, as he began to see how it all worked, he just involved more people and bought in more drugs. Now he knew that this, his hold on the drugs trade, was the only thing stopping Masters from mounting an all out attack. Nevertheless it was almost ninety-nine per cent certain that Masters would get the nod from London and then he would pretty much own the town. He would be free to fuck with John as he wished and would definitely muscle in on all of the action, but John had already been to Birmingham to see Hanif and plans had already been made.

It seemed to have gone as well as it could considering that Masters was a part of the negotiations. Maybe he was calming down now things were running his way. Maybe he just fancied her. John smiled to himself; of course he did, everybody did. John just hoped that everything would go fine between Masters and Lisa. Of course they'd end up in bed together at some point, that was business, but he'd find her some agent who owed him a few favours and she'd set herself up in London or wherever, and that would be the end of it. He hoped that she would be a distraction for Masters and that he would presume that she was some kind of gift to him. He would brag and boast to his men whilst indulging in the Lisa La Truen fantasy and seeing John as a soft touch which was exactly how John wanted it for the moment. There was one thing bothering him though. He couldn't help feeling responsible for Lisa. The sex that they had shared somehow bound them not as lovers but....but as something else, as friends but more so. He couldn't quite explain it to himself.

He had observed Masters very closely especially when he mentioned Zak and Fat Stuart but if he knew anything about it he wasn't giving anything away. He suspected Masters everybody did. If he got anything concrete then he would have to sort the whole thing out, even if that meant tackling Masters head on. Zak had been a good runner. Anything that happened that was unexpected could be traced back to Masters. He acted strangely and made what seemed to be crazy decisions as if he was trying to make sure that nobody knew what he was going to do next. And then when he fucked it all up, which was unavoidable it seemed, he used simple force and intimidation to see him through. It had worked up until now even though he must have been close to being nicked. He was riding his luck for the moment but John was ready to wait, wheels were already set in motion. He had is plan and he was sticking to it and that meant that for the time being he just had to sit back and watch things unfold around him.

He allowed his thoughts to drift to Harry because Harry was his main priority. He wanted to leave all of this shit behind and live with Harry. They had a lot of love to share and he needed to be off the stage so to speak. They needed to be together. He wanted Harry so much.

Masters lived above the restaurant. It was a large building of three floors and lush green ivy had grown over the walls covering two thirds of the exterior walls. It had large square windows like huge unblinking eyes. The restaurant had a reputation as being the finest in East Anglia. It was, of course, expensive. Inside upstairs on the second floor was a small kitchen, a bathroom and a huge long room that was Masters's office. On the third floor was Masters's bedroom and three other large rooms. One was kept as an entertaining room, it had a table set out with glasses and plates all of which looked regal and ostentatious. The other two rooms had beds in and were used, or would be used, in an emergency. If there was some heat on then Masters could have his bodyguards and soldiers around keeping watch, and sometimes when he was feeling particularly vulnerable he would have some of his men keep watch. He had guns hidden throughout the house. Masters had had bricks removed in certain parts of certain walls. Usually one brick was removed a small hand gun, already loaded, was placed carefully and securely in the hole left by the brick. This was then covered over by a thin sheet of polystyrene insulation and then papered over. Masters could quite simply punch his hand through memorized points on certain walls and hey presto he had a gun in his hand all ready to go. You are right to think that his conception of security is nourished by obsessive paranoia, and you are right to keep this thought to your self.

Lisa was sitting in the designated entertaining room. She had looked at the laid table and the lavish decorations and she had made her mind up that Philip was a wealthy man. It was surprising the amount of wealth and good taste that she had come into contact with in this small town of Colchester. They were out on the rural outskirts of the town now and she was standing by the window staring out trying to focus on something outside. Her mind was wandering and she glanced back at the table with all of its silver and cut glass and ornate candle stick holders, and above was a chandelier and the walls had large printed pictures on them, none of which she recognized. She looked around at them all, and read the titles underneath. The first was a strange fat squat creature it was called *The Toad* and was by Picasso. She had heard of this artist before; she could not remember where, or when, but she took some satisfaction from the fact that she recognized the name. The next picture was a huge blown up photograph of two frogs in a copulatory embrace. It had no title. The frogs were wet and warty, quite repulsive, but Lisa liked it, it was erotic she thought. The next picture was called *Gluttony*. Two women, one with warts, the other with frog's feet and webbed toes, were roasting and frying up small children. Lisa quickly turned away from it. The next picture was by Coljin de Coter and was called *The Damned*. There was a mass of naked human bodies and in the foreground was a naked woman. There were flames blazing up from her vagina. A man was biting into the flesh on her arm. His teeth were just about to break the skin. She had long red hair and held her left hand up to her eyes which were streaming with tears. A frog, or was it a toad, was slothfully crouched on her left bosom. Lisa cringed. Masters returned holding two large brandies in two of the largest glasses that Lisa had ever seen.

You've known John a long time then?

Well we were at school together, but we haven't seen each other, well hadn't seen each other, for quite a few years. He came to University down here and we hadn't seen, or even heard of, one another since. Mind you, as I was saying, I did go off to do a spot of globetrotting.

That's right, America. That must have been....very....great....it must have been very great.

Oh I had the best of times, really! It's quite a place you know.

I am sure that it is.

There was a rigid silence, almost unbreakable. Masters regarded her and her looks one more time. In order to sit at the top you needed to have more power and more money than anybody else. This in turn meant that you had to spend more money and exercise more power than anybody else. Masters knew that one of the best ways of expressing power and wealth was to collect beautiful things. If you stopped spending it could be seen to be as detrimental as not earning. It was important to feed those around you, to throw crumbs from the table. Masters had to give thick straining envelopes full of paper notes to the people who flocked around him wanting to help. A beautiful thing was a little different to money but it worked on similar principles. If he had the most beautiful object it was a symbol of his power. It showed the world what he was capable of. It brought respect and envy from those who coveted that beauty. He looked at Lisa as she was gabbling on about her experience as a model. He looked closely at her and he thought about her connection to John, that queer fucker. It seemed to be good that he had introduced them. It would add to the evidence that was growing which suggested that John's time was over and that he was being eaten up by the pace and vitality of Masters's operation. He didn't want to fuck her but the thought crossed his mind that he had to fuck somebody, and he could tell that this woman, more than any other, was somehow a product of male lust, as if she had been born from the dreams of men rather than some cold musty womb. If men wanted her, and it was obvious that they did, then he had to have her. He was going to have to force himself. At this point there was no choice.

Lisa could see that he was scrutinizing her, watching her. He was finally paying her the kind of attention that she was accustomed to. It made her talk quicker and take shorter breaths and soon she was blowing out long winding sentences using only fractions of her lung capacity and the words just kept on coming out. She was trying to work out where his eyes were resting. She was unsure if she was pushing her bust out enough but her back was aching a little from arching it, up and out through lunch. She decided to sit down and stretch out her legs and divert his attention for a little so as to give her back a rest. He led her over to the comfortable chairs and pulled out a low table for her to set down her drink. She unfolded her legs and made herself comfortable. She made her sensual smile and drank her brandy. She allowed her bum to wiggle slightly as the alcohol hit her stomach. His eyes were still on her bust, she thought, and she struggled to keep them pushed straight out annoyed that he had not been bothered by her legs. He must be a breast man she told herself. She continued talking but in her head she had forgotten all about modelling, all she could think about was Philip, his strong voice, and his large hands. He got up to get them both another drink and she managed to get her breath back after having been talking none stop for what seemed like hours. She liked the way that he moved; slowly but with immense power and force. He was a giant man who appeared to be constantly aware of his physical strength and was careful so as not to knock down walls or to mash furniture into flotsam and pulp. She imagined how he would deal with flesh. He would be tender but at the same time he would be unable to hide his strength and during bright flashes of desire he would momentarily forget himself bringing his whole body weight to bear down upon his lover. She had watched him move with the economy of a robot and when his limbs worked the movement did not simply occur from beneath the flesh but could be watched through the taut muscles that prominently showed through all of his clothes. When he moved his finger it was possible to see every working sinew and Lisa liked that very much. She wanted to feel that flesh and blood under her finger nails, or if it turned out to be steel and paint she wanted to feel how cold and hard it could remain whilst between her legs. That was too much, she reprimanded herself with a self-inflicted smile. She had to keep her mind on the task at hand which was to get herself some work. She had promised herself that this would not happen. She remembered to tell herself that this guy would have had thousands of little sluts throwing themselves at him and if she wanted to do herself a favour then she had to try and be a little different, kind of interested, and definitely interesting, more challenging. She had to be modest and she had to be professional.

Masters stood outside the door of his office. He had no choice, no choice, no choice, the two words echoed through his mind as he braced himself for what, he knew, had to be done. There was no escape he told himself as he tried to fortify his mental circuitry against the foul act that he must see through. He was trying not to conjure up the image of that crude weeping hole but he knew that he had to face it, and all of its rancid and clammy odours. He would have to take it and fuck it and make it his. He pushed open the door and stepped into his office. It was a large and long oblong room. There was little light as the ivy had been allowed to grow over the room's only window. His desk was at the far end of the room and he moved towards it like a smooth electronic impulse. Next to his desk was a headless and legless Mannequin carved out of Mahogany. It had a well proportioned right arm with a useable elbow and wrist, and it also had four fingers and a thumb all with knuckle joints. The left arm was longer than the right as if it had been stretched by some hideous torture technique, and it was not made out of wood but metal, smooth shining chrome. The left arm had no joints. It was just one straight and thin cylinder with a sphere attached to the end like some gross self-deformity. The Mannequin was mounted on a platform so that its head, if it had one, would stand at approximately five-ten. He sometimes had nightmares in which the Mannequin came to life and threatened him with its long left arm but he was trying not to think about it. He had enough horror downstairs spread across the sofa, lying in wait. On the other side of his desk, to the left, there was an electric chair. It was large and had leather straps for the ankles and wrists and a kind of Roundhead helmet fixed to the back of the chair that could be adjusted to sit higher up or lower down depending on the height of the person sitting in the chair. The circumference of the helmet could also be adjusted so that the head could be held securely. He had picked it up from an eccentric collector who had another identical model. It was something of a curiosity and was worth a considerable amount of money. It was heavily insured. The electric chair was originally, if you like, bought out of the same considerations that now overwhelmingly pressurized him into feeling that he should have sex with Lisa. It was expensive and unusual and people could not stop looking at it and thinking about it whilst they were in the same room as it. Next to the chair, and running alongside the entire length of the wall, was what looked like a shallow glass aquarium and opposite it a small table with the Pioneer PDR05 CD player that allowed its user to record, or "tape" as some fuckhead once explained, onto CDR discs. It had hardly been used but was certainly a beautiful machine. Its reflection could be seen on the glass aquarium wall. The bottom of the aquarium was full of soil and rocks and small pools of water. There were large branches of trees, that were constantly changed, laid across one another. There were UV lamps shining hot onto the moist fecund soil, and onto the shallow basins of water, and the lush tropical leaves on the tropical branches. Amongst all of this could be found a small collection of frogs. Each one displayed its own interpretation of the rainbow. They were beautiful almost beyond belief. The colours shined on their wet backs which made them look glossy and all the more vivid. Masters looked at the deep crimsons and the cool sapphire blues. He marvelled at the blinding yellows and the impenetrable blacks. He smiled, happy at last, he was alone with his babies. He began to shiver with delight. It was a delight that only he knew. It was a delight that was unequalled in its sublime magnificence. He was there, with his frogs, watching, and for once, truly alive. The delight, the purest of delights, was made all the more attractive and appealing by its dastardly chiaroscuro. The only light was from the UV lamps allowing Masters to remain undisturbed within the shadows. His mouth was salivating uncontrollably, his eyes trying to look at all of the frogs at once, his mouth formed a lewd and vulgar smile. Here, surrounded by his frogs and toads, he could not hide his obscene rapture. He was like a fat man in a Bangkok brothel. He thought about the bitch upstairs waiting for her fuck, waiting to cover him with her decrepit saddle of womanhood. It was enough to make him retch but that was something that he would not do in front of his babies, his frogs. They would help him do what he needed to do, what he had to do. Once again he would find his life in them, these ancient, and most noble, creatures who bore their gifts to their prince. From the shadows the prince moved lowering his hand into the kingdom of the frogs. He picked up a small scarlet spotted black frog with wet skin that seemed to glow in his hand. He quickly moved the frog onto the back of his hand and stared at its spherical eyes. Its only movement came from its throat. His hand started to burn red were the frog was squatting silent yet holding Masters in its calculating bufine glare. Masters sniggered to himself and to the frog but he held the rest of the world at bay, holding the secret closer to him, nearer to his chest. He could feel the tension beginning to leave his body and take residence elsewhere, somewhere, maybe with that disgusting bitch and her festering cunt. He was free now, free forever. He lifted the potent wisdom of the frog to his lips and he kissed its head unable to control his need of it. He licked its hind legs and its back and its neck and he rubbed the moisture, the thick slime, all over his face. He drank the magic from the world. He imbibed the beauty of the frog; its amphibian milk. All of its magnificence was his. He laughed out loud as he put the frog back and selected another. He stepped back into the shadows to drink and he looked over the lighted kingdom and he closed his eyes and he trembled with satisfaction. His hands and face were beginning to burn up and he knew that he had to move quickly before the disfigurement. He put back his second beauty and strode out of the room.

He crouched, tightly wound, outside the door of the room where she was. He was on all fours. His hands were spread out in front of him but his thumb and little finger, on both hands, were drawn back out of sight so that there were just three long digits fanned out before him. He opened his eyes as wide as he could and concentrated on not blinking. He moved as he had observed them moving with small tiny adjustments and then a leap. He held his hand to his mouth so that his juvenile giggling could not be heard, and he wiped some of the frog mucus from his face. He stood up and entered the room.

Lisa saw him enter the room. She had been worried. He had been gone for some time. She turned around as she heard the door open and saw his face and the blotches of red that covered his features. Before she could speak he was upon her. He pushed her to the table and pressed his lips onto hers. The polished silver cutlery rattled and fell to the floor and the cut glass tumbled safely onto the carpet. She could not believe what was happening. She decided to push him away but she couldn't. She didn't want to. She didn't want this but that seemed to make it all the more exciting. He quickly and roughly spread her legs apart. He ripped down her panties tearing them off with what she thought was a frantic need for her. She thought that she could smell desire on him like on no other man that she had ever encountered. She had never been wanted this much before. She supported herself on locked elbows that hurt the heel of her hands. He was biting into her neck and she forced herself into relaxing with the pain and accepting it expecting him to stop at any minute but praying to herself that he wouldn't. She had never experienced the pure untempered passion of a man. He had no time to think of her comfort because he was a man possessed and she liked this. It was wrong but the more that she thought about that the more she enjoyed what he was doing. He pulled his trousers down and was looking at her exposed body. She tried to find or to grab some part of him so that she too could communicate how she felt but there was nothing to hold onto. She tried to open his shirt to clutch at his chest or neck but it was like a cat trying to claw its way up a wall of marble. She ripped open her shirt sending electric blue buttons across the room. Her breasts sat up in her bra, but still he showed no interest. He had his erection in his hand now and she could not believe that this was happening. He held it in his sore red giant hands. He looked, longingly she thought, at her vagina. She wanted him inside her right now. She could not wait. He opened her up with his swollen fingers. She exhaled the pleasure that she was experiencing. He had no condom and this worried her but somehow it seemed to go along with the whole mood of this lusty union. She knew that she was going to have to say no as his thick hardness got closer to her moistening body. She was waiting for him to make the uncomfortable break, to put on his condom, but he didn't seem to be thinking about that. Suddenly the idea that he wasn't going to bother held her in a state of limbo. She had to stop him but she didn't want to stop the way that she felt. She wanted to feel it. And then she could feel it and she screamed something between pain and pleasure as he drove his entire self into her, forcing her legs, forcing her, wide apart. She felt the danger of him unsheathed and free within her. He immediately began to rock himself in and out of her as strong and as forceful as he could. He threw off the whole dinner service with one passing swipe of his arm and pushed her back more whilst thumping his brutal hardness into her with more and more force. The hard wood of the table hurt her bones and her skin but the throbbing pain that he was giving her was exquisite and made the contact with the table bearable. He forced her legs wider apart and held her open with his fingers so as to get deeper within her, grimacing with his effort to give it to her as hard as he could. She wanted to look up into his eyes and she strained to look at his face, but he didn't seem to notice her. He, she thought, had too much passion and desire to be released before he could think such thoughts.

Her perfume had worked its way into his eyes and hurt. He could tell that he was losing his vision and he pictured the frog in his mind. He saw the bitches forked snake tongue twist out of her mouth in unending oscillations. It flicked out and it darted in smooth serpentine coils. The whites of her eyes had turned a sinister mustard colour and her pupils looked dilated. She was showing him her true face. The one that he had suspected all along. His vision got worse and his eyes watered from the perfume. He was left alone plunging his body into an unending pit. He saw the pictures in his mind swirling around him and the bright beautiful colours bathing him in brilliance. He squeezed his eyes together tightly while his body flushed hot and cold at intervals that seemed like hours but were probably splinters of seconds.

He clenched his teeth together and drew his lips back, grimacing like an aggressive chimpanzee. Their sweat covered them as if they were two sticky garden slugs. He seemed to be crying as he fucked her, made love to her. She watched the tears jerk down his face with each thrust and she watched them disappear or fall down and splash upon her. No man had ever made her feel so needed...

Chapter 11

5-hydroxy-N, N-dimethyltryptamine

Some Tree Frogs, from the species *Hyla* and *Phyllobates* secrete a range of chemicals from their glands, onto their skins. The glands work to cover the skin of the animal as a kind of defence mechanism. These secretions contain the following: batrachotoxin, steroidal alkaloids, serotonin, histamine, and bufotenine (5hydroxyN, Ndimethyltryptamine). These chemicals, particularly bufotenine, can bring about hallucinations.

These creatures should not be handled without protective clothing. Tree Frogs' secretions can bring about burning sensations, uncomfortable rashes, and can seriously damage unprotected skin. It is important that eyes should be carefully shielded. A standard set of laboratory goggles are recommended. If these substances were to come into contact with the eyes they would produce an extremely painful inflammatory reaction. If consumed these chemicals could well bring about violent vomiting and incapacitating abdominal pains. Any prolonged use of hallucinogens or psychoactive substances is likely to evoke chronic depression and acute paranoia.

There are other Frogs, of the species *Dendrobates*, *Physalaemus*, and *Rana* which contain similar substances in different proportions. There are many Toads too whose secretions have comparable properties. The Toad secretions do tend to be much more potent, and much more toxic.

Unfortunately these potentially dangerous animals are open to abuse. They should be handled with the care and respect that their potency deserves.

None of this should be taken lightly. It is not merely frivolous indulgence. The Frog, and the Toad, symbolize some very important ideas which are cemented back in time to the very beginnings of human communities, civilization itself. There is a considerable number of contemporary theorists who believe that the ancient shamanic cultures were the germ of the great religions that we have all been practising for thousands of years, on which, even today, many of our laws and morals are based.

The Shaman stood at the door between the people of the tribe (the group or community) and the spirit world. The Shaman's key to unlock this door was hallucination. The Tree Frog, the Frog, and the Toad, were, therefore, vitally important to the Shaman, and the people. The amphibian itself could be added to a brew of psychedelic mushrooms (hence the term "toadstool") and so improve its strength.

There are other characteristics that make the Frog, or Toad, a most celebrated, and revered, creature. The process of metamorphosis, that these amphibians all go through, can be seen as a miracle of nature. The Frog, or Toad, like the butterfly, goes through a natural drama, a rite of passage, that has great significance even today. Today we have our eighteenth, or twenty-first, birthday celebrations, when we traditionally become an adult. Ethnographers and anthropologists will tell you that these rituals are fairly universal throughout human societies. Then of course there is the cannibalism practised by many species of Frog and Toad, symbolizing some macabre life-through-death cycle. There is also the, not unrelated, process of moulting in which Frogs, and Toads, shed their skin, eating it as it is removed, digesting themselves over and over. Once again it is life and death forged together in one image, one action. The whole moulting and consuming process turns the creature into a metaphor for Mother Earth. The Frog, and Toad, represent the synthesis of these ancient obsessions.

There are many examples of Frogs and Toads in the art and mythology of MesoAmerica. Tlaltecuhtli was a powerful anthropomorphic being off whom the skulls of dead humans hung. She usually took the form of a squat humanoid with Frog, or Toad, like features. Her mouth was the gateway to the underworld. She swallowed up the dead and at the same time sent forth new seed from her womb. Tlaltecuhtli was maybe the most important of all of the MesoAmerican mythical creatures. She was creation itself. One half of her was the heavens and the other half the earth.

These small amphibians have allowed us to unlock the door to the spirit world, and have enabled us to make some kind of sense out of the natural world in which we once lived, and in which some of us still do live. They served us then, and they serve us now, but theirs is a remarkable power, a truly fantastic gift. They are to be cherished. They are awe-inspiring; and like all great and beautiful things they carry, within themselves, the ability to destroy all that they come into contact with.

Chapter 12

Gillian-Record

I ask myself Where is my job? Where is my future? What has happened to all of the promises? I have kept up my part of the bargain. I got the grades. I got the manners, the polite smile. I understood, and so sought the long term rewards over the immediate rewards. I mastered the correct mode of speaking. I taught myself how to play the games of the intellectual. I have done it all. I have worked hard. But I have nothing and there is nothing on the horizon. I can quote from William Blake, Emily Dickinson, Hart Crane, Sylvia Plath and Gregory Corso. I can recite passages from novels that can make you weep with joy and laugh at misfortune. I can tell you a million million things that I have stuffed into my head, all beautiful things. But who cares for my expertise? Who cares about me and who cares about you? Who cares about what we have got to offer? You have to make your own life. You have to find your own way to put up with it all, to survive. If it is good or bad what is the difference? You have to do whatever you can...

I am sitting on a toilet masturbating. It is a part of the act. What am I thinking about? Who am I thinking about? I am not really aware of the answers to your questions. I am gradually getting bigger. The veins are swelling. My body is covered in olive oil, she says that it has to be olive oil. I smothered it all over my body just before I began masturbating. My cock is becoming similarly unctuous from the residue of olive oil that remains on my palm. I spent nearly two and a half hours at the gymnasium this morning working on heavy weights and my muscles are still very pumped up from the exercise. I must admit that I like the way that I look. All of my body is tense and hard and greasy. I seem to be fully erect now. I take out the tight elastic band from my wallet and wrap it around the base of my penis. I manage to stretch it around my circumference three times. It tightly coils around it. The aim is for it to cut off the circulation so that even though I am no longer aroused my penis still looks extremely big inside my jeans and boxers. Gillian insists on seeing a bulge.

I leave the cubicle behind. I am feeling very uncomfortable but I have to keep up the service and Gillian, who first informed me about this trick, is my most important client. The oil is making me hot. I am sweating and my clothes are sticking to my skin. I am blanking out from my mind the pain of the elastic band on my cock. I leave the building that I am in and move outside. The fresh air blasts me and I feel a little faint, unsteady. I walk past the university's hexagonal launderette and then up some steps to the right. Gillian, Professor Datisse, is the Dean of Students. She is in control of the campus, the buildings, security and the students. She has the power to have people removed from wherever she pleases to wherever she pleases. She is supposed to look after student welfare but she rarely practices the benevolence that is required for the post. She is waiting for me at the top of the steps. She does not greet me but just tells me, with an impatient and agitated tone, and in her usual faultless BBC accent that intimidates even the most acclaimed academics, to get a fucking move on. Walking up the steps has made me feel very dizzy. I can feel sweat pouring out of my brow, running down my face. I struggle to keep up with her and her stout belligerent strides. She spits out over her shoulder something that I don't quite catch but which I guess to have been that she hopes that I've been working out. I am glad that I have. We walk up to the first tower Rayleigh Tower. It has fourteen floors. The first twelve are for students and the top two floors are for couples, that is, supposed to be for couples. There are four other tower blocks on this side of campus. She nods to the small man at the bottom of the tower. I think that he is some kind of warden. I try to smile at him but I am feeling very ill, kind of dizzy whilst being both hot and cold at the same time. I am trying to remember every detail so that I can play the whole story back to myself later but I am having problems keeping up, keeping conscious. Gillian gets into a lift and waits for me to get in before pressing number 14, the top floor. I feel worse in the lift, coldhotstifled. Gillian is not looking at me and I can see my mutant reflection in the security camera that is looking down. I decide not to try and make conversation. We arrive at floor 14 and Gillian puts her hands on her hips as she waits for the doors to open. She has neither brown nor blonde hair but somewhere in between. Outside in the sun it looked more blonde than anything but now as the doors open, and as I seem to be gasping for oxygen, I could swear that she is probably brunette. We leave the lift for the corridor and Gillian takes out a set of keys that she holds in her pugilistic fist. She is at least half a foot shorter than I but she is stocky, not fat, mesomorphic. But am I seeing this? I do not know what is happening I feel dull as if my senses are breaking down....losing it. She opens the door and sternly motions me to enter. As I walk in I am shocked at how hot it is....and there seems to be a dull.....*falling*...I reach to pull down my collar....I...*falling*.....I feel heavy.....I try....*falling*

I am looking up at an imperfect white....an imperfect white ceiling....Gillian is holding my head and she is pushing it between my legs and shouting COME ON YOU FUCKING PRICK. I put my hand up to my head instinctively examining the cut that I am not aware of, that I got when I hit my head as I fell. I think that I just passed out a few moments ago. We are in another corridor that has two doors, one to the right and one straight ahead. I am shaking, trembling rather. I remember now that we are in a flat on the campus of the university. As instructed I take the door on the right which I know leads to the bathroom. CLEAN YOURSELF UP YOU LITTLE PRICK, she yells, AND GET A FUCKING MOVE ON.

In the bathroom I splash cold water on my face. My penis is swollen, puffed up and distorted. I cannot get the elastic band off. It has sunk into the skin and the now discoloured flesh. I rub my nail desperately hard against the band to cut it. It worked, to my relief, but I now have an ugly welt around my cock. I dab cold water onto this insidious red line but it does not help the pain it just feels cold. I study my face in the mirror above the sink and allow myself a "wishing you good luck" expression. I go back into the corridor and the overwhelming heat. I am nervous, very nervous, so much so that I want to be sick. I feel this unexplainable need for Gillian to approve of me, to like me, to like what I do. I want her to think that I am beautiful. I feel as though if she was to find me vulgar, or not to her taste, that I would break down into a spastic fit of self-hatred. I open the door to the room that Gillian is in. They are all self-contained single room flats with a small bathroom. Inside it is even hotter as there is a line of technical looking lamps shining down onto many giant Marijuana plants. The plants are everywhere and the smell is startling, but unrefreshingly thick, making the air heavy and sticky. The plants look as if they are very healthy and well cared for. The whole room is covered by pots and trays containing these plants, all except for a chair, which Gillian is siting on, and a small tape player. You're not dead then, eh, not yet. Gillian was not showing me the compassion that I expected after having passed out like that. I am giving my apologies for that accident. She is replying, telling me to take off my clothes. She has already done this. I dare not count the number of rolls of fat that hang from her waist like unnippled udders. Gillian's skin sags and creases and stretches in its attraction to the force of gravity. She is wearing a matching bra and panties set. They are made out of a stretch material that has a waxy shine to it. I strip off hoping that she is going to comment on how good I look, but she pays me no attention. I am wearing a pair of briefs that match Gillian's underwear. The same material and the same colour: dollar green that shines as if it were coated with vaseline. I am coated in olive oil which should have a distinctive smell but it cannot be made out because of the strong smell of the plants. Gillian, with a serious countenance, that I associate with a soldier performing manoeuvres, pulled down the material on the cups of her dollar green bra that are held by press studs. This reveals large pink nipples through the large peep holes. Her panties are crotchless and dollar green. The large violent V that is missing from the panties shows off her straggling pubic hairs. She begins to talk.

Did you go to the gym today? Lazy fuck Did you? Okay run your fingers over your cock through your underpants like I've shown you....that's it....good, good.....that's good....now open the studs and pull down the pouch that's it....is your cock shrinking?....(blowing out with disgust)....what's the fucking matter with it....come on....come on, fucking gay shit....that's better....the oil is okay, nice to know that you can get something right stupid prick....come over here now kneel down....that's it....I'm not sure exactly what kind of mood I'm in so I want you to finger fuck me for a while until I make up my mind....put on a condom first so that I don't have to be disturbed later....hurry up for fuck's sake....dozy little shit....what are you doing?....WHAT THE FUCK ARE YOU DOING?....finger fuck me I said....did I ask you to rub my clit? Did I? I'm asking you. Did I ask you to rub my fucking clit?....I don't think that I did did I? NOW FINGER FUCK ME....(she slaps me across my face)....good....better....in and out, in and out and in and out....come on.....harder than that you fucking bastard....COME ON..that's it.....Mmmm....yes....that's much better....I'm almost liking this now you fucking fuck....fucking shithead....yes....good....oh yes....I'm feeling better....much better....(she stamps on my left foot as I am crouched before her)....STOP, what are you doing? My right foot, remember? Right foot means tits. Left foot means suck my cunt, remember? HELLO IS THERE ANYBODY THERE? HELLO?....stop pissing about....right foot is tits....How many times have I told you this? How many times do I have to tell you? How many times? How many? Tell me how many? Fucking dipshit. CARRY ON WITH THE FINGER FUCKING....Did I ask you to stop?....No I didn't, did I? Did I? I didn't ask you to stop did I? (I nod in agreement)....Buck up your ideas you lousy bastard....(I can feel blood trickling from my wound which stings from the oil and the sweat on my skin) Oh yes...I like this fucker, fucker I like this....both nipples at once....again...again....more....more...,yes, yes, yes, it's good, it's good,...two fingers fucker....two fingers....deeper....and again....harder fuckhead.....yes, yes...,keep it deep, keep it deep (she stamps on my right foot)....that's right good boy....lips on my lips, tongue in, thumb on clit....you're not such a dumb little prick....faster with the tongue....come on....what's the matter with you eh? What's the fucking matter with you?....you want to get paid don't you you miserable bastard cunt?....Don't you? Well faster, more....more....MORE....don't stop, good, good....Mmmmmmmmm, oh yes, oh yes, yes....oh....oh....When I say....are you listening fuck (she slaps me hard across the face making some blood from my head splash onto my arm)....When I say, when I make the sign I want you to sit down on the floor....When I say, not before....okay got it fuck....not before, not before...oh yes....yes....yes, good, good.....shithead is a good shithead aren't you....you are aren't you....good little fuck....Okay on the floor (I sit on the floor)...I've changed my mind lie down (I lie down and she sits down pushing my cock up into her, she is sitting on top of me riding me with her back to me, she is reaching down with one hand and rubbing her own clitoris while sliding herself up and down my cock).....don't move shit, don't you move you shit, you fucking shit....keep that little prick of yours up straight....oh yes, yes....yes, oh yes, YES, (she is panting heavily) okay, okay....push a couple of fingers up my arse, WAIT UNTIL I TELL YOU YOU CHEAP BASTARD....okay...yes....you like this don't you?....fuck likes this don't you, fuck likes this, oh yes he does....further.....that's it....yes......yes.....oh....oh yes....oh yes....oh yes....oh yes....that's it, that's it, that's it....yes....yes...yes...YES...YES...OH YES...Oh GOD..OH GOD YES..OH..OH OH OH OH OH OH   OH   OH

OH OH OH OH OH OH OH OH OH OH OHAAAAAAAAAA AAAAAAAAAAAAAAAAAAAAAAAAAAAA.......................
....Oh....
..Oh......Oh...............................Oh.

I have tried to watch and observe but I do not want to be here. I do not want to have to speak, or put my clothes back on, or acknowledge this meeting. I am just looking at the plants. The beautiful green leaves and the cotton soft buds. The room is full of hot bright light but as I am lying here it seems so dark. I am lying in a shadow of something immense, at the centre of something that is larger than I can imagine. I look around this room, this bitter hole in the sky, and I look at the riotous plants growing in the air far away from the earth. I want to leave this moribund heart of dark turpitude and these giant uncontrollable plants and their odour of intoxication. I strain to look out of the window but Gillian's relaxed mass holds me to the floor so that it is just not possible. I try to fill the vacuum inside, and outside, of myself with thoughts of myself, but fear sits alone repelling all of the usurpous pictures that I can conjure up. I close my eyes and I tell myself that when I reach five in my mind that....one....then I will....two....put my hands together....three....and be able to....four....fly, fly, fly away from....five....here, and all of this. But I do not. As much as I wish it still does not happen.

Chapter 13

The Hunter's Arms

Chris is looking as good as ever. His trousers fit perfectly around his long slim legs and his jacket, very Carnaby Street that it is, looks sharp across his shoulders and pinched around his lithe young torso. He has to see Moz about something that they've got going together. You are not sure about this. Moz and Chris look as if they would have nothing in common. They talk as if they have nothing in common. It is the strangest partnership that you can imagine. Besides this though is a suspicion that you have about Chris. You haven't mentioned it to anyone, not yet just in case, but you can't help thinking that he's a bit of a bullshitter. He never seems to be in on anything. You've never been involved with him before and you, like Chris, are a newcomer and it all seems unbelievable; that you don't really know him; that he never has anything to offer; that he seems to have no connections, apart form socializing with the right people (just as you are doing, trying to get ahead), but nothing that is concrete. Now all of a sudden he's talking about all kinds of shit. It pours out of his mouth like he's fucking big time, as if he's gone from tiny time to big time overnight! And now you're entering The Hunters with him and he's talking about some business shit that he's got going with Moz. You didn't mind listening to his shit but now your expecting him to ask for Moz, in his cocky London boy way (even though he's from Chelmsford), and he, and you too cos you're with him, are gonna get laughed out of the fucking boozer.

And then it'll be goodbye big time, hello tiny time forever. But on the other hand he reckons that he went on some secret trip with John and Moz and not even he can believe that he could get away with serious bullshit like that, so he might just be in to, or in on, something, and you need to make sure before you ditch him.

He's already at the bar, leaning against it and talking his fake London boy crap. Penny, Moz's missus, does seem to know him (what a relief) as more than just a regular, and she also, more importantly, seems to know what he's talking about. Maybe this is your big chance after all. Maybe he is involved in something with Moz. Maybe he did go on a trip with John and Moz. Maybe he has met Adam, the top boy and living legend. Maybe he is moving up and he's chosen you to go with him.

It's early and there's nobody in the place except for a couple of old gits playing doms. You stand next to Chris beginning to show your support and indicating your presence. Chris lights a Marlboro and it seems too early in the day to be smelling smoke. It's ten twenty-two. You're looking around the place listening intently to Chris and Penny's conversation. Penny is quite a large woman with a happy looking moon face, too wealthy to give a fuck about being overweight. She lights up a Silk Cut. She is very reassuring. Penny takes you into the lounge which is kept locked up until lunches are served. She tells us that she's going to get Moz and that if we wait a minute she'll send Chloe in to see to our drinks.

The lounge is at the back of the building next to the spiteful looking car park, all broken glass and eroding tarmac. If you look out over the frosted section of the windows you can see the car park and even in the light of day it looks sinister. There are a few cars parked outside. You are not really paying any attention. Then you think that you see somebody near a red Citroen, Moz's daughter's car. You know that you recognize the man. You think, and watch, but as you searched your mind he left your view, or hid, or vanished. You are still trying to think who it was when Chloe comes in behind the bar and says hello to you both. Chloe is one of Moz's girls. She works in the pub and she works the shops for him signing stolen cheque books and fake credit card receipts. Moz likes to talk about her as if she's some calendar girl that can't keep her hands off him. She is of course not quite calendar girl material. She wears leggings with heels. She's got tar stained teeth and always smells of last night's booze and fags. Her hair is split and she has tried to remedy this with a cheap frizzy perm and do-it-yourself highlights. Although she is not grossly fat she does have a drinker's belly and her flesh jiggles as she walks as if she's ready to start swelling up at any moment. You order a short because you don't want to be off for a piss halfway through talking to somebody as important as Moz. Chris goes for Irish Whiskey, the only thing that he drinks since he got infected with bullshit, and so you follow suit. Chloe stretches up to the optics giving you both an eyeful of wrinkled nylon leggings and a skewed panty line. She is saying, as flirtatiously as she can without taking her clothes off, that she bets two lads like us would like big ones. As she turns her head to look at us, whilst still reaching for the optics, she focuses on our faces and then down to her arse as if she's following our gaze, as if we're interested. You two she whines as if her cunt is being tickled. You are glad to see that Chris is as repulsed as you are. She calls you around the bar so that you can go upstairs. She stands firm in the shallow walkway of the bar so that you both have no option but to brush past her as you make your way to the stairs. You notice how she manages to rub her tits on Chris's arm as he goes past and you make sure not to give her a chance to do it to you.

Upstairs you try to remember who it was that you saw out on the car park but you keep it to yourself. You enter a large room with, pathetically obvious, fake wooden beams on the walls and ceiling, and a large, similarly fake, open fire. There are lots of brass ornaments scattered around the room which clash sadistically with the gold and red flock wallpaper. Moz's daughter Mary is sitting on the red draylon sofa brushing the hair of their white poodle. Hanging up on the wall behind her is a piece of fabric inside a frame on which Mary has embroidered:

J
E
S
U
S

IS OUR

SAVIOUR

AND

REFUGE

Mary is repeating over and over, in a voice like a pull cord doll's, You don't have fleas you're a pedigree, You don't have fleas you're a pedigree, You don't have fleas you're a pedigree.... Moz hates the dog. It obviously offends his masculinity as a poodle is not respected as a guard dog or a gun dog or anything, and he is always talking about how Adam can get him a first class pit bull, one that he can fight on the circuit, but Mary will have none of it. Moz calls the poodle the rat and has threatened to kill it on numerous occasions that you've overheard whilst drinking in the bar. The dog is lucky because Mary is its guardian and that probably gives it a life expectancy beyond your's and Chris's.

You've heard a lot about Mary. You've caught glimpses of her now and then but only for a couple of seconds, apart from that all you know about her is what you've been told. Moz adores her. She's his princess. To even mention her to Moz is to set off a huge bleep on his keep-your-daughter-a-virgin radar. He pulled her out of her first year at the comprehensive after two weeks and put her into an all girls school, because he didn't like the way she was talking about her form tutor Mr. Norman. The word is that Moz paid him a little visit. Mary gets just about everything that she wants, and its only "just about" because there are some things that she would like but they are never likely to get past the strict censor. She is still, at eighteen, exactly how Moz wants her. She talks like a six year old. She's got a pony presumably to work off her frustrations (....but if Moz knew...). She's got a dog. She's got that car outside even though she's failed her test twice. She goes on holiday, with her mother and a friend, at least three times a year. She's got a permanent sunbed tan, though if Moz knew that it was an all over tan there would be a row involving him against Mary and Penny that would last for six months. She's got several bank accounts that, of course, she cannot touch. She goes to ballet and tap and has been since she was old enough to walk. She's got perfect long hair, and a lock of her hair goes into a large photograph album every time that she gets it cut (they've just started on album number three). The locks of hair are put in a plastic sheath along with the date and a polaroid of before and after (although to Moz and Penny's annoyance the first ones, taken eighteen years ago, are beginning to fade). She's slim, wholesome looking and attractive. She's clean and well spoken. In the family portraits around the room she stands out from her two brothers. It's as if she isn't the daughter of Moz and Penny. She's not overweight. She doesn't look menacing. She doesn't look cheap and she doesn't look from this world.

She turns to look at you breaking from her mechanical litany. You recognize that Danielle Bowden smile immediately. Hello Christopher she calls across the room. Hello Christopher's friend she calls at you. She puts down the brush and stands up with the poise of an Olympic Gymnast on having finished their routine. She is wearing an electric lemon dress that is made up of two layers. The outer layer is see through. It is a light material that floats in the air as she moves. It has black leopard spots printed at authentic enough intervals. The inner layer looks like a short plain vest that just about keeps her modesty. You are a little bit worried that you are paying too much attention to such details, and you begin to sweat that Moz might be able to read your mind and that he is in the next room right now polishing up some cartoon like, but nevertheless effective, blunderbuss that is just waiting to blow your head off. Mary pirouettes her way, in a way that makes you recall the term "pleasure model" from *Bladerunner*, across the room to where you and Chris are standing. You try not to have the same thoughts about Mary as you had about Daryl Hannah.

I've got on my favourite dress Christopher. Do you like it?

Now you really are shitting it, hoping that just for once Chris can keep his head. She beams out a smile as Chris nods his head and tries not to lose it.

I love citrus colours. Do you? I do. I love all citrus colours. I love citrus fruits. I love the way that citrus fruits taste. Do you?...(pause)... Cat got your tongues?

Yes, yes.

We both make sure not to offend her and try to make sure that our tone conveys this.

I don't know if you can tell but I even like to say the word citrus. I keep on saying it don't I....citrus, citrus, citrus, citrus citrus citrus.

She began to pirouette on the spot.

Citruscitruscitruscitruscitrus. Mmmm citrus. I can almost taste it. Would you like to taste it Christopher, after all you picked this dress out for me didn't you. Daddy told me that you helped. So you must like citrus fruits. Would you say it for me Christopher? Would you?

You are beginning to feel very uncomfortable. Your cock is beginning to wake up and you try desperately to think about something, or somebody, else, like Moz and the blunderbuss.

Wot? Wot? Say wot?

Citrus of course.

There's a humid silence and then Chris forces himself.

Citrus?

Thank you.

And at that she pirouettes back to her seat, picks up the comb and starts all over again. You don't have fleas you're a pedigree.... Your heart, and you suspect Chris's too, is racing at a hundred, maybe two hundred, beats per minute. You look at Chris who is looking at you. You smile at him for a job well done when suddenly you turn and see Moz standing in an intimidating pose in the doorway of the room. He looks like a great unmovable sumo wrestler only bigger. Sheer physical power emanates from him and his voice is more of a boom than anything that could be recognized as communication.

Mary go and sit with your mother for five minutes.

His voice is so commanding that you too want to obey him, show him that you are compliant with whatever he says. Mary lets out a long unappreciative breath and stares petulantly at her father. She stands up and picks up the dog. Her voice is full of dismissal.

Come on my little sweet thing we don't want to stay in here now do we. Let's go and find some frogs to kiss, (staring at her father) we might find a nice prince...

There is silence until she leaves the room. Moz closes the door behind her and stares at you a little longer as if he's accusing you of something, or as if he's making up his mind as to the most fitting kind of torture for young men caught unashamedly breathing in the same air as his daughter. You are invited to sit down. You, like Chris, take the sofa but Moz remains standing. You are sitting, trying as hard as you can, without saying anything, to show your respect for Moz, his family, and his house. Chris puts out his Marlboro.

Moz nods in your direction and asks Chris, "Is he all right?" Chris over elaborates just to prove a point to you, "Yeah, yeah, couldn't be sounder Moz old mate."

Moz looks out at you intently. He stares and you can see your reflection in his eyes. You look lost inside his black pupils, lost and alone.

Can I ask you something?

You remember to act casually.

Yeah course.

You are starting to sound like Chris. You look at him for support. He is trying to look reassuring.

Good. It's nothing personal you understand not yet (he looks at Chris and laughs making Chris laugh, you start to think about joining in too when it stops abruptly). You see, I don't know ya. People I don't know make me nervous, don't they Chris? (Chris is nodding and obviously enjoying it but you guess that he's been through this shit himself so you start to tell yourself that everything is going to be fine and that tonight you'll be sitting next to Chris in some boozer spouting the same bullshit as him and loving every minute of it) Now, I can solve all these problems quite easy see. You've just gotta pass a little test, okay? (You nod) It's just a few questions all right? Are you ready? Now you've gotta answer me cos I don't tolerate ignorance. Understand?

Yes. Yes, I do.

You are trying to give the right impression, whatever that may be.

Okay, question number one: Do you wannna be my friend?

Yes Moz.

You nod as you speak.

Good answer. (looks at Chris) He's good at this ain't he? Okay are you ready now here comes question number two: Do you wanna help me out?

Anything you want, anything, I'll help ya.

You hear yourself slipping into an imitation of Chris's fake London accent. You hope that it will work for you in the same way as it seemed to work for him.

Hey, perfect answer. (looks at Chris) You've found a good'un here. He's scored two out a two so far, bloody marvellous! Okay now question number three, sort yourself out, steady on here goes: Will ya run a little errand for me?

Yeah definitely, no problem, you can rely on me.

Well done. Okay if that's what you want I've got something for ya, wait 'ere.

Chris taps you on the arm and tells you that it's no bother, that you're in. All you've gotta do is deliver a package, it's all routine. Moz comes back into the room with a small package in brown paper. It could be drugs but when you have it in your hand it feels like a pile of cards all wrapped up. Tony, Moz's son who is lucky enough to work with Adam Bishop, top boy and practitioner of weird sex rituals involving strangulation like in that video you were talking to Chris about last night walks in with a similar package.

Dad he said he wanted two lots, not one.

Moz looks at you burning his gaze into your eyes.

Well now do you think you're up to two packages?

Yeah. (you try to laugh as if you're laid back, cool, as if you're not scared but nobody else joins in) Don't worry about a thing, it's taken care of.

Good, I like that. (Moz pats you on the back shocking you with the power he can generate in such a small movement) Now our Tony's gonna tell ya where to go and what to do. It won't take long so I'll see ya back here in about half an hour and we'll have a little chat, alright?

Chris gives you an it's going-fine-wink as you leave the room with Tony. You feel pretty pathetic following this spotty fifteen year old kid. You are totally disempowered in the presence of these people but you hope that soon you will earn some respect in whatever way you can. Soon you will have respect, and money, and girls, and friends, and favours to ask and grant. It would come soon.

You step out onto the car park squinting in the natural light. You've got the two packages from Moz. You've got the car keys from Chris. You've got the address from Tony, written on a smooth glossy scratch card that Tony got from behind the bar which has a picture of a frog and an apple on it. Then you see that figure again. The one that you saw from the lounge window. The guy who was hanging around the car park. You approach steadily but as you get nearer you recognize who it is.

Fat Stuart The Poof has been missing for a few weeks and so has his boyfriend Zak. Everybody was starting to think that they'd been whacked. They were pretty important people especially Zak. You can see Stuart's shiny super clean white skin as you get even closer to him.

Is Serge in there?

He looks desperate. He looks ill. You can see that he has two huge black rings around his eyes that even he can't scrub off with his obsessive washing. You tell him that he isn't in there. Fat Stuart The Poof looks like he's going to collapse. You help him stay on his feet using the side of the car to help balance him. He keeps repeating over and over that he needs to see Serge. You tell him that he's not in the pub and that you have no idea where he might be. You open the door of the car on the passenger side and make him sit down for a second. He starts to crouch down in the car whimpering that he musn't be seen. Now you can't get him out of the car it's all going wrong. He is pleading with you now to help him, to take him to Serge. You are not sure about this but you need to get going before Moz starts checking on your progress. You get in the car and turn on the ignition. Fat Stuart The Poof is ducking down snivelling to himself. You don't know what to do so you just keep on driving. Fat Stuart The Poof starts with his explanation.

Zak's gone.

Where to?

He's gone you fucking asshole.

He says asshole like an American, not arsehole like most people, it must be a queer saying you suppose. You are not sure how you feel about being called an asshole by Fat Stuart The Poof but there are too many other things running around in your mind at the moment to voice your protest.

And the fucking Bishop....I'm in real danger....and Zak....what they did to him....

Who? What? Did Bish do something to Zak?

No, no, the Bishop's after me. He wants to whack me.

All of a sudden you don't want Fat Stuart The Poof in the car. You're glad that he's ducking down because there is no way you're going to do anything against Adam Bishop, no fucking way. Even thinking about crossing him is enough to make you shit it.

I owed him some money. I didn't know what was going on at the time. I thought that Bish was on our side. I owed him, I owe him, nearly twenty K. I was in a club in London....it was Zak's favourite....

He starts snivelling again. You look at him crouched down in the car looking ridiculous with his black rimmed eyes that were now puffing up with his sobs. You make a face as if you're shrugging your shoulders and you pass your handkerchief to him. He looks up and smiles, and then he blows his nose making a loud resonating trumpet screech. He starts to pull himself together a little.

Anyway who walks in but Adam. Thinking about it now I realise that he was looking for me, for us, he knew something had happened. He could see that I was upset. He bought a few drinks, and then a few more, and he kept on asking about Zak and I knew that if I told him that I would be in deep shit with John deep shit! But well....he offered me a deal....We ended up back at his house, the big one in Suffolk. It was the early hours when we finally got back and I was having second thoughts and I was scared to be around at his, but I figured that if I was going to get whacked that John was going to be giving the orders and while he wasn't around, and wasn't aware of where I was, I was safe. I told him that I was in big shit and that Zak was dead. Like I said he offered me a deal....when I think about it now that steroid freak. He said that he could see that I was in a state and without Zak around I might struggle and so he offered to wipe my slate clean, twenty K just like that forgotten....he said that he'd do all that he could to help me out. The thing is now that I can't help thinking that I've betrayed Zak by sharing the secret with Adam.

You are starting to get annoyed. You are implicating yourself in all this. People can disappear for just looking at the wrong person let alone driving him around. You want to know what has gone on.

Well tell me, tell me, you're here in this car. Now fucking tell me you whining fucking faggot.

Fat Stuart The Poof looks up at you his face flushed with a potent venom that you never suspected him capable of, probably because you know that he's a queer.

Look you little shit, and I mean little, don't get too happy with yourself. What are you doing? Ferrying Moz's fake credit cards round to some other fat old man. You're nothing (he sits up now and you are getting worried, seriously worried) and don't fucking forget that. You don't call me faggot ever....You see you haven't earned my respect. You ain't earned nothing. So you just sit back and listen little boy. You are going to take me to see Serge and I'm going to get this sorted right, and if they're gonna get me they're gonna get you too right. Right?

That voice in your head is saying, "Oh shit!" He ducks down again as you drive down The Hythe.

Adam, the walking penis that he is, or should I say the walking tattooed penis that he is....Did you know that he's got COBRA tattooed on his cock? Anyway the precious Bishop is a man of strange tastes, very strange tastes. You must have heard about him and his strangulation orgasm that he has apparently perfected. Well it doesn't all end there let me tell you, oh no. He's trying to get round me, flirt that he is. He takes me down to these bunkertype rooms that he's got sunken into the grounds of that fucking great ugly house that he lives in. He's got these kids down there, God knows where he's got them from, and, of course, he's got all of his filming equipment down there too. He'd got this one girl, he said that she was fourteen, she couldn't even speak English. A Catholic girl and he assured me that she was a virgin. He even patted that big cock of his and said down boy. He'd traded her with some guy off of the continent. He joked how she was going out to some politician from the home counties. He called her "prime cunt". We looked in on her. She was bone thin, poor thing. She smiled at us and clung to us grabbing at my crotch as if she was demented, but God only knows how long she'd been down there and I don't even want to think about what that sick pervert had been doing to her all that time. Anyway he just laughed at her and said that I was the wrong kind of client. Then he showed me two boys, one of them was only eleven. They were sitting in a room, with no furniture and none of the rooms had windows, holding each other and rocking themselves back and forth. He was trying to push them onto me and even suggested that I have a free go on them. I dread to think of how many other poor children are down there. They looked dead to me. They were like zombies, empty spiritless shells. I'm sure that they wanted to escape, to leave those rooms, those cells, but they looked terrified every time the door opened. They looked terrified of me. Those poor souls. Bishop's a nasty bastard.

You are only all too aware of this fact, and now you know this superfluous piece of evidence you might be next on his list of enemies.

Anyway, I was upset, scared, and I'd lost Zak....I can't believe that he's not here....It's like some terrible nightmare that can't possibly be true but I can't wake up....I can't find him....Why did this have to happen?.... He got it out of me that nasty nasty Adam Bishop. Now he knows about Zak and Masters and I'm in shit....and Zak's gone.

The tears are running down his face. He's blowing into your handkerchief again. You feel sorry for him in as much as you could find yourself in his position easily. It only takes one wrong move, a careless glance or roll of the eye.

So now Adam says to fuck with our deal and if I don't pay him he's going to squeal to John. You know how it all is between John and Masters, everybody's smiling at one another biding their time. It's all sweet pink candy floss on the outside, but there's going to be some serious trouble very soon. Zak liked to take risks....oh he was a man, a great beautiful man who took his chances....oh Zak I want to be with you...

Things are deteriorating fast. Fat Stuart The Poof is turning what you hoped would be an informative chat into a nightmare that has been haunting you ever since you decided that you wanted a career. You look at Fat Stuart The Poof and his sorrowful black eyes and tear stained cheeks. You try to tell yourself that he's just camping it all up for your benefit but deep inside your head, somewhere where you don't have to admit it to yourself, is a solid black tumour of fear. The package is on the floor at your feet remember all that you have to do is deliver it.

Zak had been a friend of Masters for a long time. The Bishop has worked for Masters everybody accepts that though, but for Zak to do that is...was... against the rules. Zak was the best runner that John had. John looked after Zak. Things were getting out of hand. Zak was fucked up all the time he had a real habit. Masters couldn't stand being frozen out of the drugs trade. He had the power but John had the money because of his runners, because of Zak.

Yeah but Masters does business with John right?

He hated it. He hated having to deal with him. He was always trying to get Zak to sell him information or change sides....always trying to bully him and then flirt with him....but my Zak was too smart for that beast....too smart....oh God....oh Zak if only we could be together again... I'd gone round to the restraunt to pick Zak up. He was busy with his little sideline scam that he'd got going with Masters. Nothing big see just a little just for the excitement....that's how Zak liked it. When I got there Masters was flirting around him as usual trying to talk him into all kinds of shit. Zak, well everybody, was totally coked up except for Masters who seemed to be on something completely different. Zak put his arms around me when I got there....that was to be the last time....I....I'm sorry this is very difficult, but now I've started I need to tell somebody....people need to know, somebody needs to know....please listen to me.... (he wipes his eyes with a clean corner of your handkerchief) So Masters, the fiend, takes him off into another room and I'm sitting waiting to leave, but not daring to say anything. I'm playing shoot pontoon with some of Masters's cronies. Then Masters comes back in without Zak. I'm not saying anything at first because I know how easily Masters can get aggressive, how he can turn on you. It was after midnight when I got there and I just wanted to get Zak home. A few minutes went by and I'm dying to say something but I know that I need to stay calm so that I can help Zak, only I didn't know for sure what was happening. And then that evil black headed fairy breaks out into peeling laughter that just went on and on and on, bruising my ear drum shattering my nerves completely. And so I ask him, no I beg him, to tell me where Zak is I can tell at this point that something's wrong......oh it's so awful....(Fat Stuart The Poof tries to compose himself, he tries to get on top of his emotions so that he can tell his story) When we go into Master's office Zak is in there....oh God I can....oh God....it's....oh....(he swallows hard) Zak was tied to a chair, it looked like an electric chair with these manacle things for his ankles and wrists and Masters was laughing his laugh again. He'd beaten Zak. Zak was bleeding from his mouth and nose, and his eye was swollen....his left eye....he was stripped naked and jumping over him were these tiny coloured frogs....they were all over him....and he was covered in these bright red marks and he was shaking, not registering that we were in the room with him. Masters kept on saying to him that he wanted to know, he kept on that he wanted to know, and the frogs were jumping around and when one jumped off Zak Masters picked it up and put it right next to Zak's face, right up against him....pressing it against his eyes and mouth and he just kept on laughing and repeating that he wanted to know. Zak began to have some kind of spasmodic fit. I threw myself on the floor in front of Zak and pleaded with Masters to stop it, whatever he was trying to do. His men grabbed me and held me down, what they thought I might do I don't know, what can anyone do against Masters. Zak's tongue started to loll out of the side of his mouth and his eyes flickered and flickered and then they rolled back into his head showing blank perfect whites where his pupils should have been. They dragged me out of the room and we sat back down and played cards again and Masters kept acting as if nothing had happened turning his flirtatious self onto me.... playing his charming role. Later on he said that we'd be going in to check on Zak's progress. And in that beastly voice he kept on saying that he wasn't really going to hurt him.. that he didn't like queers coming on to him that was all....(Fat Stuart The Poof is very distraught weeping almost relentlessly before pulling himself together) .... It wasn't long though before I knew....it was as if Zak came to see me before he departed, just to let me know, just so that I could save myself. His soul somehow lingered in that house just long enough to let me know so that I didn't have to worry any longer. It was Zak's last act of love (he bursts into tears again, continuing to speak through distraught sobs). His last communication before he left. They thought that I'd never leave without Zak. They were right of course but they didn't know how close we were. They underestimated us and our bond, Masters always had. Ever since that night Adam has been trying to contact me. How he knew that something had gone on I don't know. But now he knows because I told him, I trusted him, and now you know too. And Masters wants me dead now because he doesn't want John to know anything. And Adam wants to find me to squeeze me for some money because he knows that if John finds out what Zak was up to with Masters that he'll get Adam to whack me, and probably Adam wants to whack me anyway because I could make things difficult for him with John. But if I can just tell Serge, put it to him straight as I just have done for you, maybe he'll see that the true villains are Masters and Adam Bishop, not me....and not my Zak. And maybe one day I'll be able to get Zak's body back and I'll arrange a nice service for him and...

You don't like the sound of this, it's all way above your head. All you know is that you don't want to be an accessory to anybody who's bad mouthing The Bishop, it's just too scary. You should open the door and kick Fat Stuart The Poof into the gutter but you don't even want to get that involved. You just want to deliver the packages and get back to the pub.

Chapter 14

The Silver-Grey Haired Man

His acquisition of the dirty blonde slut had had the effect that he supposed it would. His men were further convinced of his ability to destroy all those who stood before him. The dirty blonde slut's obvious glee at opening her legs for him rather than the queer, who no doubt preferred his nigger, had been the final piece of evidence in his favour, the final embarrassment for the queer. Wherever she went she stole the attention of those around her. Everybody was talking. His own men laughing. John's men were outraged that such a thing could be allowed to happen, even they were starting to believe the rumours. Serge and John, Harry and John, Lisa and Masters no matter how you looked at it John's mask of power was slipping. There were people floating out towards Masters every day. Things could change quickly. You had to make sure that you were on the right side. Everything, as Masters liked to tell those around him, was beautiful.

He was glad to be alone without her and her dumb fucking voice. The radio was turned up full. He did not have to worry so much about having his car bugged but it was good not to pick up any bad habits. 'It would be easy to get caught out". The music pounded out of the speakers and forced itself into his ears, hammering his ear drums. He moved his swollen bright red hands around the steering wheel as he turned the corner and the DJ spoke over the top of the music:

Well there it is the one you track you can't get enough of, the track of the summer, the one that you've all been listening to, dancing to, and I'm sure that you've all seen the film Trainspotting, that was Underworld, that was Born Slippy, and it's taking you all the way to the news and back again. It's three twenty-seven what's been going on in the world follows...

His watch shows a quarter to midnight, which judging by the night's sky is accurate. He has to breathe in slowly and deeply to stop himself from kicking in his Kenwood stereo. He clenches his blistered fists tightly around the steering wheel frantically miming to the words, that he does not know, that are being spoken as if they were coming out from beneath the thumping drums. He tries to enjoy it. He tries to allow himself to be cajoled along by the DJ's veneer of happiness. He cannot pull it off. He ejects the cassette that he his listening to and puts in another that also has random radio taped on it. The DJ, a woman this time, introduces The Prodigy's *Firestarter* in a similarly jovial tone. He tries to mime to this too, but he is weeping slow tears because he can still hear the numbingly happy voice of the DJ. He realises that the strain of being around that bloodsucking bitch is too much. Always, always she was wanting something, some kind of attention, or to be touching, or to be talking, or doing, or fucking, always fucking. Always having to fuck her because the queer couldn't. That's what kept happening and happening. His body begins to shake and he tries to concentrate on driving. The road seemed to oscillate in front of him like a rug being shaken in the wind. He feels his heart racing faster than his car, faster even than his mind. He can't keep up he just can't... Despite all of his frenzied thoughts, and the bizarre images that flash before his eyes, he is making ground towards the meeting point.

The kiss of the frog can easily change a person. The fiery moisture that the frog can proffer to your deep, intimate, osculating tongue can turn you into someone else. The Mr. Hyde that has always slothfully hung off your shoulder can take you and allow you to rest, make it all easier for you. If that is what you want. Masters was preparing to become another person, the other person that he knew a long time ago.

He pulls his car over next to a gate to a field that allows the road to widen. There are no lights out here and when he turns off his headlights Masters can see nothing except for the ghosts of light that, although gone, leave tiny traces of thermal colours dancing before his eyes. Masters watched these patterns for as long as they kept his attention. His eyes began to get used to the darkness and his amusement at the multicoloured patterns ceased. He got out of the car trying to remember who he was and who he was pretending to be. He made sure that he remembered to pretend, yes that seemed to be right. He straddled the iron gate and walked through the mud to the black van with the tinted glass windows that was parked some way out into the field where it could not be seen from the road. All that he had to do was convince this man, that was it. He could not fail, just let the other one out for a while. It all seemed to be much clearer in this dark anonymous field. He stamped through the mud towards the van. There was something in his coat pocket that was quite heavy and which made his coat fit unevenly across his shoulders. He looked through the darkness into his pocket and saw the blonde slut's book that she was always carrying with her or rather, as was evinced by it being in his pocket, she was always getting him to carry for her. Masters did not know that the book was Ovid's *Metamorphoses*, and that Lisa's book mark was poised in Book III between lines 400 and 450. Masters did not know or care about such shit. Why should he? He cursed her under his breath as he got nearer to the van. He stopped his profane curses as his reflection loomed before him in the tinted glass of the van. He noticed how he did not look like himself, or maybe he looked more like himself than he had done recently. He could not work out which it was. He knew though that his appearance was not familiar. He resembled a brother, that he had never had, or never known, maybe older, maybe younger, or maybe identical. He was fascinated by his reflection but at the same time its presence seemed to render him, the man standing before himself, as void, null, inauthentic, as if he were a cheap fake or a cloned artificial being. He tried to focus on himself. The self that he must be for this short time. The van door slid open. Brilliant white light roared out of the van and enmeshed Masters, stifling, and encumbering, his step up to get inside. He fought through the light, shielding his eyes from the sudden contrast, and sat down in the empty chair opposite the man with the silvergrey hair.

Masters begins to answer the questions that the man opposite him asks. The man has very pale skin, but not pasty or youthful even, and there is a stillness about him that makes Masters remember the man that he, himself, was, the man that he is supposed to be. The silvergrey haired man nodded through most of what Masters had to say. He scrutinized Masters's glance watching him look at the van's interior. He grinned as he contemplated Masters's grimace that accompanied his eyes gradual adjustment from the cool darkness of outside to the sharp glare of the inside. The silvergrey haired man tapped the wooden arm of his institutional style metal framed chair and beckoned Masters to lean forward. As Masters complied the man began to speak again. He opened his mouth and thick white traces of saliva strung out in lines in the two opposite creases of his mouth. Masters became focused on these stretching bands of spittle as the man moved his mouth to form words. Masters watched them elongate and then shrink back. He sat engrossed fidgeting his chaffed and blistered hands, blinking inconsistently into the man's words.

Chapter 15

The Bishop

You are in The Hunter's with Chris. It seems to be way past closing time but you're getting another round in. You slur out the order to Chloe the barmaid and turn back to look at the table where you're sitting. The lads are all pulling your leg, telling you to try and pull Chloe. Of course there is no way that you are going to do that but they are just having a laugh, seeing how drunk you are. You have to admit to yourself that you are completely smashed.

When you get back over to the table with the drinks there is a new bloke in your seat. Chris grabs you a new seat, from the bar, and you sit down. Chris gives you a serious look and then introduces the guy. His name is... Well you didn't catch his name, but he looks hard. He is unshaven, a big man, just out of prison. Serge gave him some work with Adam Bishop and Steve Vickering. All of the others at the table would love the chance to meet The Bishop, let alone work for him. The hard man is talking about his time with Bish, what he knows about him, what he's like. His voice is both enthusiastic and aggressive, and he speaks with a heavy accent, so much so that you are having to lean forward and listen carefully. You, Chris, and all of the others, are hanging on to his every last word.

The geezer's a fackin' livin' legend. Any facker'll tell ya tha'. Well 'e's The Bish ai'n 'e. You've gotta admire the bloke. I first worked wiv im, wiv Tony, ya know Moz's kid. Yeah facking straight ap. 'E got us filmin' sam birds, 'ouse wives n'tha', ya know, doin' it for their asbands like. Fackin' great it was, I rememba' im pickin me ap.

Adam Bishop's BMW breaks sharply with a loud rubber screech to let the guy in, who quickly jumps in the back with young Tony Draufer. Adam is driving. His thick bull neck is straining under the tension of his heavily muscled arms having to be held out so that he can steer the car. He twitches his neck, tightens it, and then tries to relax his neck, arms, and shoulders, trying hard to relieve the tension. His large muscle bound fingers tap the beat to the *bt ima* CD that he's got on. He is wearing a tight white stretch nylon shirt with an open, and exuberant, wing collar. The shirt is strained to its limit over his torso and limbs so that you can see his press stud brown nipples through the white stretch nylon. The shirt is short, finishing right on the waist of his tight black satin trousers and their kitsch white disco belt. He looks up into his mirror and says, "alwight tweacle" to the cut out of a woman from a porn magazine that he has stuck around the arm that holds the rear view mirror in place. The person in the front passenger seat, Steve Vickering, leans over to look up at the mirror and speak to the picture. The woman in the picture is naked and is holding her legs open in the obligatory fashion of such magazines. Steve points between her legs, touching her cunt, and says, in some comic voice that only he and Adam appreciate, "You're a fackin' cant." Steve then holds his hand over his mouth and does his insidious whispering Mutley laugh (just like the dog on the cartoon). Steve has virtually no chin and a long bulbous ended, beak hooked, nose. He has small perpendicular ears and heavy hard crusted acne on his cheeks, brow, and neck. He has an acrimoniously prominent Adam's Apple that completes his unfortunate anserine look. He reaches into the glove compartment and pulls out a handful of porn magazines and flings them into the back, "This month's," he offers without turning around. He searches for a specific magazine from his feet, where there is a small pile of about five or six, and then turns to the back seat, where there is a stack of about twenty of the same issue in a bundle and about seven or eight various ones on the top. He finds the one that he wants. He opens out a folded poster that has a woman on it. She is naked and in virtually the same pose as the woman on the mirror arm, except for that the paper between her legs has been ripped out. Steve holds this up to the guy in the back and puts his tongue through the hole flicking it up and down and he screams, "aaaaarrrrrrhhhhh!" through the glossy paper. The guy in the back points at Steve's tongue, and mimics, "You're a fackin' cant!" They all burst into laughter.

Every facker admires 'im, Bish tha' is. I'm tellin' ya e's a fackin' genius, tha's righ' fackin' genius is wot e' is. I'm mean in bizness e finks o'fings tha' normal people couldn' even dream abou', like I said e's a fackin' genius. E's always got sam new plan. E' works fackin' miracles wiv money n'tha'. E'wen'a' see John n'tha Serge like, put a few facking propasishions to'em bowf.

John and Serge are sitting in their office taking counsel. This happens once in a while, usually when they have decided to change things around or when, as is the case in this instance, somebody has an idea that they want to discuss. Serge and John are seated in their office letting Adam do all the talking, putting his case to them so to speak. He is sitting in front of them explaining, "It's a winna boss. I know it is. I (he pauses and points at his huge chest for effect) guarantee it. It's just like in tha' film *Palp Fiction*, tha' place they go to in the film? John Travol'a and that lavlee dark haired piece? You know?"

Serge slowly and mockingly, in a very subtle way, nods his head for himself and John, who is dumb with disbelief. Serge sits up in his chair to let Adam know that he is about to talk, he looks at John before speaking, and seemingly there is no communication between them, but then Serge speaks, "So the idea is that We, through our professional relationship with Masters, set you up with a place in London..."

"When he gets the nod like..." Adam interrupts.

"...Like you say when he gets the nod. And you're going to open a bar-stroke-restaurant-stroke-club on an idea from a film."

"You've got it," he condescendingly pats Serge's shoulder, and continues, "But don't miss ou' the best of it. We ain't basin' it on the fifties, Baddy Holly n' tha' shit, no way, we're gonna base it on murderers n'all tha'. It's perfect. Everybody lav's it. Every fackin' film tha' cam's out is abou' sam fackin' serial killa. Think abou' it. Charlie Manson servin' the drinks, eh, eh, Charlie Manson servin' the drinks. Okay wot abou' Peeta Satcliffe, or Ted

Bandy, waitin on your table, or even Fred fackin' West. Cam on, 'Annibal Lecta' bringin' rarnd the deserts is worf it on its own innit?" He holds his hands in the air as if he has just proved a mathematical formula and is saying Q.E.D.

N' Steve e's a crackin' bloke n'all. E's a bit quiet n'tha' bat e's alwight, like I say e's alwight. E's been goin' out t'Thailand wiv all tha' slanty cant abou', e lav's all tha'. E' was seein' some Thai bird for a while bat it didn' work out. E' sen'er'a capla fousand quid, oh yeah e' was gonna marry er n'tha, 'e laved 'er an' e wern bovered tha' she was a Chink or anyfink. fackin'dou'abou'it. E' start'd makin' plans straight away for'er t'cam over. Next fing the poor bloke knew he'd got a narsty bou'a the fackin clap, no fackin lack Steve. I gotta admi'it' to ya I felt fackin sorry for 'im, like I say 'e's alwight.

Anyways, I was tellin' ya abou' Bish wern I Said she was the best fack e'd ever 'ad, straight fackin ap I'm tellin' ya. Anyway she writes back wiv sam bullshit abou' not been let in the cantry, an says tha' if e' sen's 'er out anafa caple a grand tha' she'll try again like. Well the chinky slat was tryin' it on like. So e' wen'ova t'see er, e'said e'was gonna get 'is fackin maney ou'ov'er, bat Adam said tha' e' was in lav wiv er like, n'tha was why e'd gone back over. Wen'e' caught ap wiv 'er she was back on the fackin game again like. Well they don'fackin care over there. E'met sam atha bird anyway, even betta than the last one e'reckoned. E' stayed on for a few extra manths, set'er ap n'tha, blokes gotta 'art'a gold like. E' cam back showed ass all the fotos like, she was a fackin'looka n'all, fackin'gorgeous, no... We ad sam fackin day tha' firs'time I work'd for 'im fackin 'ell did we. I mean I fancied the fackin idea ov filmin' sam nice pieces ov cant, show me a bloke wot don't. Before all tha' tho' 'e, Adam like, ad t'go rarnd all the schools duein the lanch 'our. See sam' people like.

Adam drives the car slowly down the road adjacent to the school yard's wire mesh fence. He spots the girl that he was looking for and stops the car near to her and pushes the button to slide his window down. He looks out smiling. The girl, that he has been looking for, is with a few of her friends. She looks about fifteen sixteen and she exaggerates her surprise at seeing him again for the benefit of her friends. She turns around blushing until her friends, who are all swarming around her, talk her into walking over to him (even though she was going to anyway). She is holding a bag in front of her and has pulled in her arms and shoulders to her side in a gentle shrug. Steve has already noted the "talented" ones amongst her friends and thinks that this is a good group to hit on. He whispers, "Kerry," to Adam as she approaches. Adam gets out of the car (Steve holds his hand over his face and hisses out another Mutley laugh) and stands on the other side of the fence directly opposite her. He throws in a few icebreakers, a few smiles, and a few long desiring looks, for her benefit. Then he begins to go to work, exercising his most imploring of voices.

"Look I'm really sorry about this but I was passing and well... I'm sorry Kerry but I just can't stop thinking about you. I know what you said about your dad, and that he'd kill me if he even saw us talking but... There's nothing wrong with us being friends is there. Him and your mom they can't stop us from being friends can they... It's not fair just because I'm older. You know that I had no idea that you were still at school, you are just so mature for somebody your age. Believe me this is as wild and as crazy and as, I don't know, as wonderful for me as I know that it is for you. I know that we haven't got to know each other yet, but that's all I want to do, get to know you. If I was going to try and pressure you into something that you didn't want to do I'd have tried by now wouldn't I..."

Kerry was smiling rocking her shoulders from left to right, "Well I suppose so..."

"Cam on, I mean come on Kerry I wouldn't do anything that I thought might upset you. I'd never hurt you, never. One of the reasons that I lo'..., (well acted pause with the hint of a lover's blush) I like you so much is that I know you, what a strong person that you are, and I know that nobody could make you do something that you didn't want to do. Please I'm begging you, please just give me a chance. You can't let your parents ruin your life can you?"

Kerry finally agrees to meet Adam for a coffee in town on Saturday. She walks back to her friends who all tell her how gorgeous he is; and she is the centre of attention for the day; and everybody tells her how lucky she is; and everybody tells her how they wish that he was their boyfriend; and then she decides not to tell anybody that he isn't her boyfriend, or rather wasn't until just a short time ago.

Well, we got t'the nex'school like an'e'd got'anafa one, only this one was waitin' for 'im. Then, like the fackin genius tha'e'is, 'e shoots rarnd the back t'see anafa one, two at the same fackin school. Like I keep tellin' ya, fackin genius.

Adam's car is now at the back of the school only moments after he said goodbye to the second girl he had visited on that day. They are all busily looking to see the girl who will be the object of his third meeting of the day. He met her through the second girl, who has no idea of their clandestine arrangement.

"Yeah lads, I 'ad no choice like bat to move this one on sharpish. Markit forces an' tha'. Were the fack is she?"
Adam impatiently drums his steering wheel with mechanical regularity. Then the guy in the back speaks.

"Ther' ain't no facker abou' 'cept f'fackin' Susie Wong over there."

"Where?" Adam and Steve shout out together. The guy in the back points to an oriental girl who is loitering in a sheltered position by the teachers' car park. Adam laughs to Tony, Moz's son, and the guy in the back, "Tha's 'er. Like I said lads markit forces innit." Everybody finds this funny.

"Yeah sam panta', wait for it," he pauses and waits for Steve to correct him with "You mean CANTa'."

"Yeah sam canta' as' been askin' abou' orien'al bitches n' tha'. Steve spott'd 'er like, an' we decided to pat 'er frew a bit quicka."

The girl has seen them and starts to walk towards them. The men sit and watch her.

"I've never facked a Chink," the guy in the back offers. "Mind you she looks like she could draw the fackin' spank ou'ov'ya," he adds.

"Well this time nex'week you'll ge'a chance to see. It'll cost ya forty fackin' notes mind (everbody laughs). Anyway, seriously now, she ain'a Chink. She's a fackin Nip, or Korean, or fackin Hon' Kon' or whateva ya call those cants." He looks at Steve, "Well?"

"Well wot?" Steve replies in an agitated tone.

"Well you're the fackin exper' wiv these slanty bitches." More laughter roars in the back.

Adam starts to prepare himself, "CoCo innit? Or fackin' YoYo, or samink like tha'. Fack wot is it...CoCo? KoYo...fack, fack, fack..."

"Kyoko," Steve assures him.

Adam looks at Steve and nods, "Kyoko? Kyoko righ'? Yeah Kyoko, Kyoko, tha's it." Adam makes a large gesture of holding his crotch and, shaking his cock, through his tight fitting satin trousers, as he shouts out, "It'll be fackin COBRA soon, if ya catch me drift lads..." He repeats the word "COBRA." over and over in a loud robotic whisper.

He leaves the men in the car, and Tony, Moz's son, laughing heavily together. Their laughter was charged with a wish to keep Adam happy, and it continued as they watched him greet the girl. Adam, or The Bish, stands with perfect composure in front of the girl. His industrial musculature is rigid and visible through his tight fitting clothes. The men in the car are still laughing especially Steve and are dwelling on the significance of the similarity between the girl's name, Kyoko, and Adam's cock, COBRA.

The final visit that they made was to a girl who was already waiting for them. She was sitting outside on the school wall. The girl's crepuscular eyes were sunken and surrounded by heavy foul black rings. She swung her legs backwards and forwards with impatient deliberation and waited for Adam to keep his word.

As Adam drove the car to this final meeting point he asked the guy in the back, "Pass one ov those parcels off the back will ya."

"Which one?"

"The same fackin one I always giv'em. Well, arry fackin' ap abou'it, f'fack's sake." The fact that the guy in the back had no idea which were the same fucking ones that he always gave them was not lost on Adam. He was allowed to get angry with people. He was The Bishop. He liked to wind himself up. He got off on it. He liked hard doses of testosterone and had diligently injected himself that morning. A good needlefull could set him up for the day. The fact that the guy in the back had no idea as to which of the parcels Adam was talking about only wound Adam up further. And then of course instead of the guy in the back voicing a protest he simply said nothing because, after all, what could anybody say to Adam Bishop, and this too wound Adam up. Steve pointed to the brown paper parcels that Adam was talking about and the guy in the back passed one to him. Steve put the brown paper parcel on Adam's lap who was still enjoying the aggressive feeling that was burning inside him.

As the car pulled up at the school the girl jumped up off the wall with a languid and stroppy lunge. She stood impatiently, turning away from Adam's wink and blowing out her chagrin in long juvenile sighs, taking pleasure only in the fact that he had arrived but still miserable because she had not got what she was waiting for. Adam reached into the glove compartment and took out a large white paper bag. He took from this a small wrapped parcel and a couple of, what looked like, wraps of speed. He looked into the bag took out another wrap, thought about it, and then put it back. He got out of the car with these and the larger parcel that had been passed to him, which was the source of the stone silence. He slammed the door leaving the men, and Tony, Moz's son, in silence, except of course for Steve's hissing laugh. The girl made no steps towards Adam. She held out her hand quickly as he got near enough to pass the small parcel and the speed, or what was probably speed. He managed to kiss her, just about, as he passed her the drugs. She immediately turned around once the drugs were in her hand, finally allowing herself a smile.
"Have you got any more whizz? Please", her voice was laced with acidic petulance.

Adam holds out his hands and says, "Sorry lav. Anyway you wanna go easy on it. I'd hate t'see ya fack yerself ap." Adam listened to his own words and was pissed off that Steve had not heard him say that. He was imagining Steve's Mutley laugh nevertheless.

"Well I hope that this isn't a short measure," she was holding up the small brown package, "I had to buy some off the street last week."

"Stop wavin' it like tha'. If ya don't be careful you'll get yerself nicked... I've got samink for ya, samink special like. Jast for you." Adam hands her the other package.

"Don't open it ere, it's special, samink nice, samink t'wear. Wear it t'night, he'll like it I promise. Now make sure your on time for me t'pick you ap."

The girl has no interest in anything that he is saying. She is holding the large package indolently under her arm, and looking at the small packages in the palm of her other hand. She looks up at Adam who simply ignores her dark ringed eyes; her tarnished complexion; her derelict and limp hair, strands of which fell lank and feeble about her eyes.

"Are you sure it's all here? You promise you haven't given me any small measures?"

"'Ey look 'ere don't ge'fackin smart alwight, don't ge'fackin smart...I've bought you samink nice ain'I...pick'd it out for ya special like, jast for you. Cam on I'm lookin' afta ya, lookin out for ya, don't ge'frowin'i'back in my face. I lav ya don't I for fack's sake, more than anyone else could. Don't warry abou'anyfink. Jast turn ap t'nigh' an'make sure ya wear this special presen' won't ya. Preten'it's for me ya wearin' it. I'll be comin' t'see ya later anyway...we'll do samink special."

The girl continues to show no interest in anything that is being said when the sound of sudden breaking interrupts her. A man has parked just behind Adam's car. He has got out of his car, his haste making this manoeuvre more difficult than it should be, and is running towards Adam and the girl.

"Oh no, please," says the girl with uninterested disgust. She blows the words out as if voicing them had taken up her last reserves of energy.

The man is running towards them with the gait of a middle aged man who is used to sitting down. His navy anorak is rustling embarrassingly and impeding his stride. He is rather stout, overweight in fact, balding, and running head first with the assurance of his own mind knowing that all you have to do to a bully is stand up to him. He is out of breath before he reaches Adam and the girl. He clutches his chest with one hand, his other hand is pointing at Adam as if he is about to say something. He finally calms his breathing down enough to just about squeeze out the words, "I want a word with you."

The girl drops her eyes in disbelief. The fact that the man is much older than Adam makes no difference. The man could have been twenty years younger and in peak physical condition but it would have made no difference. Adam, like Masters, is a heavyweight. His muscles honed by repeated exercise, heavy weights, protein supplements, steroids, ape hormones (orangutan) and a psychopathic obsession to be the best that there is. The man's words had just left his mouth, and he continued to try and catch his breath, when Adam kicked him squarely in the groin. The man fell to his knees holding his groin, now losing even more air. The features of his face contorted and conspired to give away his feeling of impotence and shame at failing to protect himself, let alone his daughter. The men in the car start laughing and cheering. Adam looks down at the pathetic man and sneers. He grabs his hair, what little of it is left, and pulls his head back holding it still for a moment, for the delight of the spectators in the car, and then butts him full on with his forehead. The man's head and face could be seen twitching for a moment with blood spouting from a large cut on the bridge of his, now broken, nose, and from various other smaller cuts. The man then falls face down onto the pavement with a sickening dull thud where he lies motionless for about a minute before starting to convulse and finally come round. By the time that he manages to drag himself to a sitting up position two people have walked by, both having ignored him, the blood stains, and his shaking body. Before this though the girl leans over her father's cold body and tells him to, "Keep out of it Dad. It's my life and it's got nothing to do with you. Why do you keep doing this all the time."

Adam grabbed her roughly by the arm and walked her into the school grounds watching the prostrate man over his shoulder. The girl shouted after her father as she was being frogmarched in the opposite direction, "Leave me alone...stop trying to make a fool out of me..."

Adam tells the girl that he will be back to pick her up in a couple of hours and that she should meet him outside a nearby pub that they both know. He tells her that he loves her and that she is not to worry and he returns to the car.

Steve's laugh echoes around the car as Adam gets back in. Adam pulls away quickly in the car and tells everyone, "Tha's the pow'a of the COBRA."

The whole car is laughing again, the tense silence broken, whilst Adam's dilated pupils try to focus on the road.

After thirty seconds, maybe a minute, Adam looks at the guy in the back through his mirror. The guy in the back nervously swallows his saliva. He had hoped, had been hoping, that Adam would have forgotten his earlier confusion over the parcels, but, obviously now, he hadn't. Adam watched him for a while looking straight into his eyes. He took one hand off of the wheel for a moment and held his finger up to the mirror. Then he moved his finger up an inch or so, so that he was pointing to the picture of the woman on the mirror's arm, and said, without taking his eyes off of the guy in the back, "You're a fackin' cant." Adam, Steve and Tony, Moz's son, all started laughing, and when the guy in the back realised that Adam wanted him to laugh too, he joined in.

Yeah fackin' great day n'all, fackin superb like. Me an' bish av always got on well like. Afta tha' 'e wen'fru the job wiv ass, and dropp'd ass all off rarnd the birds 'ouse, me, Steve an' Tony, Moz's kid. She was a bit of an old slappa like. Tits like fackin fried eggs, decen'bit a' minge on 'er tho' mind you. Adam wen off to sor'out anfinish'd bizniz like. She wern't bad as it appens. You would'n believe wot arf these 'ousewives get ap to...

You start to open your mouth, to tell everyone, because you're drunk and you want to show off, what you know about The Bishop. Chris looks at you sternly, reading your mind, and you remember just how dangerous a thing to do that would be.

Chapter 16

Sally

I am sitting in a candle lit room visiting Sally again drinking red wine, that has stained everybody's teeth and tongues, and smoking countless reefers that we are taking in turns to get together. We are all sitting in a circle facing inwards. I am sitting next to Sally, but she is sitting nearer to Benjamin than she is to me, and has been all night. Benjamin is sufficiently tanned and wears smart, clean and well ironed clothes. He is not too flash a dresser. His trousers are not too short and not too long. All of his clothes fit him well and his socks match his shirt, which is something that Sally finds very important, and something that I am sure that she has already noticed. He has a lot to say for himself. In fact he has been talking for most of the evening. The girls, Sally, Juliette and Karen, do not seem to mind that Benjamin tries to hijack every conversation. They all seem to be in tune with his opinions. And I am all too aware of the fact that Sally is still sitting nearer to him than she is to me.

On Benjamin's left is Juliette and Karen. All three of the girls have edged nearer to him as the evening has progressed. Now he is poised invitingly between the three of them. Their faces turn in towards him whenever he speaks; capturing uninterrupted attention. Juliette sits with her knees, and ankles, together, her legs and feet visible but beneath her body. She is wearing an expensive and gorgeous according to Sally, Karen and Benjamin blue dress, which to me is too high in the skirt and too low cut in the top. She is wearing makeup, has curled her hair for the evening and put on a pair of cripplingly high patent leather sandals. It is not a look that I appreciate. She is obviously selling herself as a sexually available female, pandering to the fetishes of men whose libidos are wallowing in the festering images of the stereotypical whore. It's a shame because I like Juliette. She is intelligent, pretty (some might say beautiful but in a room which contains Sally she does not shine quite so brightly), well-travelled (she's French, used to live in Canada, and has been living in Britain for about four or five years) and friendly. Karen on the other hand dresses like a whore and acts like one. Karen has taken her trainers off and is sitting, sometimes lying, on the floor barefooted and in a shiny pink satin miniskirt that, from where I am sitting, reveals her sluttish black Agent Provocateur g string style knickers, or fuck-me-panties as some people call them. I wonder if her rich daddy pays for those. Of course as soon as I noticed this I made certain to always be looking directly at her face when she spoke so as not to become involved in whatever little flirtatious game that she was trying to play. She is wearing a tight baby-doll style Tshirt that is pale blue with two large pink handprints that cup her stiff high breasts. Mark The Twat is sitting next to her unable, it would seem, to stop himself from looking at the handprints, Karen's breasts, or Karen's long legs and smooth thighs. Karen is ignoring him, blanking him, but purring over Benjamin's every word.

Mark, or Mark The Twat, as some people in the bar call him, is the kind of unfortunate whose life, and shortcomings, are predictable and obvious to the point of being humourously absurd to everyone else, but Mark himself never sees this. In ten years time when the Nineties, like the decades before it, gets slammed as being the decade of bad taste (has this always happened to every decade?) by a new band of cultural critics and ironic comedians, the enduring image of bad fashion in the Nineties will be a photograph of Mark. His wardrobe is a terrible mix of the nastiest of fake designer clubbing wear (that do not compliment his skinny milk bottle white arms and low beer paunch), alternative new age ethnic wear, which all looks as if its been made for a special range that is being promoted at Kwik Save (he likes to make these two fashion concepts clash with shameless regularity), and he likes to wear black leather (which may be imitation) Bastard Trainers. He is pretty much a lost person who knows so little about anything that he has the constant look of somebody who is struggling with a Rubik's Cube, although he still has a Rubik's Cube and if you go to visit him in his room over in Barnes Hall he will instruct you on the different methods of solving "The Cube". Nevertheless Mark has made an effort tonight. Somebody loaned him a copy of *American Psycho* and so he has bought a pair of loafers, a copy of *GQ* and some Clinique selftan and moisturizer. Mark The Twat really enjoyed the novel but thought that it was strange that the bad guy was so "cool". He was puzzled as to why a writer would make a bad guy out to be so "trendy". Mark said that he "had" to buy a pair of loafers after reading the book. I told him that Patrick Bateman and his brother Sean could be seen as the products of Reagan's 1980's America. Mark The Twat replied in agreeing tones that the Eighties were "some decade" and that he hoped that Stallone was going to make another Rambo film. I was about to protest when Sally skewered me on her don't be a culture fascist stare. This left me feeling uncomfortable. Later when we, that is Sally and I, went to the shop for more Rizlas, cheap red wine, and chocolate bar munch, Sally said that I had no regard for Mark's feelings and that I was just trying to show off. I said that I thought that Mark had no regard for Bateman's victims' feelings, or the feelings of the victims' families. Sally said that it was pretentious and boring to talk about literature all of the time. She said that I am too far up my own arse. At least I knew that Mark The Marxist (the other Mark in the room) agreed that Bateman was not "cool".

Everything was pretty easy for Mark The Marxist. He did not have to justify or articulate his opinions because everybody already knew what they were, somebody had already written them down for him. He always told the girls that he was right behind them on gender issues. He was a friend to anyone who believed themselves to be exploited. He liked to wear black and to always be either stepping into, or out of, some dark velvet shadow. He was not an argumentative Marxist. Usually he would allow any amount of capitalist claptrap to pass by unchallenged, and he didn't wear Bastard Trainers. I thought it a little strange that Mark The Marxist wore Airwalk, but nobody else had raised this obvious point, this may be because there are a lot more pluses to Mark The Marxist's character than to Mark The Twat's.

Mark The Marxist will stick up for anybody who was arguing against the established order of things as if Marxism, in his mind at least, was equal to anarchism. He liked to invite people, usually girls as far as I can tell, around to his room for a one-on-one-chat. He liked to sympathise with the oppressed and point out other ways in which his guest was getting fucked over by the government, capitalism, The Tories, The Labour Party, high culture, popular culture, sport, drugs, their family, friends, and even their selfish boyfriends who would not allow them to be the woman that they wanted to be. He seems to be a popular guy.

Sally is wearing Levi's and a Quicksilver sweat shirt that her mother bought for her. We are supposed to be going to get ready to go out at some point, but so far this has not happened. We are all getting more and more fucked up on the booze and smoke. There are people waiting for us in the bar who we have made arrangements with, but we are all feeling so smug because we are having such a good time, or at least the girls and Benjamin are, that we do not see the point in disturbing our fun. We feel socially superior. The girls, Juliette and Karen, also have the opportunity to dress themselves up, or rather tart themselves up, on the pretence of going out, but can get Benjamin's attention without having to compete with people in the bars or the clubs. I know that both of the Mark's, especially Mark The Twat, are almost getting off on just being in Juliette's room, let alone being able to talk freely to the girls.

At this moment I am talking. I am talking about one of the courses that I am on.

"The course," I am telling them, "is called Imagist Poetry. The poets have some really great ideas. I am really enjoying it. They believe that we have all lost our ability to appreciate the everyday things which surround us. So, they write poems about wheelbarrows and pine trees, and that is all the poems are about. You are forced to look the thing itself. Actually one of the poets, William Carlos Williams his name is ("Trippy name," says Mark The Twat), has a famous dictum: 'No ideas but in things'. You see it is as if we have lost the joy of our senses and these poets, Pound, Williams, H.D., Flint, are all trying to resuscitate our senses...forcing us to look closely at...a chair...or a table...or anything. In one poem, again, by Williams, he has written a poem that is a note on the fridge door to the person whose plums he has eaten. The thing is that he has, in the verse, reactivated our senses so well that we can still experience the sensation of eating the plums, it is really great the way he has done it. It is almost like a kind of virtual reality. Read the poem and taste the plums but you do not take in any of the calories."

Sally replies irritated and ready for an argument, "Yeah that's great. Read this poem about a spliff and don't get stoned. Read this poem about a bottle of wine and don't get pissed."

Mark The Twat butts in, "Ha, ha, ha, right, read the poem about Pam and don't get laid, ha, ha, ha..."

I look at Mark The Twat laughing and I am angry that Sally is joining in too. I cannot really argue with him though as I seem to remember that he has a few supermodel pinups on the walls in his room, and I cannot believe that he gets many offers for casual sex, I am pretty sure that he has never had sex, and if, by some miracle, he had a girlfriend he would not be here ogling the hand prints on Karen's tits. So I suppose that he is right, only he should have said: "Buy the poster and don't get laid". I have to tell myself, and content myself with the knowledge, that he's a twat and that that is all there is to it.

I continue, "Okay, okay...but remember this was all happening around the turn of the century and it is an idea that is being used today, virtual reality etc... The idea, I think, is excellent. We should wonder at how well a chair is made. When was the last time that you looked at something and really appreciated it? I think that we take everything for granted. No honestly they're a good bunch of people, or, sorry, they were a good bunch of people. If you think about it anybody could be a poet. The inspiration is all around you if you adopt this perspective. So they, the poets, are not only revitalizing our senses but revitalizing poetry too. We can all be poets. Poetry has been sold as this form of writing that is somehow unreachable, unattainable to most people. Everybody thinks that it is a privileged form of writing written for the privileged, but it does not have to be that way. If we could get everybody writing, everybody becomes a poet. And that has got to be good. At least it might stop people from reading The Sun."

"Well," Sally says in her irritated tone," who are these people to tell us how to look at a chair or what plums taste like?"

"Surely honey," Sally looked very pissed off when I said the word "honey", "the point is that you can write your own perspective of the chair or the plums."

"Come on," states Benjamin as if what I have said is totally wrong, "huh, please," all of the three girls shuffle in their positions so that they can look at him clearly, "poetry is dead. Whatever functions poetry once performed are gone. The poet was probably an important person in years gone by but you have to move on. Films and TV shows are a more dynamic and, let's face it, a more convenient way of reading/watching a story. We've got comedians, novelists, sitcoms, computer video games, pop groups and singers...really what need does anyone have for poetry. I think that as far as most people are concerned poetry shot itself in the foot with all of those modern poets writing purposely opaque, complex, and obscure poems. Nobody likes a smart arse."

The three girls are all looking intently at Benjamin. Sally passes him the joint that she has been smoking. They seem to make a point of touching hands as the joint goes from one to the other. Benjamin is silent as he returns Sally's gaze, and he takes a long pull on the joint as if he were performing for Sally's benefit. Sally, whilst certainly paying Benjamin a lot of attention, is not dressed up like Juliette and Karen, and this seems to make him more interested in her. It is as if Juliette and Karen have already been won. It is just a matter of time before he picks them so to speak. Obviously though he does not seem to feel that he has quite won Sally over yet, and so he is trying especially hard with her. What he does not know of course is that Sally and I are devoted to one another. He continues his speech.

"You apotheosize these poets and vilify The Sun. You talk about 'everyone' being a poet. How many copies of *Des Imagistes* do you suppose were sold. Why aren't you studying somebody popular like Robert Frost or Longfellow. It's all right for you to scribble down a few lines and call yourself a poet but you're not. If none of your contemporaries read you it is because you do not speak to them or for them, you are irrelevant. A teacher is somebody who earns a living through teaching, a milkman, sorry (looks at the girls) milkperson, earns a living delivering milk. You, who scribble down a few lines, earn nothing, you are a student, or you are on the dole, but you are certainly not a poet. If

The Sun is the most popular 'newspaper' in Britain it is so for a reason. I am not saying that there is necessarily any answers to life there, of course not, but the fact that something is the most popular surely tells us something about the population that are buying it. We can learn more about the people of the time, and how they viewed their world, if we read *The Song of Hiawatha* rather than your intellectual poets who nobody really read. William Carlos Williams was a paediatrician wasn't he?"

Sally is staring at me again. Her eyes are like the fangs of a viper daring me to make my move but threatening to strike if I do. For the sake of Sally I allow the conversation to be taken over by another subject, and for the sake of harmony I allow Benjamin centre stage. I bite my tongue holding back the retort that my mind has already formulated.

We never actually "go out". We sit together puffing away feeling increasingly more superior to anybody not in the room with each joint that is passed around. I eventually manage to talk Sally into leaving at around three in the morning. The hash running out finally clinched it. Just before we left Benjamin told Juliette that he thinks that she's really interesting and that he'd like to trip with her sometime. He managed to speak in a tone that also told Karen and Sally that he'd like to trip with them too. Karen and Sally responded and suggested that they should all trip together on one of the evenings in the week. Mark The Marxist does not do hallucinogens, and Mark The Twat was, conveniently enough, in the toilet when they were discussing it. We, Sally and I, do eventually leave and start on the ten minute walk home together. I am aware that Sally is pissed off with me, and so is Sally, but I do not think that she can remember why. She is very, very, drunk.

I try to keep the conversation on subjects that we must agree on, like how cool we all are that we don't even need to go out to have a good time. I try to tap into the feeling of superiority that had pervaded our little party.

"I had a great time tonight," I offer. "I am not really bothered that we did not go out. It didn't matter, well it doesn't matter when you are having such a good time. Poor Karen and Juliette though, they were all dressed up for nothing."

I am trying to be nonjudgmental. I am trying to raise Sally up from the belligerent mood in which she seems to be stuck in.

"Wasn't a waste."

"What's that?"

"It wasn't a waste for Karen or Juliette."

She acts as if she is defending them, as if I have just insulted them. I make my tone much softer, trying to avoid an argument.

"Well I didn't mean that it was a waste..."

"Well it wasn't, okay. I'm sure that Mark liked it."

"Which one?"

"Karen of course."

"I'm sorry, I meant, which Mark?" I am angry at myself for being so nice when Sally is being so pedantic. When I look at her though she is so radiantly beautiful that I cannot bare to upset her in any way.

"Little Mark," she slurs. Sally has never referred to Mark The Twat as Little Mark before.

"Why do you say that?" I ask Sally hoping that she will not start shouting as I fear that she will at any moment.

"They're seeing each other aren't they? That's a bit of a stupid question isn't it?"

"Sorry I didn't realise. You didn't say anything."

"Karen's upset. She doesn't know whether she should put off her boyfriend whose supposed to be coming down next week."

"Telling lies just isn't worth it."

"Well it's better than lying to yourself isn't it? Oh it's really easy for you to just tell people how to live their lives. Karen and Mark love each other. It's really difficult for them and the last thing that they need is for you to be casting judgements on them."

"Karen has been seeing her boyfriend at home for a couple of years? And the last few times that I have been down to visit she has been really missing him that is all I meant. I think that if she spent more time with her boyfriend she would not want Mark. I think that she loves Graham, it is Graham? I mean that is his name, right? ...I think that she might regret it because I think that she would like to be with Graham."

"Regret it," Sally spits out the words that I used as if they are toxic. "Don't you think that we are all entitled to explore our emotions, our desires...oh you think you're an expert on everything don't you? It's fucking healthy to follow your heart."

I want to tell Sally that the idea of following your heart is not as simple as it sounds. I am thinking about Hester Prynne and

Roger Chillingworth. How the former's heart wanted to chase love, and the latter's revenge. Both of them, it could be argued were following their hearts but where can we draw the line? I want to discuss this, and more, but I know that at this moment I would only be accused of being "up my own arse". I can almost feel that phrase waiting in the chamber ready to hit me as soon as I give Sally even a semblance of an excuse to pull the trigger.

"Karen is going to attract a lot of attention...from guys. She likes to mix with the men, and you know she likes to flirt a little, only harmlessly I know that..."

"Are you calling my mate a slag?"

"No, Sally please..."

"You might want to own all women but you can't. Do you know that? What do you mean flirt? I'll tell you what you mean. You mean that you can't stand to see a woman talking to a man. That we should all speak when we're spoken to. We, the three of us, we're free spirits and no man owns us. We're free to do whatever we like, okay. Is that okay with you?"

I wish that I had said nothing right now, but even that would have been the source of some fierce diatribe from Sally. I try to back peddle, scramble for a way out. I know that it is only the wine that is talking. Karen, despite her tarty image and sexual innuendo, is, I suppose, in an orthodox glossy magazine kind of way, quite attractive, whereas Mark The Twat...well he is more...more...well he is a twat. It may sound rude, it is rude, but in the grand scheme of things she is more desirable, much more in fact, than him. I decide to follow this line to praise Karen.

"Karen is chic," I lie. "I do not really see her with Mark The Twat for any length of time."

"I don't know what's the matter with you. You've changed. How dare you say that about Mark. You hardly know him, or Karen. At least Mark doesn't go on about literature all the time as if "Literature" is going to save the world."

I can see that Sally is enjoying mocking me. I also see that there is no point in trying to be nice to her, or to agree with her; she is determined to spin everything that I say so that she can criticize incessantly. I have to say something though.

"I just thought that Karen is so fashion conscious and hip and that Mark really is not with it...err not in the same way that she is..." Actually I think, as I believe that I have already told you, that Karen dresses and acts like a tart.

"Maybe Karen is interested in Mark a little bit more than she is interested in his clothes, or how much he knows about the American Novel. You might not realise this but some people aren't impressed by you, some people think that you are up your own arse. I don't know who you think you are? Maybe Mark's a great lover."

"What you mean that it has got that far already?"

"Yes. Most people have sex you know when they're seeing each other it's natural."

"But Karen hardly spoke to him all night...well that is not what I mean, but they were hardly together were they?"

"Probably Mark doesn't feel the need to stifle Karen. Probably they have formed a secure relationship which allows them freedom to be themselves. They're not just stuck in some boring boyfriend girlfriend shit."

"Do you feel that I stifle you?"

"Do you mean that you think that you stifle me?...with your holier than holy, purer than pure, moral bullshit. You're too scared to live life. Making up your own little rules and then condemning anybody who doesn't live up to them, or who heaven forbid breaks them. I think that you're changing becoming unrecognizable. And I can't remember the last time that we had sex together."

I want to say that we made love (it was not, and never is, just sex when we are together) last time that I visited but her next outburst will be something derogative about our love making, and I could not stand to here her defile our physical and spiritual communion. I remain silent for the rest of the way home, except for encouraging Sally to remain upright as we walk up some steps to get to her block. I make up my mind to make love to Sally as soon as we get to her room, to show her my feelings, but when we get back she falls asleep almost immediately. I am leaving tomorrow.

Chapter 17

New Client

On a first date, I always suggest going to a restaurant. It is neutral territory. It means that we have to talk throughout the evening which gives me a chance to get to know the other person. I think that there is still something very special about eating with someone. It is very complimentary to be invited to dine with someone. It is intimate but not tacky, and there is always the safeguard of the table between me and the client.

On a first date I always wear a suit. It is conventional and appeals to most people without giving anything away. I think that wearing a suit is also neutral. It looks professional, and I want to make sure that they understand that we are negotiating, between my lines of ostentatious flattery, a business relationship. Some clients will want to be romanced. I am their troubadour. There are some who cannot swallow that romance and prefer a confidant, a special friend, who listens, is interested, and who makes love to them without taking anything from them. Some clients may want excitement. They want to meet the daredevil rebel who plays life by his own rules. In a suit I feel that my personality is cloaked, and therefore, that I am free to wear which ever mask the client wants me to wear. She, the client, has nothing to lose whilst I am on show. She can walk away if she chooses but that would leave me rejected. I feel inside that if she did not like me, did not want me, that I would not be able to continue. It would surely destroy me. In my role, my suit, my occupation, whatever way you want to classify my position when I meet her, I need (and it is a need that is increasing, that cannot be contained) to be liked and wanted. I am vulnerable waiting for her to ask me to have sex, or for her to communicate her desire. I have to sit across from her and wait until she decides that she wants me. I wait, desperately wanting to be bought, because to offer yourself for only money is a risk to your ego, your sense of who you are, what you are about. You can be left with nothing; paid for, used up, emptied, and discarded...

I am looking at myself in the mirror in my room, making sure that I look okay for this evening. I am going to eat out with a new client at a restaurant that she has booked. I am wearing a black pinstriped cashmere suit by Crombie. The jacket to the suit is very comfortable and well cut. It has three buttons at the front and four buttons on each cuff (if jackets have cuffs?). I hold up my right wrist to my face and then my left, and I look at my face, my hands, my wrists, and I check that all four buttons on each "cuff" are properly fastened. I have on the Dolce and Gabbana white cotton shirt that Gillian bought for me, and a plain blue Hugo Boss silk tie. This is all finished off with a pair of Patrick Cox Chelsea Boots and a splash of Egoiste Platinum by Chanel. I turn sideways and look at myself, and then I turn again and look at myself from the other side. I spent an hour and a half in the gym today pressing, curling, stretching, pulling, lifting, and then I had a relaxing sauna, followed by a good hour on the sunbed. I have lost a couple of my regular clients. One has moved to Chicago, her husband got a promotion, and the other moved to Paris, she got a promotion. I need to keep earning and saving, and so I am pulling out all of the stops for this new client, whose name is Margaret, and who has been introduced to me through Gillian. She sounded nervous on the telephone when we spoke which is good. It means that she is not accustomed to calling up gigolos, and is probably pretty normal. I am amassing a decent pot of cash from my work. Soon I am going to have to tell Sally that I've won some competition, or had a small lottery win, or something. I've decided against showing her some published piece of writing. I have decided that it has to be pure fortune and not some reward for hard work. I have lied to her and do not want to make myself into a false hero, as well as a liar. I merely want to get on with my life with Sally without seeming to be a financial milestone around her neck, without appearing to be some gold digger by the rest of her family.

It will not be long now before I will have finished my work and will be free of this filthy occupation. Something that I was reading earlier gave me some encouragement. It was in Stephen Crane's *The Red Badge Of Courage*: "He had performed his mistakes in the dark, so he was still a man." I have performed my mistakes in the dark. I have banished them all to the dark recesses of my mind, erased them totally from my consciousness. I am still a man, a whole person, alive and fighting my own demons. The problems with Sally hurt me, but I know, and I know that she knows, that it is only the distance between us that is causing the problems, and once that ceases to be the case these problems will simply disappear. Love like ours cannot be broken. But nevertheless I am aware of my infidelity, physically, if not spiritually or sexually. I will make it all up to her. I will be the perfect partner. The quicker that all this is over though the better. Sometimes I dream about the women and myself engaged in acts which, although I cannot remember, I somehow recognize. It is as if I have not managed to capture all of the details during my playback mechanism. Some things, no matter how hard I try, still slip through the net of my recall. At first these seemed to be trivial things, and I told myself that if I had not properly addressed them in my recall and playback it was because they were of no consequence. The thing is there is something of each experience, of each encounter, that clings to these tiny, supposedly irrelevant details. It may be something dormant. It may be the residue of the experience, and, as minute as it may be, it escapes me, dripping through my fingers when my clenched fist closes around it. I am frightened that these dormant, minute residues, are biding their time, soon to awaken and emerge. They may well be behind me, and I can only hear the faintest of echoes far back in this dark tunnel in which I am running for my life, but they are still there. They will catch me in the end if I do not take measures to stop them. I am struggling with this all the time. The last night at Sally's I awoke at around six o'clock in a terrible feverish sweat, the sheets of the bed all sticking to my skin like flypaper. I had been dreaming that my recall and playback was not efficient, that no matter how many times I reviewed the encounters, or the sensations, or how many times I tried to view something from a different perspective or a new angle, it was never true. I could never achieve a true account. Every fact that I constructed from my observation was a lie. I was busy catching the lies of the encounters whilst the truth was passing by, but leaving a stain on me that I could not remove. When I died the stains were all over my body. At my funeral I could see Sally and she knew everything. She was standing next to Gillian and they looked at the stains on my face as if they were medieval birthmarks, symbols of my evil nature.

I am not standing still though. I am not going to allow these thoughts and dreams to overtake me. I am taking steps to prevent any further disturbance of my psyche. I have taken out collections of short stories from the library and I am reading and rereading the same stories over and over again. I am rereading them until I know them word for word, so that I can write down the stories from memory and I do not move on to the next one until I can do this without a single error. It is taking up a lot of my time, but it might be my salvation. I have to keep my mistakes in the dark where I can destroy them without leaving so much as a mark on myself.

Now I have to be focused on this evening. The lady I am meeting is a rich widow. She lives in _____, a small town in Suffolk. I usually telephone a taxi from an out of town company that I have not used before, but Gillian has offered to give me a lift, as Margaret is such a good friend of hers. Gillian has told me to be extra nice to her because she has had a rough time since her husband died, and that she has still got a few problems. Gillian has enough problems of her own if you ask me. I suppose that Gillian understands the situation as she too is a widow, but then again she has not got a good word to say about her deceased husband. I appreciate the contact though, and I am probably being too hard on Gillian, she certainly seems concerned about this woman. She did say that she trusted me more than most a compliment I suppose. She said that she told Margaret that I was just the kind of person that she needed right now. Gillian is also looking over an article I have written, on her recomendation, on Frank Norris's *McTeague*. I think that my hard work in my studies, and professionalism in my occupation, is beginning to pay dividends. I believe that soon I will have the means to woo my Sally once and for all.

I must concentrate. I must prepare my mind, and keep it sharp so that it can inspect every detail, every sensation that I experience. I have to make a good start with this new client. I have to make sure that my mind is ready to tackle a new encounter with a new person. I also have to make sure that I am ready to meet Margaret. I have to be ready to show that I am enjoying the evening, her company, and even if it goes no further than that tonight, I have to show an interest in her. She has to believe that I "want to make love" to her.

Gillian met Margaret through the university. Margaret's husband was a lecturer there. This is what I've been told anyway. Gillian has been looking out for her since he died about eighteen months ago. Gillian has decided that I am the final stage in the recuperation programme. Margaret may still not be able to handle any kind of involved relationship, but meeting occasionally, with no pressure, might just ease her back into the social world.

Gillian's husband was in the army. He was a career soldier. He was from a military family, as is Gillian. She, so she claims, was virtually forced into marrying him. She married at nineteen and of course soon began to hate him, and her parents, for the situation in which she found herself. She refused to bear him any children, she refused sex altogether, until he financed her three year study for a degree in Literature. She went off to Cambridge with his blessing. She got a first class degree, although to hear her reminisce she cannot have had time to do much work. She then, as far as I can gather, had three children by her husband. The two girls are her pride and joy. The eldest lives in California. She followed in her mother's footsteps and lectures at Berkley. According to Gillian she has made quite a name for herself in American academia. Gillian positively beams when she recants her achievements, publications, and awards. The other daughter lives in London and works as a solicitor for some top law firm. Gillian is always talking to her on the telephone asking her about her work and prospects for promotion. They are portrayed as highflying young ambitious professionals. I do not doubt Gillian's word. I have seen photographs of her daughters and they look, just like their mother, in that they both appear to be comfortable and powerful, and full of confidence, looking squarely into the lens, ready to take on the world. "I always told all of my children to be the masters of wherever they were, of whatever they wanted, and of everybody around them. I always told them not to take any shit from anyone."

The husband was a huge man. I have seen some photographs of him in which he looks handsome, very tall, probably about six feet two, six feet three. His hair was very dark and curly. Apparently the youngest child, Paul, the only son, is almost an inch-for-inch copy of his father. The resemblance is staggering, alarming even, according to Gillian. She has no photographs of her son as a man. They fell out beyond any point of reconciliation a number of years ago and they have not made contact since. Gillian says that she does not want to see him again, and hopes that he never feels the inclination to see her either. He is a policeman, "likes to wear a uniform just like his accursed father." Gillian does not even like to say his name and has to force herself to form the sounds with her tongue, and even then spits out the "P" of Paul as if it were diseased.

Gillian's husband died in hospital, a road accident. Gillian, despite the scathing remarks about her husband, is still very bitter about what happened. He was involved in an accident on the motorway. A lorry jack-knifed and he was in the wrong place at the wrong time. It was a terrible tragedy which had a profound effect on the children, on Gillian too, a lot more than she is prepared to admit. It was the lorry driver's fault by all accounts, which, of course, only makes it seem worse, as did the fact that he, the lorry driver, walked away from the accident pretty much unscathed. Sometimes, very occasionally, Gillian will talk compassionately of her husband. There are no photographs around at her house though. It is as if she has erased him from her mind, as if he never existed, maybe it is her way of coping.

Gillian lost a lot of money in the legal case that followed, nothing could be proved beyond reasonable doubt, the wet road surface served as a cover for the truth. She tried though, and for that I admire her. She did receive a decent sum from the army, her husband was in the higher echelons by the time he died. There were insurance pay outs and other financial support from his family. This was all about fifteen years ago now. She did not have to do anything after that. She was an extremely wealthy woman even after the dent in her bank balance made by the failed legal case. She went to work so as to be a model to her children, to instil in them a work ethic, a will for power. Now she just enjoys the position that she has made for herself. She has nothing to prove to anyone, except for herself.

I can see Gillian's Land Rover turning at the corner of my street. I check myself in the mirror for one last time. I turn off the lights in my apartment, enjoying the cool anonymous darkness. I check for my wallet, and then I go outside to meet Gillian.

Chapter 18

The Meeting

It is eight o'clock in the morning. Adam is standing outside his car talking on his mobile phone. He is at the university car park. He is wearing jeans, black boots and a bulky black leather jacket.

Yeah, well y'll keep me in tach won't ya Phil?

We should'a neva let the li'ul shit out ov'ar sight.

Okay cheers.

Adam takes the phone, that looks so small in his huge hands, and taps in Steve's number. He puts the phone to his ear and waits.

Steve, alwight.

Any news on Fat Stuart The Paff?

Shit.

We gotta find im. It's windin me ap...It really is...I'm lybull t go fackin ape at any moment.

Wot left the cantry!...I would'n put anyfink parst that li'ul shit.

I danno...

E could ruwin i'all fer ass. We gotta get im sor'id.

Alwight, alwight, keep tryin... I'm gonna fack im ap when I catch im.

Yeah, yeah, see ya later. Yeah at the meetin. It's gotta be about Phil ain it? They're all shitin bricks abou'it.

Yeah I know bat we can't take any chances can we. We gotta keep lookin, an in the meantime we gotta keep ap appearances like.

Alwight I'll see ya there. Give ass a fackin call if anyfink cams ap.

Adam put the phone in his jacket, and began to walk up to the large fourteen storey towers. At the bottom of the first tower a small man, who looks like a janitor, says, "Morning" in what Adam takes to be a northern accent, probably Scottish. The man has seen Adam on countless mornings and always greets him with the same questioning gaze, the eye of suspicion. Adam did not give a shit about what this man thought was going on. Adam got into the elevator and pressed number 14, the top floor. He stood in the corner of the elevator with his back to the security camera, and counted the floors off on the display. He got out at the top and walked around the corridor. There were five rooms. He would go into them all but he started at the first room. The plants were all doing exceptionally well. He had managed to get the use of these rooms from some woman he met through the video business. She was a professor, well you met all sorts in his line of work. He could smell the sweet resin in the air. The curtains were all drawn and the air was very damp. It was very difficult to breathe because of all the carbon dioxide from the dry ice. He pulled back the curtain a little to get a look at the view. There was so much condensation on the window that all he could see was a blur. He rubbed the glass with the heel of his hand but the water gushed from the glass down his arm as soon as he touched the pane. He closed the curtain again and started to look around, inspecting the plants. The lights were off and he had disturbed the plants' twelve hour cycle of darkness, but he suspected that the plants were ready anyway. He looked and sure enough most of the plants, if not all of them, had tiny swellings at the bottom of the pistils, like little sacks. They were ready. He went through to the next room, and then the next room, and then the next tower and the next. It was time to harvest.

When he had checked everything out to his satisfaction he decided to go over to The Hunter's. He would give young Tony his first chance at harvesting, it would also give him a chance to sound out Moz. He could even go to the meeting with him. A real show of solidarity that would be. Adam smiled, sometimes he even amazed himself.

He had first made a name for himself as a bouncer. He had got interested in body building, lifting, working out. He met the "right" people and started taking steroids, just pills at first, and then he started to inject. He got bigger and bigger and bigger. Then one night he was pissed up with his mates and had gone into the chip shop; a black guy was in the queue with a white girl. A girl who Adam had gone to school with. Adam started to call her "nigger lover". The guy, obviously outnumbered, thought it best to leave. His girlfriend, remembering Adam as just a boy from school, began to argue with him. Adam just flipped. He went for the guy, quickly overpowered him and then thumped fist after fist into the guy's face. Adam was wearing those heavy gold sovereign rings, and he virtually ground the guy's skull into dust. Adam later joked that he was only showing him his jewellery. The guy had to have surgery to reconstruct his cheek bones. His girlfriend was screaming, totally hysterical. Later it came out that she was having his kid. He, the victim, recovered physically, after having a lot of painful plastic surgery, but he did not recover mentally. He could not walk down his street without the fear of attack. He certainly could not go into a bar, or a club, or a restaurant, or anywhere. A prisoner in his own home; he was quite literally forced into going to court. He wanted to stay indoors and see nobody. The viciousness, and, above all, the meaninglessness, of the assault was too great for the victim to fully recover from. He became more and more disturbed and split with the girl. He has deteriorated and is now institutionalised. She has got a beautiful little boy, he must be about seven or eight now, and he has never met his father.

Adam went down for that. He served four months because, well mainly because, he hit a policeman in the struggle to get him off the unconscious guy. When he got out, as soon as he got out, he signed up with a firm who recruited the "right kind of people"as bouncers and doormen from inside the prisons, and employed them as soon as they were released. Adam can often be heard remarking that doing time was the best career move he ever made. He worked the doors at a few clubs around London, he did a bit of dealing. He took more and more steroids, eventually moving on to testosterone, obsessed with lifting heavier and heavier weights.

One night someone caught a young kid, about seventeen or eighteen, who was already inside the club and dealing ecstasy. The Rave scene had started to hit the clubs. Adam was having a great time. Whoever caught the kid with the E's lost him for a second and he still had all of the gear on him. Adam, whizzing off of his tits, was searching people on the door. He liked to move the girls away from the queue and touch them up a little. Some of them got upset and stormed out, most just looked confused and frightened, not sure of what had just happened. Occasionally one of them actually enjoyed it, though as far as Adam was concerned they all enjoyed it. The guy ran straight through the congregation of doormen, and was chased by one of the bouncers out onto the entrance courtyard and car park. A second bouncer was soon behind them. Adam watched the chase and saw the guy lose the bouncers and crawl under a car. He went outside to tell them but before he had chance to say anything one of the bouncers, in anger, said, "He's carrying a fucking sack full of pills. A small fucking fortune." Adam said nothing other than that he would watch the front while they ran around to the back. They were gone in seconds; off on their empty pursuit. Adam drove his car parallel to the one underneath which the kid was hiding, opened the passenger door and told him to get in. The young kid scared beyond comprehension jumped in, it was a way out and it was being offered to him. Adam drove him away from the club. The kid was scared and asked to be let out. He realised as soon as he had got into the car that he was trapped. The kid began to empty his pockets. He had got bags and bags of E's. In his jacket, in his trousers, down his fucking pants, everywhere. Then he starts to take out rolls of tens and twenties. He had got two or three thousand rolled up, and probably four or five times that amount in pills, the kid was a walking chemist. Adam told him to throw it all on the back seat. Adam drove at full speed down towards some local building site where he sold steroids to some of the young men who worked there, all brickies, labourers, scaffolders, roofers,...all looking for that little bit extra. Adam knew that there would be nobody around. He slammed on the brakes. Adam's seat belt caught him but the kid, with no safety belt, hit the windscreen hard, not hard enough to shatter it, Adam did not want that, but hard enough to hurt and disorient him for a second whilst Adam dragged him out of the car and hit him until he was unconscious. He delivered each blow without flinching, enjoying hitting the defenceless target, making himself angrier and angrier with each blow that he administered, so that each time he hit the kid it was with an increasing sense of malice. When the kid was finally out cold Adam began to kick his head taking a step back each time and swinging his heavy leg and foot and kicking his toe into the head of the kid, who was by now totally unrecognizable as the kid who had been sitting next to him only moments before. He aimed his kicks around the ears and temples of the kid's head. Adam, whilst calling the dead kid a fucking bastard, dragged him into the boot of his car, in those days an Orion Ghia, and locked the corpse in. He drove back about ten to fifteen thousand pounds richer. Nobody noticed that his car had been gone for twenty minutes. He told the others that he had seen the kid running off and had chased him but that finally the kid had given him the slip. The others laughed at what they perceived to be Adam's relative inexperience and over zealousness. One of them had said that it was just best to let them go, but everyone agreed that Adam was a good bloke.

Adam went back to Southend, where he grew up, shortly after that. He used the drugs to make the right connections. He did not want to stay in London because he did not know who the kid was. He seemed too young to have that kind of money and that amount of pills. Adam wanted to lie low. The kid could have been working for someone big. He ground down the pills and put the powder into capsules that way there was no connection at all. If someone was on the lookout for tablets with a heart stamped on them then they were not going to pay attention to the capsules that he was selling. He met John and Serge who were starting to make it big at the time importing from Amsterdam. Within a month he was doing runs for them. Within six months he had carried out his first hit. He was on the payroll.

Adam drove Moz and Tony, Moz's son, to the meeting that John and Serge had called. The car stereo was, of course, on full blast. Adam was talking to Moz, exchanging pleasantries, but he was thinking about Mary, Moz's daughter who had been sitting watching TV when he arrived. Tony, who was in the back, did not seem to notice the peculiarity in the size of the two gigantic men in the front seats. It would be strange, and fearful, for most people to see such physically impressive men sitting so close to one another, but Tony was not most people, he was Moz's son. Moz loved the fact that Tony worked with Adam, as far as Moz was concerned he could not be in better hands. He understood, and appreciated, the way in which Adam worked, all aggression, intimidation, and violence, the oldfashioned way maybe, but it was still the best way. They were going to Serge's office. A large room above a Florists in a building which he owned in partnership with John. Occasionally they met here. Usually they met at The Hunter's but Moz suspected that a few plain clothes coppers had been around recently and that it might be better to move this meeting, as it was only going to be short, to Serge's office. As they got out of the car Adam's mobile began to ring.

I'll be ap in a minit lads alwight.

Moz and Tony went through the back door greeting Andy "Baz" Rogers and Johnny "Two" Cox as they opened it for them. The "Baz" was because his nose had been broken so many times that it no longer had any form, it was simply a huge ugly mess. Adam put the phone to his ear hoping for good news. He had begun to feel nervous, agitated, going to this unusual meeting with Fat Stuart The Poof on the loose. He had underestimated the little faggot shit, but now he hoped that he been picked up. Adam was anxious for news and it showed in his voice.

Yes...who?...ahem wot is it?

Farnd wot?

Wot the fack was it doin in yer fackin bag?

I don't give a fackin shit.

Tell im ya boyfriend's a fackin diabe'ik.

No.

No way...No.

I've jast told ya wot t'say. Tell im ya boyfriend's a fackin diabe'ik....tell im e needs it for is fackin insulin shots....I've told ya not t'carry yer works in yer fackin school bag...For facks sake.

No, y'll afta sort it out fer y'self...Don't call me about this kind'a shit again.

I'll call you. Now fack off.

Adam had hoped that it would be Steve on the phone, but Steve was already waiting upstairs. Steve shook his small pinhead very slightly so that Adam would know that he had had no luck. John and Serge were both their sitting on chairs that faced the rest of the group. John smiled and said hello to Adam just as he always did, and Adam, for the moment, was appeased.

Everybody was their; Andy "Baz" Rogers; "Sick" Simon; Dave; Moz; Tony; Chris; his mate Gary; Terry "The Pusher"; "Mad" Rex; Paul "Morse"; Johnny "Two" Cox; "Dirty" Brian; Selvin "Thrills". They all pointed their gnarled heavy faces, creased with the lines of wrath, in the direction of John, as he began to speak. These men were the villains. They were yobs with enough muscle and intimidation behind them to get themselves in a position of power. There were others. The business men who did not attend these meetings. They provided the veneer of legitimacy and allowed the operations to be run, seemingly, within the law. It would jeopardise their position if they were to attend such meetings. John and Serge pretty much talked to those people in private, in a one on one situation. They were not needed anyway. They were businessmen and could be relied upon. They wanted money and an easy life. The men in this room wanted more than money. They had all got a point to make to themselves, and to the people they dealt with. They loved violence and power foremost and wanted the kind of respect that people pay you when they fear you. They were unpredictable. Their pride and egos got in the way of everything that they did. This made them dangerous, very dangerous, not only to anybody who happened to cross their path, but also to John and Serge. There had been many times when one, or more of them, had ruined one of Serge's money spinning plans. These men were responsible for blowing countless opportunities. John and Serge had to call these meetings to order them, so as to instruct them on what to do, and more importantly what not to do.

John and Serge were the brains but it was John who dealt with the men. They were the two at the top. Moz rated very highly too. He had been around some time, was a big nasty looking fucker, and spoke the same language as these men, shared their views and opinions. Above all he had always earned, always made money, and he was loyal, always had been, and always ranted on about being loyal. He was an example, a good example to the other men, of how far loyalty could take you. Adam was the new power, extremely visible, had a lot of operations, and was respected and feared by just about everyone. Sometimes it seemed that not even John could have kept him in line, not if Adam decided to turn against him. Adam was ruthless, his business was growing, as was his influence. It was difficult to contain him in John and Serge's operations so his work for others, Masters for example, was tolerated. It was them showing him respect.

John stood up. His hair had been freshly cut that morning. His inch and a half long hair was immaculately groomed. He looked splendid standing in front of the hushed crowd of villains. He looked around at the men and searched his mind for a second or two before beginning. He made sure that he knew what he was going to say and how he was going to say it, and then he began, "I'd like to open this meeting now. There's not much for me to say but what I have to say is of vital importance to our well being in the immediate future. It is no secret, no secret whatsoever, that Masters, who we have had a good working relationship with, is set to get the word from the men in London. (John waited, as he had already expected that he would have to, for Moz's sighs of protest to end before continuing) This will bring about a change in the present situation. The boys in London need their supplies to be regular and reliable. Masters will have to be organized. He will have to be ready. They want someone to oversee the local operation so that there are no hiccups. We still have the right connections on the continent to run our service. Masters is going to have to use us, and we will be happy that he uses us, (John looks at Moz making it plain that there will be no debate on this point) and we will all continue making money. We will keep our considerable local interests and we will have a small, but increasing share of the London market. We, through Masters will receive benefits, small favours, from our new friends in the capital. It is a time of great opportunity, but we cannot afford to fail our new friends, and we cannot afford to fail Masters either. This acknowledgement of Masters, this embrace from London, brings with it certain dangers. Masters now has the full backing of his new associates. He belongs to a bigger team. A team that we simply cannot afford to upset; a team that will stop at nothing to protect those who are a part of its whole. At the moment I have an assurance from Masters that our operations will continue as before except that we will help him out with the large deliveries up to the city. Serge and I are ready to overcome all difficulties that may arise in our friendship with Masters. We can all prosper from the new allegiance that is forming. (John looked over at Serge to check on how convincing he was being. Serge's slow but serious concentration told him he was doing fine.) We do not want any problems to arise with any of Masters's men. They are going to be cocky, shooting their mouths off; they are going to be even bigger pricks than they usually are, but nobody, I repeat nobody, is to retaliate to the mouthy bastards. I want you all to keep away from them, okay. I want you to all settle down. Let them mouth off for a while what do we care? We'll be making more than ever, and that's good enough for me, and for the time being it will have to be good enough for all of you. I'm sorry if you don't like it but that's the way that it's going to be do you all understand? I don't want anybody doing anything for the next month, not without the go ahead from either me or Serge. Now I said that this was going to be short, if you've got any questions

Serge will be hanging around to help you as best as he can. I've got to leave now. Don't forget what I've told you. I don't want anyone messing this up do you hear? Anybody who fucks up will get no protection from me. This is too important we're all too near the big time now. I promise now to deliver. In a few months time you'll all be able to retire gentlemen."

A laugh went around the room. It was too dangerous for them all to be in the same place for too long. It would be too easy for the police, or a gang of rivals, to walk in and take them all out. The irony was of course that Masters, their so called new friend, the very person whom they had gathered there to discuss, was the prime enemy. This irony was not lost on the men and they were quick to voice their protests to Serge. John stopped at the door before leaving and turned to face the men, "You can all piss and moan about it as much as you like but it doesn't matter. You are not to fuck around sit tight and wait for the word from me and Serge before you do anything." John closed the door behind him and began to walk down the stairs.

Moz went straight after him.

"Yes Moz?" John asked.

"Look John, I promise ya, promise ya now, I ain't gonna do nafink, nafink, alright. You ave my word on it. I just wanted ya t'know...that's all."

"Thanks Moz, and don't worry about anything it's all under control."

"We ain't gonna do nafink either boss," Adam interrupted, Steve's face just showing around Adam's shoulder. Steve desperately wanted to hiss out his Mutley laugh but knew that it would get him in trouble if he did. Having shown his head he hid behind Adam where he was free to at least make the right facial expression, if not the insidious noise. There was a pregnant silence. John and Adam looked at each other for a moment, a moment that passed Moz by, it somehow slipped beyond his senses.

"Thanks Adam. If only they were all like you guys. This...all this," John gestured a large and magnificent circle around himself, "it is all based on you two. You are the foundations of our power. And you Steve." Steve's head slid guiltily around the side of Adam. Steve's irreverent smile flashed for a moment and then he shrunk back behind Adam. "I'll be talking to the three of you very soon. If you have any problems talk to Serge." John went to carry on, and then checked himself he repeated, "If only they were all like you. Everything we have is built on you... ...I'll be in touch."

Chapter 19

The Telephone

The world, for Philip Masters, had become very flat; not just simply flat but depthless. There was no echo to be heard on this endless surface. There was only a deafening hush; a pervasive silence which numbed Masters to the marrow of his soul. It was as if the air was thick, difficult to negotiate, difficult to walk through, and it stifled sound. Everybody acted like a heavily painted mime; everything was silent and yet melodramatic. Masters felt that he was moving through a ghastly film frame by frame, in which people were purposely reticent, secretly plotting quiet tortures, but objects were loud and obnoxious and insulted you to your face, and then they laughed in histrionic paroxysms behind the hands of your ambitious inferiors.

Masters was naked. His dark olive skin was developing like photographic film, his form appearing to the eye slowly from the brilliant, and dazzling, white sheet that he was lying on like a polaroid. He was surrounded by female faces, each one benign enough, looking on with the "safe" intentions of the mother, or the grandmother, or the sister. He was safe amongst these women. They were not predatory. They were not men who he had to kill. They were not people who wanted to steal from him. They offered him a kind of sanctuary in the circular fortress that they made around him.

The telephone began its hammering tones. He rocked back and forth desperate to pick it up, desperate to stop the piercing ring that was causing him so much pain. The telephone appeared and he made as to pick it up with his right hand, but his arm suddenly locked tight. He concentrated on trying to move his arm but he could do nothing. He fell back trying to remove himself as far as he could from the excruciating noise of the ringing telephone. His mind, so focused on the repetitive ringing, could not control his body. He was no longer able to make the most infantile of movements; he could not so much as make an audible sound. All that he could do was stare upwards and above him at the figure of a woman, a tall giant woman who moved her hips in a soft slow circle. Masters was unable to move. He was down, down, down below, beneath this huge woman looking up from the secret, and protected, depths of her skirt. He could not tell where this woman had come from but he knew that he had immediately felt nauseous as soon as she had appeared. He could not see her face. He did not, or tried not to, recognize his torturess. The telephone was still ringing. He watched the hideous arabesque circle that her hips scored in their delicate but sickening motion. Then her hands appeared. They were unsettling company for Masters in his nest of safety. He watched them too. They fluttered around him like a brace of pure white cuckoos. The telephone was still ringing. He tried to struggle free. He tried to move but his mind was stuck in the pain of the telephone that was still ringing. The hands mocked him in their slow fanning rhythms. They forced him to look up as they began to remove the blank panties that he had sought not to notice. The telephone was still ringing. The hands removed the panties from the woman's crotch, slowly. Then as the blank panties descended down the tight thighs of this giant woman Masters felt a violent retching in his stomach. The black area that they circumscribed hovered above Masters like a stagnant miasma, a void of perception. The telephone was still ringing. The hands left the panties stranded half way down the thighs. This exacerbated Masters's nausea. He was left on the shelf of this void, hardly daring to look into it. His warm and secure haven had been contaminated. He, and his private thoughts, had been violated in his safe dark hole. And now he began to choke. The telephone was still ringing. He was lying on his back drowning. His cries for help were muted by the ringing telephone. He could not move the thick liquid the black liquid from his lungs. The woman above him lowered her giant frame closer and closer to him. Dark black crimson blood bubbled out from his mouth. Thick globules stained his skin and the white sheet. The lunar blood got thicker and heavier. The viscous fluid was gushing from his nostrils spilling into his mouth that could hold no more of the foul womanblood. The telephone was still ringing. The women in the circle turned inwards to watch him choke, sniggering and making strange faces at him. Traces of the blood stained his skin, covering him in more darkness. He was wet all over with the internecine broth of these dancing women. They moved in closer and closer. The telephone was still ringing. The women moved in closer and closer. The giant woman moved closer to him. The circle got smaller and smaller and smaller, constricting his breathing. His lungs began to burn. They were ready to burst and expurgate his intense fear; his personal ambivalent terrors. He could see the contorted faces of the women getting ever nearer. He tried to roll over but they surrounded him. Closing in. Closing in. It was about to happen. His being was taught, ready to split in two. It was now. It was now. He was tearing himself away from himself, soaked in blood, stained in his irrefutable sin...

He awoke. The telephone was still ringing. He was doused in his own steaming sweat. He was stuck to the bed and the bedclothes like a roach in a motel. A flash of scalding coldness shivered through his body. He looked around confused. The telephone stopped ringing. Someone was talking. It had been a dream a nightmare. He was very disorientated, dizzy, he tried to find something to hold onto, to steady himself, so that he could locate his centre. There was nothing at hand. He sat up feeling his sticky sweat making his skin clammy, and both hot and cold at the same time. It had been just a dream. A fantasy gone wrong. He was fine now. It had only been a dream, he told himself over and over again. He knew that dreams were supposed to be important. They were riddles that required deciphering. All that he had to do was think about it, work it out. It was like junior school algebra but with images instead of letters; it was as easy as that. He tried to remember what he had witnessed, but it was already distorted in his mind. He had already contrived to forget the too familiar thighs and buttocks of the giant woman. He had already substituted this writhing female with an octopus. Its crooked one eyed gaze became the mysterious and meaningless source of tempered horror. Its imperfect blots of ink, or perhaps its female blemish, and deep absorbent suckers were the only traces of the disturbed mind. Masters merely skipped over these details, allowing them to decompose without further contemplation, until all that remained was a silhouette of what he thought his dream, his fantasy, his nightmare, had been. It was all a lie even before he began his mindless algebra.

Masters remembered the telephone. He could hear Lisa's voice. He was certain that she was doing something behind his back. He was sure that she was scheming against him. He put on some shorts and walked out of his bedroom. He followed the voice stealthily padding forwards on his bare feet. He could hear Lisa's guilt in her meandering tones and lingeried words. He noticed tiny patches of dampness on the carpet each one succeeding the other, marking out the slut's footsteps. They were proof; proof of something and there was no doubt about that. He stopped outside the dining room, the room that the voice was coming from, the place where he had left the telephone. He crouched down to look through the crack in the door. His movement was swift, undetectable; crouching on his legs with his great arms straight out with his fingertips touching the floor. He held his head up, pointed his square jaw out at the world, and revealed his throat, swollen with misconception, poised to sing. He could see Lisa wrapped in a towel, another twisted around her head, speaking gleefully into the telephone. He thought about the man with the silvergrey hair, what was she talking to him about? How did they know each other? And if it wasn't him then who was it? Who had he got to make the phone call? Who else was working for him?

Lisa had heard the telephone ring and ring and ring, and had called out to Philip. When he did not answer, and the telephone had continued to ring, she had jumped out of the shower, thrown a couple of towels around herself and skipped along to find it. John was on the other end. She had been pleasantly surprised to hear his voice, the feeling seemed to be mutual. She remembered that he had been very charming, and after all he had introduced her to Philip, who she had fallen in love with. Besides that though he had always, even when they were at school together, treated her with kindness and respect. She was enjoying talking to him whilst wearing just a towel. She liked him a lot even though she had found the man of her dreams. There was no conflict between the two as far as she was concerned. John was more sociable, more fun loving, but he was not Philip. Philip was a man who did not have time for laughter. He was a handsome brute with a harshly defined chest and torso. He was a man, rash and bold and rude, but in control, and powerful. Lisa found Masters an irresistible turn on. He was like no man that she had ever met before. He did not fawn over her. He did not have strings of other women around him. He was good to her but he was not like some of the puppy dogs who, once having slept with her, became neurotic, totally paranoid, scared that she would leave them. When he made love to her it was out of this world. She knew that Philip loved her so much, and wanted her with a passion that was beyond his control, because he pleased himself. Other men when they stroked her body stroked their egos. They would push and pull to get at her clitoris, only wanting to assert themselves through her orgasm. And then talk about it afterwards as if she had probably never orgasmed before, how they had been entirely responsible for it rather than her favourite Brad Pitt fantasy that she loved to playback over and over again. They expected her to be eternally grateful. And when they parted company they acted as if they believed that she was upset. They thought that they were something special, maybe they thought that they had been the first to discover the female orgasm. She got none of this with Masters though. His passion was such that he had no time to consider her, or anything else. He would hold her in some interminable death grip and push himself into her abandoning everything except for his will and his instinct. He needed her, that was apparent enough. She had never known such physical muscular sex. Philip was different. He loved her like no other man. The story that he created was pure and perfect. He took her and held her. There was no need for words, or to push her clit as if she were an electrical power point. They existed together in a kind of primal glory.

Lisa enjoyed chitchatting to John. He was happy to be aroused by Lisa. It was surely better than talking to Masters. He was happy to have caught up with her again. He was pleased to hear that he, Masters, was helping her career. He was certain that she would move on sooner or later. Lisa was far too beautiful, too provocative to stay with Masters. He was quite obviously not up to the kind of competition that Lisa would attract. She was a great girl. She was a fantastic lover. She knew exactly how to please a man. It would be easy to become obsessed with her. She was a perfect distraction for him because any sane man would either be too busy in the bedroom to be anything other than impotent in business, or too busy trying to keep her happy, and too busy trying to keep the crowds of men from the door.

Lisa was curling a loose tendril of hair around her index finger not saying anything but suggesting her responses with ethereal sighs. She put down the mobile telephone and went to find Masters, who she thought must be in the bedroom. Masters watched her carefully put down the telephone and leave the room without noticing him. She was still wet, covered in beads of water. Her skin had seen the attention of rigorous soaps and sponges but as far as Masters was concerned she reeked of her dark filth. He stood up simian like, outraged at her betrayal with the telephone. He now knew who it was, and it did not matter, not now he had received confirmation from London. The evening, the whole ceremony, was set up for the weekend. He was going to get canonized. Then he was going to kill the queer and his nigger, or rather, he smiled to himself, he was going to have them killed, and probably by their own men. This bastard was on borrowed time, for once Masters could take some quiet satisfaction in talking on the telephone.

Lisa came running back into the room to tell John that she could not find Philip, but there he was standing in front of her; a colossal figure of masculinity. All of the charm and grace in the world could not make up for the magnetic attraction and mutual passion that existed between them. Of course John was a nice guy; he was not Philip though. He had none of Philip's isolated and terrible perfection. Philip was hers, and she was his, the evidence was undeniable. She shook with desire. She wanted him. She caught his attention and mouthed, "I am going to dry off." Lisa rubbed herself with the towel to demonstrate her message. Masters nodded unconcerned and continued to talk to John.

Lisa went back into the bathroom and applied hair serums, curl revivers, hair gel, eye gel, face packs, moisturizers, antiwrinkle creams, deep cleansers, body lotions, oils, depilatories, powders and perfume. She thought about Philip, why she thought that she loved him, and she considered the memories that speaking to John had triggered off. It was true that sex was powerful with Philip, but it was also a little primitive. This had been a part of the attraction, and she still craved his hard controlling lunges. She was under no illusions, so she thought. Their relationship needed to change, not drastically, but subtly. She liked the wild passion of Philip more than anything, but she, they, needed more than that. John was a considerate man. There were some things that Philip had yet to learn. He had to pay attention to her from time to time. Of this she was sure. She did not want to lose him. She could not bear to even allow the thought to cross her mind. She needed to mould him a little. She had to change him by making him want to change. She had to slow him down, show him new delights, and make him chase after them. She was partly to blame she decided. There had been too many dresses, too much skimpy black underwear. She had painted her lips too prominently. What was called for was a softer approach, gentle but suggestive persuasion. She had proved her point. She had got him. Now she had to polish her raw diamond. It had to be done with the slightest of pushes and the most exhilarating of rewards and incentives. She put on a bathrobe, tying it neatly around her waist. She looked at herself in the bathroom mirror as she blow dried her hair. Maybe she should start right now. Maybe she should go in there right now; let her bathrobe fall at her feet and step out towards him. He would be forced to look at her, forced to appreciate her, petrified by longing whilst in the middle of his conversation. That was not right though. He would let go of the telephone and would be carried away by his passion. No, it had to be something uninviting, something he could not be a part of. She had to force him to sit back, distance himself, so that he could see clearly how to move on to the next stage of their love affair. She would sit with him, even if he protested and she would touch herself. She would open her legs very slightly, just enough so that he could see her pearly finger nail on her clitoris; stroking herself. The robe would be only ever so tenderly parted so that a person had to be standing in a certain privileged position in order to be aware of what was happening. Yes, she would show him. She would tutor him in the kind of love that she needed from time to time.

Masters was enjoying telling the queer specific times, dates, and venues. He revelled in the notoriety of the names of the people who would be there. All John, the queer shit, could offer were congratulations. This meant that he was absolutely gutted. He had lost and he knew it. They had completely overlooked him in favour of Masters. How it must piss him off. Masters was very content. He had even got the girl. She might be a pain in the arse slut but he had got her, and every man that came in contact with her wanted her. She was a trophy. She was a representation of his power and influence. To be the best, to have the most, you had to show the most, spend the most. Whatever went out was as important, at times more important, than what came in. He, Masters, was considered to be the best. He was on top, and everybody, including John, knew all about it. It, he, was right in their fucking faces.

Lisa walked into the room wrapped this time in a bathrobe. She sat right in his line of vision. she seemed to be scratching. The dirty bitch had probably got some undesirable rash or was infested with some parasite, something that served as retribution for her disgusting activities. He could see her hand through her robe that was opened an inch or two. She was moving her fingers back and forth across, what he thought was, her pelvic bone. Slowly she tilted her head back and made sick silent faces. She made no sound but her chest heaved and her lips puckered as if she were going to cry out in pain at any moment.

Lisa began selfconsciously, a little afraid, but it got easier and more enjoyable. She had only ever done this a couple of times before, never exhibiting herself, it had always been alone. She had intended to entice Masters but now she was finding intrinsic pleasure. She had begun to do it for herself, concentrating on what she liked. She felt herself leapfrog plateau after plateau of pleasure and aroused excitement. She closed her eyes and kept going even when she told herself that she should stop. She did not want to stop. She forgot all about Masters and her plan. She lost herself to herself. She rubbed her clitoris until it pulsed, and then teased herself with long firm strokes using the entire length of her fingers. She had never before realised the gift of herself. She had not thought of her own worth, not understood the power of control. She had made herself into an ecstatic circle of bliss.

Masters was outraged. She was pestering him again. What was she trying to prove? He fucked her whenever he had to, and now she wanted more, like this. She was perverse. How much more evidence was required. She was a sick slut; there was no other alternative charge. He was going to have to do it again. He was being forced. He had no choice. She was a damned witch who he despised. She was a part of the life. She was an unfortunate necessity. Now he had to prove again that he was capable of fucking her. He had to prove it to her and the queer. What had they been talking about together? What devious plot were they incubating? This depraved show of the most obscene form of self-appropriation was a challenge he had to meet. He was too close now to be put off. He had made too many sacrifices to give up now, and one more sacrifice, however repulsive, however repugnant and loathsome, would have to be performed. He felt the blood curdle in his veins. He put the telephone down and rushed reluctantly over to her. Lisa's hand was grasped and moved away. His grip was biting and he had caused her to accidentally graze the skin on her inner thigh with her nails. He pushed her down hard on to the table and her spine soon became sore on the flat wooden top. Lisa's elbows hurt, her pelvis hurt, on the completely flat surface. Masters forced her legs open as he always did. He pulled his shorts down knowing all too well of the dreadful dance he was to perform. He held her shoulders down, forcing her shoulder blades onto that unforgiving table. Lisa was shocked. The pleasure that she had found for herself had been taken. It was dissipating, draining from her body. Where to? She felt no excitement as she usually did. She wanted herself back. He seemed to be so unaware, so unconvincing, when compared to her own sensitivity. He was hurting her. His weight was too much. The telephone, which she had not expected Masters to put down, was ringing again. John presumed that they had been cut off as he was in mid-sentence when the telephone went dead. He was calling back. It was ringing now, and again, and again.

"Philip...no...please..."

(RINGRING)

"Please Philip...no....the telephone...no Philip..."

"Okay Philip...let's go into the bedroom...let's go...let me go...let me go...."   (RINGRING)

"No...stop...stop...the telephone..."

"No! No! You have to have a condom...no Philip no..."
(RINGRING)

Lisa tried to push him off. She strained herself. She tried to look for herself again to find the resources to throw Masters off. She began to feel responsible. She had brought this on herself, she could see that. He was trying to get inside her. And she knew that he was only following the pattern that they had forged since they met, but it was not good enough now. It did not fit, she wanted something better. She could not see his face, only his chest and neck. He was far too tall to make eye contact with her. The telephone was still ringing. Lisa did not want to ruin it for herself. She did not want to hurt Philip. This would be the last time. She began to move herself on him trying to make it end quickly.

Masters, he was sure, was doing what she wanted. He was proving to her and the telephone that he was strong, that he would not falter now. He would do whatever he had to do. His fingers pressed blue bruises into her flesh wherever they clasped her. He had succeeded. He had turned his lowest point into a victory. He continued in his reckless act, chilled to his nerve endings, revolted by her inane mutterings of sex. He moved himself to a conclusion. The telephone was still ringing. She had tried to involve herself with him. She had tried to engage his interest in her. He had not given her a second glance. He had not so much as kissed her. She held on waiting for the end, and he grimaced and looked straight ahead telling himself that soon, very soon, it would all be over.

Chapter 20

The Bishop's Mission

Serge was in his office above the florists waiting for Adam. It was an empty room. There were no pictures on the walls. The furniture consisted of plastic backed institutional chairs and an old desk. There was no typewriter, no computer, no paper work or filing cabinets, just an electric heater and a small push button telephone. Serge was wearing a starched white shirt and black narrow leg trousers. He was a handsome man. A man who commanded respect. He had been working with John for nearly seven years now, and they had been friends for even longer. The two of them had had some great times but they both agreed that it was important to get out now. Masters was too much of a flunk. He was totally unpredictable, simply too dangerous to work with. There was no way that they were going to get nicked for his carelessness, and if the police did not get to them then sooner or later someone was going to take a pop at them. They didn't need that shit. It was definitely time to get out, to retire.

He had started the runs to Amsterdam with John. They had formed a sound working partnership and remained friends throughout. He often remembered some of the capers they'd been involved in, and when he did his handsome black face broke out in an involuntary smile. They had single handedly taken control of the drug traffic from Amsterdam to this area. They had made pots of money. It had been one great adventure. John's face had fronted the operation because his face was white like most of the men, but they were equal partners, and Serge was pleased that he did not really have much to do with that collection of lowlifes. For a while they had both been blasted on chemicals, E's and coke mostly, and money, and success, but they had pulled themselves out of it and only dabbled from time to time these days. Serge, every now and then, still liked to lock himself up in a hotel room for the weekend with some decent coke, a little bit of smoke, and a wicked blonde or a talented West Indian lady. He even did that less and less though.

Over the last four or five years they had not been involved in any runs. They paid people to do that, and Harry had everything under control on the other end. When John first met Harry it had been a worrying time. Love could fuck with you at the best of times, and John and Harry were not your usual couple. John had managed to keep a grip and things had moved along smoothly. The more runs that were made the richer they became, and the richer they became the less hands on involvement was required. Whilst they could both be implicated in a whole number of crimes neither of them had actually, physically speaking, got their hands dirty for quite some time. These had been the easy years, but they had worked hard for them. They were still in danger every minute of the day, and probably even more so at night, in the dark. The problem was the easier it got, the more power that they got, the more complacent they became, the easier it would be to get to them

A lot of their money was tied up in clubs, bars, restaurants and cafes. Leaving the life and the area would prove to be difficult. They could not just up and leave. There were too many people with an interest in their business, and besides neither of them could get at all of their money without dealing with people, psychos, who would be left in the lurch if John and Serge disappeared without leaving their connections on the continent with someone. No they were leaving but they were going to do it right. They were going to do the right thing by everyone. They were making sure that they did not owe anybody anything. When they left there would be no comeback.

Serge was waiting for Adam so that he could instruct him on his last mission. Adam did not know of their plans to leave the life, nobody did. They had already put the first part of their plan into action when John had gone up to Birmingham to meet

Hanif. A working factory in your own country eliminated the risks that always existed when you had to cross national borders. Masters was probably already working to squeeze their Dutch contacts out of the people who did the runs. Zak had gone missing, and so had his boyfriend Stuart. Masters could take over the traffic as soon as he got his London endorsement and where would that leave them? Serge had quickly realised that it was the end for them one way or another. John had taken some convincing, not because he doubted him, but because John had always loved the life so much. They were going out to St. Lucia to stay with Serge's family. Serge was going to settle out there. John was going to take a long holiday and then decide what to do with himself from there. In the meantime they were sitting on a huge pile of stuff that had been delivered by Hanif's men. Things were going to get very hot on the borders for a while. They were going to sit on it and sit on it until Masters was at breaking point and then they would sell out and split. In the meantime they owed something to their Amsterdam connections, Harry would sort that out, and then there was Adam. He looked like the person who was most likely to benefit from all of this, and they certainly owed him too. They had to keep him in the dark as well as the others. They had one last task for him to perform, one last favour, before they paid him off.

Adam and Moz had been their two greatest successes. Moz had the respect of the old guard. He kept them in line; and once they realised that they were being treated well by Serge and John there had been no complaints. Adam commanded everybody's fear. The old timers liked him and his straight forward intimidation. The new kids looked up to him, and just about everybody was shit scared of him. He could not be held back, not anymore, and he was such an essential member of the team that they allowed him to freelance. He was their man, Adam had always expressed the fact that he was their man, but he was too good to keep to themselves without risking offending other large operators, and so they allowed him to work for other people too. He helped out Masters with specific problems. He knew a lot of important people in London, and had made himself popular with his gifts and his efficiency.

Serge thought about Adam Bishop for a moment. What did he know about him? He liked coke. He virtually ate steroids. He was one big motherfucker. He practised auto-erotic asphyxiation, and always wanted to loan out videos on the subject to anyone in earshot. He had a sleazy porn business, that Serge found distasteful, but there's always someone willing to get involved in that filth. Recently there had been rumours that he was also involved in some kind of child pornography ring. John had gone mad when he heard but with no proof, they could not question Adam, not without raising his suspicions, there was nothing that they could do. He, apparently, had COBRA tattooed on his dick. He knew some woman at a nearby university who helped him to grow grass, but that was a small time operation. He ran around with Steve Vickering; a runtish factotum who looked, and acted, as if he had spent all of his life in the vacuous selfmade dungeon of sexual frustration. Serge had dealt with Adam as little as possible. Serge did not like him, and it was obvious that he did not like Serge too much either.

There were footsteps on the stairs. Serge stood up looked through the slits in the blinds and saw Adam's BMW, the black one, parked out back next to his own Mercedes. The door opened and he walked in. It did not matter how many times you met Adam you were always taken back for a moment by his immense size and this time was no different. Serge motioned to Adam to take a seat. Adam turned the chair around defiantly and sat on it so that he could rest his arms on what was supposed to be the back rest. He stared straight at Serge who began to speak.

First of all thanks for coming Adam. I know that John usually briefs you on any assignments, but what I'm going to ask of you today is a little different. John thinks, well he's decided, that he's too close to this one. He doesn't want to know about it; he just wants it done. He needs someone that he can rely on, someone that he can trust, someone who can do the job.

An tha samone is me right?

That's right Adam, although we think that Steve should go along with you as added support. You two are, after all, the finest partnership this side of The Old Kent Road... (Adam sat up, he was enjoying this)...Now we need to cleanse our operation. With Masters taking over we've got to show him that we can deliver the goods. If you like we're vying for a new contract. We can't afford to let Masters down. So we want to make our first delivery double safe and so that's why we want you to go...to Amsterdam.

Amsterdam!

I know, I know, you don't do runs anymore. We're...er John's not asking you to do the run. He wants you there for security. Our usual runners will take the risks. You'll be there for extra security like I've said, and there's one other favour that John wants to ask... But, before I go any further, have you heard from Zak, or have you heard anything about him?

Nafink, nafink a all. E's problee wiv Fat Stuart the Paff samwhere, yeah they're problee doin a caple ov rent boys as we speak. (Adam laughs appreciating his own little joke)

Well yes... If you do hear anything we need to see them as soon as possible. You see we can't afford to lose our best runner like that, and we certainly can't afford to lose another one. That's why we need you to just oversee the whole shipment.

Wot's this other fing then?

Well, I was just getting to that. I know, and so does John, that there's been a lot of talk about him recently. There's a lot of bullshit floating around about him and Harry. Well first of all you'll be working with Harry.

I'll finally get ta mee im?

You'll finally get to meet Harry that's right. Harry's got a lot of good connections out there. Harry knows what's going on. You see Adam we want you to know the whole operation. We think its time that we moved you up. It's time that you joined us at the top of the pyramid. (Adam is obviously shocked by this, he tries to show his appreciation through his perplexed frown)

Oh...fanks...err...fanks...Serge mate I danno wot t'say...

Of course it all depends on how this little matter goes, but we don't foresee any problems, and John has asked me to let you know that you'll be receiving double your usual rate, a gesture of our goodwill, recognition for all the services that you've offered over the last five years.

Fanks...fanks a lot. Like I say Serge, I jast donno wot t'say...

The thanks are from John, Adam. Now the other thing. There's this girl, a cheap bitch, whose been running off her mouth. She's fucked on smack most of the time and we want rid of her.

My pleasure...

Well it's a delicate thing Adam. Not only can we not afford for there to be any link between us and the girl, we are also very aware that the police could easily ask a few questions and make the link with the import business we've got going, if you catch my drift. There's one other thing. She can't just disappear. You see John used to have a thing going with her. It's a very sensitive issue with him. He wants her to have a proper grave, a proper funeral. He wants to know nothing about the details of her...accident...He's got himself all wound up about it. He's scared that if she doesn't go into the ground with a proper funeral that she'll come back to haunt him or something. He can't quite settle this with his conscience you understand. I thought, and I'm only suggesting this to you Adam, that we could bring back the serial killer...you know make it look like some sicko pervert had just grabbed a random person and you know...

Yeah I do. (Adam smiled at the memories that it brought back for him)

Adam used to really enjoy the hits, and to confuse the police he liked to fuck around with the corpses, so that they thought that it was the work of some anonymous, isolated, serial killer. He kept up the work, making the victims appear to be random people who just happened to be in the wrong place at the wrong time. The victims were supposed to be canvases, as is the fashion, for a sick form of art. The police never even got a sniff.

Well John is adamant that she is not to be harmed in that way, not until she's dead, and then, well then, you've got to do whatever you've got to do. He wants her done cleanly, no unnecessary pain. After that it's up to you to make sure that the police are lead to believe that its the work of a depraved mind. (The police had been so utterly convinced of this in the past because Adam loved his work so much, it was convincing because he was motivated, it was convincing because it was authentic, it was as if Adam were born for the part, and if not he had definitely been socialized into the part) But remember not until she's passed away.

Course, course...(Adam was getting erect, his mind was already remembering, thinking up new ideas, new dramas, to play out with the victim)...who is it?

You'll meet Harry here. (Serge hands Adam a piece of paper with a date, time, and place on) You'll also be picking up the girl in this country. When you meet Harry you'll be put in the picture.

Ang on a sec. This is fer this weeken...wot about Masters's big do ap in Landon?

John's sorry about you having to miss it Adam, but this is urgent, there's nobody else who can do a job like this. Masters's big welcome party is going to be something, but this is the most important shipment in years. This is your chance to make it big. We want you, as our new partner, to reacquaint yourself with our people out there, and meet our new colleagues. Come on Adam what do you say?

I ain' gonna let ya down now. Course I'll do it, an I'll make sure that Steve cams along too.

Good we've always had perfect results with anything we've asked the two of you to do. Now the girl's going to be bringing the gear back through customs. She's not to be touched until she's back, safe and sound, on British soil, okay?

No problem Serge.

Good. I want you to call me as soon as it's over. I'll put John's mind at rest. And while you're gone I'll sort out everything you need for your new role. John will come and see you and he's going to be working on the thing, you know the thing we spoke about, the thing over in India. He's going to be working on the proposal for the club in London that you've already put to me, and we're very confident that we can put that through. Adam this is the beginning of something very very special...

Later on, in his car, on his mobile telephone, Adam is speaking to Steve.

Yeah...ironik innit...

Ha, haaa...We'll be back on the Sandee. We go over on Fridee night...

Danno mate...

If we get back late on Sandee...get rarnd t'see em in the early ours of Mandee mornin we'll jast be in time to watch the black barstard enjoy a nice lime barth...

Yeah an' it'll be is larst...Too right...fackin pissin meself I'll tell ya...

Chapter 21

Lust

The prominent V-cleft on the heads of frogs and toads has, throughout history, been identified with the external features of the female reproductive organ. The frog and toad have become universally accepted manifestations of female fertility. The wide, open, mouth of the frog is symbolic of the vagina, swallowing up life and all of its pulsing hardness, and spitting out death and all of its limp impotence.

The skin of the creature splits down the hunched spinal column, and up from its underside. The frog or toad then swells and shrinks its body making the skin stretch and snap. It is then sucked off and eaten, peeling away from the body with a perfect symmetry. The old frog is quickly eaten by the new frog. It is reborn from its death, playing out the ancient cycle of birth death rebirth. In this way the frog offered the ancient peoples a perfect synthesis of the trials of life.

The female sex organ, the pudendum, female sexuality, fertility, orgasm, are all things that have been scaring men shitless ever since Eve realised there might be someone else around who could offer her some action. And who was it that put the idea in her head as she slept? Satan. And how did he make his lusty approach? You might have been led to believe that he writhed around in his snake suit, playing the cunning serpent. You might even believe that he crawled around the Garden of Eden in his finest black leather thong and silver studded dog collar. He did not do either of these two things. According to the great poet John Milton, in *Paradise Lost*, he was:

> Squat like a toad, close at the ear of Eve,
> Assaying by his devilish art to reach
> The organs of her fancy, and with them forge
> Illusions, as he list, phantasms and dreams.

Eve lay sleeping whilst our Bufonine friend, soon to be the living motif of female lust, reached down with his damp webbed digits to "The organs of her fancy", and whispered a few smutty observations into her ear. It does not say much for Adam, living in Eden, total paradise, no work, no hardship, just him and his mate, and he lets her fall asleep with enough energy, and desire, left in her tight fertile body and soul that she could be brought off by a toad. A toad, can you believe it, all slime and warts. The poor cow, she must have been desperate.

Chapter 22

Lisa's Plan

Okay, fine, she admitted it to herself. She had been wrong, terribly wrong. It had been her first attempt and she had got it wrong, but she was a big enough person to hold her hands up and come clean with herself. At least she had learnt something.

It had been about time that she took control. She had been entertained by men's narratives often enough, and not all of them had been good, not all of them had had the desired effect. They had all learnt from experience and that was what she had to do. She could not blame Philip. She had been far too provocative. What man, or woman, worth their salt, if in love with her, could have reacted in a different way? She would not make the same mistake again though.

She had made the first step. She was taking responsibility for herself. She was no longer just a face in someone else's narrative. She was the author of her own story, and next time she would do better than last time. She was not going to lose him, no way. She begun to look inside herself to see what the problem might be. She was also making efforts to accommodate Philip, and the things that he enjoyed. She had started to look at the frogs. At first she thought them slimy and hideous but now she was starting to see their beauty. Philip was always picking them up. She had even overheard him talking to them once but she could not make out what he was saying to them. If they were so important to him then she would at least learn to appreciate them. She did not think that she would ever be able to bring herself to pick one of them up, but still...

Her mind went back to the first time that they had made love. It had been wonderful. It was like nothing that she had experienced before. There was no performance, it had been pure emotion. Oh how she loved him. She could never make him see what a wonderful thing it was that he had done for her. She would try though. She had been walking around blaming him for not taking his time to love her as he should. Well it was not his fault. She could see that now. She had been flaunting herself around the place, all flimsy dresses, short skirts, tight blouses, silk underwear and high high heels. All of that hadn't just been for show. She liked to look glamorous, but it had been too much. How could he love her like that? She could see it all so plainly now. He was only reacting to her.

She had not been offered any modelling, but Philip was trying to work something out for her. The thing was she did not care. She did not care about it. She was not getting any younger. She had not quite made it yet and she could not help thinking that by the time it would take from now to get established she would be too old. Lisa had felt obliged to make something up to John just because he had spoken to her as if he were responsible for her, as if he were waiting for her to tell him that Philip was in some way mistreating her. She had made something up to appease John. She did not care if she never got work again. She felt that now she had met Philip she could forget about all of those ambitions. She had him now and she was happier than ever.

It was his big night on Saturday. She was going to make him proud. She was about to go shopping for her outfit. Philip had arranged for a driver to take her wherever she wanted to go. He thought of everything. She had a picture in her mind of what she was going to wear. It had to be in a pacifying white, or soft cream, and it had to be a soft comforting fabric, something that you could snuggle up to. A creamy cashmere dress would be perfect. She would buy shoes with only a gentle heel, and if it what was what he wanted she would wear tights, no more stockings, she would risk thrush for this one night, just for him. It was time for modesty. It was time to think of someone else for a change. She was going to make this thing work. She was tired of all the games, now that she had met someone who loved her, truly loved her, she was not going to lose him. She felt as if she had been waiting for this man all of her life, and now she had something, someone, to work for. They were connected, linked together by indissoluble ties. They had made love time and time again. The first time and the last time they had not even used a condom; that had been a part of the initial thrill of self-abandonment. They had both thrown their bodies at the other and cast the consequences into hell. What did they care. It was as if as soon as they had met they had known each other, as if they had always known each other, and they had risked everything in order to make their point to one another. Now she thought about it she understood what had happened. He had tried to recapture that moment again, for her. She could be pregnant, in fact she was due on any day. She would just sit and wait for the time being. There was no need to worry, not now she had Philip. There was another thing though, something she had thought about last night whilst lying next to his heaving body. She knew nothing about him, well she knew about the important things, she could tell how he felt about her, sometimes the absence of words, the missing details of a story, made it all the more poignant. She knew nothing of his past though. He did not like to talk about his family. He was protective that was natural enough. She did not know about his past loves, past relationships. She knew as little about him now as when they had cemented their fates together in that first meeting, their first reckless, but defining, union. Now what? She might have AIDS. The thought had crossed her mind several times. It was something that you had to think about in her line of work. There was always casual sex being offered. You had to be careful, but even with these thoughts in her mind she felt safe. The last time she had had unprotected sex had been with her boyfriend of the time's boss at his firm's Christmas Party 1991, and the time before that, well she could not remember that, it had been a lifetime ago. She had been pretty careful... She told herself that she was in no danger from Philip, and if she were pregnant then so be it; they had called on, no they had invited, the forces of life to grip them, seize them, and do as they would. She did not regret a thing.

    She went over to the window and pulled the curtain back just enough so that she could see if the driver was waiting; he was. She could see him leaning against the car smoking, he snapped out the end of his cigarette and looked up. Lisa waved and nodded her head, she was ready. She grabbed a jacket and her handbag. Philip had told Jimmy, the driver, that she was to have whatever she wanted. He was so good to her. She felt guilty for being so demanding of him. She was going to make it all up to him though. She swung her handbag over her shoulder and made downstairs for the car. She loved shopping. This was going to be a great day...

As soon as the door had closed, and Lisa had stepped outside, Masters entered the room. He too went to look out of the window. He could see her getting into the car. He stepped back out of view. He was safe now behind the curtain. He had made a small protective pod with his two palms and now he opened them very slightly to uncover a small but distinctive black and red frog. It sat quite still, unmoving. Masters dragged his tongue along its back and then flicked it repeatedly across its head, pressing his tongue into the sharp Vcleft high up between its eyes. It was so sweet to him, so immaculate. This was the room that he had been sharing since Lisa arrived. He was showing it all to his amphibian familiar. He was moving silently around and around trying to look at, and show the frog, everything at once. He tapped the hollows in the walls where he had the guns hidden, each one was dormant, resting beneath the thin wallpaper, but ready to be fired at any moment. Masters felt some relief during the split seconds in which he touched these small hideouts.

The room smelt very differently these days. It set something off inside his head. A memory; a memory that he believed but which he did not know if he remembered. He had believed in this memory, that he was now recalling, believed in it longer than anything that he could remember. He felt the presence of his mother in the sweet smelling woman things that surrounded him. He looked around at the room. It was orderly and tidy and it was full of her. He opened drawers and found piles of soft-woman garments, pink and white. He looked at the neat rows of makeup on top of the chest of drawers that Lisa was using as a makeshift dressing table, on which a small adjustable mirror stood persistently reflecting a panel of silver-white light on the ceiling. Masters showed his companion its reflection. It stared at itself irresolutely, before anxiously plodding its tiny bulk away across his palm. "How beautiful you are my child," Masters' deep grating voice shattered the brittle silence. He sorted through her various cosmetics until he found a small pot. It was like a miniature urn and inside was a smooth sticky translucent pink coloured something, sweet smelling and sickly, difficult to eat, and surreptitious. Masters did not read the label which would have told him that it was Lip Balm. He smeared it on his teeth, and tongue, and lips, and chin, until his face glistened and became hot. His eyes glanced across the rows of lipsticks and selected a pink-woman coloured hue which he applied with juvenile laughter. He painted thick broken lines across his mouth and he laughed, and he licked his teeth and lips tasting their indigestibly sweet pungency. If only she could see him now. He could never tell what she wanted. He had been a confused child, and what had she done but disturb his confusion, exacerbate it, and force him to go beyond the curtain. Here he was again looking for the curtain that had both saved him and prevented him from ever entering the other side, from unlocking the attic. He heard a voice, footsteps. It was happening again. He stood frozen for a moment transfixed on the threshold of time, ready to shrink from her wrath, ready to become that criminal of perception once more. He broke from his stillness and hid in the white fitted wardrobe. He squatted amongst the soft woman garments looking through the dark at his precious frog. They were still again, unmoving to the sounds that cut through their makeshift hideaway.

Lisa had forgotten her tampax holder. She did not feel that she was going to need it but you could never be sure. The missing lip balm and lipstick went unnoticed. She did not think that she had left her drawer open but Jimmy was waiting... She quickly felt around in the corners until she found it. She checked to see if it was loaded...fine... Masters pulled himself inwards, squatting closer to the ground, putting his chest on his knees trying to make himself disappear. The pink lip balm and lipstick that he had swallowed, that he was swallowing more and more of, began to work against one another, his stomach jolted with severe cramps, and noiseless retches. He began to sweat. Then he realised that he had been sweating for some time. He could see himself sweating. He could see her watching him now, and he could see her watching him then. She had made him hers, encouraged his passive surrender, only to accuse him of something terrible later on, much later on, like now. He could hear her speaking, calling him back from his memory, from his belief, to his childhood. He had not taken this much before. Perhaps the animal in him had known that too much would make him sick; perhaps the human in him had known that too much would get him caught, caught again. He was fighting for control of himself, trying to prevent the vomiting that was sure to follow. Lisa closed the drawer without consideration for him, allowing a mean high scratching sound to tear through the air and settle caustically in the pit of his twisted stomach. Lisa snatched her tampax holder and rushed out to the stairs, not wanting to keep Jimmy waiting.

Masters squatted there for some time, content in his pink woman smelling obscurity beyond the thinning curtain. He drew more pink lines across his face. He swallowed more of its, and the lip balm's, pungent sweetness. He waited for her to scold him, but he had not seen her for so long. How could she know? How could he know? He could only believe.

Chapter 23

The Pick Up

There is a bright blue sky overhead, not a cloud in sight. It is about eight o'clock in the evening. Adam and Steve are sitting in Adam's BMW, not in the black one with the pictures and magazine cut-outs stuck everywhere, but the metallic grey one. They are parked on a supermarket car park, waiting for Harry. They are both very excited at the prospect of their latest job. They have found it difficult, impossible even, to talk about anything else. They have, for once, differing opinions on how they should proceed with their task, and have been debating for some time. Adam wants to do one thing, and Steve another. Adam is in the driving seat. He turns to Steve.

Adam: This is gonna be the best job we've ever dan...Wot could be betta? I don' care what you fink...It's jast gotta be dan...

Steve: It ain' worf it Bish...too risky...forensik tests n'all tha...It's too risky I'm tellin ya...

Adam: Well I'll av to be careful won' I. You carn expck me t'turn me nose ap at the charnce to fack the boss's bird...cam on be realistic...specially as the boss ain' gonna be ararnd fer mach longa. This is the oppachunity of a lifetime innit.

Steve: Bat they'll av records n'tha'...It's mach safer if you wait till she's dead, pat the clin'filwm rarnd 'er, 'n then do wot cams natrally, n' when it's all ova we can jast dispose ov the clin'filwm. Averwise they're gonna know too mach abou' ya. These scientists they can do fackin anyfink these days ya know. You could be givin 'er sam dick right enaff a bit ov air or samink falls off ya, jast a bit of air tha's all they need these days, and they pick it ap, do sam tests n' tha'...nex' fing ya know fackin bang! they got ya. They know abou ya DNA n'all tha', wot ya look like, 'ow many inches ya packin, wotever they want'a fackin know. Clingfilwm's alwight...it ain' tha' bad...It's betta than when we used t'jast wrap 'em ap in black bin liners...at least you'll be able t'see 'er...Anyway, if you arsk me it's more fan when they're dead innit...

Adam: You ain' bin listinin av ya...First ov all its sam bird tha' John's been knockin' off...'E ain' been doin' er in clingfilwm 'as 'e...I wan 'er live mate, I've gotta do it. Doin' the boss's bird is one fing right...bat fink abou' it...

Steve: I carn stop fackin finkin abou' it...an' it ain worf it I'm tellin ya...

Adam: 'Ow can you sit there an' say tha'?...'Ow can ya? 'E don't even like birds as a rule...everyone knows tha'...so its gotta be a decent piece'a cant ain' it?

Steve: Bish mate don' tach it, don' fackin tach it...If that homo's been all ova 'er I dread to fink wot she might av. Let's jast bamp er off, wrap er ap, give er one, (he pauses so that they can both say, or rather shout, together: "I'd give 'er anava n'all, wahey!) n'then jast piss abou' a bit...ya know cat off 'er nipples...cam on you always like tha'...'Ow abou' we cat off 'er 'ead, keep it wiv ass for a few extra days, jast t'make you 'appy...Cam on Bish...I've brought the camcorda...it'll be a laugh...

Adam: Look Steve I ain' arguin wiv ya, alwight (raises his eyebrows and puts up his hand)... I jast want'a do 'er long 'n 'ard...give 'er a really goodun jast so she knows wot she's been missin all this time...then bang!, no messin...

Steve: Wot abou' this 'Arry geezer? Wot abou' if he finds out? 'E knows she ain' s'posed to be facked...not while she's still alive anyway.

Adam: Fack 'im...Wot's 'e gonna do abou' it?

Steve: Well all I mean is 'e's an anknown quaniee ain' 'e. 'E might be alwight abou' it then again 'e might not. We ought'a sass 'im out first n'tha'. Let's pick 'im ap...'E'll tell ass where to go next right...so let's sound 'im out...see wot 'e's gotta say abou' 'er..

pick 'er ap from whereva...an' then play it from there...It makes sense don' it?

Adam: Look Steve fack 'im...'E might be alwight...'e might not...either way wot do we care...'E ain' gonna fack about wiv the two of ass is 'e...So wot else is 'e gonna do...tell John, tell the fackin Golly Wog...I don' fink so...'An anyway so wot if 'e dass, both ov 'em'll be dead soon...We'll problee, wot... see 'em again once more t'pick ap payment, then wot? They ain' gonna be ararnd for mach longer...Phil is 'avin is fing in Landon tommorra...it's all ova for 'em...Besides Serge is obviously really jealous ov 'er ain' 'e...I mean if old Johnny Boy's been servin' the cock to this bird then Serge ain' gonna be none to pleased...If you fink abou' it we'd be doin' 'im a favour...You carn please evEryone right, so we might as well please our fackin selves...

They look around the car park, waiting with caimanine patience, commenting on various people that they see; pointing out specific women who walk past, alone, with their families, with their loved ones. They verbally fantasize about these women, what they would do to them, how they would use the camcorder. They make no allowances for looks, or age, or children, or race, or disabilities. There is nobody who is not a potential target. Unbeknown to the people, coming and going with their loved ones, they are all at some time covered by the cross of the gunsights, the wicked imaginations of these two monsters.

A woman starts to walk into view. She is walking parallel to the lines of parked cars. Once or twice the headlights of reversing cars illuminate her figure. At such times it is possible to see her comfortable gait; the ease at which she carries a large holdall and a suitcase. She makes great strides in her pale grey pin striped trouser suit. The jacket fastens up high and she has a silk scarf knotted around her neck. She moves with an underestimated sinewy strength, gritting her teeth and moving, searching onwards. When she recedes back from the headlights she merges quickly with the darkness, her face and your memory of it making no image on the screen of your mind. Her lithe steps and ethereal body clashes with her firm handling of the holdall and suitcase. She goes unnoticed by everyone, and then...

Steve (pretending to be holding a microphone up to his mouth, imitating a sport commentator's intonation): An' there goes a nice piece a cant, and anava, and anava, they're all out today mate...

Adam (playing along with Steve): They certainly are...There's a lavlee piece to our right jast bendin' over t'pat the shoppin' in the boot...quite remarkable I'd say Steve...

Steve: Well spotted Mr. Adam Bishop...lavlee indeed but she'd look a lot more camfortable wiv half a roll of marskin' tape wrapped ararnd 'er wrists an' ankles and then slang in the back of our motor...

Adam: Nice fought, very nice fought my friend...bat don' you fink tha' you should take the precaution of gaggin' the dirty bitch before slingin' 'er in the motor?

Steve: Ho, ho, ho, you're right again Mr. Bishop, that's simply marvellous, a fine observation...She looks as though she'd gag on twelve inches...what's your opinion?

Adam: Oh perfect readin' ov the siuayshon Mr. Vickerin'...absolutely spot on...

Steve: Well there's a lavlee piece a' cant approachin' at two o'clock, check it out, an' it's over to you Adam...

Adam (discarding the commentary): I do like that...I fackin do...I gotta say mate I still lav the challenge ov a bird, you know, intelligen' n' tha'...sexy bitch tha' one...

Steve (persisting with the commentary, holding his pretend microphone under Adam's chin): Could you jast ran fru' tha' wiv ass Adam Bishop...(Steve hisses out his Mutley laugh, he was enjoying himself)

Adam: You can see it on 'er face, fackin sexy bitch...Wearin' a suit n'that' ya can tell she's an intelligen woman, profeshionul like...you can tell cass she's wearin trarsers...I lav t'fack yappies, nafink betta...

The woman in the pale grey suit continues along her narrow locus, looking simultaneously at everyone and no one. Adam and Steve provoke increasingly disgusting violent fantasies from one another, all of which include them and this woman. Then another target comes into sight and their attentions are switched to a couple of older ladies in their late fifties early sixties, they laugh at the women having restarted their perverse commentary. The back door of the car suddenly opens and the woman in the pale grey suit dumps her holdall and suitcase on the back seat, and quickly joins them herself. The mirth that had allowed her to take Adam and Steve by surprise has now vaporized. They change their pace like ancient reptiles moving from relaxed loose inertia to sharp slick predacious movements. They both turn on a reflex, leaning over into the back seat, both of them have their hands on guns that they have concealed underneath their jackets. They stare for a moment as their minds process the information that has crept up on them. The woman in her mid to late twenties has cropped brown hair, white unblemished skin, slim well defined, but unobtrusive, features, and razor sharp cheekbones. She bats her eyelashes affectedly and disarmingly smiles at them both.

Adam: Swee'art I fink you've jast read my mind...

She began to speak. Her tones were placated, neutral, well controlled. She spoke using English vocabulary and phrases, but a thin trace of east coast America could be detected in her accent, but this was far from obvious. It would take Adam and Steve several hours in her company and at least two private discussions between themselves before they would work this out, or at least make some kind of guess. The woman, making a point of turning away from Adam, looked exclusively at Steve saying that she was told to meet them here, that they all had business in Amsterdam. She addressed Steve as Adam, and Steve once more let off his Mutley laugh.

Adam (Adam and Steve look at each other a little confused but slowly the realisation that this was the intended victim caused a sinister smile to form on Adam's lips, and Steve to hiss his laugh): Right...right...sorry lav, we fought, well we were told tha', we were pickin ap 'Arry first, an' then we were camin to pick you ap, bat bein' as tho' you're 'ere 'ow abou'...

She held out her hand to Steve, and kept a straight face, managing to smile inwards, despite his acne, despite his unfortunate anserine appearance, and said, "Please to meet you Adam. Let me introduce myself, I'm Harry, Harriet Thompson Mann." Steve made no attempt to shake her hand but made another Mutley laugh and very steadily withdrew behind the head rest of the passenger seat. Adam reached over for her hand.

Adam: 'Scuse me lav I'm Adam, Adam Bishop...And let me say I am very, very, pleased, in fact 'onoured, to meet you.

Harry (retracts her hand before Adam had chance to touch it, she leans back in the chair): Sorry about that but they told me that Adam was the good looking one (gives a smug smile that lasts for a fraction of a second; Steve is trying to keep his hissing laugh high pitched enough to be barely audible but he finds this difficult and almost chokes on his appreciation). I don't know who has told you that there is someone else joining us, or whether you've made it up, either way it does not matter. You will take orders from me now. Is that plain and simple enough for you? (silence) Good, very good boys. Now let's go to the port shall we?

Adam and Steve exchange a silent but pregnant glance. Adam was thrilled. He could not have set up a better story line in his own studio. He was so glad that Steve had brought the camcorder. This was going to be the best job that he had done in years. He had made up his mind for sure now. Steve's argument went out of the window. His mind, and Steve's too, were full of unspeakable stills, mind photographs of the fate that was in store for "Harry". Adam turned the ignition key, glanced at Steve one more time, who had the face of a feeding imp, blotched red, with a carnivorous grin. When Adam was sure that they were both thinking the same things, he allowed himself a smile, pulled out of their parking space, and moved out to the exit amidst the queue of traffic.

Adam: Well it's nice meeting you 'Arr...err...Harry. Amsterdam's a lovely place innit?...Ever been there before?...What am I saying, course you have, you're our contact right. Sorry I'm not thinking straight...ahem...We've heard a lot about you, all good like...And I must say you're quite a legend...We're very impressed ain' we Steve...

Steve (wriggles in his seat): Yeah...Oh yeah...got a lot of respect for ya...an' all your work an' tha'...

Adam (interrupting, why else would he have addressed Steve in this situation but in order to be able to interrupt him in front of her, for her sake): Like I was saying beautiful place Amsterdam. Maybe me and you might get a chance to get to know each other a little better. You're a very attractive woman and it's a very romantic place. Me and you could have a real good time together.

He watched her reaction in the rear view mirror. He knew that she would not like it, not yet. It was just a start, an icebreaker. She was intelligent, Adam had already realised that, she had to be to be doing what she was doing. The problem with intelligence was that it stopped people from doing what they wanted to do. It urged them to consider possibilities before acting on decisions. He could see her intelligence holding back her attraction for him. It struggled in the flickering of a moment before being subdued. It did not matter though, while there was a struggle of sorts, and he had just witnessed that, then there it was, it was just a matter of time, a matter of cajoling, of finding the right angle. She responded swiftly, unnervingly easily, to Adam's approach, with a merciless feline thrust, pushing a cold metal barrel against the back of his head. Steve was slow and she caught him reaching but not quite ready.

Harry:You freeze (Steve). You keep driving (Adam). Now before we embark on our journey let's get one thing straight DON'T FUCK ABOUT WITH ME. Don't be fucking foolish. Don't take any risks boys. This lady does not have time to be interested in you two pitiful lackeys. Keep your mouths shut and I won't, or rather I might not, BLOW YOUR FUCKING BRAINS OUT..............I'm going to put my little friend, here, away, and then I'm going to get some sleep. My advice to you two is not to disturb me; not to piss me off; keep it in your pants boys and we'll all arrive back here safe and sound in forty-eight hours time. (She took the gun away carefully)

Adam watched her arrange her holdall as a pillow and make herself comfortable for sleep. He also caught a glimpse of her looking at him. She did not know that he had seen her. She had betrayed her feelings with a smile to her interior. Would he get her consent before he had to kill her. One thing was for sure once the goods were in their, in his, possession, he could, and would, do as he pleased with her. She took something from out of her holdall.

Adam: What's this...more 'idden weapons. Is it a stick of dynamite this time?

Harry (not being able to stop herself from smiling, which makes her smile even more): Not quite... Here put this tape on...It's my favourite...

Adam (in a mock chastisement of Steve): You heard the lady Steve, pat 'er tape on...cam on show it sam...we've got a guest.

Harry curled up and closed her eyes and hummed along to the songs on the tape. It was Gainsbourg her favourite and she hummed along to:

> Hello Docteur Jekyll
> Non je n'suis pas le Docteur Jekyll
> Hello Docteur Jekyll
> Mon nom est Hyde, Mister Hyde...

And so they drove out to the port...
As Adam drove the car up onto the ship, Harry woke up. The tape was still playing and she heard Gainsbourg and Bridget Bardot singing:

> Chaqu'fois qu'un polic'man
> Se fait buter
> Qu'un garage ou qu'un banque
> Se fait braquer
> Pour la polic'
> Ca ne fait pas d'myster
> C'est signie Clyde Barrow
> Bonnie Parker
>
> Bonnie and Clyde
> Bonnie and Clyde

Harry (with an exaggerated yawn): Hey, they're playing our song Adam.

Adam (his cock bulging): Oh yes...

Harry (smiling and gathering her things together): Okay boys I took the liberty of booking you two into a nice two berth. One of you can bunk up and the other can bunk down. I've booked myself, as is my custom, into Commodore De Luxe. I have some phone calls to make and do not wish to be disturbed. (She opens the door and puts down her suitcase and holdall before getting out and standing next to them.)

Adam: What about us?...

Harry: I'll see you down here ten minutes before we are set to dock...

Adam: And in the meantime?...

Harry (in a faultless French accent wasted on Adam): Vas te faire voir chez les Grecs.

(Steve hissed out his Mutley laugh as Harry disappeared amongst a small crowd of passengers.)

Later on, in her three birth couchette that she was sharing with Juliette and Karen, Sally was applying her last coat of lipstick. Juliette came in and asked, "Are you ready now?"

"Sorry Jewel, I'm trying to make the best of myself."

"You look great, but you'd better get a move on. Karen's already moved in on a real dish. He's got muscles on top of muscles, drop dead gorgeous. You know Karen though another half an hour and she'll have already had all the decent men."

Sally laughed in agreement. "Oh Jewel, I'm so excited. You know I'm going to make tonight my night. I'm going to stop at nothing. The night is mine." She put her lipstick back in her bag.

"I'm not going to stop until I've conquered half the continent. Now come on quick."

Juliette was dressed in a short blue and gold dress that she had bought especially for their weekend in Amsterdam. Sally had on a tight fitting purple sweater with a baby blue double line across the chest and arms. She was wearing a new pair of black trousers that she had dared to buy in a smaller size than she usually felt comfortable in. She crossed her fingers and squealed "Let me at 'em!" as they left the cabin.

The drinks kept coming all night. Sally remembered paying for a round at some point because she remembered flirting with the barman, but apart from that one certain encounter she did not know where the drinks came from, only that they kept on coming. Large G and T's all round they would say when somebody asked any one of them what they were drinking, and sure enough whoever had asked the question promptly delivered large G and T's to the three of them. There was no time for alcohol's melancholy to set in as they drank one after another, after another, and when they were not drinking they were laughing at one of the other two's comments on some guy who was trying to pick them up. There were men from all over Europe, all over the world. It was wonderful. Karen was trying to ditch Mark The Twat for the evening as he too was a part of the Friends Of Amsterdam Society and had decided to tag along on the trip. He would pop up every now and then and Juliette or Sally, or one of the guys who they were talking to at that particular moment, would tell him that she was in the bathroom, or on the dance floor, or anywhere, and then when he went off to find her she would sneak back from wherever she had been hiding and they would all laugh and laugh and somebody, the guy who had made up the their excuse perhaps would get them another drink, and they would drink it and call for another, and Karen would say "thank you" much deeper and slower than she ought to, and would sit on the guy's lap until somebody else took her fancy, or bought her another drink. The DJ was playing Soft Cell, Yazoo, The Human League, Duran Duran, Eurythmics, Spandau Ballet, Depeche Mode. They danced with anybody who asked and sometimes just moved in on pockets of dancing guys laughing and taking exaggerated swigs from their drinks. Karen had finally managed to ditch Mark The Twat who had OD'd on Southern Comfort and Grolsch and was puking up in a toilet somewhere. She was now clamped at the mouth to some Dutch guy in the middle of the dance floor. He had one hand up her skirt and Sally laughed a warning to his friends not to let him take advantage of their mate. Juliette pretended to scold Sally "If only," putting on her most seductive French voice. They climbed up to the bar. They grabbed two empty stools and looked around at the ferry's clientele. They decided to take a breather from the action and they spied around the bar at men, at guys, who were looking for them, looking to see what interest they could get on the drinks that they had been paying for all night, the drinks that the two girls had been throwing down their necks all night. They ducked below the bar and laughed in spasms of alcooblivion. The Dutch guy Willhem walked past holding Karen up in one hand, showing off her, desperately scant, pearly white semi-see-through silk Agent Provocateur panties to his legion of friends in the other. Karen shook her head so that her hair jumped around and she shrieked in histrionic delight, "See you two ladies later...much later..." She left with the Dutch guy Willhem, both of them laughing, falling into one another, each carrying their similar, but different, trophies on their respective arms. Sally and Juliette fell about themselves. Karen was outrageous. They all were...

"Oh God," said Sally, "if I wasn't holding my fanny I'd have pissed myself laughing by now.."

A drink, a drink that's what they both needed now, another drink. They leaned drunkenly against the bar, thinking about what to order. The barman came over with two chilled fizzy drinks that were a curious transparent brown colour, nothing seemed strange about this, they just accepted the brown-gold hue, or maybe it just went unnoticed.

"These drinks were sent by the gentleman across the bar. He asks that you enjoy them and perhaps you would like to join him?"

"What's in them?" slurred Sally.

"Vodka and PommeTizer...a...a...a kind of apple juice, all quite normal."

They looked over.

"Sally, Sally, it's that guy...You know... The one Karen was talking to earlier...I told you...Before she met Dennis Bergkamp...It's him. The muscle man." Juliette raised her arms, acting out "muscle man," pretending to flex her biceps. Then realising that he could see her they both began laughing uncontrollably.

"Sally listen, he's a bit creepy."

"A bit creepy...a bit horny you mean...I think he going to come over. Shall I call him..."

"I'm not sure." But Sally was already in the act of calling him over.

"Oh Jewel he is gorgeous...I like his trousers...what a jaw...(putting it on a little) what bone structure...oh dear...I'm all overcome."

They both pretend to revive themselves from a swoon by fanning themselves with their palms. The man in question had a shock of blonde hair, parted fashionably, and flattened around his ears. His swagger, inevitable for someone with so much muscle, was exaggerated by his rolling neck, and brawny arms. He introduced himself and sat down. Juliette commented on his accent. He guessed straight away that they were students and decided that it was best to be, or seem to be, impressed by the two of them. Sally commented on his tight fitting velvet trousers and ran her palm up and down his thigh and then made a loud remark about the firmness of his flesh. She ran her hand up again and invited Juliette to do the same. They both agreed that his flesh was very firm, very tight, very tidy. He called the barman over. He'd ordered two vodkas with PommeTizer so where were the girls' scratch cards? The barman apologized and brought them over. Sally and Juliette giggled. They quickly scratched off the panels, not paying any attention to the brightly coloured frog staring at them from the top right hand corner, and then suddenly wham! Sally won herself a drink, which was good because she had spilt most of the last one down her sweater when she had been stroking the guy's velvet leg. They cheered in unison. More drinks please, and they went off to the bathroom together. They needed to piss. They promised that they would be back and so he ordered another round as an incentive for their return. On their return they threw back the drinks and the guy, like some little puppy dog they thought, ordered some more drinks. Mark The Twat came over. He had sick all down the front of his Michael Jackson T shirt and was giving off a strong smell of Southern Comfort. He began to engage Sally with his 'I'm drunk and I've lost my girl friend' routine. She did not want to deal with him. She did not want him, the big sexy blonde, to move in on Juliette in the meantime. She wanted him for herself. He looked as if he were an experienced man who would know how to please a girl. She needed a man not these young male students, what did they know about life, about love. She wanted him to take her in his strong steady hands where she would be safe. He, she was sure, would know exactly how to treat her; how to make love to her. As she was getting rid of Mark The Twat's unwanted conversation she watched him, the blonde with the profile. He was looking at Juliette, really looking at her. She felt bad. For once, just once, Sally wished to be the starlet in the dress, that dress, any dress, showing off smooth tanned legs. Sally watched his large man hands pick up his glass, hold it for a moment, and then take confident assured sips. All that she had was her useless boyfriend. What she needed was to be undressed by those careful hands. She bet herself that he would have no problem releasing her high pert bosoms from their tightly binding lace bra. She reckoned that he would be able to have her undressed easily, gracefully, in a couple of seconds. Her imagination began to work. Her clothes were all lying around her bare feet like a trap door to her old life, her old romance. She stepped off this trap door and into the Hollywood muscles of this sexy, experienced, considerate, man. Oh she could not, would not, deny herself this pleasure. She moved over to him and Juliette in time to here her saying to him, "Give me a call when you're the last man on Earth, until then fuck off." Her English was excellent, but you could always tell that she was from the continent. The bitch was putting it on for his benefit, trying to push Sally out, but Sally was not going to let her win. Juliette moved away and whispered in Sally's ear that she should do the same, but what did she know, this was her night and nothing was going to stop her, nothing. It was tough if she, Juliette, had lucked out, but there was no need to try and put her off. Sally ignored Juliette and moved closer and closer to the hunk on the bar stool, until at last he happened to mention that he had got some hash, draw was what he called it, in his cabin. They could go for a smoke if she liked. She liked...

In the cabin, out of the bar, Sally began to remember that they were on board a boat. It seemed rather strange. The guy opened a bottle of red wine and made her drink a glass of it before he rolled up a joint. The wine sat obliquely in her stomach, contradicting the gin and the vodka. The tobacco in the joint made her head spin. She was lying on the bottom bunk, he was sitting at the foot of the bed. She could not hear what she was talking about but she could tell by the way that she was holding the joint, the way she kept on having to re-light it, and the way in which she was taking it back that she was doing a lot of talking. They were kissing on the bed, his large hands were all over her tight sweater. The music from the disco was still audible in the cabin. Tears For Fears were playing and then The Clash and then... With her sweater pulled only half way over her head, leaving her arms flailing and her sight limited, he began to remove her trousers. The cool air cascading down her legs should have felt decadent, luxurious, but she was feeling a little sick now, and the wind outside now merged with the music making it sound as if it was being played at too slow a speed, as if the DJ was playing old vinyl singles on 33 rather than 45. Suddenly Sally did not know if she wanted this to continue but she was drunk, too drunk, and the room was spinning on and on, endlessly never stopping for a second. Her trousers were off and she had managed to wriggle her head from out of her sweater although her arms remained enmeshed inside it, stranded above her head and shoulders. She could see herself and for a split second she thanked Karen for lending her that pair of black lycra g string fuck me panties. At the moment she was happy looking down at her leading lady underwear and young concupiscent figure. This did not last for long though and soon she was trying, struggling, to keep all of the drink down whilst the muscle man covered her body with his cold wet mouth. She could hear herself making the sensual moans and groans that were expected of her. She felt him opening her with his fingers. He even almost touched her clitoris. He clumsily held his cock in his hand and forced it into her. He fucked her hard, sucked her tits until they were sore. He held back her arms by the wrists and there was simply no protest to be made against this giant. She was naked he still had his clothes on. The cold zip up the front of his shirt chaffed her belly and chin as he moved up and down inside her, fast and hard. The sound of Iggy Pop's Lust For Life from the Trainspotting soundtrack was playing in the disco, the thought that she was living her life in someone else's film not even this could belong to her crossed her mind, a distraction from the pain of this rough copulation. The fucking began to hurt more and more, never ceasing. She kind of blacked out for a while. She could not tell how long it had been for. There were voices in the room. She heard broken lines, "Is it workin'?" and, "Did ya charge the batt'ry." Somebody, something, grabbed her feet and she was pulled off the bed. She saw a grotesque face covered in sharp red spots like pock marks. The face grinned at her, mocked her. She felt as though she had lost the power to hold her head up, as if she had no control of the muscles in her neck. She was in the dark in the bathroom. She was covered, all over, in a sticky oil, and she could feel the cold surfaces of the bathroom against her skin. The big blonde was on top of her. She tried to smile at him. "Get the light wiv yer other 'and." "Close ap, close ap," she heard over and over. The fucking was hard, her skin felt feverish. Somebody was pointing something in her face, a TV, or a camera and then the bathroom light kept coming on and going off, quickly, epileptic, like a strobe light. On-and-off; on-and-off; black-and-white; black-and-white; on-and-off... And she was being sprayed with water from a shower head and the big blonde was now pointing something in her face and another thinner figure was on top of her rolling in and out of her... She remembered being sick at some point or at least she could smell bile and alcohol on herself the next day... Her head hurt. Her hair was matted. It smelt as if it had been burnt in places and was full of ash and half smoked tobacco. Her cunt, tits, and rectum were sore, her mouth dry. She had been taken into the corridor outside at some time in the morning, unsure of where she was, or who she was talking to. He had been a thin man, tragically ugly, probably one of those nice guy types whose looks prevent him from meeting women. The kind who do not have the arrogance that comes with male beauty and so are polite and courteous because nobody, no woman, would put up with them being otherwise. She thought that she recognized him from last night, maybe from the bar. He disappeared.

Sally half dressed, clutching the ripped clothes that she was not wearing to her chest, walked steadily, totally lost, uncommunicative in the early hours of Saturday morning. A crew member found her and took her to her room. Five minutes later he was describing her to his work mates. They were all laughing, recalling similar scenes that they had witnessed over the last year or two. Stories, little anecdotes, like that made the job more interesting. Something to write home about.

Chapter 24

Gillian's House

Outside the taxi it is dull and dark, a light mist hangs around the trees of the narrow winding country lane that I am travelling down. The atmosphere, even inside the taxi, is damp, and oppressive. The driver is making haste through the gloom, his accelerator forcing us onwards cutting the air before us in two.

Gillian's house is out in the country. It is difficult to guess how near, or far, we are from her place in this darkness. We are going, that is she is taking me, to a party of some sort. She likes to have me on her arm for these occasions. She says that I am good at conversation, even if I do only talk about fine novels, avant garde music, and cult B-Movies, though I would like to state that I do not, there are thousands of subjects that I can talk about. Well she was not quite honest about Margaret. She is a widow, but her husband, far from being connected to the university, had been some kind of notorious big time career criminal in London, south of the Thames. She had been nice enough though and obviously missed her husband, and loved her grownup children too much to begin a new relationship and introduce a new man to them. This, of course, makes me the perfect solution.

As the taxi pulls into Gillian's long gravelled drive, approaching the house, I remember Sally. All of this will be over soon. The little pile of money that I have been saving has grown quite substantially. I am becoming a wealthy young man, and this is giving me hope. A shaft of light is beckoning me forwards, ultimately to wash my hands of my sordid involvement with Gillian and all of these people. The time when I hold Sally in my arms and we live together, forever, is not so far away. I miss you my sweet angel... She telephoned to say that she was going on an organized trip to Amsterdam. I wished her well, but really wished that I were going with her. She said that they had booked only hours before, otherwise she would have arranged for me to go along too. It had been a spur of the moment decision. She was going with Karen and Juliette, not the kind of people I would like her to go with, especially not Karen. They go tonight, Friday night. They will be in Amsterdam tomorrow. They come back late Sunday evening early Monday morning. Amsterdam is a wonderful city, but like all cities there are dangers, and dangerous people. I told her to watch out. I know Sally though, she is a sensible girl. I cannot wait to see her. I am going up to visit on Tuesday. She promised to tell me all about her time in Holland. I have to get through tonight first though, and the early hours of tomorrow morning. And tomorrow evening I will be out with Margaret again. She needs an escort for an important function in London. She will be meeting associates of her late husband, business men, who she, through her husband's will, still owns a part of. I do not like doing so many dates so close together, but I realise that I cannot do this for very much longer. I need to get out, be with Sally. It is not good for me, all of this... But the more that I do, and the quicker that I do them, the sooner that I can put a stop to it all.

In the meantime I am listening to the crunch of the gravel underneath the tyres. Gillian's house is large, really too large for her to still be living there alone. I think she enjoys the room though. She definitely likes the feeling of power that it gives her. The large rectangular windows, bordered by ivy, remind me of eyes staring out, bleakly observing all that dare walk up the steps to the grand antique front door.

The taxi leaves. The driver had already been paid. I take a few moments to survey the land at the front of the house. The water in the manmade pond is undisturbed, perfectly still. The pond is large, a huge expanse of water as smooth as glass, maybe some twenty yards wide. The house is reflected in the water as if cloned. I ask myself how deep that pond is, maybe only a few feet, maybe it went right down to the centre of the world. I did not know. A small noise began and was followed by others. There were frogs croaking around the large pond. The tyres on the gravel must have quietened them they do not like sudden unrecognizable sounds but now they had begun to sing again. I moved towards the steps and the front door. The noise of my footsteps obviously spooked the frogs, and they were silent again, perturbed that I was ignoring them and that I was resuming the last few steps of my journey.

Once inside Gillian looks at me critically. She is wearing an indigo dress that is too young in style for her. It is quite revealing, with a large cleavage hole cut into the middle of the chest, totally unsuitable. She does not look good, but she thinks that she does. She is shaking her head. She does not like my suit. It is by Joe Casely Hayford, in a kind of military style, it is quality, very dashing I think. Gillian says that if it does not shine then it does not work, and that I am not to show her up tonight by wearing it. She leaves me with a single malt and after a short time returns with a shining silver suit made from some kind of rubberized silk. It is fashionably cut, but looks more like an artistic statement than something that you might actually wear. She tells me to try it on immediately, and starts tugging at my jacket. I push her off. This is my favourite suit, okay she does not want me to wear it, but I can't afford to ruin it, and besides I like it I do not want her to ruin it. This silver space suit is not really the kind of thing that I would wear but it is Gillian's night and I have no choice. My cuban heeled slip on loafers are no good either, apparently. Gillian leaves and comes back with a large white box. She gives it to me and I open it. To my horror there are a pair of white boots inside, my size, with spiked stiletto heels. No way! No way, I am telling her... ....Listen you little shit they cost a lot of money. She laughs right in my face. Why these boots, these beautiful boots, cost more than you do. Now I suggest that you stop making a scene and put them on like a good little prick..............NOW!!! ...Don't be silly, all you have to do is slip your feet into them... I am beginning to lose my patience with you shithead... Are you listening to me shithead... Then why aren't you putting them on?... I don't fucking care you spoilt bastard. After all I've done for you, you ungrateful piece of shit. David Bowie wore heels like these at that music awards ceremony. Not good enough for you though eh? You spineless cocksucker... What do I care... What do I care about a no good prick like you... I could not, do not, give a shit about you or how you feel... I've bought you shithead...I've bought you and paid for you shithead...and now I fucking own you, you shit...NOW PUT THEM ON... PUT THEM ON... I ordered these boots from fucking Katharine Hamnett, now put them on... What are you talking about now fuck?... What did you say fuck?... Sorry can't hear a fucking word you're saying fuck... We've been wearing them for decades fuck... In China they used to bind the girls' feet, break the toes and fold them back so that they could have small distorted feet. It was thought to be beautiful, and small feet were attractive to a man looking for a wife. This is no big hardship for you is it....for one fucking night that's all I ask... You bastard... You shitty little prick.. You might as well go home you shitty bastard..and take your tiny little cock with you... Why?...Why?.. Because you're a cunt, and cunts have been walking around in them for years... It's simple; cunts wear them... Cunts wear them, and YOU ARE A CUNT...

She threw the boots at me. And eventually I conceded. What else could I do walk all the way home for the sake of what, my principles.

I am walking up the staircase in her house, holding onto the carved banister, trying to get used to walking in stiletto heels. My feet look awkward. I am taller but feel as if I am on show, as if I am here to be stared at. Gillian is staring at me, shouting at me: turn this way, shorter steps, longer steps... I feel vulnerable with the extra inches of height. I have been wearing them for nearly ten minutes now and my back, calves, shins, and ankles are all aching. My back is especially hurting, filling the rest of my body and limbs with a daunting fatigue, and we are not even at the damned party yet. Gillian is, unaware that she is, chuckling small spit balls down the front of her dress, rarely have I seen her so happy. I move clumsily, making heavy deliberate footsteps, resembling the first movements of Frankenstein's Monster. I feel over conscious of myself, as if my purpose is to be looked at and watched without being consulted. I am slow. I have lost my ability to move swiftly and freely. I cannot get away. All of my escape routes have been cut off. I find it very uncomfortable to move any distance at all. This is how I go out for the evening. This is what I must endure.

At least Gillian had a good time. She was vibrant. I watched her running around, stuffed ridiculously into that dress, moving from one group to another, calling me over, introducing me to people, showing me off like a collector's item. She did go missing for a while. She said that she had laddered her tights and had to change out of them. Her bawdy grin and the, only partially visible, but nevertheless incriminating, stain on the back of her dress gave her away but what do I care...

Back in the house, at about two in the morning, the silence constantly contaminated by the whirring of central heating radiators coming on and going off in various rooms of the house, Gillian took me upstairs. We had done it in all five of the bedrooms as I remembered, downstairs too. Gillian stopped outside of a door that I had never been through before. She unlocked it, felt for a light switch, there were some stairs behind the door, a whole new staircase that seemed to lead up to an attic, and she sent me up first. I feel nervous, restricted by the white boots, unable to command my centre of balance as I am used to doing. I hold this less elaborately carved banister as if my life depends upon it. Each step that I take is unsteady, unsure. I am near the top and Gillian is pushing past me even though there is not really enough room for her to do this. She is feeling for another switch it would seem. There is a blinding flickering of light for a moment, and I can now see that this staircase leads directly into a room. The room has polished floorboards and a huge fur rug, that disappointingly looks genuine, and is laid across the floor. The room is dominated by a large bed with a solid wooden, and somewhat sombre and intimidating, headboard. Next to the bed are two cameras on tripods, one on either side. There are spotlights trained on the bed, one of them is on, emitting a lugubrious white haze. On a small table at the bottom of the bed is a large tube of KY Jelly, and two giant looking plastic dildos, moulded with foreskins and authentic looking vein configurations. One is a generic plastic pink, the other an iridescent black, if black can be iridescent. The bed is roughly in the centre of the room, and behind it is a table with a large dazzling arrangement of dried flowers and a photograph in a silver frame. It looks as if the picture is of her children. A rare one which has her son in too. The children look very young. Her son, is crouched in the middle of his two older sisters, and is holding a large bouquet of flowers, not unlike the dried ones in the vase that sit next to the photograph. Gillian moves straight to these dried flowers, quite guiltily I think, and she takes them, and the photograph, away, puts them out of view. For some reason I am aware that I am not really sure what is happening. Maybe the extra couple of giddy inches of height have brought on paranoid delusions. I make a mental note to proceed with care. Gillian is telling me to take off my clothes and lie on the bed, but she is telling me to keep my boots on. I cannot believe this but I might as well see this thing through now it has started. It is just the two of us now. It is her pathetic game not mine. It cannot be more embarrassing than it already has been. I take off my clothes as instructed and place an unopened condom on the pillow, for when, and as, I need it.

I have to be careful when I am at Gillian's house. She is obsessed with filming the two of us having sex. I have not, and will not, ever consent to this, and she knows it, but it does not stop her offering me more and more money nearly every time we meet. I think that my reasons for declining are obvious. If I were filmed the moment could not be erased in my mind. I would have no control of myself. The film could be shown over and over again. I could be made to perform over and over again, forever even. It would be like buying me permanently. I may be available for evenings and days. I will accept an offer for a weekend but I cannot be bought for anytime longer than that. I agree to perform once, exclusively, and if the client would like a succession of single, exclusive, encounters then that is okay too. I am not prepared to be filmed, or recorded, or photographed, and I am telling Gillian this so that I can be sure, and so that she can be sure. Gillian retorts with her usual name calling but it is quite tame for her. She, seems to have accepted that I will not allow her to film us, and so just enjoys making the threat. It is something to annoy me with.

Gillian leaves the spotlight on and turns off the more powerful main light. The darkness, or at least some of it, is allowed back into the room. This soothes my eyes which are stinging with tobacco smoke from the party. The white boots, next to my lightly haired calves, make me look washed out. The whiteness drains me of any vitality that I have left after the painful experience of walking around in these boots for the evening. It is nice to be off my feet, and I stretch out seductively across the bed. I lie back and clasp my hands together and tuck them behind my head. I try to look as if I could not give a shit. You know, detached, unconcerned, waiting for my moll to undress. Gillian has decided that she does not want to undress, not yet. She says that we are going to play a game of cat and mouse, and she cannot hide her excitement, unable to stop herself from spraying a fine drizzle of spittle into the air as she says the word "mouse." It is not strictly cat and mouse, she is now telling me, but pussy and mouse. I tell her that her little pun is shamefully poor for a Professor of Literature. She tells me not to be so pretentious! She kneels up by me and asks me to warm her up. She bends down low and pushes her behind in my face. I kiss her buttocks through her dress. Then I very slowly lift up the dress over her legs and up to her waist, stroking her naked skin as I push it up. It remains snagged, quite naturally, over her thighs and around her bloated waist. The fake tan has not been applied so evenly on her buttocks and her skin is unevenly coloured, resembling large nicotine stains. She has no panties on although I am certain that she went out with some on, but, like her "laddered" tights where are they? In the inside pocket of some handsome twenty something's Gucci jacket? Who knows? Gillian seems to be especially happy and I guess that she is heavily coked up, and she would not have invited me over if she did not have enough to see her, to see us, through the rest of the night. I have made a promise to Margaret though and must take it easy, well relatively easy. I promised her tomorrow night.

I am stroking between her legs up and down, up and down, very slowly, allowing my hand to linger, lightly brushing her clitoris, gently parting her vagina's lips, making as if to push my finger, my hand, inside, but then drawing back watching her sadistic smile. She draws her lips apart and shows off rows of teeth. The more excited she gets the more she does this, and the more intense her expression. When she comes she presents a whole set of yellow-white teeth, chattering them together like an aggressive chimpanzee. She moves her arse up a little trying to persuade me to push in to her cunt, but I am biding my time. There is a distinctive smell of latex rubber even though I have not opened the condom on the pillow yet. She has clearly already been fucked once tonight. I can see her smile increasing as if she knows that I am just confirming this in my mind, and it gives her some weird kick. I push my middle finger into her, and quickly withdraw it, only to push it in again and withdraw it. The next time that I withdraw it I find time in the rhythm to push her clit from left to right a few times, just as she likes it, before plunging it back into her. Gillian is breathing heavily. Her cunt is very moist. There is probably some spermicide in there from the stuffed condom that fucked her earlier. Gillian is panting now. I move ahead opening her legs further and kneeling between her knees. I lean forwards so that she can feel the warmth of my body on her buttocks. She responds with a couple of short sharp intense breaths before settling back into her own rhythm. I have one hand on her clit moving it left and right, tweaking it in sequence with my other hand which is now pushing two fingers into her warm dribbling cunt. Her buttocks jiggle and wobble. I can feel her clit swelling slightly. It is now the size of a small bead. I push down on it heavily and vibrate my hand very quickly, rapidly and firmly, twisting it one way and then the other. She lifts her head slightly making her back arch. She is starting to gasp for air, she has joined the oxygen race.... ...Stop, oh God stop not yet, not yet, oh fuck that was good, but not yet....not yet... I want to play my game... Gillian gets a piece of string, which she tells me is the mouse's tail. She wants to "ever so gently" push it some way up my rectum, so that I have a tail. She is going to do this whilst I lick her cunt. I am not happy about this. I do not want a mouth full of spermicide and I do not want to taste latex rubber for the rest of the evening (and most of tomorrow). I tell her that I know she has already been fucked. She does not have to labour the point. She grudgingly agrees to get under the shower and wash out down below before proceeding with the game. She curses me as she pulls down her dress and goes running off down the stairs to the bathroom, one of the bathrooms. I walk over to the picture of Gillian's children, my heels triptrap across the floorboards. She had put it out of sight in a corner of the room where the darkness dwelt at its thickest. The two daughters, in their late teens, are quite pretty. The son is rather different. He has a furrowed brow, looks uncomfortable in front of the camera. He is looking away as though he does not want to be apart of the group of three. I put it down where she left it. This attic must be the studio that she is always talking about. I go back onto the bed and lie on the white satin sheet. I feel tired. I will need some coke to keep me up, to keep me going for the rest of the evening. I lie here for a while until Gillian returns. She has taken off her dress and has put on a purple bodice. It is tied up at the back with what looks like a crisscrossed shoe lace. She bought it from Button, Boot and Spatterdash on mail order. It is shaped very artistically. A designer's masterpiece no doubt, but on Gillian, and not really in her size, it makes her look like an amusing parody of an erotic dancer. She steps out of a Chiffon thong that she bought from Elysium. I was with her when she bought the thong. She throws it at me sexy, like an ambitious third rate actress. She entwines the white string, the mouse's tail, around her hands and then snaps it tight between them, holding them up at throat height and advancing forwards as if she intend to garrotte me.... ...Put on a condom...now please....that's right, be a good boy... Now I am going to just slip this piece of string up your dirty arse so that you have a little tail for me to play with. I might lick and suck your balls a little, if the fancy takes me, but I am not touching your cock....you've probably got AIDS and I don't want to catch it, especially not off you... And you've got to put a condom on because I don't want a face full of your hot toxic gism... Am I making myself clear... Do you understand? Can we continue?... ...It is very tiring being spoken to in this way, but this is how she likes it. I slip my cock into the cold condom. A face full of hot toxic gism indeed...huh...little does she know, that is the last thing that is liable to happen. I know that I am taking a risk licking her exposed genitalia. I could be the one who catches AIDS from her! I do know that it is unlikely, but it could happen. I concentrate on her clit, lapping it excitedly like a dog. Her freshly rinsed cunt has dried up a little and I move my fingers, three of them now, in and out of her until she starts to show her teeth again. I am lying on my back and she is bridged over me. I begin to push my tongue across her now, moving it like before. My fingers squelch in the self-lubrication of her cunt. I stop the licking for a while and talk to her. I tell her in secret whispered tones how much I fancy her. I tell her that I lie awake at night wanking over the image I have of her in my mind: bending over in her office with just a pair of black leather crotchless panties covering her juicy cunt. She loves this story. She loves any story. I think she just likes to hear dirty words. I stroke her cunt and lick her clit harder and faster. Her neatly trimmed pubic hair sticks to my tongue and scratches my face as I press my nose into her cunt, and press down on her clit as hard as I can with my tongue and shake my head capriciously. Her body jiggles and she begins to shriek as if I am trying to hurt her. Maybe it does hurt her. I continue with the story about her and the leather panties and my mind drifts back to Sally, and the last time I visited, and somehow I recall the black lycra g string panties that Karen was flashing at me all night. It must be my mind bored, shuffling with images I thought were discarded. I push this purposeless image away and try to concentrate on Gillian, and on what I am doing. I have to stop briefly and count to five every now and then because Gillian is repeating not yet, not yet, so I let her calm down and then raise her excitement back up with condescending strokes of my tongue across her swollen clitoris. Each one sends her into shivers of pleasure. Her mind and body crying out simultaneously for me to stop and to continue. I can feel Gillian's hand pushing the string up my rectum. She has licked her finger, quite professionally, so as to ease the passage up through my tight sphincter. I can tell that despite the pauses in my licking that she cannot hold off an orgasm for much longer. A sustained ten seconds of rubbing, licking and sucking of her clit and cunt would set her off. I begin to bite into her inner thighs. I aim to keep her suspended in the thrill of it all for another minute or so... Her finger is moving further up my rectum and while at first it had been mildly, well fairly, enjoyable, it was now making me feel uncomfortable. I will have to bring her off before she can go any further. I regulate my breathing with hers. I regulate my clit licking and cunt rubbing with our breathing. She cannot hold herself back. I am struggling to keep up with her short unbreathing breaths. We race our lungs together. I pause the licking for a fraction of a second and resume and her body tightens and she struggles for air and she calls out she screams "There's no net. I'm going to open the parachute." I feel a tearing inside my arse and her hand reaches up as if she is going to rip out my soul by the scruff of its neck and my body begins to jolt in some spasm of hot pain and cold ecstasy and she pulls out the string which burns with friction and is followed by small bleeding and my cock jolts too and my body bucks and I can hear Gillian squealing with pleasure and perverse glee and my milky essence shoots into the tight suffocating rubber bag that is stretched over my cock and the string is out in her hand and a trail of blood followed by another spasm wracks my body as my sphincter opens and a loose stool of dark foul shit expurgates all over the white sheet I writhe in painful disbelief seeing nothing except for Gillian who is holding her throbbing twat in one hand and pointing, laughing, with the other at the consequences of her terrible plan... I have been caught, milked like a sidewinder, and rendered harmless, abused and scorned, and finally ridiculed. The tears form in the corners of my eyes, and it stings. And my arse, the inside of my arse, is burning and I can feel the trickle of warm bitter blood coiling its way down my insides, reaching the air becoming visible, matting the tiny hairs together, flowing out into the rank shit, that is still and unmoving. Gillian is laughing at the corporeal mess on the white silk sheet. I hold my cock with my hands trying to hide my sperm from her, from me. I curl to protect my cock and cover myself. I look down at the shit and the white boots. Gillian is still getting her breath back, pointing, holding up the string like a tapemeasure, as the instrument, the culprit, as if it were evidence of some kind. It is half white, the virgin half, the other half is dark, shitcoloured, streaked with bloody crimson, foul moments had stuck to it and would not come off, it was frayed now, unravelling at one end.

Chapter 25

The Coronation

Lisa, all dressed in white, just as she had hoped, was led, on the great bestial arm of Masters, into the huge main room of the club. The lights were dim, the air filled with smoke and chitchat. Clusters of beautiful women, madeup and squeezed into the most exquisite of outfits, were perched beside their men, smiling, talking, laughing, working. They wore the most wonderful colours that she had ever seen. Every hue, every nuance, of every colour was represented here, there, somewhere, on somebody. She wanted to look at them all, acquaint herself with everyone. She felt slightly envious of the magnificent and colourful array of women. A small part of her wished to join them. She was encased in this cute, but functional, completely white number. She was with the man of the evening though, and really that was all that mattered, well that is what she told herself.

It was like a dream. Everybody wanted to congratulate Philip. Wherever they sat, or stood, people flocked around to shake his hand, kiss her cheek. The men paid Philip compliments by complimenting her, which felt wonderful, and they took him to one side and discussed business plans with him, the size, and importance, of which she could not even imagine. She spoke to the beautiful women and she lost count of all of the famous people, and all of the beautiful people, that she was being introduced to. She met Actors and Actresses, Singers, Musicians, Dancers, Models, Super Models, Writers, Producers, Directors,

Sportsmen, Sportswomen, TV Personalities, Doctors, Lawyers, Professors, Tycoons, Landowners, Hoteliers, Promoters, Agents, People who owned giant companies, the list was endless...

It was like being a princess. A child's fairytale was unfolding before her, and Philip was the handsome prince. He seemed a little strange. The eczema on his hands did not look too bad. His hands were not red or blistered as they usually were. He smiled at people. He looked at them when he spoke to them. He seemed to be charged with life, and it had rubbed off on her. A particularly famous Boxing Promoter sent over champagne. They sat on plush velvet seats with chrome frames, with three legs instead of four. The tables were three legged too. The table tops were made of polished glass smoked black, and they reflected the lights as if the lights were divinity itself. She became dizzier and dizzier, taking gourmet gulps of champagne, and smoking long cigarettes that she would have described as being sophisticated. She had arrived. This was her dream. This was where she wanted to be.

Suddenly, quite unexpected, she heard someone calling her name. She turned to see Kelly Saunderson running down through an aisle of tables towards her, with her arms outstretched, a look of, what was supposed to be, happiness and surprise was etched onto her face. Kelly looked like a complete belle. She had on the exact white knee high leather boots, with the elegantly shaped heels, that Lisa had had to talk herself out of wearing. She was wearing a sleeveless dress of sequins which caught your sight and threw it back at you in a thousand different ways. Her hair was dark brown, almost black, parted in the middle and dragged unevenly down the sides of her head, then combed into tiny scattered stalagmites, giving the impression that she had only moments before stepped out of the shower. They too exchanged compliments. Lisa loved her hair, and her dress, and well it was so nice to see her again. They had not seen each other since L.A. Kelly said thanks, that, yes, she loved her new hairstyle, wasn't she a gorgeous little bitch; but she thought that Lisa looked great; what a good idea to come in virginal white; who was she with? When Kelly realised she held her fingertips to her chest as if she was lost for words. Oh my God, Kelly could not believe it. She was *so* happy for her. Now she understood the white dress. Kelly said that she had not been so far off with her description of virginal white then. She pretended to pull an imaginary rope, accompanying her mime with the sounds dingdong, dingdong. Lisa blushed. If only she told herself. Philip came over. He shrugged off Kelly's flirting and apologized to her, but he had to take his seat at the table at the front, next to the stage, and he wanted Lisa's company. Kelly said goodbye in her throatiest voice, but Philip led Lisa to the front without so much as batting an eyelid.

Philip pulled her chair out so that she could sit down like a lady. There were some of Philip's men on the table with them, and others; handsome men who looked as though they had spent their whole tanned lives in sharp tuxedos and brilliant white shirts. Lisa began to feel a little uncomfortable. Her back was aching and she was pretty sure that she needed a new tampax. She excused herself to Philip and the others. They all stood up before she had chance to make a move. She leaned over to kiss Philip. He accepted and reciprocated the kiss. She went looking for the bathrooms, walking on air, looking at all of the faces, swimming through the crowds of wealthy, beautiful, people

She went into a cubicle, pulled up her dress, pulled down her tights and panties and sat on one of the white, electrically heated, toilet seats that had been imported from Japan. Typical, thought Lisa, she was on the rag on what was quite possibly the finest evening of her life, so far. She hoped that it would not spoil Philip's evening. Most men didn't care about such details, but there again her Philip was not most men. She took the loaded tampax holder out of her bag. She held the fresh tampon in her hand. It was white too, just like she was. She pulled out the old one and dropped it in the disposal unit at the side of the toilet. Using the applicator, she pushed the new clean tampon inside. She flushed the red water, in the toilet, away. She was not pregnant. That was one thing, and she did not itch, or feel any infection of any kind, but she could not help thinking about AIDS. She never knew. Nobody ever knew. And she certainly did not know enough about Philip to be sure. He could have slept with hundreds of women. He had said nothing to the contrary. There were always prostitutes hanging around these kind of places. How many of these parties had he attended? She had to talk to him about it. When it was the right time they would have a real head to head, a heart to heart, discuss everything. This wonderful night was the start. She had only one more tampon left until they got back to the hotel. She hoped that she was not going to be too heavy. She left the cubicle and washed her hands. She looked at herself in the wall length mirror over the wash basin. She was wrong, the tampon was not white like her; she was white like it. She was, not only, on the rag, but walking around like one. My God if ever she was to leak it would be hideously obvious in this...this..all of this whiteness. She squeezed handfuls of blonde curls in her tiny mighty fists, leaving them just so, like dancing cherubs, and she went back to her seat.

Margaret is speaking to some old friends who knew her late husband. She is enjoying seeing all of these people again. It certainly is an ostentatious event. The guy, who all of this is in aid of, is standing up on the stage. He has been up and down for most of the evening so far. Saying hello to people as they came in; making small announcements about his intentions for the future; making sure that he has thanked everyone. He was called up as a volunteer for the illusionist. He calls down to some woman, his partner I suppose, to go up and join him. She is bashful, but charmingly so; all dressed in white with a mass of blonde curls heaped carefully upon her head. A whisper goes up as she gets up onto the stage. The people at the tables are discussing her, critically examining her clothes, her poise, her voice. She is remarkably attractive. I cannot help but notice how this woman seems to drink up the whole atmosphere, the music, the low hum of conversation and laughter, the pervasive sparkling glossy sheen of glamour, and the lusty slothful decadence that is accepted at parties such as this. She does not come close to my Sally's beauty but I have never met anyone that does. This woman is the subject of scorn because she is so attractive. The guy she is with is a big man, very dark, tight curly hair. I feel as if I have seen his face before but I cannot quite work out where. Probably on a wanted poster if what Margaret has been telling me, about most of the guests I have met so far, is true. The man seems to stoop a little under the weight of his heavy looking arms. I must say that it is not very often that you see such a giant person, and the woman at his side is so petite, well at least that is how it looks when she stands next to him.

The brass section of the band starts up a fanfare and a man in a white coat comes from behind the stage curtain. He has a stethoscope around his neck. Everyone seems to know him. The guests are all laughing, saying things like, "about time," and "been waiting waiting for this since we arrived," and then laughing at one another's comments. *Ape Man* by The Kinks starts to play over the speakers and everyone is clapping now. The song is frighteningly apt. Is this all being designed by someone I ask myself? Is someone else, some great puppeteer, trying to draw my attention to the large, apelike, man standing on the stage? The man, the apeman, looks a little confused up there. The man in the white coat, the doctor man, goes back behind the curtain and everyone else leaves the stage. The doctor man comes back out, the curtain rises, *Ape Man* resumes, and there are a line of chimpanzees on the stage. They begin to entertain and do tricks. It is all rather absurd.

The dinner things have all been cleared away. I look down at myself in the black coloured glass table top. This is the end. I have had of enough these kind of people. I do not want to be a part of this whole scene. What happened last night was not good. I cannot continue any more. This will be my last appointment. I am not sorry that it is all over. I only have to look around the room, this vacuum of superficiality, to realise that this is not where I want to be. I have betrayed Sally. I have betrayed myself. I have been betrayed by Gillian. I have to be with Sally, spend my life with her, and I will have to lie to her. I still cannot believe that Gillian would do anything so vile. A middle-aged rich looking man and young woman, with fake looking tits, that appear to be squeezing out over the top of her gown, are laughing and clapping their hands. The man is saying that they are going to be there at any moment, just like he said they would. The woman is turning in her chair looking all around. A chimpanzee comes running down the aisle. The man holds up a blue disc and the monkey throws out, from about ten yards away, a small folded up wrap of paper, and then runs back to the stage, urged on by the crowds' applause and the gesturing doctor man, who seems to be responsible for this act. The man spills the contents of the wrap of paper all over the table top. I guess that it is coke. The man and woman do thick lines of it. They kiss at the table. The man grabs one of those fake looking tits, pinching the nipple through the gown. They laugh together, and speak at a hundred miles an hour until they get dry mouth. Then they make a horrible plashing sound with their lips as they talk and thick strings of saliva hang like girders between their upper and lower lips. The man wants some more, and orders more of the blue discs from a passing waiter. The men in their monkey suits laugh at the apes who run around feeding them coke, excited like children in a zoo. One man, further down our aisle, jumps up on the table as one of the chimps go by. He bends his knees and scratches under his arms and calls out at the chimp. All of the people at his table think that this is hilarious. The apes take no notice they just do their job in the midst of all of these people.

Do you really need me to tell you why I am so sickened? It is not just this, but the whole social environment that I have been working in. I am appalled by it all, and by myself. I have to live with my betrayal, but after tonight I am starting a fresh. The rest of my life begins on Tuesday, that is the next time that I will see Sally.

Eventually the chimps finish their act and the narcotics are now brought out, for those that want them, by the waiters. Lisa has had a little, but only after Philip had some first. The night was going well as far as she could tell. Philip seemed to be happy. He was very popular that was for sure. Masters was looking around. He was looking for the silvergrey haired man. Would he dare to show his face? Masters didn't have to listen to him any more. He was finished with all of that.

Masters spotted John and Serge looking on with a calmness that he was about to disrupt. Their aloofness was ill advised because they would soon be quietened forever. They should really take their last chance to say something, to do something, but Masters expected that they would do nothing as they moved downwards, on an inescapable escalator, towards their fates. Everything was set up now. He laughed to himself inside his own head, they'd be better off in the toilets together, doing their dirty disgusting dance while they still had chance... John and Serge regretted that it was not one of them who was being called up on the stage, receiving all kinds of good wishes from the guests, being offered all kinds of deals, all kinds of favours. What could they do? It was his day. There was no point in being sour. The only way to maintain their dignity was to join in the congratulations. They went over earlier to shake hands, exchange pleasantries, but Masters had made it clear that he did not want them snooping around for contacts amongst the people that were surrounding him. Again, what could they do? This had all been laid on for him. He was on the inside now. In the movies they would describe him as being untouchable, and this was what he was now, untouchable.

The compare introduced a comedian. The comedian a short stocky man with slicked back hair adjusted the microphone down to his level and began with the obligatory hello to Masters.

It's nice to be here with you beautiful people...(applause)

And I'd just like to say well done Philip. It's nice to have you on board, round of applause please ladies and gentlemen...(applause)...stand up Philip please stand up...(applause)

And you know I could not help noticing your beautiful friend tonight... I hope you don't mind me saying that, but I think that everyone agrees that she's a beautiful woman... But let me give you a little advice Philip, don't take it the wrong way, but you've got to be careful... Oh yes they're all beautiful until you marry them (laughter)... Oh yes... You may laugh ladies and gentlemen... You may laugh, but it's true... For instance, take my wife (pause)... Please for God's sake, someone, take my wife, take her away...(laughter) Get her out of here...(laughter) I take her everywhere but she always finds her way home again...(laughter) I never want to see her face again...(laughter) Ha, ha, ha, you're a wonderful audience... D'you know that?... You're the best... But seriously, ha, ha, ha...(laughter) Seriously, please... I got home from work the other day... Yes *work,* it's true, believe me (laughter)... Ha, ha, ha, I got in from work and my wife is making love to some guy on the sofa... It's true my wife was making love to some guy, who I'd never seen before, on our sofa... (points to someone in the audience, playing at taking offence) What do you mean that's funny?...(laughter) So she's making love to this guy on my sofa... (in an outraged tone) my sofa, my sofa (pointing to himself)...(laughter) So I said to her, I said, "Hey, what's going on?" You know what she says? Do you know what she says? I'll tell ya... She says to me, "Don't worry he's paying for it?"...(laughter) I say to her that that's as maybe but when I get home I don't expect my wife to be making love to some strange guy on my sofa, (in mock disbelief) okay (laughter)... *I* want to come home and make love to *my* wife on *my* sofa, (pressing the point home) okay... She says back to me, "You can sweetheart, you can, (bats his eyelids and folds his hands over his heart, motionless for a moment) (laughter) (walks away in disgust) as soon as you pay me what you owe from the two times last week...(laughter).. Please, please, you're too kind... (laughter) Please, please, ha, ha, ha (laughter) Please, please, really, really, I wouldn't mind, I wouldn't mind if she did something around the house... A little dusting, a little cleaning, a little cooking would be nice, but does she? Doe she? (rolls his eyes in disgust) (some laugher) Huh! I lean over to take a piss and the kitchen sink's full of dishes from last week...(laughter and applause) You are a great crowd, a great crowd...(applause) Seriously though guys you've got to keep your eyes on them. Have you heard of this new disease that they're all catching, heard of it? It's called Feminism, Women's Lib...(laughter) Ha, ha, ha (laughter) They catch it off their friends...(laughter) What are you laughing about? It's true..(laughter) You can tell carriers they swell up all fat (puffs his cheeks out) (laughter), they get lice and have to shave off their hair, and they get obsessed with overalls (some laughter) Only they call them dungarees...(laughter) It's true, ha, ha, ha, I wouldn't lie to you people... She comes in, my wife, after visiting one of these Women's Lib Lesbians, (aside) now that's something I'd like to see when I get home from work (laughter), she says to me (he waddles across the stage shaking his ass like a drag queen, speaking in a high pitched voice) (laughter), "I've been speaking to Tina. And I've learnt a few things. And there's gonna be a few changes around here...(laughter) Don't think I'm gonna walk around in these shoes anymore...my feet are gonna be in touch with the Earth...(some laughter) And I ain't gonna wear any more of that sexy smelling perfume you bought me...(laughter) Why," she says, "it ain't natural." (back in his own voice) I told her that neither were the plastic tits and ass I bought her last year from Doctor Johnson what's she gonna do about that..(laughter and applause) If they catch the bug though there is not a lot you can do about it... Seriously guys, I'm speaking from experience... If she's wants to burn her bra let her....just make sure that she's still wearing it...(laughter) ...Oh you're too kind (laughter) (holds his hands out and turns to look off stage) I love these people...(applause)......

Backstage the comedian's voice can be heard but his exact words cannot be made out. The ears of the band follow the intonation, the pitch, and then the laughter and applause. The lead singer, boyish and handsome, looks too much like Blur's Damon Albarn for him to actually be Damon Albarn. The waitress who is bringing over a tray of flutes for their champagne has convinced herself that he is, that the whole band are, lookalikes. She still kind of fancies him though, but concentrates on putting down the flutes and getting on with her job. The band raise their glasses and toast one another. They were all bewildered by everything that was going on around them. There were fierce looking chimps running around the backstage corridors and dressing rooms, and there were fiercer looking men standing around smoking cigars, sipping scotch, covered in gold, speaking out of the side of their mouths. It was all even more bizarre than last year. They finished off their champagne and asked for some more, but before it reached them they were called onto the stage. The lead singer, who looked too much like Damon Albarn for it to be Damon Albarn, made his way, with the others, to the stage. They, the compare, the audience, wanted to speak to him, the band that is, before the band played their two songs and left. They were playing elsewhere tonight, it was already set up, but they could not refuse this invitation and so agreed to a couple of numbers, as a gesture, before shooting off.

They were introduced and ran on stage to a rapturous reception. The compare stood aside to share the microphone with the guy who looked too much like Damon Albarn for it to be Damon Albarn. The compare began:

For those of you who were lucky enough to be here last year... You may remember that we all paid our respects to the late, and great Ronnie Kray...(respectful pause) And our good friend here took up our challenge to put Ronnie's name in a song, as a tribute, and put him in the Hit Parade. Well he did it...just... And now I would like to hear a huge round of applause for these boys (applause)...Thank you...

The band go into their song, the singer into his routine. Lisa jumps up and down excitedly in her chair. Some people get up to dance at their tables. Masters looks on; annoyed. He is appalled by Lisa's behaviour. He did not like the way that she encouraged men to talk to her. She did not excuse herself, or back away, or even just stand there with her mouth shut. She was supposed to be blonde not talkative. This was all that he needed. He would have to sort her out later. Despite her making a fool out of both of them, he was not totally unhappy. He had got what he wanted. He had won. A strange feeling would not go away though. He felt as if this was not his. That he would never be able to enjoy all of it, especially as the silvergrey haired man was still keeping tabs on him. He often felt as if he were not real, as if some day, someone, would find him out. What then? He had worked hard for all of this. There was no way that he was going to lose it all, not now. He had been the one taking all of the risks. Why should he do anything but enjoy, recline into the fruits of his labour and take what he was due. He had got everything; wardrobes full of clothes and shoes; the right kind of woman, the right looking kind of woman; the right kinds of cars; the right way of treating people; he coveted beautiful things as men in his position did; he had all of the details of power. There were still a few insects to swat and stamp on, but then there always were. The music and the dancing that was all around him made him sweat. He undid his bow tie and unfastened his top button. He signalled to a nearby waiter and ordered more coke. He was going to need a lot, a hell of a lot, if he was going to get through the rest of the night.

The band came off having finished their numbers, and their brief encore. They ran down the back stage corridor into a Limousine that was waiting to whisk them away to wherever. They ran past the waitress who sighed to herself, if only she had asked... She shook her head it could not have possibly been, surely not...

The house band struck up some ambience as the applause died down. The compare announced that a film was being shown, sent by two absent guests, Adam Bishop and Steve Vickering, close friends to many people present. They wanted to send their best wishes through him, the compare, to all of the guests, and said that they were sorry that they could not make it, but would be here next year. A large screen came down. It was some twenty feet square of solid, undisturbed whiteness. The lights dimmed a little. The hum of conversation could be heard below the gentle music of the band. The projector started rolling and the film was showing, without the sound. Most people merely glanced at it and went around to meet other people. It was just something that was available to fill in the time between the band, that had had to leave so quickly, and the High Priestess of Dance herself: Mademoiselle Hermione. She was going to be dancing and singing tonight. She was understandably top of the bill.

John and Serge looked on with interest. They left their table for a while a little concerned as to what the film was going to show, but it turned out to be okay. It was just one of Adam's skin flicks, with him, as usual, in the leading role. It was all a bit tongue in cheek, and it was much much softer than the stuff that they suspected, and had been told that, he was in to. He was dancing, to some soundless tune, around a bed, in just a g string. His body was oiled. His body hair freshly shaved. Some of the women cooed at his beautiful ersatz chest. He smiled at the camera. A great row of teeth filled the screen, each one the size of a person. Eventually, of course, Adam whips off his g string, and yes, there it is, with black blue writing down the side. Adam is pulling his cock up and down, and as it enlarges the word COBRA can be made out. There is a close up of this, so that the word COBRA now fills the whole screen. Some laughter echoes around the guests.

Adam, now fully clothed, looks at a ring on the side of some desk, that just happens to be in view. There is a close up of the glittering ring. It is all rather poor really. Adam slips on the ring. he walks into an office, which is obviously just a cardboard set with a desk, he looks around and bingo! he can see through all of the women's clothes. There is a close up on the ring and a close up on Adam's lecherous smile, so that we know that there is some kind of magic at work here. Strangely all of the women have their clothes on again now. They come up to him one by one and stroke the ringed finger. There is another close up of the ring. The close up remains for about five long seconds and then the ring starts to move around. The camera moves back so that we can see the whole picture. Adam, wearing the ring, is behind some stout middle-aged woman. They both appear to be naked. One of Adam's hands reaches over and starts to play with the woman's tits. He mugs the camera and winks. There is a quiet laughter around the room from those who can be bothered to watch it...

I cannot believe what I am seeing. I cannot believe that this is happening. There is a film being shown on a large screen, some kind of home porn movie. I am sitting at my table watching this monstrosity, and before me, projected, to at least twice her normal size, is Gillian, and she is being fucked by some huge, young, very athletic looking, guy. I turn around to look at Margaret who is just pulling her head away from a fat white line of coke. She sniffs, looks up at the screen, and smiles. She laughs loudly and then says, with what sounds like genuine admiration, but bear in mind that she is totally coked up, that Gillian is, and always has been, beautiful. The most erotic woman of her generation, or something like that, is what Margaret says. She is staring up at the giant projection as if it were a balcony and she some spellbound troubadour. This is the end. There is enough malice inside me to bring myself to fuck Margaret. I can at least do that. I will at least have some form of revenge on these abominable... What should I call them? People, Animals, Machines, Demons, whatever... I will not dance to their tune any longer. It is time for me to do what I want. It is time for me to seize the life that I want.

All of these fucking grotesques were shouting and screaming around him. He felt a vague sickness, one that he recalled from only a few days previous. It was a tepid nausea that had lodged itself in the very pit of his stomach. His mind was numb. He needed more coke. He would get that sweet prim and proper little slut to call the waiter over. She did not seem to be at the table. Where was she? She was with that queer cocksucker and his black lover. That much he was sure of. He looked around at the distorted rubber faces of the others at his table. One of them made a gesture towards a neat line of coke. Masters's eyes glazed for a second and then he smiled, as he knew that he should, and went down on it. He felt the white shit shoot up his nose at a million miles an hour and explode into thousands of ice cold sparks in his mind. He groped out a thank you. Somebody was laughing pointing at the screen. There it was. His eyes watered. His mind went into convulsions. His eyelids flickered uncontrollably for a while. He shuddered through a recurring image of something that should never of happened a long time ago. There it was. There she was, his mother, HIS MOTHER, being fucked from behind by The Bishop, his Bishop. He sat transfixed. A close up of Adam's cock sliding into her moistened cunt. Then a cut to her over made up face, mouth open, tongue lolling out, lapping across her scarlet lips. She blinked, opened her eyes, she knew what was happening, happening to him, and she was cloaked in her whoredom. She closed her eyes and smiled, moving her chest up and down with muted inhaling. A cut back to the cock penetrating the cunt. The word COBRA appeared and disappeared again, again, again, again. The lines of the letters seemed to blur with each thrust, as if they were not tattooed on, but were rather painted on in some non-permanent marker. It cut to a close up of Adam and, despite the fact that there was no sound to the film, he could hear him saying, "Phil, Phil, she's fackin' great. Look at 'er, she's fackin lav'in' it. You kept 'er quiet for sam time, bat we're all entie-uled to fack 'er nar ain' we, ha, ha, ha, ha, ha, ha, ha................"

The laughter continued. Lisa came back and went down on another line. He went down too, but the line of coke turned into a long, thin, snake wriggling penis of perfect whiteness. The penis forced its way into his nose and he could feel it moving inside his alimentary canal, poisoning his body. He choked and sneezed and coke flew all over everyone and everyone laughed and ordered more and more and Lisa slapped his back and he coughed and sneezed some more and his mother was coming her flesh shaking with her sick orgasm and the penis was in his mouth choking him and Lisa slapped his back harder and more people went down on their coke and penis and and Adam and his mother turned to face each other and they did the missionary and put their arms around one another's necks and began to strangle each other and their faces turned red and white and pale blue and a lifeless purple and they kept coming their eyeballs ready to pop and he felt a hand on his shoulder pushing him down and he went down on more coke and his mother and Adam fucked and fucked and fucked...

The lights went out. There were a few whistles from the crowd. The compare stepped out from the wings. A spotlight followed his path for the eyes of the audience. A microphone magnified the sound of his voice for the ears of the audience.

Ladies and Gentlemen it is time for me to introduce tonight's very special guest. She has come here, for your entertainment, from the cities of Milan, Rome, and Paris. She is, by popular decree, the most renowned dancer in the world. She leaves on Monday for New York, but tonight, and for one night only, she is going to perform for us, here in London Town... She is, I think you'll agree, one very special lady. She is Mademoiselle Hermione...

The lights go down low. There is an expectant hush. The curtain goes up. Six men and six women pull themselves up from off the floor moving in time with the echoing, reverberating, sound of a plucked bass string that keeps making more and more sound. Each woman takes a man's hand and leads him in a circle around and around. They stop for a moment and spin their male partners into the centre of the circle, where they meet and rebound back to their female partners. They continue with their dance to a tinkling piano. The suspense builds as everyone cranes their necks trying to be the first to spot the infamous Mademoiselle Hermione. Suddenly she is there, right at the front. The other dancers have on silver shorts, and the women bras, but she is dressed with much more panache. She has brown hair all piled up on her head like an enormous beehive with a couple of perpendicular sticks in to hold it up. She has on thigh high silver boots with vertical heels, a silver basque tied at the front in a double bow and very short silver shorts that dig in tightly to her thighs. She is holding a microphone and, against the distorted shimmering sounds that emanate from the stage, she begins to move. A piano starts to play the most beautiful music and she begins:

> It's safe in the city
> To love in a doorway

The crowd applauds. Everyone stands to get a better view of her. She glides around the stage:

> Boys, boys, its a sweet thing
> Boys, boys, its a sweet thing, sweet thing

She unwinds her arm that is not holding the microphone and she fans it across the crowd as if she is welcoming them. People are competing for space on the table tops. There is a lot of pushing and pulling going on. White powder is being kicked up off the tables, by leather soled shoes, into the faces of those lined in the aisles, up on tiptoes. There is an electricity in the air, a mesmeric miasma.

> On the street where you live
> I could not hold up my head

> Because I gave all I had
> In another bed
> On another floor
> In the back of a car
> In a cellar of a church
> With the door ajar

The male dancers rush over to her and run their hands all over her body. Then the women dancers rush over and run their hands all over her body. They pull the two sticks from out of her hair and it falls down into a symmetrical parting. She screams banshee like into the microphone, her fine hair jumps around her face like a lion's mane. The hairs under her armpits, dark and straight, lap up like flames around her arms. Her pubic hair bristles over the top of her silver shorts. Her figure is smooth, curvilinear, a moving ball of liquid mercury. The long unshaven hairs on the inside of her thighs rub warmly against one another as she sways, and moves, and dances.

> I guess we could cruise down one more time
> With you by my side it would be fine
> We buy some drugs
> And watch a band
> We jump in a river
> Holding hands

The whole scene is sublime. The dancers move with the precision of machines, never making an error, never missing the beat, always synchronized.

The first number finished. Feet stamped on the tables. Hands clapped together furiously. Shouts went up. There were calls from every corner. The lights were dimmed and then came on again as she went straight into the second number. She sings into the microphone.

> If I was your girlfriend

Mademoiselle Hermione went into a tight spin. Then she pulled out of it and backed off into a troupe of female dancers who removed her bodice with a mean rip and left her body exposed except for a silver bra. The hairs on her stomach were quite visible, and so they should be, after all they were her trademark. The crowd roared as her semi naked firm hairy flesh writhed, tossed, twisted, thrashed and distorted before them. She was a wonderful mover, very impressive when she was in full flight. She continued to sing and backed off into a troupe of male dancers who ran their hands all over her feminine curves, as if she were the most voluptuous woman in the world. She began singing again.

> If I was your girlfriend
> Would you remember
> To tell me all the things you forgot
> When I was your man

On the word "man" the male dancers that were surrounding her pulled down her shorts, exposing her to the audience. There, in the spotlight, in full view, was her, small, pink, only slightly retarded, penis. The crowd began to clap in tune with the song. Her breasts and penis bounced freely as she moved across the stage, first this way and then that and then this again. The song finished and once again the lights dimmed. She waited for the applause to die down before addressing the crowd. She spoke in a kind of hybridized European accent, introducing herself, her dancers, and her band. Then she looked down at Masters who was in total awe of her. She said that the next one was dedicated to him. She began, alone this time, no dancers, no dancing as such.

> You want to know
> How it will be
> Me and him
> Or you and me

Her voice was haunting like Grace Slick's rendition of the song. She began to make long strides to the front of the stage and descend the stairs seductively, casting her gaze at anyone who dared to meet it.

> What can we do now we both love you
> I love you too
> I can't really see

> Why can't we go on as three?

She makes a beeline for Masters. She kicks up her foot on the table pushes her breasts into one of the other men's faces, then pushing him off, she gives Masters one hundred percent attention. Masters begins to sweat. She rubs her limp penis against his leg as she squats next to him. She ripples her stomach, highlighting her dark brown hairs and leans as close to his face with her chest as she can without touching him. The crowd is in a frenzy, urging her on, urging Masters on. Lisa sits, trying to see the funny side, her hand over her mouth in naive shock.

> You are afraid
> Embarrassed too
> No one has ever said
> Such a thing to you

She looks deep into Masters's mind, she reads it, smiles indulgently, and delivers the next line with the flicker of lust in her eyes only seen, and even then rarely, in the greatest of Motion Picture Vampires.

> Your mother's ghost stands at your shoulder
> Face like ice
> A little bit colder
> Saying to you
> You can't do that it breaks all the rules
> You learned in school
> I don't really see
> Why can't we go on as three?

She moved behind Masters so that he had to move in his chair to see her. She danced for him holding the microphone above her head.

She finished the song and it was as if the walls of the building were going to collapse under the immensity of the cheering. She took her place back upon the stage and bowed to her adoring crowd.

Back in the hotel room, Masters, shoes off, shirt undone, smoking a large joint, was watching the TV. It was a strange colourful film. He was not really watching it, but at the same time he was totally engrossed by it. Lisa was talking on and on. It was the coke. She came out of the bathroom to continue her sentence, make her point, and then disappeared back into the bathroom. A guy, a horribly good looking guy, with blonde hair, his hands tied behind his back, was lying on the floor laughing at another guy with dark hair, and long side burns, in some kind of Superman, Superwoman, suit... Lisa once again interrupted the film, stealing his attention. Masters tried to ignore her and get back to the film. The guy with the dark hair has a sword and he takes it in both hands and cuts the blonde guy's head off, it rolls dumbly across the floor. Masters shivers. Lisa is looking at him expectantly, as if she has just asked him a question and is awaiting the answer. He tells her, simply, that he does not know. She seems to be quite happy with this and goes back into the bathroom and continues talking. Once again he tries to get back into the film.

Philip...(she whines from the bathroom)

Philip...

What?

Why don't we celebrate?

We have been.

No... Okay yes, we have been, but we don't have to stop now do we? Why don't we turn down the lights, slip underneath the sheets and make love like we've never made love before?

You've got your period haven't you?

Yes... but we could always put a towel underneath, keep the sheet clean, please, what do you say?

Fuck off... Dirty slag... On your fucking period... There's something the matter with you slag.

Lisa walks over to him, clenching her tiny mighty fists. She looks down at him defiantly.

You'd better take that back... I'm no slag... I've been surrounded by trash all my life but I've never been trash, and I won't put up with trash any longer, now take it back Philip. I'm warning you...

Okay, okay, but I'm not going to fuck you, you can forget about that. I don't want to touch you whilst you've got all that blood around. You might have AIDS for all I know. Don't forget I know what you models get up to...

Lisa fights to hold back the tears. She chokes on the swelling in her throat.

How can you say such things?

Lisa begins to flail at him with all the strength that she can muster. Masters aims a heavy kick at her midrift. It throws her back across the room and she hits her head against the wall and falls to the floor. She lies motionless for a moment. Blood trickles out from between her legs as if she were a cracked urn. Masters springs to his feet and drags her up by the neck.

Now listen to me you piece of TRASH.

He slaps her hard across the face with his free hand.

Don't you ever try to hit me again. I don't let TRASH touch me see.

He slaps her across the face again, harder this time.

It's been a good night and you've had to spoil it.

Lisa tries to squirm out of his grip. Her heart is pounding with fear.

I could smash your skull with one hand, do you know that? I step on TRASH for a living. That's right, I round up all of the TRASH and lock them up. That's why I'm here. That's why I allow you to be here. So don't talk to me about TRASH, because I'm a fucking expert on it.

He throws her down on the bed.

Now if you lie down like a nice girl, instead of mouthing off like a piece of TRASH, then I might just forget about this little episode, put it down to experience and too much of that white shit that you've been snorting all night. It's your choice Lisa. It's all up to you.

Chapter 26

Adam's Apple

Where was he? He had looked in the cabin. He had looked in the bar, the restaurant, the casino, the top deck, and the dutyfree shop. Steve was nowhere to be found. Adam was losing his patience. It would not be long before they reached England, maybe three hours, maybe less, and he wanted to fuck that Harry bitch while she was still alive, and he wanted Steve to hold the camera. Where the fuck was he? This was going to be Adam's "coup de grace", his masterpiece. He was going to fuck Harry, who had turned out to be a decent looking bird, the boss's missus, or rather, soon to be, dead boss's missus. He could not really tell that much about her. The trouser suit that she had been wearing hid most of her body, and they had hardly seen her whilst they were in Amsterdam, but he did know that she had good looks, wasn't overweight, and had enough mouth on her to guarantee that he was going to enjoy making her squeal. He had already said that he wanted to give it to her long and hard, real hard, just so that she knew what she had been missing all of these years. He couldn't think of anything else, hadn't been able to since she had introduced herself. The thing was that he had not seen her in the last couple of hours either. The last time that he spoke to her she was going to have a word with the lorry drivers, probably arranging their fees before they took the shit through customs. He decided to try the bar again.

Adam was wearing tight PVC silver trousers, through which you could make out the tight elasticated lines of the dollar green posing pouch that he was wearing underneath. He had on black Base boots and a black nylon V necked top with sleeves that tapered out to the wrists, with a small hole cut out in the body, so as to show off his tight brown navel. He looked around the bar; no Steve; no Harry. He went to turn around, his face a tense shade of sanguine, his fists clenched with rage, when he noticed a long pair of slim, smooth, legs, that were crossed invitingly. The person was sitting up on a high stool at the bar, bolting some spirit or another, and ordering a new measure. When he finally got around to looking at her face he realised that it was Harry. He gave out a heavy boxer's sniff and walked over to her.

She looked very different. She was wearing a tight green micro skirt, little green Converse trainers without socks, a beaded anklet, and a stretch green lycra Tshirt that revealed some of her delicate cleavage. Around her neck was a gold necklace with the legend "Harry" in the middle like a pendant, a kind of identity necklace. Harry had a cute gamine look, very charming, quite sexy. Her short brown bob shone as she turned to meet Adam's greeting. He pulled up a stool, took another look at her legs, and ordered an Irish Whiskey.

You ain' seen Steve ararnd 'av ya?

I've been in my room. I came out to the bar about twenty minutes ago. I haven't seen anyone since I've been sitting here... apart from that (pointing) friendly barman whose been serving me with Vodka.

You look like you're goin' for it. I saw ya knock one back from over there... An' wot's all this in aid of?

Adam makes a gesture to her clothes, her appearance.

I fought you was one o' them Women's Libbers....ya know...don't get me wrang you look lavlee, really lavlee likc...

Thanks...

She raises her glass to Adam's, their glasses chink together, and she bolts down another and calls over the barman. Adam drinks his down too and insists on paying for the next round. After some hesitation Harry concedes. She watched Adam as he ordered the drinks. He had a profile to die for.

Sometimes, Adam, a girl just wants to put on her WonderBra, shave her legs, and show the world that she's still got what it takes.

Well you look great lav, like I said really lavlee... Wot about John though? Wot would 'e fink abou' it?

She gave out a dismissing blast of air.

What do I care... I'm not sure about the two of us any more... I mean when was the last time that you saw us together?

I take ya point...

We never see each other... We hardly spend any time together... He's too busy running around, worrying about Philip bloody Masters, rather than giving me any attention...

I find that difficul' t'belive... I mean, no disrespec' or anyfink, bat, well, you're a lavlee lookin' woman. If I was 'im (and I soon will be he thought to himself), well if I was 'im, I would'n wanna let ya out me sight... 'E mast be mad...

She was a little taken back by his compliment. She looked deep into his aqua blue eyes trying to detect if he really meant it or not, but she found herself being drawn in by them. She had to force herself to blink in order to pull away from them and their enchanting allure.

So 'ow did the two of you meet then?...you an' John like...

She begins to smile as she remembers how they met.

Well I'm from The States, Illinois originally, but I spent my youth in Boston, you can probably tell...

Me an' Steve we fought that you were'n English like, bat we were'n sure where you was from, we fought you was problee American... You can't really tell your accen', you've lost a lot of it ain' ya... An' wiv you speakin' French an' tha' it's a bit confusin'. "Geez we didn't know for sure if you was Amarycan".

Harry laughs at his poor attempt at an American accent, but she manages to hold it back, so as not to offend him. Her laugh is mild enough to make him smile, and he beams a few pearly white teeth at her.

I wanted to see some of Europe. I was hearing all about this Rave thing, and Techno, and all kinds of good things, and I wanted to see it for myself. I hung out in Paris for a while, and I spent some time in Rome, looking around, sending postcards, the whole tourist deal right... I got to Amsterdam, I took an E, I went to a Rave, and pow, it was... it was... it was just fucking amazing... I couldn't stop myself. I loved it. Suddenly I had thousands of new friends. I was taking more and more E's, clubbing every night, I met some cool guys, I did some cool things... Then one day the money ran out. I met some English guy. We hung out together, had a rad time. He looked after me, bought my drugs, took me to all of the right places, it was a blast. He had to go home though. He was on some year out thing and was going home to a nice job, and a nice girl. He gave me the last of his money before he left and then he got on the ferry and sailed off into the sunset...

Shit...

Yeah well he never made any promises... I should have gone home but I just loved the life. I spent the last of the money, that Dave left me, on E's, and I started dealing. The problem was that I'd get off my tits, take more and more, and give half of them away to friends, to anyone who danced with me for more than five minutes. The next thing I knew I had no money left, again. I phoned my dad to wire me some cash but I found out that he had gone away with his secretary for a couple of months, to some hideaway in the Caribbean. My mother's second husband and I don't get on. I think that he was probably wiping out the messages that I was leaving on their answer machine, anyway fuck him, they're divorced now. I started stealing but I wasn't very good at it, and there are only so many shops that you can steal from before they recognize your face and stop letting you in. There was only one thing for it...

Wot... You wen' on the game...

Adam tried to stop his eyes from lighting up, but he was sure that they had anyway.

Well yes... But I was lucky... The first person to take me seriously was John... Before I had picked up a client I had got myself a new boyfriend. He was good to me, real nice you know. It was as if he saved me. He was my gallant English knight in shining armour, my Lancelot... But you know I think about it now and I realise that I would have sorted myself out. He didn't save me. If we hadn't have met I would have found another way out. To hear him talk it is as if I have to thank him for saving my soul... As if he was the only person standing between me and Satan himself... The more that I think about it the more that his attitude pisses me off you know.

Typical ov sam blowks tho' innit... Jast wanna take all the credit n' all tha'...

Yeah... (starting to pick up his intonation) Well I had a lot of contacts. I introduced him to people who could introduce him to the people that he needed to meet. I helped him out. He forgets that now, but I was the one that set him up. He wouldn't be half the....bloke....that he is now if it wasn't for me....and I've been overseeing things on this end ever since. We see each other, a weekend here and there, a holiday in Spain occasionally, apart from that it's long telephone calls and the odd bunch of something from Interflora.

He mast be stupid...

It's okay Adam...

She put her hand on his to quiet his protests. Her hand looked so small next to his giant paw. She stopped for a moment and imagined what a giant's hands would feel like, if those hands were all over her body, and him standing there a huge tower of strength ready to move down onto her, and into her. Once again she had to pull herself away from her thoughts. She told him that she was not going to put up with it for any longer and that she had decided to leave Amsterdam, and would only return there to pick up her belongings. She was finished with it all. She ordered two more drinks. Adam insisted on paying for them. It was kind of sweet of him to keep insisting so she let it go, if it made him happy... As the barman poured the drinks she told Adam that he was a real gent. He got up to go to the toilet. She watched his cute and tidy ass move as he walked. She could not stop looking at his VPL that was showing through those tight revealing silver trousers. Nobody had made her feel like this since she had been a teenager. She was now twenty five, drunk, getting drunker, and enjoying herself. She made a pact with herself not to check out his crotch area when he returned to the bar. She giggled and took another sip of Vodka.

Adam took out the COBRA and pissed into the porcelain basin. Where the fuck was Steve? He'd got that slag eating out of the palm of his hand. All he needed was a cameraman, and to buy her a few more of the same. Time was running out. If it came to it he would have to fuck her without Steve around, just leave the camera on the side, and point it at the bed. Shit the camera was in his room and they would probably go back to her more luxurious cabin. Shit, maybe he was going to have to be satisfied with a fuck for now, and they could film some scenes of the two of them together once she was dead.

When he walked back in he noticed that she was looking at his crotch, the bulge in his trousers. She had probably turned herself on imagining the COBRA in his hand as he took his piss. He looked around, no Steve, maybe he'd bumped into those posh student birds again, Adam smiled to himself, that dirty fucker. It was either that or he had met some slope-eyed Chink at the roulette wheel. He sat back down on his stool and moved it right up next to Harry's. There is an uncomfortable silence. They both take large sips from their drinks.

You've 'ad it raff then ain' ya?

You could say that...

I 'ad t' cam ap the 'ard way n'all. I'm a self made man like. I've 'ad t' do everyhing for myself. It's the best way I s'pose. I've been workin' for John too. There've been a lot of good times, I can't say there 'ave'nt been, bat I'm sick of doin' 'is dirty work too, ya know... I'm like you...

Are you?

Yeah, course... I'd like to leave all of this behind you know... It don't appeal to me any more... Don't get me wrang, I ain' 'ad it as 'ard as you like, bat it ain' been no bed 'a roses either.

He finishes off his drink.

Cam on let me buy ya anafa, please, I'm enjoyin' myself, on me, we'll drarn our sorrows together, wot d'ya say?

Okay then....okay....why not? Let's make a toast to us. We're taking no more shit right...

Right!

They put their empty glasses down on the bar and Adam signals to the barman.

'Arry....ahem....Harry....

Please call me Harriet. I'd like you to call me Harriet I only wear a skirt on leap years and even then only for one evening, so you're very lucky, or hadn't you noticed?...

She looked at him trying not to try too hard to be seductive.

Fanks, it's a lavlee name tha' HHarriet. Anyway wot was I goin' t' say....err......oh yeah....that was it....I want you to try samfink special....a little cocktail I've made ap. Don't warry it's great like....you'll like it, I promise ya. It's made wiv apple....You know that new drink Pommetizer....look there, the one with the Frog (pointing)....That's right...You'll like it I swear....It's French right, "Pomme", apple, right?... Should be right ap your street like...

He orders the drinks from the barman, reminding him to bring over the promotion scratchcards with the frogs on.

I wondered why there were all of these pictures of toads everywhere.

Frogs ain' they. You know like the French, and frogs like, d'you get it?... Like the French they eat frogs n'tha' don't they? So we all call 'em frogs see?...

The drinks fizz as the barman pours in the Pommetizer.

So what do you have it with?

Anyfink really....Vodka's good....or Bacardi....or whateva you like...

I like Vodka...

I fought you did, you've drank enaff ov it.

They both laugh together. Harry, sorry I mean Harriet, watched those aqua blue eyes sparkle as Adam threw his head back in appreciation of his own little joke. She felt dizzy, as if she was disappearing into his eyes. She was in a soothing trance, deep in appreciation of his irises, those cool blue pools that she just wanted to dive into.

You are absolutely sure about this then?

Yeah course...

She looked at Adam sincerely, as if she were about to ask the first question ever asked by a human being, and then she asked the question.

Are you sure about the apple Adam?

Don't warry about it. Jast keep it t' yerself like. We don't want everyone to know now do we?

He gave Harriet an encouraging wink and then watched her take her first drink before he, too, tasted it, just for the record. The bubbles fizzed and Harriet gave out a burp that made other people standing, or sitting, at the bar turn around. She held her hand up to her mouth, rather embarrassed, and they both fell into fits of laughter. Adam urged her to drink it off whilst ordering another.

I don't know about you but I haven't had this much fun for as long as I can remember.

Me neither...

Look I want to apologize for being so abrupt, you know, when I first met you. Look I'm sorry, it's just one of those built in defence mechanisms that we all seem to have, in some form or another.

I've already forgotten abou' it, 'onestly, don't warry... Wot did you 'av to be so defensive abou' anyway?

Well....I was....err... (she is blushing)

Wot?

I had heard a lot about you and...well...

Well wot? Wot was the problem?

You're embarrassing me now...

Spit it out fer God's sake, it can't be that bad...

It was just that....you know....well....oh dear... It was just that I did not expect you to be so good looking okay....there I've said it now...(blushing even more)

She looks up at him with large doe eyes.

Yeah, fanks, I quite fancied you n'all like.

You're just saying that to hide my blushes.

No I ain'....I would'nt do tha'.

She hooks her feet into the rest on the stool and hunches forwards looking at the frog (toad) on the scratchcard. She is silent for a moment, as if she is listening, as if the toad was whispering some secret that was meant only for her.

You know what Adam, I think I'd like a cigarette. I haven't had one in....oh....ages. Have you got any?

Yeah, bat 'ow about we go back to my cabin. We could smoke sam ov the draw, cigarettes are are alrigh' bat they don't make it speshal like... We could get camfortable... It would be really nice n'tha'.

Are you asking what I think you're asking?

Yeah I am. (staring calculatedly)

Well I don't know, what about John?

You said yerself that you're sick ov 'Im. You don't owe 'im nafink. Wot about it? Me and you?

He looked down to where her skirt ended and her legs began. He could feel his cock pushing out hard against his tight trousers. He wiped his lips on the back of his hand. Harriet sat and thought about it.

Okay but listen let's go back to my cabin. It's cosier. We don't want your friend coming in and disturbing us.... (actually that was exactly what Adam wanted) And I've got some coke, personal, good stuff...

Let's go...

Wait Adam (her speech had noticeably degenerated into a drunk's slur) there's something I have to tell you first. That story, about me, you know....well John wasn't the first person....you know...when I was short on money and all....I.....I....just wanted to let you know. I was a broken woman for a while, and it may sound foolish to you, but I thought that John was going to put me back together, and at first he did, kind of, but... I just want you to remember that I'm fragile.

He held her head in his great hands, and he looked at her face, and she thought that she was going to faint, her heart pumped faster than she could count.

Like I said, don't warry about nafink, alright... I'll pat you back togeva

They stood up together without breaking their eye contact, until Harriet suddenly got an alcohol rush and stumbled blindly to the side. Adam caught her with one hand and she looked up at that hard handsome jaw of his as if she had swooned. It was perfect, like the fairy story that she had been waiting for since she had been a little girl. He stood her back up on her feet. They began their walk to her cabin. As they descended a flight of stairs Adam remembered that they had forgotten their scratchcards.

Come on Adam, forget about them...

He wanted to have one more look for Steve, but even he realised that it was a lame excuse. They continued.

Adam Bishop I think you've gone and got me drunk and now you're going to take advantage of me...

"I sure do 'ope so maam."

They laughed together at his second attempt at an American accent.

They stood outside the door while she got her keys out of her purse. Then she reached up on tiptoes and wrapped her arms around his neck and kissed his mouth. They stood locked on to one another, each exploring the other with their welcoming tongues. He was a great kisser, maybe the best she had ever had. She made a move to draw away but he followed her. She enjoyed his persistence, and his firm controlling grip. She moved away again and this time he allowed her to move away. His cock made him impatient to get inside her room. Her eyes sparkled as an idea suddenly came to her.

I've got an idea.

Wot?

She put the key in the lock.

I'm going to treat you to something special. Close your eyes and let me lead you... That's it, no peaking... no peaking I said... She sat him down on the edge of the bed. He squinted out of his left eye, but it was pitch black in there.

Wot is it?

No peeking you. I'm just going to put on some music, just to get me in the right mood.

He smiled at this, but was then a little startled as Harriet turned the radio on full blast. Janis Joplin was screaming "get it while you can" and above this he could hear Harriet shout.

Okay I hope you're ready for this.

His cock was throbbing with anticipation. As he opened his eyes she turned the light on. It was bright enough to hurt. He shied from the light for a moment, squinting, and then realised that she still had all of her clothes on. It was all a bit puzzling. She nodded at something behind him. He turned around to see what it was. He was surprised, a little disappointed, yet quite relieved to see Steve lying on the bed behind him, sleeping. Steve had a thin pale smile on his lips. The dirty fucker, Adam thought to himself again. How could Steve sleep through this great fucking din. He went to reach over to wake him up, when Harriet did something that caught his attention. He turned to look back at Harriet who was lifting her skirt up to him, showing off a nice pair of lily white panties. She put her skirt back down. She had a cute shiny 38 in her hands with a pretty pearl handle. She shouted over Janis Joplin once more, her speech was suddenly clear again, sober.

You stupid prick.

She fired the first bullet into his head throwing his body backwards, but he was so heavy, so immense, that he began to slump forward again. She let off two more. One hit him in the shoulder, the other in the throat. He tried to say something, but no words came out of his mouth only thick hot red blood. She took a step back as he fell face forwards onto the floor. She put the smoking barrel down onto the back of his head, pushed her foot into his back to steady herself, and let off one more, just to be thorough. Then she turned the radio off. She put the gun down, picked up a mobile phone and dialled.

She held the phone up to her ear with one hand, the other rested on her hip which she stuck out to the side in a gesture of defiance, but to whom she could not be sure. The telephone had chance to ring out only once.

Serge... Yes...

Both of them.

(repeating what Serge is saying) A blue Ford Cabriolet soft top. (pauses, waiting for confirmation)

She put the telephone down, and put the gun away. The back of Adam's head had cracked and collapsed like a china bowl. There were thick sticky strands of blood, and what looked like mucus, which had burst out from the back of his head, and had all entangled in his blonde hair in abstract spiders' webs. She brushed off tiny shards of skull from her smooth shins and cleaned off the warm spray of blood from her ankles and her Converse. There was a knock at the door.

Harriet opened the door and a thin man in his late twenties walked in. She locked the door behind him. He was wearing the ferry company's uniform. His face, and features, were slim. His arms, and legs, were skinny, but honest. He looked at the two fresh corpses and the pool of blood that was increasing in size second by second.

Oh my God...

She reached over and held him close to her, squeezing him tightly.

Harry what's going on?...

It's the end. I'm leaving Amsterdam. This (she points to the two dead men) was my last job. I'm going to London for a few days and then I'm leaving Europe. I'm not carrying anything through, it's over.

You can't just leave... What about us?... For God's sake, what about these two bodies?...

He was beginning to feel sick as the idea of being next to two murdered men began to sink in. He began to realsie that the blood on the walls, over the bed, and all over the floor, was real.

We'll clean this shit (points to Adam and Steve) up, but that's it. I won't be taking anymore ferries. I'm going to leave these two somewhere where they can be found in a day or two's time. You are going to help me. I'm going to leave a decent sized stash of coke with them. The police are going to be all over the place. Nobody is going to be able to move anything through here for quite some time. That guy I told you about Masters he's not going to be able to do anything. He will not be able to bring anything in, and it will be John and his associates who hold all of the cards. I've given the right gifts to the right people in Amsterdam, smoothed things over with them. The drugs are going to be made in a factory somewhere in the Midlands. John made a deal with an old friend of his. They're an Indian group, reliable, professional; they don't make mistakes; they don't get careless, not like these two. So you see the operation no longer needs me, and I no longer need it. You know that I've wanted to leave it all behind for, well, for as long as I've known you. I'm sick of working in all of this filth. I'm taking my ticket out of here. I'm going to start again.

Don't go Harry... Please... Please don't leave me... Take me with you but don't leave me here...

He stood in silence as tears fought their way down his cheeks. He blinked through his sobs, trying to maintain his dignity.

I love you Harry... I'm begging you please...

Harriet stepped away from the expanding perimeter of blood.

Look, I love you too, but don't you see it won't work, it can't work...

It can... It can...

No, Gary, it can't. You see what we had was special, really special. The thing is I could make you happy, for a time maybe, but it wouldn't last, and I couldn't do that to you, I couldn't. You see, my angel, none of it works for me, not any more. I can't enjoy love...

Because you won't let yourself, but I'll make you, you'll see, just give me a chance...

I can't, it's not that I won't.

What have I done wrong?... What is it?... Just tell me please...

Don't blame yourself. If you want to blame somebody blame these two (she looks at Steve and Adam, she kicks Adam hard with her toe). This bastard, you see this bastard, there are people at his house now freeing poor souls, poor children, who he has tormented, interfered with, and beaten, whose lives he has ruined forever, forever... Those children how can they know love...

You mean how can you know love? But what you really mean is how can you love me? Is that it, you just don't love me any more? If it is then why don't you just say it?

You're not listening to me... It's not that... It's not that... It's not you, it's not your fault. I can't do the things that you want me to do. I can't be the person that you want me to be, that you deserve. I love you Gary, as much as I can love anyone. When you've experienced something bad, something real bad, things are never the same again, no matter how hard you try. When you wake up one morning and the whole world is shaking, the very ground beneath you is no longer still, but moving, the walls of your house crumble and the roof caves in, what do you do? You get up, you cry, you weep, you dust yourself off, and you start again. You build a new house, and you try and make it as best as you can, but you're never the same, because as much as you like the new house you know that at any moment, without warning, it's going to all fall apart again. People like me we play a different game, with different rules, and all that we do is hurt people, beautiful people, like you.

Show me Harry... Please show me... I want to be people like you...

His pleading brings tears to her eyes, but she cannot quite let them materialize, cannot let them fall, and she knows that this is why she must leave him.

You're going back to him aren't you?....to John....is that it? Is that what you want?

It's got nothing do with him, but I'm not going to lie to you. I have to do what I have to do in order to survive. It's not because I don't love you, or that I love him more, it's not about that... It's about me. I've spent my life on the rapids jumping onto each and every log that looked as though it was going to overtake the one that I was on. It's the way it has to be for me. Don't upset yourself any more Gary.

She touched his face with her hand.

Now, my sweetheart, I have something for you.

She hands over a large white package full of fifties.

Here you go. This is your pay off. They have two options. They either kill you or pay you off. I argued your case. There's a lot of money there. Take it home to your wife. You've said yourself that she's a good woman. She looks pretty enough in all of the photos that I've seen. On your way home buy her something beautiful to wear; a dress so beautiful that you know she'll never get chance to wear it, make her see that she's desirable, make it work with her, because it can't work for us, it just can't. When it all dies down stop working here; spend more time with her. There's enough money there to start a small business, a new life, work together. I know that she loves you, that she will look after you.

She leaned over and kissed his forehead.

I'm sorry my little puppy. I'm truly sorry. I was a broken woman, in need of repair, I had fallen apart, nobody cared, and then you, you, put me back together again. You are the one true selfless person to have ever touched upon my life, and you have left ripples of love that will go on until the end of time. I was damaged goods, and now I owe everything to you. (with tears in her eyes she kisses him again) I'll always, always, think of you.

Chapter 27

Harry

You and Chris are sitting in the front seats of the blue Ford Cabriolet soft top that Serge gave you the keys to. The two of you have to pick up some woman who is on the ferry from Holland. You are parked up on the carpark. Things are going pretty well for you, especially since you made the delivery for Moz. Things are going pretty well for both of you. You seem to have caught on with John and Serge's outfit. You're even doing a job for them. Serge spoke to you, he actually handed you the keys. You are no longer a wannabe...

You are not quite sure though. You've discussed it all with Chris over and over. There are lots of things happening. Masters finally got the nod from London so he's the main man now. Everybody knows that Adam is John's number one man, yeah Moz is useful but he's getting on, he's part of the old school, he just wants an easy life. Moz has got his family to think about. Adam and Steve though they're a team, and it seems as though it's all going to come down to them. If they stay loyal to John then, with his drug business being very healthy, he may well be able to keep his power. After what Fat Stuart The Poof had to say though you and Chris are pretty sure that The Bishop is soon going to be working for the other side, and you and Chris, and everybody else for that matter, can't see how John and Serge's operation can keep going without him. He's too powerful, has too much support, too many people are too scared of him to oppose him. And yeah sure you've caught on but Serge has got you running around picking up some poxy bird from the port, hardly the stuff of your comic book fantasies now is it...

Chris thinks that you should play it cagey. After all you're both moving up in within John's group of associates. The thing is not to commit yourself to anything major, stay loyal but keep in touch with the opposition, don't burn your bridges so to speak. If you need to jump ship you'll both be ready. For the time being you're willing to sit tight and see what happens, enjoy yourself a little, because this is what you wanted. Just because John may soon be history doesn't necessarily mean that you will be.

You would both really like to sit here in sun glasses, looking cool, with the top of the car folded back, but there is a light grey drizzle emerging with the beginning of the day's sunlight, and Chris has had to put the soft top up. The two of you seem to have done a lot of waiting around since you started doing jobs for Serge and John, none of it is quite how you expected it to be. Chris turns to you.

This looks like her (pointing).

A woman in a rather chic grey pinstriped trouser suit is making long strides towards you. She is carrying a holdall in one hand and a suitcase in the other. She opens the back door of the car, on the driver's side, throws her luggage in, and then gets in herself. She holds her hand out to you, and then Chris.

Hello I'm Harriet...

She shakes hands and then, between the two of you, she dangles over a bunch of keys and an address.

One of you has to deliver a car. I parked it at the end of this row. It's a grey BMW. It's okay Serge knows all about it.

Chris takes the keys which are on a Playboy Bunny keyring. You remember now that Serge had mentioned something about another car. Chris gets out of the driver's seat.

I'll call you later...

You get into the driver's seat and turn the ignition. The drive back is pretty uneventful, silent except for some tape of some French singer than the woman wanted on. She's nice enough, but you are too knackered to keep up any conversation with her, and you keep on wishing that if you have to be the pickup guy, that Serge could at least give you a few important jobs, a few major players to pickup, whose brains you could pick for advice, or who could at least give you a few entertaining stories. Never mind at least she wasn't some crazed axeman, or cold blooded murderer. You are aware that violence is a big part of the game, and you've told yourself that when the time comes you'll be ready. In the meantime you drive back in a trance of fatigue. You were out all of the night before with Chris. It's what, six o'clock in the morning now, so you missed another nights sleep too. At least your career is moving you tell yourself.

When Harry got to John's she said goodbye to the taciturn young man with the baggy eyes, who looked relieved to be off on his way, and she walked up to the door of John's country home in He came out of the house to greet her and wrapped her up in his arms lifting her off the floor. Well at least he was happy to see her. Inside he had prepared bagels with cream cheese, avocado, and smoked salmon her favourite. There was a glass jug full of chilled orange juice, champagne on ice (a little over elaborate, but a considerate touch), and fresh coffee sitting invitingly in a squat cafetiere. She could just about handle a coffee but the rest would have to wait until she had cleaned up. John was very understanding and went off to run her bath. He was certainly making an effort, but then again she'd been here before. He would talk about quitting, make plans even, raise her hopes up, when really all that he was doing was softening her up. It was quite possible that the next thing to come out of his mouth would be: "I just need you to do this one thing for me..."

She sat back in the creamy white suds of her bath, closed her eyes, and felt herself relax, really relax like she hadn't been able to since she got messed up in all this business. Maybe he did really mean it this time. Her mind wandered to Gary. It had been so awful leaving him behind, but she knew that she had made the right decision. He was a good man. Maybe things could have worked out for them, but her instinct told her that it wouldn't have. He had a pure soul, as she had had once, and a pure soul needs love. She knew too much about the world and its evils to be able to live like that. She could love, she was capable of that, but she could never be sure of how long it would last. She would have broken his heart. She had broken his heart but at least she had not made a mess of it all. He still had a life to go back to. She had tried to make him understand, and she thought that deep down he did understand, that he had always known really. In a final unselfish act of love he had let her go. Another time, in another world, who knows?...

John came up into the bathroom with two flutes bubbling with champagne.

Sorry, couldn't resist it... Come on have a glass....indulge me eh?

She smiled and nodded. John whipped out an envelope from nowhere and inside were two tickets to the West Indies. He explained that they were really going, that he was selling up, that they could stay with Serge and his family for as long as they liked, take some time out for themselves. She started to enjoy the chamagne and drank an expensive slither of cold dry bubbles. Her flesh was pink from the hot bath water. She looked at John hard and suspicious.

Do you mean it? Do you really mean it this time?

Yes I do.

John had been feeling terribly guilty about the whole Lisa La Truen thing. He didn't regret what had happened. In fact it made him realise what he wanted. It made him realise how he felt about Harry. How good things could be between people. He had had to have Lisa. He could not miss an opportunity like that. You can't turn down a fantasy, not if you were honest with yourself. Anyway he had been brought to his senses by Lisa. The thing that he had wanted from the life, when he first started, had been long mornings, and longer nights, in bed with a beautiful woman, having breakfast together, with money no obstacle. He had lost sight of that for a while, it had become a job like anything else, a business that required constant attention. Lisa, Serge, and Hanif, had all shown him what was obvious now he thought about it. He didn't need any more money, and he certainly didn't need any more stress. What he did need was a companion, someone who he could love, respect, maybe start a family with. He had, with all of their help, put his house in order. He had stopped blaming Harry for their problems and started to scrutinize himself. He still felt guilty about Lisa though, but he'd make it up to Harry. He just wished that Lisa had moved to London by now, anywhere as long as she wasn't with that beast. Even though he told himself that it was out of his hands he still felt responsible for Lisa. If anything happened to her... He told himself that she'd move along soon enough. When Masters's money and power dried up. They had already limited the opportunities for imports. The people that he and Serge were going leave behind were sitting on a pile of shit that would keep the clubs in tablets for quite some time, and as long as they paid Hanif what he was asking there would be no problems. He could disappear, Serge too, and they would not have to spend the rest of their lives looking over their shoulders for snipers in the garden, or hit men disguised as taxi drivers, or policemen, or priests, or whatever... They had taken care of everything.

As much as he wanted it, there would be no final showdown with Masters, Serge had finally made him see the folly in that. Masters would be left shaking a couple of dice with no spots on them, and by the time they stopped rolling, their blank faces on all sides adding up to a big fat zero, he'd be on the other side of the world, rubbing sun tan oil onto Harry's topless back. Masters would have a whole new cast of enemies to occupy himself with. He'd be too busy chasing his own arse to work out what a thorough whipping they'd given him. It was perfect, just when it seemed to everyone that him and Serge were finished...

I'm sorry for all of the other times Harry. All of those times when I let you down. It won't happen again.

It had better not or I'll be out of your life forever.

John grimaced at the thought.

It won't. I love you Harry.

She smiled, scooped up some of the foam from her bath onto her finger, and dabbed it gently onto the end of his nose. Her movements were playful, feline, full of poise and grace.

We're going to make a go of it this time aren't we?

Yes, I promise.

She stood up and he passed her a large soft bath towel. She wrapped it around herself and held her arm out for another which she twisted onto her head in the fashion of a turban. She stepped out of the bath. He moved straight to her, embracing her and all of her wet skin. She laughed. He kissed her gently on the lips and as she responded he started to remove the towel from around her firm slim body.

Not yet... I'm sorry but I'm not ready.

John backed away, held his hands up.

It's okay... I understand... No pressure...

We've got a lot of talking to do. I really want to make things work. We may have to take our time.

That's okay, really, please, we need time, and we'll have plenty of it on the beaches of St. Lucia.

She looked at him, her eyes sparkling.

You do understand then. You do want to help me.

He nodded.

John, I'm a broken woman, I need your strength again, to put me back together again, like you did before (John is visibly moved, he struggles to keep his emotions in check). I need to be looked after John. Do you want to help me? Do you want to put me back together again? (He found himself nodding, trying to swallow the lump in his throat) I hope that you're not going to let me down. I need your strength (John was straining to keep his tear ducts dry, she was getting a little tired of her well rehearsed speech and even half hoped that she would be rumbled, but she wasn't, and was probably never likely to be). I need a big strong man John. Can you do it? Can you help me?

John's answers were fast, imploring, he had never wanted anything, or anybody this much before. He needed her to move with him into his new life, his retirement. His voice was full of pure, genuine, totally sincere, and true, emotion. He grabbed her hand, kissed it and held it to his cheek.

Yes I want you and I want to look after you. I want to be with you. I'm going to make it all right again, trust me, please. I won't let you down. I've never been so certain of something in all of my life.

He kissed her hand again. Harry smiled and padded off into the bedroom to get dried up and changed. It was all going to work out fine.

Chapter 28

Philip Masters

Looking at her reflection in the mirror she thought to herself that her eye wasn't that bad, a little swollen yes, but there wasn't that much damage. It was discoloured a purple-blue, and her eyes were cracked red like an old oil painting, but it could have been worse, he must have pulled his punches, that was something, wasn't it? At least he cared enough, even in the state that he had been in, not to put his full weight behind the blows that he had delivered. She tried her best to cover it up with makeup and other cosmetics but it hurt whenever she touched it, and made her eyes water, and then made her eyes run, streaking the makeup that she was applying, so that it looked even more repulsive than before. She pulled the light cord in the bathroom, making herself disappear, making it all disappear.

It was early Monday morning. She had woken up to find that Philip had already risen, and presumably gone out to see someone or another, maybe he was downstairs getting one of the cooks to make his breakfast. He wasn't in any of the rooms where he could usually be found. They had not spoken about the incident in the hotel room in London, not on the way home, with her one eye closed to the world, making it impossible for her to look out of the passenger seat window. He had not mentioned anything when he came in last night (this morning) at around three. He had disturbed her restless uncomfortable sleep, and had slipped in, unnoticed he thought, and had slept right on the edge of the bed, as far away from her as he could. He was probably ashamed of himself she thought.

She was wearing nothing except for one of Masters' shirts, it quite literally dwarfed her, and billowed out behind as she walked into his special room, the one with the desk, and the mannequin, and the chair, and the frogs. There was a book on the desk, *The Book of the Toad* by Robert M. Degraaff. She read the title and the author's name out loud to herself. She peered down at the enigmatic frogs. They were the answer, but what did they mean, what did they mean to him? Somehow they connected to his tortured soul. He could let them in, share his secret with them, but not with her. She could not help but think that if she could work them out, decipher their message, expose whatever it was that they symbolized, that she would be able to reach him, help him, sort it all out. She had heard it said on Ricki Lake that wife beating, domestic abuse, was a circular process, like the full turn of a wheel. The victim became the villain, the villain had once been the victim. She wanted to share his pain, to help him. If only she knew what to do...

Lisa looked down at the glistening frogs. Their wet amphibian skin reflected the light from the window and the artificial sun lamps, up into her eyes, so that it was difficult to see them properly, as if looking at them was like looking into the sun. You could see them but you could never really look at them, not in detail, not in the light, maybe this was what Philip liked about them. They always appeared to be so slimy, so wet, she couldn't imagine how one would feel in her hand.

What's the matter with him?

She hoped that the frogs would reply, not in words as such, but maybe a croak, or leap, or something, anything. They didn't know, or they weren't telling. What was she going to do?

Why don't you tell mommy?...

She asked of the frogs that which they could not tell. They sat basking in meaningless crouches, in the dumb silence of the morning light. Suddenly she heard movement behind her and turned around to see Philip standing up, his whole height drawn up before her, magnificent and threatening. His hands were red raw, fidgeting, a small green frog hopped from palm to palm, as Masters tilted it one way and then back again. His eyes were swollen, popping out of his head almost. His face look strained, gaunt, and pale, as if he had just been sick. He moved towards her filling up the entire room.

He'd followed her into his room, their room, and just in time too. She was disgusting. Was there nothing that she would not do? Was there no disgrace from which she would shy from? What was she going to do now? Walking around with her blood weeping shame between her legs. The slut was trying to contaminate his frogs, his babies. What she had said, that word, calling herself that word, "mommy." What was she up to? He had to save them from her. She was speaking. He could see her lips moving but the sound was all distorted. She was trying to fuck with him, was that it? Well he'd show her. He'd fucking show her. He put the frog down safe among the others. She was close by, her hair, all blonde curls, writhed and coiled, spitting at him like Medusa's vipers. Maybe she thought that it was funny, fucking funny that's what she thought, fucking funny. He hit her hard across the mouth, that ought to shut her up. He grabbed that mass of snakes that was slithering across her head, and he dragged her screaming, her legs twisted beneath her, from the room, so that *they* did not have to see her, or smell her foul and primitive running sore.

He threw her onto the bed and a large sod of blonde hair tipped with blood came off in his hand. He shook his hand at the floor but some of the hair stuck to his hand, and he shook it harder and harder but there was still some stuck to his hand and it would not come off. He screamed and wiped it on the quilt leaving a smear of blood where he touched it. He held his hand up to his eyes looking to make sure that it was all gone. She was up on her feet, standing on the other side of the bed, speaking in her distorted tongues, challenging him with her retreating steps. He advanced again...

Lisa took a step forward and screamed, "LEAVE ME ALONE," as loud and as hard as she could. The tears were streaming down her face. Her scalp was on fire where he had pulled her hair out by the roots. She stepped forward again trying to gather some momentum. "DON'T YOU FUCKING TOUCH ME," she shouted. He took a step back, he actually backed off from her. She just wanted to get out of that room that was all that she could think about. It was her only chance. the only way that she could save herself. She tried again, clenching her fists together, her nails cutting through the skin of her palms. She would not lie down and accept his violence. She screamed again, "GET AWAY FROM ME..." His eyes creased as he scowled through her electric howl, her only defence against him. It was brave, and fierce, and strong, but it was not enough against this terrible being.... this terrible *man*.

She was shouting, but it was still distorted. She was speaking to him but it did not make sense, nothing made sense. He would beat the sense into her, and her secret language, the code that she must be using to communicate with that queer shit, the one he was going to kill. He was going to have him killed, and this bitch, this fucking bitch, she was trying to kill him, drag him down into that lake where she would roll him over and over until he was soft, until he changed and became like her, and he would be foul too like her, like the earth. He could not allow this to happen. He had to stop her, he had to. He threw out his angry and confused fists. She was still moving spritely and he just clipped her, as she tried to escape, on the back of her head, but the force and her own momentum, took her on beyond her balance and she seemed to fold over and pitch forwards. She fell heavily. She lay still, her eyes covered by blank eyelids that were like thumb smudges of putty. Her body, that was so enchanting to all who met her, was unmoving, her smooth skin was as white as a screen without a projector. He felt safer now that she was not moving. Her hair had stopped crawling. She had stopped making those sounds. It was better this way.

It was some relief to him that she was still. He had a lot to think about but it was hard, so hard to think. He had seen her again. What did she want? What did she know? What did Adam know? Maybe Adam knew everything. He was supposed to be back by now. He was going to call but he hadn't. This is Philip Masters he's dealing with, he should have called. He should know better. Maybe he hadn't called because he knew everything. Maybe he was on his way round now. Maybe he had told everyone and now they all wanted revenge. They were all going to turn on him, take him outside, and nail him up.

He stood up and walked back to his frogs touching all of the hidden guns in the wall on his way. He needed another kiss. He reached down for one of his frogs and he brought it up to his face, looked it straight in the eyes, before wriggling his tongue down the frog's back and then up into the cleft in its head. The frog began to croak nervously and so Masters had to clamp it tightly with his swollen rubicund hand. There was some drying blood from Lisa in the grooves of his fingers which mixed with the poisons. He tilted back his head in some celebratory gesticulation, a show of primal worship, and he drank down the frog's gift.

He would get them....He would get them all....the whole fucking lot of them. He wasn't to be fucked with....didn't they know that....didn't they know... What did they know? Where were they? Where was Adam? What did he know????

And that man, the one with the silvergrey hair, maybe he had told. No he couldn't, but maybe he had... The man was after him. He wanted him back.

Chapter 29

Coital Imagination

I had lunch with Margaret the day after our night out. I was professional to the end. She seemed to be a sad woman and I think that if I had mentioned sex she would have wanted it. We went shopping instead. She bought me a shiny black button down shirt by Hugo Boss. I did not ask for it, and I felt guilty with her not knowing that she would never see me again, but it seemed to make her happy. I told myself that she could afford it so I just accepted it, kissed her, and paid her lots of believable compliments.

When I got home I called Gillian no answer. I left a message on her machine. I told her that it was over; that I was getting out; that I was finished making house calls; that I wanted nothing more to do with any of that shit. Before I left for my journey to Sally's I received a telephone call and I allowed the person to speak on my machine, as though I had already gone. Gillian's laughter came through the small speaker. She said that of course I was going to retire, as she put it. Then she laughed harder and said that if I wanted my work published that I had better meet her at The _____ in_____ on Thursday. I was instructed to wear a suit, to make sure that I was covered in olive oil, and that she was sending me a pair of her panties in the post which I was to wear instead of boxers. She laughed some more, cruelly mocking me. She asked if I had enjoyed our last meeting...

What do I care? I do not want her to pull strings so that my work can get published. I do not want anything from her, not now, not ever again, all of that is over. Gillian has used me up.

I took a long relaxing bath as soon as I got here. Sally was busy in the kitchen. For the first time, in Sally's presence, I wore some of my best clothes, the ones that have been bought for me. I put on my new shirt. The shiny fabric felt good across my tight chest and back. Sally said that I looked very nice. She cooked sea food in a wine and cream sauce, there was a salad with lemon vinaigrette, and she made chocolate mousse for desert. There were lit candles on the small table in her room and she took out one of the exclusive bottles of wine that her father sends her back to university with each term. We made a toast to one another. Sally was wearing makeup, black leather shoes, tights, a black skirt that came down just above the knee, and a striped woollen poloneck jumper. We talked and laughed and ate and drank. We took photographs of one another in casual poses around the room. We pulled face into the lens. I rolled up a joint and lit it for Sally. She smoked it like a silver screen goddess. We made fresh coffee together stoned in the kitchen giggling whenever someone walked past the window.

Sally sat on the side of the bed. Her legs crossed looking up over the rim of her coffee cup. Her eyes were beckoning me to her and when she put the cup to her lips it was as if she was drinking up my whole being. I was drawn to her, my heart beating in my chest, my eyes fixed to hers. I remember that suddenly, and I do not know how, she was in my arms, and I was looking down at her. She lay back on the bed and pulled me with her. I took time to kiss her mouth, her hands, her fingers, and I stroked her thighs, and took off her shoes. Sally was watching me in silence. She seemed to be gripped by the moment, overcome with feeling I thought, at that point where emotions mix with sensations so powerfully that pleasure shows itself in clear crystal tears of love. I kissed Sally's knees through her tights and I told her that I love her. A series of images began to flicker through my mind. I saw white fleshed women with shapeless bodies, removing straps, undoing zips, unclipping stockings, unfastening belts, pulling up skirts, pulling down trousers, taking off bras, stepping out of fallen dresses. All of these things I remembered but I did not know them. They were there in my mind walking down the corridors of my memory, their steps echoed through everything that I did. I heard them as I took Sally's shoes off, as I felt her hair, and as I sucked her ear lobe. They would not go away. I began to talk to Sally. I tried to speak over the top of them but they would not leave me. I looked down at Sally and saw a hundred different women holding and pushing out their breasts in their outstretched palms. I saw myself go down onto each woman turning them around and around in my hands. I told Sally that she was mine and that I was hers and that we were meant to be together. She started to say that, yes, "she was mine". She said that she wanted me to take her, that she liked it that way. She called out my name and said that she had always been mine. She liked me to have her, and use her, and play with her, and keep her. Her voice sounded desperate. She asked me to be gentle. She said repeatedly not to hurt her, that she was mine but I was not to hurt her. She kept on saying this only more and more desperately as my hands caressed her breasts and I pulled her jumper over her head. The jumper kept coming off, and off, and off, and going over her head time and time again, but it was as if it would never come off, as if I were stuck in some eternal film loop, so that when it did come off I did not know who would be looking up at me. I crouched above her expecting, anticipating, looking at Gillian's face all creased up in a deformed smile. I saw Margaret and Sonya and Marie and Liz and...and scores of others chattering with delight and pleading for more. I saw Sally again her eyes were screwed shut, her hand was over her brow as if she was shielding herself from some painful light, and she was telling me, no, asking me not to hurt her. There were hundreds of images flashing up in front of me. I could see myself in some act, with some woman, and the images were changing quickly, and more and more went past. I felt myself drifting. The images were rapidly playing out. How many more could there be? I saw myself in distorted poses, straining myself to reach hidden erogenous zones, my neck out to its limit, my tongue stretched out to a point. I was on top of people, between legs, behind backs, underneath vaginas, tangled in arms and hair. I was wet with sweat and covered in oil, naked, fully clothed, tied up, tied down, outdoors, beneath sheets, and in uncomfortable cars. I was a tiny piece of all that I had seen. I was lying on a bed holding my cock with a corporeal mass of shit and blood and grey sperm next to me. I had no feet, no means of escape, just a narrow point of whiteness that seemed to go on and on like the most piercing pain that I have ever experienced. My whole body becomes white and I, and the white boots that I am wearing, my white boots, merge into the white sheet with me.

I realise that I am looking up at the blank ceiling. Sally is beside me crying. Her tears, and sobs, and sniffs, are breaking up her repetitive chant, "Please don't hurt me. I'm yours but please don't hurt me..." She has pulled her tights and panties down to her knees. She too is staring at the ceiling as if it is everything else that is blank. I wonder what she is watching; what film is being shown to her. She has one hand up her skirt. I can sense its movement without having to look. Her other hand is reaching out and is squeezing and stroking between my legs. My trousers are ruffled around my knees. My penis is flaccid, limp, it does not work. Sally will not look at me but she keeps crying and asking me not to hurt her. I feel my own tears sliding down the sides of my face onto the pillow. I turn my head towards her. She turns her head towards me. Sally is still holding our genitalia. I roll on top of her. My penis is unmoving, unfeeling, it will not awaken. We lie there together crying into one another's tears.

Chapter 30

Your Time Is Up

The telephone began to ring and Masters, sitting on a chair facing the frogs, stood up to go to the bedroom where he had left it. He hoped that it was Adam calling to say that everything had gone smoothly. Once Adam called they could move ahead with the plan to get rid of John and his nigger boyfriend. He didn't want their kind around, not now that he had the power to get rid of them. They were filth and he would not do business with filth. Masters was still troubled about Adam as well though. Adam knew his mother what else did he know? He could be calling to set him up. Adam might have discovered who he was, what he was; picking up the telephone might be dangerous. He hesitated.

It might not be Adam. It might be Lisa. He did not know where she was. She had been fucking with him. He could not quite remember what had happened but she had insulted him, betrayed him. She had been up to something and he knew it, but he wasn't quite sure what it was that she had done. Maybe she knew too. Maybe Lisa and Adam had a plan, maybe John was also in on it. All of Lisa's clothes were gone. There had been a note, lines of loops in black ink on bleached white paper, but he did not know where it was now. Lisa could be calling, wanting to come back, pleading with him. If only he could remember what she had written in the letter, or where he had put it, he would at least have a clue as to how much she knew. One thing was for sure he could not have her running around opening her legs for all kinds of people, not after he had taken her to London with him. It would look bad. He would have to find her and keep her in line.

Masters picked up, and spoke into, the telephone.

Hello?

He immediately recognized the voice on the other end. The silvergrey haired man was sitting at a solid wooden desk, tapping a pencil onto a piece of paper, allowing the pencil to slide through his fingers, and then twisting it upside down and tapping it again. The pencil maintained an even pace throughout their conversation.

Are you alone?

The silvergrey haired man's voice caused Masters to break out into a sweat. He had not considered this. He was not ready for it.

Yes.

Can we talk?

Yes.

I'm pulling you out.

When?

Now it's over. I'm sending some people to get you.

No you can't it's too...

You have become a liability. You are putting everything at risk. I've been getting all kinds of reports about you...

What?

I'm not going to discuss it with you, not now... You be ready. Don't get doing anything silly you're in enough trouble as it is. Did you think that you were the only person at that funny little party that they organized for you in London? Come on, what did you think I was going to do? Pat you on the back? It's all over for you. Your time is up. I'm calling you in.

But...

I'll see you later...

The telephone was dead. Masters listened intently as it began to beep out its agony. He carefully put it down.

He told himself that this could not be happening. They could not take it all away from him. He had worked so hard for everything, the business, the contacts, the men, the cars, the clothes, the good life. He had schemed and plotted and now that he was at the top they wanted him out. How could they expect him to give in just like that? The more he thought about it the angrier he became. No, fuck them, fuck the whole lot of them, he would not give in, why should he? He took the telephone off the hook. No more communication, he was going to show those fucks. If Adam, or Lisa, or whoever, wanted to talk to him they would have to come and see him, and when they did he would be ready for them. He'd like to see them try and take him on.

Moz was having half an hour to himself upstairs in the living room. He was eating his lunch, microwaved pie and chips, from a plate that he was balancing on a cushion on his lap. He liked a lot of salt on his chips. The more salt that he put on the chips the more he liked them. Some of the salt went all over the armchair but Moz didn't care, why should he, after all it was his place, his house, his boozer. Mary had taken that fucking rat of a dog out for a walk, Penny and Chloe were in the bar, and young Tony was watching his portable in his room. Moz could hear the portable blaring out daytime TV. Tony had got nothing to do as Adam and Steve were away on business. Moz's other son, Maurice, was away too. He didn't live at home. He was always off travelling. Moz could not remember where he was, Penny knew, France he supposed, or Belgium, somewhere like that. The most important thing to Moz at that moment was that none of them where there, in that room, he was alone. The living room, empty for once, was bliss. Moz pushed down a fork full of heavily salted microwaved chips. He broke through the crust of the pie and thick processed gravy ran out all over his plate. It tasted great. He salted the gravy then he dipped a fork full of chips into it, and sucked them down. He put his knife and fork into his left hand and began to press the buttons on the remote control unit that was resting on the arm of the chair. The television sat facing him waiting to be switched on. He wanted to put the teletext on; he wanted to look at the odds for the horses.

The TV came on. It was the same channel that he could hear blaring out of Tony's portable. It was the local Anglia news bulletin. Moz was searching for the text button on the remote control unit. There was a report on about two men found dead on the ferry from Harwich to Holland. Moz's jaw dropped. His mouth was open so that a dark dumb black hole formed in the middle of his face. Moz stood up, a reflex reaction, and pie, chips, salt, and his plate all crashed onto the floor. He heard

Tony cry out in his room, and then he heard Penny's bovine footsteps on the stairs. She burst into the room.

I just seen it on the portable in the bar. I can't believe it. Who'd want to do a thing like that to Adam? And Steve he ain't got a bad bone in his body...

Penny looked at Moz she recognized that look on his face. Moz was not happy. She moved over to him, and held onto his arm, trying to pacify him.

I'll clean this mess up, just sit down and I'll make you another one Maurice okay....and then we can have a little chat about it.

There's only one person I want to have a chat with...

Now come on Maurice please you remember what John said, he don't want any trouble. You're not even supposed to see Masters's men.

I can't stand by and let this happen. Our little Tony could have been with him. No I've got to have him. He's been asking for it.

Please Maurice (Penny is tugging on his arm), leave it to John please...

Moz shook his arm free and made for the stairs. Penny tried to grab a hold of the back of his Giorgio sweatshirt but she slipped on the pie and gravy and twisted her ankle. Moz stopped by Tony's room before getting his things together. Tony sat up on his bed and tried to hide the fact that he felt like he was going to cry.

Don't you worry son I'm going to sort this out once and for all.

Moz picked up his leather jacket and his piece and ran down the stairs. Penny limped after him, her great fat body wobbling with each step that she took.

Maurice come back... Please Maurice... Come back...

Chris and his mate, the one he's always with these days, were standing at the bar both drinking Irish Whiskey. They had not been watching the portable and so were ignorant of everything that was going on. They were waiting for some people to come in. They had some job on and were amusing themselves in the meantime by taking the piss out of Chloe. She didn't seem to mind. She thought that any form of attention was good, and was happy to see them. Chloe was wearing slack leggings, that were supposed to be tight, with stirrups, a lot of makeup, and she had had more highlights put in a couple of days ago, which had made her hair go really dry and brittle. There was lipstick all over the end of her fag. She fancied both of them like mad. At first she had liked Chris the most. The other one was a little quieter, but she had seen a lot of them recently and so was getting to know him too, now she didn't know which one she liked most. She was telling them about a dream that she had had last night.

Yeah it was the same frog as the one on them scratchcards....look (Chris and his friend snigger to one another). It weren't that colour....same frog, but it was all white. It was coming towards me and as it got nearer I started to panic....well ya would wouldn't ya....and it was really big, a big white frog. I could see all of this sticky stuff all over the frog's body. It was really horrible ya know. When I woke up I was all sweaty in my bed. I felt really funny. It was like, when I was awake I knew that it was a good thing, the frog that is. Frogs are just little animals ain't they. They won't hurt ya...

Chris turns to you and starts laughing cruelly, right at her, right in front of her. You think that it's a bit rough on his part, to openly take the piss out of her like that, but, well, it is Chloe after all. You don't want to give her the wrong idea. It was probably better to be too mean than too nice.

Don't laugh. I think that the frog woke me up to something. I felt different when I opened me eyes. I felt as though it had helped me, honest. All of these scratchcards funny ain't it? This frog here, it got into my mind. I just think that it's funny how this frog can get inside your head, get into your dreams. You don't know what's inside it do ya? (pointing to her head, well actually her awful perm and highlights) I think that there must be all sorts up there, things you don't even think about half the time...

Chris is trying to make you laugh too. You are trying not to, but she seems so oblivious to his scorn, and he is pretending to try and hold back his laughter, making his eyes bulge, which urges you on into a tight smirk. You don't want to look at Chloe because the idea of her articulating anything, let alone a dream, makes you want to piss yourself. You know that she's going to be looking all serious, waiting for a reply. You know that if you look at her that your lips are going to rip open in an explosion of laughter and spittle. Frogs on fucking scratchcards jumping around in her dreams....it's just too much.

Moz walks through the bar. He does not notice anyone. He goes out of the doors onto the main road and starts to turn to go around the back onto the car park. Penny hobbles after him. She catches Moz on the street. She is screaming hysterically.

Maurice... Don't do it Maurice... Stay here... Please Maurice... PLEASE...

She grabs hold of his legs. He tries to pull away but Penny will not let go. She falls over but is still holding onto his trousers. Moz slowly drags his legs out in front of himself edging his way along the pavement to the small drive that leads to the car park. Penny is screaming and crying. Her tears have made her mascara run. She has got pie and gravy all up the side of her leg, all over her cheap nylon trousers. Moz finally pulls away and Penny is left rolling on the paving stones still screaming, kicking her legs, and crying black mascara tears. By the time that she is on her feet Moz is in his car and is about to pull out onto the main road. Penny tries to jump across the bonnet but Moz anticipates this and pulls forward so that she hits the side door and falls over again only with louder screams and blacker tears. A car sounds its horn at Moz's lurching car. Moz thinks about popping the guy right there and then, but it was Masters that he wanted. He gave the guy in the car two fingers and drove off. Penny limped after the car for a few steps and then he was out of sight.

Maurice... MAURICE...

Penny quickly turned around.

Mom what's the matter? Oh mom...

Mary had just turned the corner with the dog. Penny sobbed and they put their arms around one another. They stood there in the middle of the street, with people staring, drivers twisting their necks to see what was happening. She wept black tears onto Mary's electric lemon dress while the poodle jumped up her and licked the pie and gravy off her cheap nylon trousers.

Lisa had tied a scarf around her head and was wearing a pair of dark glasses. Her head and face hurt like hell. Philip was no good. She knew that now. He had problems; she had tried to gain his trust; she had tried to win his confidence, but just as she thought she was beginning to make progress it had all gone wrong. She wasn't going to hang around for more of the same.

Her bruises would heal and her hair would grow back. She was going to be okay. She was shook up but she knew that what mattered right now was how she felt. Yes she did feel guilty, as if it was her own fault but deep inside she knew that it would pass. A part of her wanted Philip to appear out of nowhere and plead with her to go back to him. She wanted him to plead with her, but she would not go back. She thought about AIDS. She should get tested. It had all ended up in such a mess.

The taxi was getting nearer to John's house. She had nowhere else to go, not right away. She could get in touch with some friends from there. John would help her. She could talk to him. He would listen. He was always so nice...

He'd killed Adam and Steve. He'd killed them. Moz had told John that something like this was going to happen. You couldn't let bastards like Masters dictate to ya. You had to hit them first. Well Adam was a good mate and Masters had no right, no fucking right...

This was the way to do it. You didn't need to sit around talking about it. You just needed someone to go in and get the job done, no fucking about. They'd all thank him for it afterwards. Everybody wanted to get rid of him. Moz was the man for the job, a man of action.

Moz threw open the door to the restaurant. He began a bellicose walk to the back of the restaurant where he knew the stairs were. A waiter moved over to block his path.

Do you have a reservation sir?

Moz pushed him out of his way.

Fuck off.

The waiter fell over backwards. There were only three tables in use but the people all turned to look at Moz, and his slow but powerful movements, his angry strained features. Another waiter appeared and tried to block Moz's path, while the other waiter, who had been so easily pushed aside, grabbed Moz from behind. Moz swung his elbow back slicing through the skin above and around the waiter's eye. He punched the waiter in front breaking his nose. None of the people eating said a thing. They watched in silent fear and when Moz started to climb the stairs they all began to collect their things together.

John had called someone to take her into London. He was leaving for the airport. He had offered her his place for a few days but she needed to be with friends. Lisa was angry that John was just leaving like that. She sat and told him her story. She told him everything. How she had fallen in love and how she had been mistreated, and abused, and beaten. John got angry, saying that he was going to do this and that to Philip, and Lisa liked it that he was jumping to her defence.

How could he do this to you? You haven't done anything wrong. You're the innocent party in all of this. I'm going to sort him out.

She did not want any more trouble. She knew that to have any contact with Philip was a mistake. She knew that she was still in love with him. She could be easily persuaded to go back to him, that was the worst thing about all of it. She could not simply stop loving him but she knew that she could not see him again. She needed time to forget about him.

Leave it John, just leave it.

He's done wrong. Why are you trying to protect him? You're the victim in all of this.

She suddenly felt very different. She did not want John to take over, to feel responsible for her, that he had to right the balance of justice. She was her own person. She wanted herself back.

I'm not protecting him, and I'm not the victim.

Yes you are.

No I'm not. I made a mistake that's all. I fell in love and things went wrong. Yes he hit me, and yes I tried to make it work even after that, but it didn't work. I tried and it failed. I'm not a bloody victim. I'm me. I'm Lisa.

Of course you're Lisa, of course you are, but what he did turned you into the victim.

No. You make me sound helpless, pitiful; I'm not. You think I'm the victim because I'm what innocent. Well I am innocent I didn't do anything that would have made him want to hit me, but I don't want to be a victim. You think that if I've done something wrong then I'm the cheating seductress, and if not I'm the poor victim. Well I'm not. I just want to move on. I need to think about what happened. I need to think about why it happened, but I'm not going to hang around being a victim. I just want to be Lisa and live Lisa's life.

You don't know what you're saying. I'm not going to let him get away with what he's done to you.

This discussion was making Lisa'a cuts and bruises swell with pain. She knew that her only chance to leave and put all of this behind her was to be Lisa. If she became something else, somebody else, she would be trapped. She liked John because she thought that he had not presumed anything about her. He had treated her like a real person, but now he wanted her to be something that she did not want to be.

Look this is what he's done to me (she takes off her scarf and dark glasses, John pulls an angry face). I don't want to care about him. I want to care about me. It's my life that counts now.

The car pulled up outside. Lisa was pleased, she wanted to leave as soon as possible. She wanted to be a long way away from there, from all of them. The driver put her bags in the boot. She said her goodbye to John and she left. She left as Lisa, ready to live in the vital energies life offered, to be spun in the vortex of emotion and experience, to be a part of it all. She did not want to be tied up, or locked up, in labels. She could never make it work with Philip and she had already decided that it was better to make it work with herself, that was what she was going to do.

John watched his first true love being driven away. Her scarfed head bobbed up and down in the back of the car as the driver slowly negotiated John's long drive. She had been, when he was younger, the most important person in his life. There was a time when he could not stop thinking about her. She had played such a major role in the story of his life. Now whenever he went back to those memories, looking through a photograph album, or visiting home, his old home, where his parents and family still lived, those memories would be stained. He would not see her smooth thighs, or stiff pink nipples, or her angelic blonde curls. He would see bruises, purple imprints of Masters' fists, a clump of hair missing, and a sore red scab where it should have been. Masters had ruined her, and his image of her, and the memory of those hours of fantasy and reality that they had shared together, hours that had helped him sort his head out. She had given him so much and now Masters had taken it away. He didn't care what she thought, or what she said, there was simply no way that he was going to allow Masters to get away with this. He still had time to pay him a visit. Harry and Serge were already in London. He was meeting them later. They were flying that evening. News had broken about Adam and Steve. Masters would be expecting to hear from him.

Where are ya Masters? Come on out... Come on...

Two of Masters' men, who he had put in position fearing a visit from Adam, and all that he knew, or might know, or a visit from the man with the silvergrey hair, jumped out on Moz. He butted the first but the second backed off a little so that Moz's wild swing missed. Moz shouted again.

Come on, fucking show yourself you cant. Cam on...

Moz swung again and missed. He looked clumsy this time. His anger had sapped his coordination. They were in a corridor with doors to rooms on either side. Masters had to be in one of them. Moz was wasting his time on this prick in front of him. It was Masters he was after. He forced his way along the corridor and into one of the rooms. There was a weird dummy in there, and what looked like an old electric chair, and an open aquarium full of small croaking frogs. The prick from the corridor came in and behind him, peering through a mask of blood, was the other one, the one that he had butted. One of the waiters, the one with the busted nose, followed them in. The stupid bastards would be no match for him. They jumped in but Moz could handle them. They all, Moz included, seemed to go down together, and the dummy with them. Moz was the first to his feet but Masters was there now, right next to him. He smashed his fist into Moz's face. The others grabbed him from behind. Masters aimed a spiteful kick which landed right between Moz's balls and he slumped over. The men held him down, crouched over, squatting on his legs. Moz struggled to free himself.

Why did you kill Adam?

Masters had not killed Adam, but the other men were looking at him as if he had. Maybe he had. It would be good if he had. If he had then he didn't have to worry about Adam and what he might know. He supposed that that was why he must have had him killed. He suddenly felt a lot better. This was good. Moz was trying to free himself and was about to succeed, about to lunge at Masters and bring him down, when Masters reached behind, punched through a small hole in the wall, pulled out a revolver. He steadied the barrel against Moz's temple, tightened his grip, and shot him twice in the head. Somebody downstairs screamed. There was a look of disbelief on the men's faces as Moz's warm blood spattered all over them. They let go of Moz's freshly executed body as if death was contagious. Masters put the smoking gun back through the torn wallpaper into that little hole that he had purposefully made.

Two men in sombre grey suits, driving a white Sierra, made their way to Masters' house. The orders from the man with the silvergrey hair were still ringing in their ears. The driver had a good head of wiry brown hair, and a thick moustache which sat passively above his mouth. The man in the passenger seat was tall and slim, balding at the crown, eyes deeply set, calculating, concentrating. This was a new one to them; totally out of the ordinary. They did not know how he was going to react when they walked in. They did not expect any trouble but you could never be sure...

The body was wrapped up in black polythene. The men cursed him for their injuries and complained about what a big dumb fuck he was. He had taken some shifting, but he was dead so it was only effort, painful but stupid effort, that was needed. The waiter guy cleaned the blood from the walls, and the carpet, and the glass sides of the frogs' home, and the electric chair, and the mannequin with the long chrome arm. Masters was there now alone with a frog in his hand pressed to his open mouth. It was very quiet. The people in the restaurant had gone. His men had taken the body away. They were efficient. They were paid to be efficient. The dead had to be dealt with. Death was like refuse, like shit. It was necessary. It was dirty and unpleasant but if you didn't deal with it, get rid of it, it would kill you. It would rot and draw attention to you. People might ask questions, enquiries would be made, and it would all lead back to you eventually. You had to bury it deep, put it somewhere far away from yourself, and it had to be done quickly.

Masters licked the frog's back slowly. He enjoyed the feeling of the frog's skin on his tongue. It was his favourite sensation. He felt better now, much better.

John had tried to call him on the telephone, to sound him out, to work out what was going on, maybe Masters was waiting for him. John couldn't be too careful, not when he was so close to being out of it, the whole stinking mess. He couldn't get through on the telephone. Masters always seemed to be engaged. John had thought about it. He never had to see Masters again but he felt as if he had to confront him with it, with what he had done to Lisa. It was not only that though, there was something else too. Serge's plan was faultless. It had worked like a dream but John, for all of the plan's success, didn't like it. He favoured a showdown. He couldn't help it. It just didn't seem right skulking off. It was no way to end what had been the most productive period of his life. It was certainly no way to leave everything that he had built up and worked for. John could not imagine a life that was not like the one he had now. He could not imagine living somewhere else. When he thought about the plan, the chain of events, it did not matter how hard he tried, he could not imagine himself in St. Lucia, or anywhere else for that matter. He could imagine a holiday but not actually living there. When he thought about the plan's conclusion and what it meant for him, the rest of his life, his thoughts, the images of his imagination, always brought him back here, and his life and work here. In his mind he saw faces laughing about how he couldn't handle it; how he'd run away; voices telling him that Masters had won; driven him out of town and into hiding. John did feel, despite Serge's cold logic, as if he was running away. It made him feel weak, cowardly, as if he were scared. He was not scared. He wanted everyone here to know that, so after he was gone his name could live on. There was something to be said for shooting Masters and then splitting. The tickets were booked. He had sent his luggage on ahead with Serge and Harry. Serge would have done his business; Harry said goodbye to her friends. He could hit Masters himself, one last thrill, and then he would be gone. He could disappear and enjoy it rather than feeling like a rat stowed away, living not with fear but with shame, which was probably worse. He didn't want to spend the rest of his life feeling like this, a rat, a yellow livered runner, someone who could not properly conclude his business.

The more that John thought about leaving Masters behind the more the idea curdled inside his mind. He was watching the restaurant. John was going over it all in his mind. There was no movement inside. There were no people eating. There didn't even seem to be any waiters around. He couldn't see any of Masters' men around. What was to stop him from walking in there, finding Masters, if he was in, squeezing the trigger, and pop, putting him out. Maybe he wasn't there, in that case he would have to accept that it wasn't meant to be, but that was the chance, and the fact that it was chance somehow made it all the more appealing. If he was there then it was a sign that he was supposed to kill him. He thought about Lisa too. There were too many reasons urging him to go ahead. He would have to be quiet. He would move quickly and any hint that he might get, if it was too difficult, or too dangerous, or whatever, he would leave, get out, and go directly to the airport. It was the right thing to do. He got out of his car.

They could not believe it. John Tomilary was entering the restaurant just as they pulled up. This was a great opportunity. The balding man looked at his watch, just for the record. The man with the moustache made a note of the time in his notebook, again, just for the record. They spent a few moments looking around to see if there was anybody else around. It looked inconspicuous enough. The only other car they could see, apart from their white Sierra, was John's. They got out and followed him in.

He had to do it properly. There was no need, and no time, for an arrogant speech, as much as he would like to give one. He had to do the job. Do the job and get out. Do the job and get out... He spoke these words to himself over and over. The tingle that comes from adrenaline was just beginning to charge his muscles. He drew his gun which he had attached a silencer to earlier, when he had only thought about how he would do it. Now he was here in Masters' lair, about to do it. This was where he had done those terrible things to Lisa. This was where he had killed Zak, and turned Adam against his own men. He silently moved up the stairs.

Masters was feeling sick. He had severe stomach cramps, sharp waves of pain passed through his fast beating heart. The silence seemed loud to him. The colours in the room too bright, blurring his vision so that all he could see were bright blinding clouds of colour. He was sweating. He was covered in sweat. He was lost inside a room, a mind, a memory that he wanted to forget but couldn't. Someone, something was in the room with him. He turned to see a blurred and distorted image of the queer before him. The fucking queer with his shitty little gun pointing at him, at Philip Masters, the man who had been embraced by the big shots in London. He would not be so stupid as to think that he could get away with something like this, take on the whole of London. No he didn't think so. The queer hadn't got the balls. He couldn't handle it. He was probably going to shit himself, right there, right now. Masters curled back his lips over his teeth. He reached out behind to punch a hole in the wall where he knew he would find more help but John's finger was too quick. There was a muffled sput as the bullet, stifled by the silencer, cut through the air and hit Masters in the left eye. Blood squirted out in an indolent red fountain. Masters clutched at the pain in his eye. He fell backwards onto the glass frog house smashing the thick glass under his weight, sending vicious shards of broken glass all over the room. He lay on the floor squirming, waiting for the next one, the one to end it all.

Two men ran into the room. They knocked John's aimed gun from out of his hand and pushed him straight up against the wall, his arm twisted behind his back.

Paul? Paul?

The tall balding man tried to roll Masters over to see what had happened, where he had been hit. He saw, through Masters' hands that his left eye was gone, the eye socket was cracked. The balding man decided he should play down the injury to Masters. He didn't want to panic him any more than was necessary. Masters was covered in broken glass that was cutting into him as he writhed on the floor in pain. There were some small weird looking frogs hopping all over him. John started to shout.

Who the fuck's Paul? What's going on? Who the fuck are you? Get the fuck off me.

The tall balding man rang for an ambulance. The man with the wiry hair and moustache showed John his identification. The protective transparent plastic sheet, that covered his identification card, reflected the light from the windows into John's eyes so that he had to squint to look at it, to see it.

JohnTom, caught, with the gun in his hand... You're under arrest. Anything you say..........

The balding man put down the telephone and went back over to check on Masters.

It's going to be okay Paul. They're on their way. Don't worry, this scum (pointing at John) will be going down for a long time. You finally nailed him. Just sit tight Paul. You're going to come through this. You're going to be up for promotion.

(smiling) You've given the boss a few extra grey hairs mind you. But you're going to be okay. He says that he's going to the hospital to debrief you and send you off on holiday. God knows you've earned it.

Chapter 31

The End

You wake up shivering, with a particularly nasty case of alcohol poisoning. Chris is pulling back the curtains in a room that you don't seem to recognize. You are cold, and dehydrated, still tired, even though the clock says that it's twelve thirty. The light streams in as Chris pulls back each individual curtain making you feel sick. There is a thick layer of cold sweat all over your body. You cover yourself in the quilt, wrapping it all around. You are hungry but the thought of food makes you want to throw up. Chris opens a window and the sounds of the street follow the light into the room, compounding your misery. Chris sits in a chair facing your bed and lights up a Marlboro. It seems too early to be smelling smoke but you reach over for a Silk Cut, not quite Marlboro, but you have managed to build up a dependency for them. You light up the cigarette and hold it in your hand, folded at the knuckles. You shiver again. The tremors cause the blue line of smoke from the tip of the cigarette to zigzag in the air.

It's a hotel room. It's London. You are starting to remember. You can smell hairspray mixed in with the cigarette smoke. You realise that there are other things in this room that are not yours, female things you tell yourself.

Where am I?

You scratch your head but the light and the air from the open window seem to burn your flesh. You put your arm back underneath the quilt, so that only your head, your hand, and your cigarette, are exposed.

Where are ya?

Chris's new, and improved, accent jolts your memory.

You're in Landon. Don't ya rememba?

Chris philosophically pulls on his fag. When he starts to speak it is as if he is rallying you, building you up, boosting your morale. You sit, hunched up in the quilt, shivering and smoking and listening.

We're wiv the girls. You came along for a favour....a favour to your best fackin mate like.

He taps some ash on the floor.

I'm here doin the sights, and bright lights, of Landon Town. I've brought Mary along wiv me.

Mary? Mary, Moz's Mary?

Yeah we were like two flaffy little bannies larst night, when we got back from the clab like. Let me tell ya she lived ap to all my expektayshuns, lavlee. And you were wiv Chloe, jast as a favour for me n'that.

Your head is hurting. You don't want to be thinking about Chloe, about you and Chloe.

They're downstairs right now, aving samink to eat.

You can see them both in your head, sitting at the table eating. Mary is holding her knife and fork cutting her food into small dainty morsels, putting her knife down, putting her fork into her other hand, chewing elegantly on one of the perfectly cut pieces of food, patting her lips, drinking her coffee without a sound. Chloe is looking down at her plate, her coffee cup is stained with ketchup off her lips from where she has partly chewed her sausage and eggs before sucking them down. Chris can see that you are thinking.

Yeah I know shame about Moz and that innit? It's a fackin shame bat life goes on don't it? I mean when there's a fire....one of them big forest fires in America, it burns everyfink down, but after it gives the yang shoots a charnce to grow don't it....new life n'that....that's nature innit? One way or anafa there's been a lot ov trees burn down ain't the. Serge's gone; John's gone; Masters's gone; Adam's gone; Steve's gone; Moz's gone; Zak's gone; Stuart's gone; it's a shame yeah, bat it's an oppachewnity ain't it....for the two ov ass like... Moz ain't around to look after, or to provide for, is little girl anymore. Mary knows it, yang Tony knows it, even Penny, poor old girl, she knows it. Mary knows I'll look after er. We're goin ap West later. I'm gonna treat er to whateva she likes. I can do that now. We (meaning you too) can both do it now. There's a lot ov room at the top all ov a sadden. The drugs, rememba me tellin ya about the trip I went on wiv John and Moz?....Yeah well I'm the one, the only one, wiv the contact, no other facker knows anyfink... We're on fackin easy street from ere on...

He stands up takes a long draw on his Marlboro. He walks over to the open window continuing to speak to you even though he is looking at something, fixing his eyes on something so that they glaze over; looking at, focusing on, the horizon, the skyline, of whatever part of London you are in, the future?

Suddenly Chris is waving a gun around. You've no idea where he got it from. It is a sturdy looking black revolver. He's looking out of the window down the barrel of the gun, moving it around as if he was training it on somebody. You think about making a protest, or asking where he got it from, when he starts to speak.

See all these fackin people they look down on ass....bat really we should look down at them. They're the lazy ones. They're the ones who accept wot's given to them. They might moan in front of the telly when the news is on bat not even their own wives, or asbands, or kids, listen to them. They might make a stillborn protest in the works canteen bat they still panch their fackin card in every mornin and again before they go ome. They're all fackin stupid....livin in little boxes, rannin on the treadmill, jampin frew oops. It ain't for ass, no way. We're different. There's lines see, a great grid of lines everywhere, you can't see them bat they make millions of squares....and we all stand in the middle of all of these squares, bat wot we want is on the other side of the lines....me and you though we ain't scared to cross over those lines....we're gonna take whateva we like, and we're gonna take it right there and then....and if samone, anyone, don't like that then we're gonna hit them, or even betta we'll get samone else to hit them, and we'll have them hit so ard that they're gonna curse their own mathers for givin birf to them. No we ain't afraid....we ain't afraid to step over the line and take wot we want...

You put out your cigarette and try to tell yourself that it has made you feel better. Chris's speech is unnerving you. Everything seems to have happened so quickly. Everything is different. You are not sure if things are better now, or worse, but you suspect that they are pretty much the same, it's just that things are happening to different people, different faces; the only thing is that it's your face, and you see your face in your mind, just for a moment, and you're not unnerved any more, you start to believe Chris. You do believe him. You watch him squint as he smokes. You listen to him, and the endless hope in his voice, and he seems so sure.

I looked out ov the window in my room this mornin, jast like I'm lookin out ov this one now, and I said to myself, I said Chris me old mate, Chris, look at it all, look, it's all yours, it's all yours.

Chapter 32

Life

You expected the door to be ajar. You thought that you would see my two feet, at eye level, turning clockwise and then anticlockwise, in a slow, ever reversing, death circle. You were ready to cut down my hanged and damned body, but there is no sound of twisting and untwisting rope.

I am looking at you trying not to imagine how it would be between us; trying not to wonder if you like me or not. I am still trying to forget all of those encounters. I do not want to keep asking myself if you like me, want me, if you approve of me and what I am doing, or rather, what I have done. I have to tell myself that despite whatever has happened I am alive. The blood still pumps around my body. I can still see, and hear, and taste, and smell, and feel, and love.

All along I have tried to tell the truth, not only to you, but also to myself. It has been a difficult, an impossible, task. Somehow, no matter how hard I try, the truth, or tiny fragments of what I believe to be the truth, are missing. I have tried to think about all of my experiences, work out what I am missing out, what I am denying to myself, but it keeps bringing me back to the same problem the truth. I think, and have thought, that I have it, but I don't quite trust my senses, does anyone?

I am leaving. I am going to move away, a long way from here. Sally said that we had to talk, and talk we did. She shared a secret with me; something terrible that happened to her. She tried to tell me the truth. I think it worked. I took her in my arms and she told me a story, the story, that has made her so unhappy. Now I know, and now I know that I have to tell her my story too, that is if things are going to work out for us as we want them to. I have not been quite ready though, and I am sure that she is not quite ready to hear it, but I will tell her. I will tell her tonight. I have to because then, and only then, will the memories, and the black silk clad phantoms, be wiped clean, or at least rendered harmless. If you can confront something with words, form the sounds with your mouth, vocalize them, it is a start. I have thought about all that I have told you, all of the words that I have used, and I think that now I could tell Sally. There is a part of me that cannot wait to tell her. She knows that something is wrong, has been wrong. She is ready for bad news. She knows that I have a secret. She says that she is ready to hear it, whatever it is, and I believe her. We are closer than ever before. We need each other.

Sally says that we can go away. We can go anywhere we want to go. She wants to go to Japan. We can teach English there and we can be anonymous, but most importantly we can live together. I have never really thought about leaving before, and Japan is so far away, but it sounds interesting, tempting even. I think that we will go and have a year there and see how things work out. The past is all behind Japan. It is looking to the future. It is exactly what I need because I have been looking at the past for too long. The more I have looked the less that I have seen. Maybe the answers are in the future, beyond the millennium. I am not certain but I think I am going to look for them there from now on.

I will not be able to take my books with me. I will have to leave them behind. I have a few empty brown boxes into which I am going to put them all. I am going to stack them all up, on top of one another, pushed up tight right next to each other, all arranged neatly and efficiently like honeycomb. They will all have to make room so that each one of them can fit in. It is going to be strange living without them but I will see them again. I think I will buy a thick paperback at the airport just before we go. I will not think about it beforehand. I will have whatever is on sale. I want to read the author's name on the front in big gold letters. I want to be able to put it down and pick it back up again whilst not thinking about it in between, just for once, just for a change. I imagine that the leading lady will be just like Sally, just like you, beautiful and confused, but with a big warm heart. And the hero? Well the hero he will be just like me, just like you, handsome and sad, full of failures and successes, but with an incorruptible belief in love that will go on and on.